EXTRAORDINARY PRAISE FOR

EVERYTHING IS NOT ENOUGH

"Brilliant. . . . Lọlá Ákínmádé Åkerström has a sharp voice in the world of nuanced contemporary women's fiction."

—Jennette McCurdy

"*Everything Is Not Enough* is a heart-racer of a sequel. The passions, regrets, and vulnerabilities of Black women ignite each smartly crafted page. A very satisfying read!"

—Deesha Philyaw, award-winning author of *The Secret Lives of Church Ladies*

"*Everything Is Not Enough* presents a fascinating and complex kaleidoscope of women's lives in Sweden, asking crucial questions around career, love, family, and the definition of success. There are no easy answers in this book—the characters are real, subtle, and surprising, and you root for them the whole way through."

—Kathy Wang, author of *Impostor Syndrome*

"Incendiary, emotionally devastating, absolutely wonderful."

—Onyi Nwabineli, author of *Someday, Maybe*

"*Everything Is Not Enough* is a searing account of three women struggling through heartbreak, deception, and the scars of their pasts to find their rightful place in a society that isn't eager to make space for them. Lọlá Ákínmádé Åkerström writes with clarity and fearlessness, baring ugly truths amid the strength and resilience of women who come into their own while also coming into the beauty of hope."

—Charlene Carr, author of *Hold My Girl*

"International best-selling author Lọlá Ákínmádé Åkerström's second novel, *Everything Is Not Enough*, . . . turns expectations and stereotypes of Black women on their heads. Åkerström creates space for characters to become fully realized, allowing them to make mistakes and embrace anger or selfishness in ways they're not always allowed."

—Shondaland

"Åkerström carefully examines the loneliness of frequently feeling like an outsider and how this can draw the most disparate of people together. Balancing the trauma and turmoil of being judged and appraised based on the prejudices of individual people and societies, this fitting follow-up dwells on the comforts of finding a community on which to depend."

—*Booklist*

EVERYTHING IS NOT ENOUGH

ALSO BY LỌLÁ ÁKÍNMÁDÉ ÅKERSTRÖM

In Every Mirror She's Black

EVERYTHING IS NOT ENOUGH

A Novel

LỌLÁ ÁKÍNMÁDÉ ÅKERSTRÖM

wm
WILLIAM MORROW
An Imprint of HarperCollins*Publishers*

This is a work of fiction. Names, characters, places, and incidents are products of the author's imagination or are used fictitiously and are not to be construed as real. Any resemblance to actual events, locales, organizations, or persons, living or dead, is entirely coincidental.

HarperCollins books may be purchased for educational, business, or sales promotional use. For information, please email the Special Markets Department at SPsales@harpercollins.com.

A hardcover edition of this book was published in 2023 by William Morrow, an imprint of HarperCollins Publishers.

FIRST WILLIAM MORROW PAPERBACK EDITION PUBLISHED 2024.

Library of Congress Cataloging-in-Publication Data has been applied for.

ISBN 978-0-06-331698-0

24 25 26 27 28 LBC 5 4 3 2 1

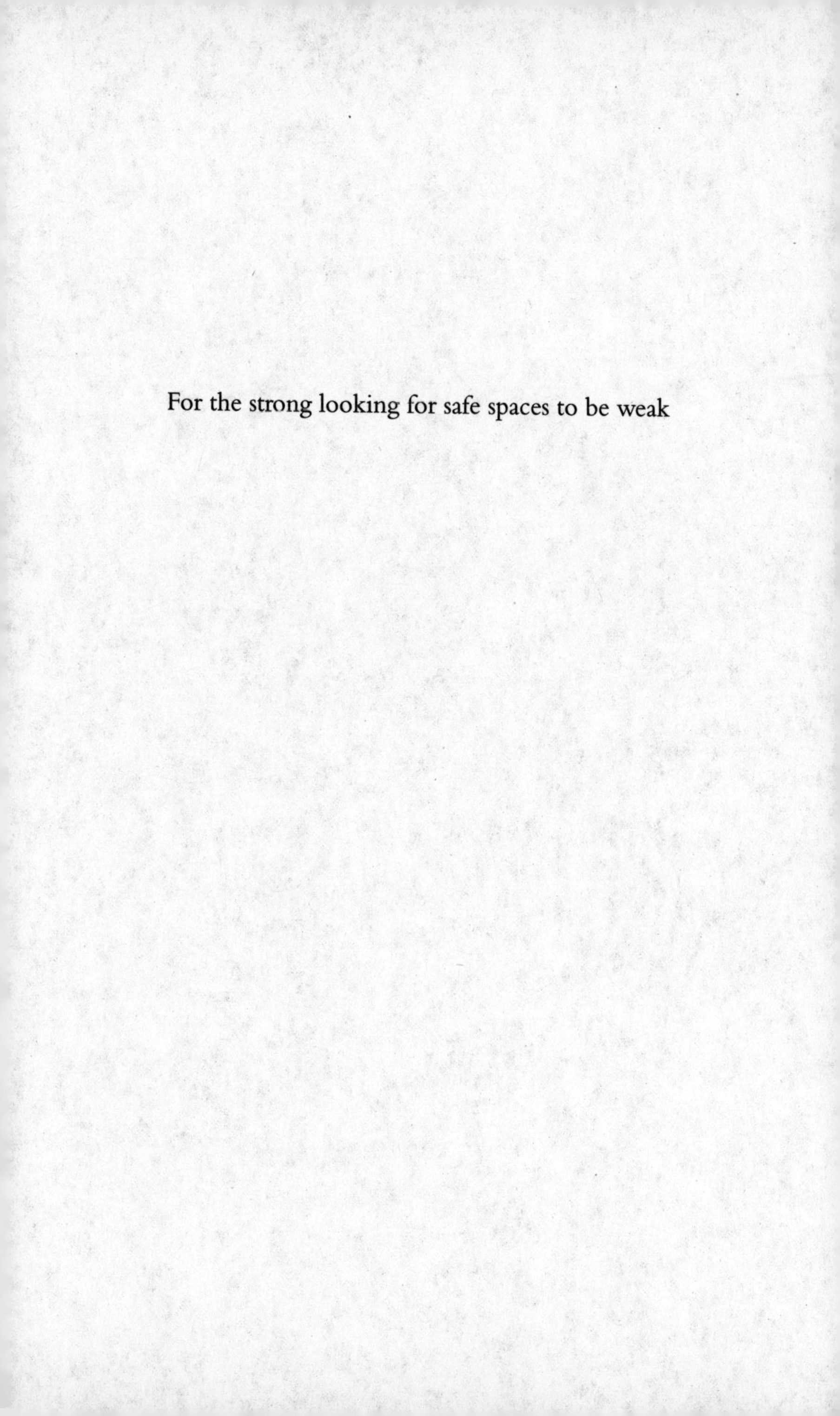

For the strong looking for safe spaces to be weak

AUTHOR'S NOTE

Trigger warning: Please be advised, this novel discusses issues of infidelity, sexual assault, infant loss, and suicide.

PART ONE

ONE

YASMIIN

Yasmiin watches the police officer's thin lips. They're still moving, spewing words which are making no sense. The room plunges into ear-popping silence as the loud ringing in her ears drowns out the officer's words.

The last time Yasmiin sat in a police station was years ago in Rome, Italy. The body of a Togolese girl—late teens, early twenties maybe—had been pulled from the Tiber, which flows through the city. The police didn't share details of how she'd been murdered. They simply wanted to talk to her "friends." The pack of girls who had strolled the same block.

Yasmiin had turned eighteen just a few days earlier and was scared shitless. She sat wearing a faux leather miniskirt which covered nothing and required strategically placed hands for modesty. She recalls an Italian officer screaming in her face, demanding answers he knew she didn't have. Intimidating her. When he finally took what he wanted from her in a backroom of the station in exchange for the freedom she already had, her fear had already taken her choice and reason with it.

Now the officer in front of her, a blonde woman with clear eyes, is staring her down, watching for signs of evasion. The air around them suddenly shifts and Yasmiin swallows.

"So, you haven't seen Muna Saheed in over a year, is that correct?"

"That is correct."

The officer scribbles words in a notebook. Yasmiin watches her write.

"But your husband"—the officer keeps writing, not looking up at her—"he had contact with Muna Saheed, is that correct?"

Yasmiin hesitates for a few seconds, then nods. The officer asks again, forcing the words out of her.

"Yes, he told me Muna used to come see him at the kebab shop," Yasmiin explains. Pen moves over paper some more.

"And how often did your husband say Muna used to come see him?"

"I don't know."

"Every day? Once a week?"

"I don't know." More scribbling. "Maybe once a month? Two months? I don't know."

"But you haven't seen Muna in over a year, is that right?"

"I told you already. Yes."

"So why would your husband be meeting her without telling you?"

Yasmiin swallows. She knows where the officer is heading. Why had Yagiz been meeting Muna at the kebab shop? She knows it couldn't have been an affair. Maybe he pitied her?

"He told me he didn't want me and Muna hanging around together because she was a troubled woman."

"So, you let him pick your friends?"

"No! He said he was protecting me from her."

"Why would he need to protect you from her? Was she dangerous?"

"No."

"Did she have radical leanings?" the officer asks. Yasmiin frowns at her. "Is that why your husband kept her away from you?"

"No!"

"Why do you think Muna Saheed would do this? When you were friends, did she mention these thoughts to you?"

"No. She never mentioned anything. Yes, she was sad and

depressed because she had no family. But to do this to herself? *La Samah Allah!*"

"Was Muna ever violent?"

"Never," she exclaims.

"Do you know that minutes before she jumped she attacked a young man, fracturing his skull?"

Yasmiin's hand flies to her mouth. None of this is making sense.

"The man will survive, but his injuries are severe," the officer continues. "His family decided to temporarily withdraw their charges against Muna when they found out what she tried to do to herself." The officer takes a sharp intake of air. "They are waiting for her to recover before deciding whether to proceed."

Yasmiin sits back in her chair. Muna? Attack a man? He must have provoked her in some way. Yasmiin is sure he must have said or done something vile for little Muna to have fought him and broken his head.

"Here is what I think, Mrs. Çelik." The officer drops her pen and links her fingers, resting them on her notebook. "I think your husband was having an affair with Muna Saheed."

"How dare you say that!" Yasmiin sits on the edge of her seat. "Yagiz would never touch her. He called her a little girl. He pitied her and said he only gave her food whenever she came to the shop." Yasmiin continues breathlessly. "She worked for him. His cleaning company. Maybe that was also why they had contact."

The officer relaxes into her own chair, listening as Yasmiin rails on.

"And how many times did you say your husband saw Muna Saheed again?"

"Maybe once a month? I don't know!"

The officer leans forward again. "Mrs. Çelik, you know I spoke to your husband before you?"

"Yes, I know. He's waiting for me in the lobby."

"According to him, he hasn't seen Muna in over a year."

Yasmiin's heart sinks. "Now, why would he lie? What more isn't he telling me about the nature of their relationship?"

After ten more minutes with the officer, Yasmiin shuffles to her feet. Muna had survived. A few broken ribs and limbs, but lying in a medically induced coma at Karolinska Hospital.

Alive. *Korttåg. Short train.*

It had been slowing to a stop when Muna jumped, a fact that had saved her life, the officer explained. Yasmiin's heaves come in fits and starts, a mix of elation and relief at the news.

When Yasmiin rushes back to the lobby, Yagiz springs to his feet.

"*Aşkım?*" *My love.* "How did it go?" He scans her face, trying to get a read on what had transpired between her and the officer. Yasmiin stands frozen, her gaze to the ground, her mind racing. "*Aşkım?*"

She peers into his dark eyes before wrapping her arms around his neck, jerking him down for a suffocating hug. He lets her take what she needs until she eases out of their embrace.

A few more moments of silence.

"She made me her next of kin." The words make their way out of Yasmiin. "Before this, before all of this happened," she continues. "She made me her next of kin."

"So, what does that mean?" Yagiz isn't so much asking a question, but pondering how much more he needs to be involved, Yasmiin's sure of it. He was never going to shake Muna Saheed off, he once told her. Yasmiin now wonders if Muna kept coming to his stall because he was the only certainty in her life. The only person who didn't go away.

Yasmiin hiccups a few sobs, before responding. "It means I am her family now." She sucks in a deep breath. "Once she wakes up, I am all she has."

BRITTANY-RAE

Three forty-two a.m.

Brittany leans against the jamb of her daughter Maya's fairytale-unicorned room, a slender hand cupping her mouth to muffle tears.

A light waft of alcohol reaches her as her toddler snuggles into the familiar grip of a man she no longer recognizes. The man she shares this child with, shares her life with. One she finally realizes she really doesn't know after all.

Jonny.

His mother Astrid had sent her a photo yesterday. One she'd never seen before. A picture of a teenage Jonny with an arm wrapped around his girlfriend, his first love, taken in front of Big Ben in London over twenty years ago.

That face.

A replica of Brittany's.

That name.

Maya.

Jonny shuffles from foot to foot, rocking gently, cooing to their daughter. "*Kära Maya*," he whispers softly, before breaking into a grin. "*Min söta Maya.*" *My sweet Maya*. He swivels toward Brittany and flashes that smile of a thousand small teeth.

That grin.

Jonny barged into her life over two years ago. She knew deep down why she let this stranger in. She wanted to taste what it would feel like to be wrapped in a class above all others, where race no longer mattered. So, Brittany welcomed his advances. She wanted his privilege cloaked around her shoulders.

And Jonny had chased her meticulously. He memorized her body like topography and used it against her. A man so besotted she couldn't help but bask in this knowledge. It cost her freedom instead. A heftier price to pay.

He inches closer now, Maya drowsily clinging to his neck. His eyes roam Brittany's face, scanning like they always do, learning to read emotions better so he doesn't have to ask.

She knows his quirks. He stares intensely. Often blankly. For the receiver, it borders on hair-raising—her best friend Tanesha calls it his "*resting serial killer face*." She's grown to love him, yet his intensity still bothers her, the way he fixates on things, situations, people.

Like Maya Daniels.

Brittany heaves a breath. She feels a suffocating squeeze on her chest. "Give her to me." The words barely leave her quivering lips. "Please."

He pivots toward her with his asphyxiating gray-blue glare. "Why?"

"Please," Brittany cries, her hands reaching, grasping air, wishing the child was in her arms instead. "Stop saying her name like that." Her daughter's name. A name she now loathes.

Jonny was so attentive while they were dating. He always wanted to know how to please her. To fix anything he might have done wrong or said to upset her.

Now she knows why. He and his bevy of assistants were grooming her to be a dead woman's replacement. Because Jonny can't handle loose ends, abruptly broken conversations, and sudden breaks, he will never stop trying to make up for Maya Daniels's death.

Perhaps his only love.

He convinced her to name their daughter Maya before she ever knew of his obsession.

Now that ghost name will haunt her forever.

Fear grips Brittany once more. "Please." Her mouth crumbles into an ugly pout. "Give her to me."

"She's mine." Jonny's voice turns harsh. "You can't take her away from me."

She inches toward him, but halts when he tightens his grip on Maya, his brows dipping inwards.

"You know I'll never hurt her, right?" He's asking, not stating.

"Right?" She knows he doesn't like unanswered questions. "You know I'll never hurt her?"

She'd always thought he was a terrible liar. Another quirk. So, when he lied brazenly about knowing who Maya Daniels was when she'd confronted him, deep terror had welled up within her. What else does he keep from her?

Brittany presses her lips together, shuts her eyes tightly, and nods, switching into survival mode. She lifts her eyelids in time to catch him spin once more, Maya exhausted in his arms, Jonny reeking of drink.

"*Pappa älskar dig, gumman,*" he mutters low beneath his breath, touching his forehead to their child's.

Daddy loves you, sweetie.

KEMI

Mirrors are cruel.

They cut with truth. No sugar coating with compliments. They run honesty like blades across your skin. Slashing with each glance you cast their way. Each gaze revealing what you've let yourself become.

In the dark orange of dawn, while Stockholm quietly wakes one opaque winter morning, Kemi stands in front of her mirror. Her eyes travel her bare shoulders, still strong even though they haven't seen weights in years. They roam over full breasts, across a soft stomach that never knew flatness. They move across wide hips and sturdy thighs. They journey her length, and return to rest on eyes beginning to lose their luster.

It had taken years to train those eyes to move lovingly over the curves they own. To smile with upturned lips at the space they take up with pride.

But this morning, those eyes are drowning as she stares at her reflection. A gasp of exasperation escapes her mouth. Her eyelids flutter shut at what she doesn't want to face. That she nearly crossed the line with Ragnar, a married man. A man whose wife mirrors adore because society holds her up as its ideal.

"*Heeejjj.*" Tobias stirs in bed. He finds her standing in front of the room's narrow mirror, running her palms over her naked skin. "What are you doing? Bring that beautiful body back to bed."

"What I asked you," Kemi starts. "Have you thought about it?"

"About what?" His question is punctuated by a yawn. "I need to sleep, *you* need to sleep."

"What I asked you when I got home from the office Christmas party."

"Seriously?"

She remains quiet. He curses under his breath.

"I can't stay here anymore, Tobias."

"Why? What happened?"

"Will you move back to the States with me or not?" She turns to him, locking eyes.

He meets her with a frown. "I thought you were joking."

"I'm not."

"I can't deal with this right now. It's too early." Tobias repositions himself, dragging the covers over his head, wishing for sleep to claim him once more.

"I can't stay in Sweden anymore."

"*Men herregud!*" *Good God!* "Did something happen at that party? With your weird boss?"

Kemi shuts her eyes and shakes her head. No, not Jonny. Someone worse. She opens them to wipe away a few rogue tears.

"Just come back to bed, okay?" he begs her.

She shakes her head, violently this time, holding back tears. She had let Ragnar, her boss's best friend, back her up against the elevator wall at the company Christmas party and consume her. They had desperately grabbed at each other then. She had allowed his tongue to devour hers.

And in that moment, she had wanted no one else. Not even her dear Tobias, who now narrows his eyes at her in confusion.

"Move back with me!" she demands, her tears finally bursting through. "I'm not staying."

She watches his eyebrows dip, replacing concern with anger, his brown eyes glaring at her. Then a slow shaking of his head.

"God, Kemi. I knew you were driven," he starts. "I just never knew you were so selfish."

Tobias rips off the covers, dresses, and leaves.

Kemi pulls her coat tighter as she strolls up Birger Jarlsgatan toward work on Monday morning, her head bent low against the heavy snow shower. She isn't sure why she's going to work today. She should have called in sick. Made up an excuse. Anything to avoid going in to face them all, to face him.

Snowflakes settle on her plum-colored lips. Kemi blows them off, taking a deep breath once she gets to the building. Another long breath as an anchor, then she pushes that hefty historic wooden door belonging to von Lundin Marknadsföring AB.

The elevator doors open to silence. Colleagues mill around quietly, grabbing coffee, looking through documents, no one glancing her way. Even the receptionist who normally gives her a forced smile busies himself flipping through papers. She draws her coat in tighter, her head held high, and struts past him, her heart beating faster.

As she strides past cubicles, heads duck away. Eyes, which often hold contact, divert themselves. They all know. One source has contaminated them all like a virus. She wonders if they look past him too. She walks past his cubicle, though she doesn't really expect him to be there. Clever of him. She's beginning to settle into the fact that she makes the dumbest moves for a smart girl.

Once at her desk, she closes her eyes for more strength before taking off her coat.

"Kemi." She stops mid-task and turns to Ingrid's voice. Head of Human Resources. Kemi remains silent. "Jonny has called off our morning meeting," Ingrid continues before stepping into her space. Kemi nods. "He isn't coming into the office today." Kemi bobs her head once more.

"Thanks for the intel." Kemi meets her gaze. Ingrid holds hers. Kemi swallows. "Is that all?"

"Once you get settled, can I have a word with you?"

"Is it important?" Kemi asks. Ingrid's silence confirms its gravity. "Umm, sure. We can have it now if you want."

A few minutes later, they sit in the boardroom where Ingrid first introduced her to her senior management colleagues over two years ago. Ingrid cradles a mug of coffee. Kemi opts for water, her mouth dry.

"I like you, Kemi. I really do." Ingrid links her fingers and leans forward.

Kemi sinks deeper into her chair. "I don't want to talk about it."

"He's married. He has a daughter. His wife is pregnant." Ingrid's glare remains trained on her.

"I'm not having an affair with Ragnar." Kemi muffles out the words.

"So what happened? What did I see?" Ingrid leans back and rests her linked fingers on her stomach.

"We were both drunk. It was a stupid mistake. It will never happen again." Kemi's voice hovers above a whisper. "I swear to you."

"It can't happen again, Kemi. You both work together on one of our biggest accounts. It's unethical and could jeopardize it."

"I know, I know."

"Now everyone thinks you're both having an affair," Ingrid says with a shrug.

"Because of you." Kemi's voice pitches with irritation. Clearly, Ingrid must have started the rumors after catching them.

"Me?" Ingrid's eyes widen at her accusation.

"Yes! You could have asked me first before spreading rumors about—"

"I saw you kissing a married man," Ingrid cuts her off firmly.

"Louise saw you leave with him in a taxi. She saw you holding hands." She sharply sucks in air. "The picture fits."

"I swear to you, Ingrid"—Kemi's voice sinks lower—"we're not having an affair."

"Maybe you should work from home this week," Ingrid says, lowering her voice too.

"I'm not going to hide away. I made one mistake. I'm not going to be judged by it forever." Kemi can feel herself begin to unravel.

"I think it's best if you work from home this week," Ingrid repeats.

Ingrid holds her gaze before lifting the scalding mug to her lips. Kemi bites her own lips instead. Arrogance isn't going to get her anywhere.

"Fine." Kemi admits defeat, rising to her feet. "Fine." She turns to go.

"Kemi," Ingrid calls out once more. Kemi looks back in wordless angst. "Jonny wants you both in London next week."

"London?"

Her skin heats up. She catches Ingrid's eyes scanning her face for a reaction. A business trip with Ragnar. Kemi switches into neutral. "What's happening in London?"

"He's buying a design startup and wants you there," Ingrid explains. "You know, for diversity and inclusion."

"Diversity and inclusion?" Kemi repeats, her eyebrows arching upwards. "You mean just show my Black face there?"

"To assess the startup from that angle," Ingrid clarifies. "The owner is a young intelligent Black woman like yourself." Kemi purses her lips in response. "Jonny thinks you two might connect."

"So let me get this straight," Kemi starts. "Jonny is buying a company next week. I am being summoned to just appear in person because the owner is Black when I wasn't involved at any stage of the acquisition process. Am I getting this right?"

The air shifts and she reads Ingrid's agitation. "The other directors and I didn't think you needed to be involved until now," she says. "Especially since Ragnar is leading the acquisition on Jonny's behalf."

"I see." With no more words for Ingrid, she spins on her heels and heads toward the door.

"No one has told Jonny yet," Ingrid calls out to her before she pushes the door open. "About you and Ragnar," she adds. "I'm not sure he can handle it."

"I appreciate your concern, but the world doesn't revolve around him. I'm tired of being schooled," Kemi says in exasperation. "Plus, there is no me and Ragnar—"

"They're best friends," Ingrid interrupts. Kemi peers at her. "Stay away from Ragnar. For your own sake."

TWO

YASMIIN

Yasmiin dices pieces of tripe on a Sunday morning to make *tuzlama*—tripe soup—for the beguiling Turk, her dear husband. Yagiz grunts with each bicep curl in their modest living room out in the suburb of Hässelby, northwest of town. Their one-year-old son Mehmet, with his mass of jet-black wispy curls and matching long lashes, naps in his cot.

The sharp shrill of one of Yagiz's three phones cuts through his grunting in the living room. He curses. He runs multiple businesses and has a phone for each.

Yagizs Städning och Rengöring (YSR)—Yagiz's Tidying and Cleaning—which supplies cleaners and janitors to some of the city's most expensive office buildings. Where Muna had worked.

Çelik Kebab—his family-run kebab stall within Kungshallen basement food court at Hötorget in the heart of town. Yagiz spends his days here, managing the stall in person where, according to him, Muna often came to pester him.

And his other business, the one he'd initially roped her into. Selling khat leaves. A stimulant drug when chewed. After Mehmet's birth, Yagiz had sold that business off to a friend, an ox of a man named Özel. He now sells low-key steroid pills to bodybuilders and health fanatics instead.

Normally lean, Yagiz now uses his own body as a testbed for those steroids with each grunt.

She hears him cursing at someone in Swedish over the phone.

He drops a weight and tramps toward the kitchen, phone to his ear, switching to shooting off words in rapid Turkish. She senses him by the door and turns to find him leaning against its jamb.

His handlebar moustache and goatee are damp. Beads of sweat race down his topless torso, tattoos etched all over it, down to his deep V-cut, which disappears into well-worn sweatpants. His hair is shaved off on both sides with a lush black patch running through the middle—his "rooster" as Muna used to call it.

As she grabs a handful of tripe and tosses it into the bubbling broth, she breaks into sobs, tears overcoming her. She drops the knife, covering her mouth with the back of her palm.

Muna.

Yasmiin still hasn't seen her and isn't sure when she'll be allowed to visit. But, *Alhamdulillah*, she's alive.

Yagiz swallows when he scans her face, his Adam's apple jumping with the movement.

"Yasmiin? What's wrong?" He stares at her, brows dipped, phone still at his ear.

She shakes her head violently, muffling each cry with her hand, shoulders shaking. Yagiz disconnects his call abruptly, closes the distance between them, and gathers her into his arms.

"*Ilaahayow!*" *My God!* Yasmiin wails in Somali as Yagiz cradles her against his sweaty torso. "Muna," she cries.

"*Aşkım.*" Yagiz runs a palm over her back. "It will be alright. Allah is in control."

"Why didn't I check on her?" Yasmiin cries. "Why?" She sniffs back runny mucus. "She called me her sister, but I left her alone."

"Muna had many troubles," Yagiz says. "She was always coming to the kebab shop every week. No friends. No man to fuck her. She was a sad woman."

Yasmiin pushes out of his hug and peers at him. He lifts his shoulders in question. *Vad? What?*

"Every week? Muna was coming to the shop every week?" Her voice begins to shake. "And you didn't tell me?"

"That girl was trouble. So negative. Like a little witch. I didn't want her around you." Yasmiin bursts into tears once more. Yagiz continues. "I mean, I thought you didn't want to be her friend anymore. You left that place. You left her."

That place.

The modest government-subsidized apartment she'd shared with Muna. Strangers in a foreign land. The space in which Muna became the only person on earth who knows her secrets from Rome and what she'd done to survive.

Family for Yasmiin remains a nebulous entity on a continent she hasn't been back to in years. Memories of Somalia are buried in the foggiest trenches of her mind. She isn't sure if her family members are dead or alive, wealthy or struggling, reveling in freedom or fighting. She doesn't remember how she made it to Italy. Her brain refuses to remember that journey. They lie buried in the deepest recesses of her memory as if years of her life never happened. Never existed. All Yasmiin can dredge up is that one day she was happy, laughing underneath the hot sun in Mogadishu. The next, she was fleeing from something she couldn't quite explain or understand.

She wandered the streets of Rome in a perpetual daze, wondering how she'd landed in this ragtag family—a Togolese girl, three Nigerian girls, one Slovakian girl, and one Ukrainian girl—with their middle-aged Libyan pimp as their pappa. Even those days are logged in creases. She isn't ready to pry them out and confront them.

She ended up in Sweden five years ago because a client helped her escape from the claws of her pimp. Foreign affairs, the man had told her when she asked him, as he undressed, why he was in Rome. He'd left his socks on. He was Swedish and much older. Late fifties maybe, with greasy light-brown curls and leathery sun-beaten skin that suggested long stretches of time in the tropics. His laughing cerulean-blue eyes were framed by wrinkles. He was going to help her, he said. After all, his country opened its arms wide to refugees and asylum seekers like her. She didn't need to be walking the streets. "*Trust me.*" Those were his last words as he shuddered, letting out an otherworldly growl, before collapsing onto her back.

Her Swedish diplomat kept his promise. Within three weeks, she became his girlfriend on paper. In reality, she loathed his proximity, love handles, and breath. She didn't care to know his name. With a tourist visa secured and fastened into an emergency Somali passport, they walked hand-in-hand through security as lovers, boarded a flight to Stockholm's Arlanda Airport, and strolled into his country on a frigid winter day, his grip on her tightening once they touched land.

Yasmiin finally did learn his name. *Bosse.* The beginning embers of her disdain for middle-aged white men. Because he forced her to scream it in gratitude every day for two full weeks as payment for her freedom from Italy. Considering she didn't understand a lick of his language and knew no one in this land coated with powdered sugar snow, she reckoned screaming his name was a small price for never having to feel his vileness again after a fortnight.

Once thoroughly satisfied, he dropped her off at the nearest asylum center for safekeeping. Not without kissing the back of her palm, thanking her for the ride, and informing her he was returning to his post in Rome.

Six months later, she was assigned to that government-funded apartment with Muna.

That place.

Yasmiin keeps sobbing, her hands flying up to cover her face. Sobbing because Muna is alive and breathing, albeit clutching tightly to Yasmiin's past, all dug out and covered in dirt. Yasmiin isn't sure what her friend would have done with all that dirt, had they remained close. Maybe that was why she kept her distance too.

The steel bubble she'd been crafting around her new life with Yagiz and Mehmet has now morphed into brittle glass with the news that her former roommate has survived a suicide attempt.

One tap, a single word from Muna once she comes to, and

Yasmiin's glass paradise will come crashing down. The life she is currently weaving around her shoulders in protection to erase the scars of Rome's streets and Bosse's scent is proving to be more fragile than she had anticipated.

Yagiz pries her hands off her face and cups her head between his palms. He kisses her, his lips moving featherlight over her clenched mouth, before resting his forehead on hers in comfort.

What isn't Yagiz telling her? Why did he keep seeing Muna so often?

She teeters on the edge of losing it all, of losing him, so Yasmiin's tears refuse to stop when thoughts of an affair surface again.

BRITTANY-RAE

Brittany stirs her coffee, her silver teaspoon scraping exquisite porcelain with each revolution, her eyes on Jonny.

Her swirling motion hooks him like a homing device. Soon it begins to grate. She watches him unfurl and furl his fingers, unable to control himself. She revs up her motion instead, her gaze still on him. He shifts in his seat, his eyes drawn by the cup, his fingers reacting to the scraping noise.

His assistant Louise walks into their dining room, ending his misery. Louise's shoulders jump when she sees Brittany. She composes herself.

"*God morgon*, Brittany," she greets. "Hope you're doing well?"

Brittany stops racing her teaspoon inside her cup. She lifts lukewarm coffee to her lips, assessing Louise over its rim.

"It's Monday morning." Brittany leaves Louise's greeting hanging.

The petite brunette clears her throat before turning to her boss and launching into a barrage of Swedish. Two years and Brittany still can't keep up with their Swedish. She blames herself for not making more progress with the language. She still has a private tutor at her disposal. One she disposes of weekly, dipping into her bag of excuses. She ponders if her subconscious is rejecting him by refusing to learn his tongue.

She listens to Louise talk. Observes her gestures and how Jonny listens to her intently. He can't multitask. Eating and listening concurrently remains impossible. He has to choose. This time, he listens to Louise, his brows furrowed. He lets her interrupt his breakfast instead. What she is saying chooses for him. She pulls out a folder, listing out appointments and deadlines. She repeats them once more. Brittany knows he's mentally hitting *save*. He remembers minute details, dates, numbers, fine print with frightening precision.

Five minutes later, Louise quiets down, closing the folder, holding it in front of her with both hands. She flashes Brittany a quick glance, unsure if she should continue talking.

"*Vad?*" Jonny prods her back.

She starts again, her voice falling lower, clearly trying to avoid Brittany's ears. Brittany sets down her cup and grabs a piece of cold toast. She nibbles, busying herself, her ears perking up. She hears names.

Kemi. Ragnar. Ingrid.

Ragnar. Jonny's best friend. A man who sees her as nothing more than a gold digger. His eyes tell her this every time Jonny forces them to be in each other's vicinity.

She notices Jonny's brow arch upwards. "*Vad.*" Not a question. His voice dips.

Louise nods and Jonny pushes to his feet. Gearing up to leave, he notices Brittany still there. She gawks at him, realizing where she stands on his list. Ragnar takes higher priority.

Right after Maya Daniels. The woman their daughter is named after.

"We need to talk," Brittany says as he stands. He remains silent. "So I suggest Louise reschedule whatever appointment it is you're rushing off to." She turns to his assistant. Louise avoids her gaze and excuses herself, leaving them. The dining room falls into a hush.

"I need to go," Jonny says.

"I said we need to talk." Anger begins brewing within her. "I can't do this anymore." A loud clunk. Someone drops something metallic in the kitchen, their housekeeper Sylvia eavesdropping.

Brittany gets to her feet too, pulling her bathrobe tighter. He rounds the table toward her. She takes a couple of steps backward, halting his advance.

"Don't touch me," she says between clenched teeth. "Don't you dare touch me." He stands with his fists by his sides, glaring at her intensely. She reads it in his eyes as his brain works furiously to find the right words.

"I'm sorry I lied to you."

"No, Jonny. You're not sorry. You're delusional and you need help," Brittany says. "Your family failed you. Your sisters. Your father. Your witch of a mother!"

"Leave Astrid out of this." He clenches his jaw and tightens his fists at the mention of his mother.

"Leave Astrid out of this?" she parrots him in disbelief. He tenses once more. Brittany knows the name *Astrid* always invokes this physical reaction from him. She needs to know why. Beyond the reveal of his past. Beyond this rigid adult version in front of her. What else has Astrid done?

"How can I fix this? How can I make it right?" Jonny asks, his body relaxing once more.

She wrinkles her brows. "Don't you get it, Jonny? This isn't real—" Her voice breaks.

"I love you."

"You love a ghost," she says. "I need answers right now. I need to know everything about her," she cries. "Right now."

Jonny stands frozen as he takes her in, hands still in fists.

"Okay."

"Okay?"

"Okay. Follow me." He turns and slowly strides out of their dining room.

* * *

Brittany sits on the chaise longue in Jonny's sparse study, legs crossed, arms folded across her chest, lips biting back tears as he tells her all about Maya Daniels in painstaking detail. He wears the widest boyish grin she has ever seen him wear.

He is perched on his desk, staring at the wall, as if the girl with the "most beautiful name" has materialized right in front of him. His lips curve into occasional smiles with each memory flooding his brain. He met Maya when he was sixteen years old at an international school in London. A Black British girl. She walked into his class and he was smitten upon sight. He chased her for weeks until she finally returned his kiss, saying she admired his energy.

He describes in agonizing detail how he lost his virginity to this Maya, where and when.

How he felt. How he learned everything about her and what she liked. How beautiful she was and how her smile could brighten his darkest thoughts. He remembers exactly when he told Maya he loved her. Beneath Big Ben's glow, she repeated those same words. A stranger had helped capture that moment for them in the photo Astrid had sent Brittany.

Brittany sits through it all because she is tired of not knowing and because Jonny is tactless when it comes to reading emotional situations.

"I wanted us to be together forever. I wanted to marry her." He smiles at the wall once more. He looks at his fingers, starts toying with them. "I wanted our baby so much. I wrote a letter to my parents, telling them how happy I was. That I had found my soulmate. That I was going to walk away from everything, from this life, to be with her. Astrid wasn't happy. She told me to come back home immediately."

He falls silent, his fingers doing their dance.

"One day, Maya was sharing news of our baby with me in a letter she wrote. The next day, she was dead." She sees him grit his teeth. "And I blame them. I blame them for everything." His eyes turn serious. His study descends into charged silence once more. Brittany's heart pounds so hard it threatens to burst through her ribcage. Jonny swivels around to stare at her. She pulls her robe tighter around her shoulders. His eyes wash over her torso before settling like lasers back on her face.

"You look just like her."

A tiny gasp escapes Brittany. This, she already knows. After all, she is the dead woman's doppelgänger. But hearing those words from his mouth for the first time confirms what she always suspected. Johan von Lundin never loved her.

He pushes off the desk and trudges to where she sits on the chaise longue. He plants himself next to her. She inches away. A new type of fear wells up within her because she doesn't know him. Not anymore. A man who she assumed could never lie to her face because of his transparent mannerisms had done so boldly. With that core of their marriage gone, Jonny might as well be dead to her too. His inability to lie to her had been the main thing that drew her to him.

He moves closer. She shuffles until the edge stops her.

"Brittany." He reaches for her cheek, tracing it with his fingertips. She closes her eyes against his caress, sniffing back tears. She lets him feel her. How had she missed all the signs? Had she been so blinded by the idea of him that she'd given him pass after pass?

"Do you forgive me now?"

Brittany spins away from his gaze. He reaches for her hand. She yanks it back and shoots to her feet.

"Please leave." She swallows her tears, hands resting on her hips. He slowly rises, planting himself inches from her face. His favorite spot.

"Why?"

"I can't do this anymore."

"Do what?"

She lets out a gasp of despair. "Just go to work." He stands rooted, as if a robot. "Now, Jonny. Just go." She prods him along. He gives her a half-smile before leaving her in the study.

Once he's out of earshot, Brittany lets out a cry, rebooting her lungs once again. Who can she trust enough to share the fact that her husband has a fetish for her very image?

She's desperate for outlets. Someone, anyone, who can make her feel less alone. Over two years in Sweden, she so deeply cocooned herself in Jonny's world she barely has other friends of color. She did meet that arrogant Nigerian American who works for Jonny and had helped bring his company back from the brink of diversity death in the media.

But that woman—*Kemi*—she will never befriend. Every time they meet, or rather collide, at functions Jonny organizes, there's always an abrasion Brittany has grown to anticipate.

So it takes every ounce of humility for Brittany to call Kemi when Jonny finally leaves the house, realizing she has indeed sunk to such depths of desperation.

"Brittany?" Kemi calls out on the other end. Brittany hesitates before responding.

"*Hej*, Kemi. How are you?"

Kemi finds her voice. "I'm fine. Hope everything is okay?"

"I know. It's weird that I'm calling you, right?"

"Well, not weird. Just unexpected."

More silence from Brittany before she continues. "Kemi, I need to talk to you about something. Something important."

"Of course. Anything."

Yeah, Brittany can't talk to her about anything, but she'll take the invitation for now. She needs that divorce from Jonny and fast. She can't go to his sisters. Their allegiance is squarely to their baby brother. Antonia, the eldest, had eventually told her about Maya Daniels but only once their mother Astrid had sent Brittany that photo. And even then Antonia tried to excuse Jonny. Svea deals with it by distancing herself. She rarely even picks up Brittany's calls.

"I was wondering if we could meet for brunch on Sunday."

"Yes, I think I can make it work. I'm flying back to the States for the holidays soon."

This information irritates Brittany. She responds with a weak "Good for you."

Kemi stays silent on the other end. Brittany knows she has picked up on her sarcasm. *The smarty pants.*

"Well, I haven't seen my family in over two years so I'm desperate to give them hugs," Kemi says.

"So . . . can we meet for brunch then?"

"Yes, of course."

"Meet me at Cadierbaren at the Grand Hôtel. Twelve p.m. Sunday. My treat."

KEMI

Kemi watches Brittany eat. The other woman cuts into her eggs Benedict so daintily it feels cartoonish. They never would have been friends back in the States yet this place, it seems, is forcing them into each other's arms.

Now she sits in arguably the most expensive gilded property in all of Sweden—the Grand Hôtel—which regularly hosts heads of state and royalty. The panorama from the restaurant's window consists of direct views of the yellow ocher–colored Royal Palace on the island of Gamla stan.

She turns her gaze back to Brittany, who's wearing a tight-fitting red dress which hugs her lithe frame topped with a long-sleeved black fur bolero. Quite festive. Her lips are dyed her signature cherry red. Her dark brooding eyes look even moodier under thick black lashes and black eyeliner.

Kemi clears her throat. "Thanks for inviting me here. I've never been."

"Really?"

"Well, I have no reason to come here," Kemi adds.

"So Tobias doesn't treat you to fancy places once in a while?"

"Tobias doesn't have von Lundin money." Kemi chuckles. When she sees the look on Brittany's face, she knows she's treading on dangerous territory. She clears her throat once more.

"So"—Brittany grabs a napkin, dabs delicately at her lips—"I'm sure you're dying to know why I asked you to brunch."

"Well, considering I'm still packing for my trip back to the States soon, I'm hoping it's a super-important reason."

Brittany clasps her fingers together and rests her elbows on the table. "I was wondering if you knew any lawyers in your circles," she asks.

"Lawyers? Is everything okay?" Kemi is surprised. When Brittany holds her gaze, she knows everything isn't okay.

"I just need to talk to a lawyer, that's all."

"Okay, what type of lawyer? Is it about your US taxes?" Brittany shakes her head, then takes a sip of her Tarte Tatin cocktail. "Is it Jonny?" Kemi asks.

Brittany presses her lips together before setting the drink down. "I need a *relationship* lawyer."

"What do you mean? Do you need a divorce lawyer?" Trouble in the von Lundin kingdom? This isn't making sense to Kemi. Not after the way she has witnessed Jonny behave around his wife. This is a man so in love it borders on obsession.

"Yes," Brittany responds after a few seconds. "I'm looking into divorce. I don't trust anyone else here. Not his family. Not his assistants."

"Oh my goodness, Brittany. I'm so sorry." Kemi's voice sinks to a whisper. "Did he cheat on you?"

Brittany lets out a pained laugh before angling her face away. "If only it were that simple," she says, sniffing.

"Is there anything else I can do to help you?"

"I need to find a divorce lawyer, that's all."

Kemi watches as Brittany dabs her eyes and composes herself, slipping back into that facade, a reminder that they aren't buddies. Maybe this is the opening they both need to connect with each other in deeper ways beyond the social events Jonny pulls them to. Kemi has always been curious about Brittany's story. How she ended up in Sweden. How she crossed paths with one of its wealthiest men. How she's adjusting, integrating, and finding her place within its upper echelons.

"I'll ask around for you," Kemi says.

"Thank you." Then silence envelops the ladies until Kemi speaks.

"I want you to know you can trust me, Brittany," she says. "Are you willing to share? Maybe tell me more?"

Brittany glares at her for a few more seconds before replying, "No."

They finish brunch in awkward silence.

When Monday rolls around, Kemi decides to work from home, as Ingrid suggested, hoping the rumors rapidly spreading about her and Ragnar will simmer down.

Kemi isn't sure what she's feeling these days. Shame for sure. Coupled with something deeper. She carries the impossible. A deep-seated responsibility to show the world she's a Black woman making it in Sweden to inspire others. That unbearable weight is currently being stripped off and replaced with the fact that she is indeed human.

When they'd shared that ill-fated taxi ride after their elevator encounter, Ragnar promised her he would quit their joint Bachmann project and find something else. He understood the gravity of what had transpired between them.

Alas, Ragnar Pettersen led a conference call that same morning as if nothing had happened, his promise of leaving seemingly forgotten once the weekend was over. She joined in that work call, quiet as a fly. Nothing in his voice suggested he had heard the rumors as well. If he had, the calmness of his tone suggested she was getting the rougher end of the gossip mill.

After all, wasn't he the one who was dutifully married, and she, the society-cast slut chasing a married man? The thought of her upcoming business trip to London with him scorches her from within.

She flips shut her laptop and promptly dials her twin sister Kehinde.

"Kemi?" Kehinde answers.

"How are you?"

"Counting the days till I see your face! The kids are excited," Kehinde adds.

"Me too! Can't wait," Kemi declares.

Since Kemi's move to Sweden to take on the role of Director of Diversity and Inclusion, she hadn't been back home to the States. The job had been the ultimate ego boost. A chance to show von Lundin Marketing why she won National Marketing Executive twice in a row in the US and to help dig them out of their diversity marketing scandal.

She did that successfully with their Bachmann campaign, marketing luxury German high top sneakers. Now her days are spent twiddling her thumbs while softly rocking that one client. She craves more challenges but is promptly realizing work runs at a different pace here, punctuated by six-week vacations, sick leave, and parental leave spanning over a year. She has settled into a box of work-life-balanced boredom, while witnessing her skills blunt around the edges.

Heading back to the US for two weeks over Christmas and New Year's will be a much-needed break from a place forcing her to choose flatlined comfort in a corner with no prospects for growth.

She's sitting at her kitchen table in her pint-sized Nacka apartment. Tobias hasn't dropped by since their rift. Is he that skittish about commitment? Kemi ponders. She isn't sure why she'd asked him to move back to the States with her. To uproot all he'd ever known on a whim and follow her to prove his love. She has found the man she wants to invest in the long term with, yet her thoughts keep floating to the dead end that is Ragnar.

"Kehinde," Kemi starts again. "I'm not okay." There's a quiescence on the other end absorbing her words. "I've done something stupid."

"Stupid *ke*? What did you do? Is it you and your mouth? Did you curse someone out?"

"If only."

"If only? What did you do? Will it jeopardize your job?" Kehinde asks.

Kemi clears her throat. "There are rumors being spread about me."

"Rumors?"

"Yes, about me and a colleague." More silence as Kehinde processes her words.

"What colleague? Your boss?"

"No, no, it's someone else."

"Kemi, what is going on? What are you doing? Does Tobias know what's going on?"

"The rumors are not true. They say I'm having an affair with this man, but I swear it's not true."

"So, why are they spreading it? This doesn't make sense."

Kemi closes her eyes, dragging in air for strength. She has never faced anything like this. A defamation of character she added fuel to. What will happen when she goes in to work for her final week before the holidays? Working remotely this week isn't going to mask the fact that whatever reputation she confidently built at work is being chipped away in chunks by her sordid encounter with Ragnar, which others witnessed.

"I kissed a married man and someone saw us," Kemi shares. Silence on the other end. "I kissed him, Kehinde, and at that moment, I wanted him more than anyone else. More than Tobias. That is what I'm struggling with right now."

Still more silence from Kehinde. Kemi knows her twin. She's probably flipping through her mental Rolodex of Bible verses to quote something on adultery.

"A married man, Kemi?"

"I know, I know. I'm ashamed of myself. The HR director told me to work remotely this week. To avoid the office. Hopefully the rumor dies down a little by the time I'm back next week."

"Why would you do this with a married man?" Kehinde's tone is razor sharp.

Kemi winces at those words. "It was a harmless kiss."

"A harmless kiss that's forcing you not to show your face in the office, *ehn*?"

"I'm scared. I can't stop thinking about this man. I love Tobias with everything I have, but—"

"But what? But what? Another woman's husband?" Kehinde's words burn.

"Please stop it!" Kemi raises her voice. She hates being cornered. And she hates the fact that she still can't emotionally handle being cornered either.

"Oh, is that too real for you? When I actually mention his wife?"

"I don't want to hurt her," Kemi says, her brows dipping, contemplating.

"What do you mean 'don't want to'? Are you planning on repeating your stupid kiss?" When Kemi doesn't answer, Kehinde continues.

"Look, Kemi. Don't lose yourself in that country and forget who you are and your values. You're already living in sin with Tobias. But add on top of that, you're now kissing married men as well."

"Yes, Kehinde," Kemi replies, exasperated. "I know. I'm an Old Testament harlot. I'll see you in two weeks."

Tap.

THREE

YASMIIN

Yasmiin still has questions for Yagiz.

There are layers she hasn't peeled back from her husband. His charisma acts as a buffer between her digging into his life outside of her, and his core. Wondering why he lied about regularly seeing Muna Saheed grates on her still.

Why hadn't he just stated it like it was? Why is his default setting always to find a way around saying what he wants to say? Clearly he's keeping information from her.

Yagiz seems equally curious. Ever since she was interviewed at the police station, he's been full of questions. He wants to know how it went with the policewoman. What questions had she asked? What had Yasmiin told her?

Patience isn't a virtue of his. He wants answers right away. Even if asking while grunting on top of her way past midnight.

"So…*urgh*…what did…*urgh*…she…*hmmm*…ask you…*aşkım*?" Yagiz is breathless as he works hard. Yasmiin rolls her eyes. "*Uhnnn?* Tell me, *ughhh,*" he continues, beads of sweat falling off his face onto hers.

"Will you stop talking?!" Yasmiin yells, clenching her thighs to stop his rhythm. He yelps in pain.

"What?" Yagiz's breathing labors, his tone angry. Yasmiin has the blood-stopping upper hand at the moment, her thighs gripping him, so he obliges.

"*What?!*" She pushes him off and shimmies into a sitting position. "Is this normal to you?"

Yagiz lifts his shoulders in question. "I only want to know what that *snuten* asked you." *The cop.*

"While we're fucking?"

"I can multitask, you know," Yagiz cackles while crawling back toward her. She brushes him aside and gets to her feet.

"Why did you lie about Muna?"

Yagiz blows out air, frustrated. "I don't know, okay? I got nervous. The *snuten* was asking too many questions."

Yasmiin dons a floral-patterned robe and trots out of their bedroom toward the living room. Yagiz finally admits defeat. She isn't going to give him any more. He begrudgingly gets to his feet. He searches around for his briefs and a cigarette. He follows her, his cigarette balancing between his lips, his fingers raking through his strip of hair. Yasmiin flops onto the sofa, crosses her legs. She starts dangling the one on top.

"Were you sleeping with Muna?"

"*Allah korusun!*" Yagiz curses in Turkish. "I wouldn't touch that girl even if I was the only man alive and she was the only woman alive and we were on an island and—"

"Yagiz!"

"What? No, okay. I only pitied her. She looked so sad," Yagiz says, reaching for his lighter on a shelf. "I think maybe she even liked me. I think she wanted me."

Yasmiin rolls her eyes. "So, why did you lie?"

"I don't know, *aşkım*." He lights his cigarette, drags in some smoke, and blows it out. "I think I lie automatically. No matter what the question. Like default. Like autopilot."

Yagiz holds her gaze and sighs before continuing. "I didn't think you wanted to be her friend anymore. She probably reminds you of whatever you experienced and whoever you were before me." He pads closer to her. Yasmiin holds her breath. "You never tell me anything. About your time before me. Which means you don't want to remember. So, I didn't want Muna ruining who you are now with me."

Yasmiin takes an audible breath and lowers her head to process his words. Then she switches topic.

"The policewoman said Muna almost killed a man. Broke his head."

"*Faaannnn!*" Yagiz's fingers fly to his temple. *Damn.*

"What would possess little Muna to do that?" Yasmiin furrows her brows. "Maybe he tried to attack her? Said foul words to her?"

"This man, what did he look like?" Yagiz asks.

"I don't know. She didn't tell me," Yasmiin finishes with a yawn. Yagiz curses some more between pulling in smoke and turning to head to their bedroom. He pads a few feet away, then swivels back to her.

"So…are we going to finish or what?" he asks.

She hisses at him and turns away.

The next day, she's back at the police station because the officer has more information for her.

"*Kaffe?*" the female officer offers. Yasmiin shakes her head. Her son Mehmet balances on her knee. She starts bouncing him when low yelps of discomfort escape him.

"*Vilken sötnos!*" *What a cutie.* The officer instantly reaches for his wispy black curls, running her fingers through the toddler's hair before giving Yasmiin time to permit it. Yasmiin tugs him tighter away from the officer's touch. After clearing her throat, the officer pulls out a folder and spreads it open before Yasmiin.

"So, did you know Gunhild Andersson?" the officer asks, reaching for a photo, turning it upside down so Yasmiin can study its subject. *Gunhild*. Yasmiin's eyebrows arch. *Gunhild.* Her old social case handler from Spånga-Tensta district who had taken care of her and Muna. At least emotionally as they carved out new lives while sharing that government-assigned apartment. They had both arrived in Sweden alone. Gunhild made sure they'd settled in as best they could.

"Yes, of course," she replies, her voice heavy. "I know Gunhild. I haven't seen her in years." Mehmet wriggles in discomfort. Yasmiin readjusts him.

"That is the last known address we have for Muna Saheed," the officer says. "It seems Muna was living with Gunhild at the time." She pauses to collect her breath. "Our records show that Muna Saheed had found Gunhild's body that morning. The same day she jumped."

"What?" Yasmiin isn't sure she heard properly. "What do you mean Gunhild's body?"

"I'm sorry," is all the officer says as she watches Yasmiin's face contort before tears begin streaming down her plump cheeks. She wipes a few with the back of her hand, the other hand cradling her son closer to her chest.

Gunhild. Gone.

She pictures the older Swedish woman with her thin glasses always on the tip of her nose, her short blonde bob framing her face like a helmet. But what comes flashing through her mind are those turquoise-blue eyes with crow's feet fanning out from their edges. Eyes filled with warmth. Eyes which had fully seen her without judgment whenever they rested on her.

Memories flood Yasmiin as she weeps. How different crow's feet can look next to similar light eyes. Menacing around Bosse's. Mesmerizing framing Gunhild's.

The officer gives her a few minutes to collect herself before reaching for a small box resting on the table, shoving it closer to Yasmiin.

"What is this?" Yasmiin asks between sniffs.

"Does the name Ahmed Tofiq Rahim sound familiar to you?" the officer inquires. Yasmiin shakes her head, wiping away snot from a nostril. "Are you sure?"

"I don't know that name," Yasmiin says. "What's in the box?"

"Have you seen this box before?" Yasmiin shakes her head again. No, she has never laid eyes on it. Then again, Muna had been secretive. In their communal living room, they were sister-friends. When they retreated into their bedrooms, they became strangers once more.

"It seems the artifacts in this box belonged to a Kurdish man, Ahmed Tofiq Rahim." The officer clears her throat. Yasmiin can tell from her reaction the box is filled with nightmares. "If we can find out why Muna had his things, this could help us get closer to understanding why Muna jumped in front of a train."

"I've never heard that name before in my life." Yasmiin remains adamant. "I just want to see her. When can I see her?"

The officer holds her gaze for a moment longer before nodding. "Very soon, I promise you."

BRITTANY-RAE

Brittany unlocks the door to a low-lit hallway. The time is eight fifty-three p.m.

The living room is dark, save for crackling light from the fireplace which their housekeeper must have left for her. She hangs up her coat, zips off her boots, and steps quietly toward the flames. Its glow is what she needs. Two weeks away from Christmas. Stockholm broods. No snow yet. She pulls off her fur bolero and sits on the rug right in front of the fireplace. She closes her eyes and arches her shoulders, letting its warmth travel her face to her neck while sitting on the floor.

She had ventured off their island of Lidingö and into town to do some shopping at NK department store along Hamngatan. She'd also stopped for some sushi and wine at a fusion restaurant before heading back home. Jonny's electric car is parked so she knows he's home, but their housekeeper's hatchback is gone.

Brittany stretches some more, letting the heat course through her, before dropping her head. She knows her husband's quirks. He often moves stealthily around her like a ghost. She feels him there in the dark.

"You can at least say hello," she says, not turning back to look at Jonny sitting in the large plush armchair behind her all along.

He remains silent.

She glances over her shoulder to look at him. He's wearing a white T-shirt over jeans with bare feet. He leans forward as if in thought, his fingers linked. He peers at her intently. She turns back to watch the leaping flames as they dance. They twirl and shoot up in small bursts of fury.

"I tried calling you," he says, his voice low.

"I was busy."

More silence.

"Where have you been?"

She leaves his question hanging. Her back turned to him, she hears him wringing his fingers nervously behind her. Agitation makes them dance. He keeps lacing and interlacing them.

"Out," she mutters while rubbing heat from the fireplace into her skin.

"Where did you go?" he asks.

"Out to dinner." Silence bears once more on them like a heavy blanket.

"But we usually have dinner together." Jonny seems confused.

Brittany lets out a huff of frustration. Jonny's world is black and white. No nuance. She pushes up to her feet and spins around. He shoots to his feet too. He moves to inches from her face, peering at her, his eyes gleaming like diamonds in the absence of light. Her breath catches at the sight of him. The same way it did when she'd seen him for the first time onboard her flight. He reaches to stroke her forearm. She brushes past him instead, making her way to their winding staircase.

Once inside their bedroom, she shuts the door and leans against it, taking long deep breaths. She had asked Kemi for help at their brunch date. To help find a lawyer. She doesn't trust her, but she has no one else in Sweden she can fully trust with such sensitive news. That her seemingly perfect life is all a lie. Trapped with no clean way out from a man obsessed with a ghost.

Maya is Jonny's daughter. She deserves the life her father's wealth and privilege are crafting around her. How will Jonny handle child support? Will he cut her off because he can't get what he wants? Cut their child off? And his family? Will they sever all ties? Her relationship with his parents remains nonexistent, but his older sisters—Antonia and Svea—she still keeps in touch with on a civil basis. After all, they are Maya's only aunts.

She sheds her dress and treads lightly into the bathroom. She craves a hot shower. She needs to think. To consider her next moves. Once Kemi helps her find a lawyer, what next? She can't leave Sweden with Maya without Jonny signing permission. The authorities won't let her. She'd already tried and hadn't made it past an hour.

She turns on the shower's powerful jet sprays and closes her eyes as pins of water hit her face with force.

At least in the States, she would get half Jonny's assets because they're legally married. She isn't sure about Sweden. She'd googled and read on some expat forum that assets aren't simply automatically split in half if both spouses' names aren't tied to them. She's pretty sure his family has legal documents protecting his personal property as a result of his dating history. His total assets remain a mystery. Louise, his Stockholm assistant, dutifully transfers six figures in Swedish kronor into her account every month. Their villa is in his name, not hers. And her Range Rover too.

What exactly does she own in Sweden?

She splashes water over her body and reaches for shower gel when she hears the glass door creak. She spins around to Jonny, stark naked, who swallows up the space between them. He pulls her to fit his frame, his hands grabbing her backside firmly. His name barely leaves her mouth because he drowns her words, prying her lips apart with his.

Jonny's kiss burns fiercely. A side of him she rarely sees because he's usually hellbent on pleasing her instead. This time, Jonny gives her no space to protest as his tongue claims hers possessively, vigor in every vein. He crushes her against his heaving chest, his hands roaming upwards, over her back. She tastes fear in his ferocious kiss.

He dutifully claims her, taking control in a way she's rarely experienced before, possessing her, running shivers to her toes.

"Jonny," Brittany moans against his kiss in an unconvincing protest. He swallows his name too. She wraps her arms around his neck. He lifts her up against the wall, pinning her with his weight as hot water pelts them. He knows how to disarm her. He's doing it again in ways he knows she likes.

"Stay with me," he murmurs against her neck before trailing it with his lips. "Please don't leave me," he whispers against her skin before tightening his grip. He wraps her long legs around his waist. Brittany gasps, blinking to fully catch her breath. She opens her eyes to his locking with hers intensely, burrowing into her, challenging her to deny him.

To slip out of his grasp for good, she has to keep him close right now. To keep letting him believe he is in control. So, when Jonny begins his pounding rhythm, Brittany concedes this round.

KEMI

Tobias hasn't surfaced in a week. She desperately misses him and his grin with its small gap between the top front teeth. A grin which narrows his eyes. She misses his handsome freckled face. The waft of cinnamon when he bakes buns to appease her. His pitiful attempt at *benachin*—a rice and lamb dish—which he often makes. His full lips. His broad swimmer's shoulders.

His Gambian mother Nancy had invited them to dinner along with his younger sister Tina before Kemi was supposed to jet off to the States for the holidays. She isn't sure if the dinner is still on or if Tobias's family knows of their little rift.

Her phone beeps with a text message from him.

Mamma said we should be there by 7 p.m. tomorrow. Tina can't make it. I'll come get you.

Kemi stares at the message, basking in its promise of reconciliation, while annoyed at his flightiness. The first time she met Tobias's mother was in June during Midsummer celebrations. She had immediately taken a liking to her. Her robust laugh. Her shimmering dark skin. The same toothy grin her son had inherited. Her short-cropped hair. Nancy exuded a confidence and contentment Kemi prays she'll find someday, lest she continue spiraling into a space where nothing or no one is enough for her.

She can't wait to spend more time with Tobias's mother. To get to know him better through her. She contemplates responding right away with a wordy longing for his return. The only words her fingers type are "Okay, thanks." She bites her lower lip as she sends it off. She doesn't expect him to respond.

Five minutes later, as she inches her way toward work, a text message from him pops up.

Sure.

The von Lundin offices are practically empty when she walks in that Friday morning, save for twinkling lights and their grandiose behemoth of a Christmas tree which is anything but *lagom*—*moderation*. Most of her colleagues have already slunk off for the holidays. Returning to the office after working remotely for the entire week feels refreshing. She finds solace in her cubicle. Her best always comes out to shine within its walls.

Before reaching her own slice of office space, she hears voices coming out of a nearby conference room. She inches closer and peeks in. Espen Wiklund, Head of Client Services, sits on the edge of the table with a mug of coffee in hand, laughing at something the man with seventy percent dark chocolate hair is saying.

Ragnar.

When Espen catches her, his laughter dies. He stands and moves away from the table. Ragnar turns toward the door, his deep ocean blues taking her in.

"Excuse me," she begins to apologize.

Espen holds up his right hand. "It's okay, we were done anyway." Espen strides up to her, gives her a half-smile, and squeezes past, leaving her with the one person she doesn't trust herself with.

Ragnar rises to his feet. They stare at each other in silence. Her eyes move to his lips. They travel down, sweeping across his chest straining beneath a dress shirt one size too small. Her gaze returns to his eyes. She watches his pupils dilate, as he takes her in.

She closes the door, then takes a few more steps into the room. "I thought you were leaving the project?" she finally asks after crossing her arms over her racing heart in defense.

"I tried," Ragnar says.

Kemi swallows. Heat bubbles up within her. "Well, you didn't try hard enough." Her words taste bitter. She hopes he senses her fury because she hates him. Hates every inch of him for making her weak. For exposing her so rawly that she's pretty sure she'll never regain her footing.

He gives her a wry smile and says, "Jonny wants us in London next week for a last-minute end of year purchase." His eyes remain serious. "Something caught his fancy." He holds her gaze.

"Why do I need to go on this trip?" she says. "I don't need the stress before I head off to the States."

She watches him grate his teeth behind his closed lips. "Espen and Maria are coming too, so we'll definitely have chaperones." His eyes dance over her bust. They move back to lock with hers. "We might need them."

"On the contrary," Kemi counters. "I have self-control."

He chuckles, his glance squinting with the motion, but it never leaves hers, pinning her in place. She doesn't back down. She keeps her arms tightly hugging her chest in response.

Is this why? This metaphoric standoff? The mere thought of him stokes her competitive edge. She'll never let him win this. Whatever *this* is between them.

"Ragnar," she starts in a low voice. "There are rumors going around"—she hesitates—"about us." He stays silent. "I need you to stop them."

Ragnar's eyebrows dip into his trademark frown, one which holds the world in suspicion of everything. He glares at her, roaming her face, brows furrowed.

"I need them to stop. My career, my reputation. I've never done anything like this before," she continues in a whisper.

"I'm sorry for what happened," Ragnar says. "I deserved that slap," he chuckles. His laughter dies when he reads her face.

She cringes when she remembers. From the elevator into a taxi, they had continued ravaging each other until that slap. She'd swept her palm across his face, because when she finally refused him, he'd said: *Too bad, you would have been one sweet fuck.*

Ragnar continues, breaking her memories. "I'll talk to Ingrid and tell her I was drunk and made inappropriate passes at you."

"She saw us," Kemi says. "I wasn't protesting against your inappropriate pass." She locks eyes with him.

"I know," he agrees.

He glides toward her, looks down at her. He now stands close enough to be a colleague discussing business, though the energy between them chokes her. Memories of his mouth claiming hers, his hands caressing her, tease out goosebumps. She shivers. They take each other in quietly, chests heaving, stealing a few more seconds.

"I don't regret it," Ragnar breaks their silence with a whisper, his eyes warming.

Kemi backs up at his confession, the door stopping her as she hits it. Ragnar inches toward her, but she fumbles for the handle and opens the door, fleeing from him.

* * *

The sharp buzz of her doorbell announces Tobias's arrival later that evening.

He has a key. He can let himself in. This new distance bothers her. She fastens her earring and opens the door for him. Tobias Wikström. Wearing the same heavy aviator jacket he wore on their first date. Those brown eyes. That mocha-colored skin crowned by short kinky reddish-brown hair. The result of an affair between his Gambian mother and her Swedish professor two decades older.

"*Hej.*"

"*Hej.*"

"I brought you something." He digs into his jacket pocket and pulls out a brown paper bag.

The sweet smell of *brända mandlar*—candied almonds—fills her apartment. She reaches for it, grabs a piece, and pops it into her mouth. She muffles a *thank you* and that toothy smile, which melted her once, returns.

"I can't quit you," he says, stepping closer, gathering her into his arms. She cranes up to look at him.

"You were right. That was a bit selfish of me." She pieces together an apology. "I had no right to ask you to give up everything you've ever known, to give up your life for me when you weren't ready."

"Someday I might." He grins at her.

"But not right now," she says. He purses his lips, nods. It's too soon. Tobias is Sweden and Sweden is Tobias. His African side remains firmly parked at his mother Nancy's.

The next day, Kemi and Tobias stroll into Nancy's apartment in Norsborg, finding her gliding around in a loose-fitting batik boubou. Normally, when Nancy invited people over, it was a packed house with people overflowing from her dining table to the living room, balancing plates on knees.

This time around, she wanted Kemi alone alongside her kids. Tobias's younger sister Tina couldn't make it.

Upon sight, Nancy pulls her into a crushing hug and releases her so Kemi can catch her breath.

"You this woman," Nancy starts in a tone half reprimanding, half jovial. "You're giving my son too much headache," she says before whirling off into the kitchen. Kemi follows her.

"Headache?"

Nancy passes her a bowl of salad to carry out instead. Kemi obeys as silently commanded and returns for more tasks.

"Yes, headache." Nancy picks up their conversation while stirring a pot of *domoda*—peanut and lamb stew. "I hope you're not allergic to peanuts. I don't have any medicine for that."

"No, *uhmm*. Has Tobias said anything?" Nancy continues stirring the pot while mouthing the lyrics to a Fela Kuti highlife tune blasting through the apartment. Kemi is realizing that Nancy moves at her own pace, while everyone else rushes past her, slaving away to punctuality.

"He doesn't talk much to me," Nancy says. "Only that you want him to leave his mother and move back with you to America."

Kemi sighs. She recognizes her own mother's tactic. "I didn't tell him to leave you."

"But you told him to move to America with you. That means leaving his poor mother."

"I didn't tell him. I asked him to move back to the States with me."

"Smart girl." Nancy turns to her and giggles, revealing that toothy grin Tobias has inherited. "I see why he likes you."

"Nancy, I love Tobias and want to spend more time with him."

"You love him?" Kemi locks eyes with her.

"Yes, I do. Very much."

"*Haaa*. This is serious territory," Nancy says, before grabbing a ladle and spooning large chunks of *domoda* into a porcelain serving dish. "Have you told him yet?"

Kemi ponders Nancy's words. No, she hasn't told him she loves him. Saying those words comes with a certain finality. It means admitting to herself she would have to tune into his wavelength for a while. He has to know she does, right? Otherwise, she would never have asked him to uproot himself. She moved to Sweden looking for love under the guise of a high-powered job and finally found it. At least in the simple form Tobias is offering it to her.

Now Sweden wants something from her in return. Her job. Her career. She's realizing she can't have it all at once. She's being forced to choose between Tobias Wikström and her dreams of becoming Chief Marketing Officer for a large agency. Or maybe opening her own agency. She has enough clout within the industry to do so.

"No, not yet."

"Then why are you telling me instead? What if he gets hit by a bus tomorrow?"

"He's not going to get hit by a bus tomorrow."

"But it could happen, *ehn*?!"

"I will tell him when it's right."

Nancy spins toward her, the full dish in hand. "Look, Tobias has been waiting for you all his life. A strong African woman."

This is the second time since meeting her that Nancy has said this. The first meeting had been at Midsummer, punctuated with the fact that Tobias only dated white women before her. Kemi had processed that remark for weeks.

Is she overthinking Nancy's words? Or maybe Tobias only craves a different body to warm his bed for the time being? Like being on a diet?

Nancy's words derail her.

Over dinner, she watches as Nancy speaks Wolof to Tobias, while he responds in Swedish. At least that is what she assumes until she asks.

"Mandinka," Nancy corrects her, before spooning some rice and *domoda* into her mouth. "I also speak Wolof and French," she adds between chewing.

"Do you speak Mandinka?" Kemi turns to Tobias, who quietly

eats. He regards her with heavy brown eyes. Something is on his mind. He shakes his head and continues with his meal.

By the time they leave, exhaustion claims them. Kemi's own mother often talked nonstop, but Nancy? Chatting with Tobias's mother requires preparation and endurance.

In two years, Kemi had racked up a sizable savings account under von Lundin. She had finally invested in her own car, a hybrid, which Tobias often drives for them because she doesn't have her full license yet.

Before he opens the passenger door for her, Kemi stops him. She pulls his head down for a kiss. She always loves kissing him. The way he takes time savoring her. Her kiss is a *thank you* and *forgive me* all wrapped up with a bow of promise for later on that night. She rests in their kiss. He leans against the car and draws her closer to fit him.

Ragnar's face flashes across his and she tastes Ragnar's lips instead. Kemi gasps, pulling back.

"What's wrong?" Tobias asks, brows arching in concern, his eyes searching her face. She avoids his gaze, scared at what just happened.

"Sorry, I-I just got light-headed, that's all," she stutters, an excuse. "I think Nancy's JulBrew made me dizzy."

"You didn't drink that much." Tobias laughs. "Come here." He pulls her closer by her jacket.

But the moment evaporates. Ragnar is already a parasite within her, one now attacking every cell that loves Tobias. She needs to kill his essence. To see a therapist to rid herself of him. Of men like him.

She gives Tobias a peck and opens the passenger door herself.

FOUR

YASMIIN

There she is.

Yasmiin's eyes roam over the petite younger woman as she lies motionless on stark white sheets, her fully bandaged arms lying straight at her sides. She's covered up to the waist. Muna's face has mostly been spared. Black-purple bruises and a large burn across her left cheek. Another bandage over her head like a turban.

She has finally been allowed to visit Muna at Karolinska Hospital as her next of kin.

"We had to do an emergency amputation the same night she was rushed to us," the attending doctor had explained to her once they were in the room by Muna's side. "We didn't have time to wait for next of kin permission. We had to save her life first."

Yasmiin had spun back to a sleeping woman, her eyes traveling down her lower half. Fingers shaking, she had peeled back the covers to reveal Muna's upper left thigh.

All that is left of her left leg. She dare not peek under those pale sheets again.

Yasmiin sucks in a sharp breath, the only sounds in the room the beating of her heart and the beeping on the heart monitor Muna is hooked to.

She remembers the first day that she laid eyes on Muna. It was over two years ago when their social worker responsible for checking in on them, Gunhild, walked her over from the *tunnelbana*—the metro—to their modest Tensta apartment, northwest of town. She had given Muna a hug that the younger girl did not want to pull out of.

Yasmiin had realized the depths of Muna's loneliness in that hug. The well of isolation she must have felt. She immediately embraced her like a younger sister. Muna grew clingier as the months flew by. Never wanting to be alone. Always looking to build some sisterhood.

A few days before her visit to the hospital, Yasmiin met the female officer at Gunhild's apartment. The place oozed musty, dark, depressing. Everything was still in place, as if the older woman had simply gone shopping for groceries. Cups left untouched. A stale smell permeating the air. The officer rested against the doorframe to Muna's own room, watching as Yasmiin packed up her things. Enough to fill a duffle bag and one suitcase.

Yasmiin paused by the vanity mirror, taking in the photos tacked on it. She bit her lower lip as her eyes washed over Muna's family. Father, mother, and a brother. They all seemed so happy, their clothes and surroundings quite modest. Yasmiin herself came from a middle-class working family. Her past life had been a comfortable cocoon before she'd fled. She could tell from Muna's pictures of her family that theirs had been a sparse life, yet one filled with smiles and love.

Her eyes settled on a photo—a handsome man with an amber stare. He carried a sheep across his shoulders, his hair picked up by the wind, his honey eyes twinkling. This must be him. The Kurdish man whose wooden box of memories and artifacts now belonged to Yasmiin.

So, Muna had a boyfriend, Ahmed, who she had never uttered a word about in all that time. Yasmiin was going to make it her mission to find out why.

Yasmiin had already peeked into that wooden box and fingered its contents curiously: silver chains, misbaha prayer beads, pewter rings, burnished jewelry, a Kurdish Peshmerga flag, sheared sheep wool, a plastic container full of sand, and family photos including several passport photos.

She transferred the box, along with Muna's few belongings, to her place in Hässelby. The box needed time to assess in detail. To fully understand why Muna would have been carrying it around for years. She needed to understand why Muna hadn't shared him with her.

But first, she needed to see Muna.

Now Yasmiin sits quietly, mechanical beeping as background music. She stares at an unmoving Muna, her chest slightly rising and falling with each breath to stay alive. Observing her now, fragile and hanging on, she looks like a child. Yasmiin's heart breaks once more.

"*Gacaliye Muna*," she starts in Somali, her voice shaking with emotion, "*aad baan uga xumahay.*" *Dear Muna, I'm so sorry.*

A pained gasp escapes Yasmiin before she fully lets her tears consume her. For years, she'd known isolation too. What it felt like to be completely on your own. Yet she'd never made Muna feel safe. She realizes that now as she weeps. How love and family can give shape to nothingness.

For all his theatrics, Yagiz Çelik shaped her own void of loss and created form around it. When she met Yagiz for the first time, it was in the sweaty core of a reggae dancehall in Akalla. She'd been there by herself, not fully sure why she sought that place out, but knowing deeply that old habits die hard. It had been close to a year without foreign hands roaming her flesh and she felt weirdly alien in her own body.

Yagiz had been there with a couple of his Turkish friends. The same ones who now call her Yagiz's "*Afrikalı prenses*" whenever they see her or come over to talk business or belch on their couch. *Yagiz's African princess.* A sarcastic inside joke because his friends always say everyone from Africa claims they are princes and princesses of some tribe. He always curses them out, though, calling them idiots, whenever they come around insinuating nonsense.

She had been smitten upon first sight. They found each other, dancing and gyrating, the crowd long forgotten, she letting him know without words that his hands were at home on her generous backside. Before the night was over, they found their way outside to a shadowed corner and made out until two random Ethiopian men peeled her away from Yagiz, screaming at him that their "sister" was not a prostitute.

Yagiz had laughed off their possessiveness and handed her his business card, inviting her to come to his kebab shop. He pulled her hand up to his mouth for a kiss but the men dragged him away from her before his lips reached their mark, and he chuckled.

Yasmiin had giggled before flipping his card between her fingers and mouthing his name: *Yagiz*.

It took her a month before gathering up the courage to show up at his kiosk in Kungshallen. She found him in boisterous banter with a customer. When his dark gaze landed on her, he froze. One of the few times Yasmiin would later count as his rare moments of silence. A tiny smile lifted the right corner of his mouth in recognition before he yelled out, "*Aşkım!*" spreading both arms out dramatically.

Aşkım. My love.

She would later add that word to her sparse list of Turkish phrases. He had popped out from behind the kiosk, his customer dismissed, and beelined toward her. He stood inches from her face, his hands resting on his hips, a kitchen rag flung across a shoulder, as he peered down at her.

"You want to continue what we started," he chuckled with a glint in his eye. "Am I right?"

She giggled. "If your kebab is as good as it smells, then maybe," she teased. A roar erupted from him, head thrown backward, hands still on hips. His eyes then settled back on her. They roamed her face, crawled their way down her chest, which had been sealed tightly beneath a high-collar blouse. His smile dropped as his eyes made their way back to hers, and she took a visible deep breath.

"So, what's your name, *aşkım*?" Yagiz finally asked her.

They did finish what they started in so many ways. The very roughness which had forced her to scream in agony beneath strange hands had urged her to scream in ecstasy under his touch. In between fucking and eating, they frequented most of Stockholm's clubs far out in the suburbs, where clientele were more brown than white, his arm always thrown possessively across her shoulder to ward off potential suitors. The feisty Turk had slipped in through the cracks of her heart, filling her completely to overflowing, so that she finally left that place. She moved out of her shared apartment in Tensta and left Muna behind to fend for herself.

Barely two months after moving out, Yagiz had wept against her still-flat belly. And the second time she ever witnessed him cry was when their sand-colored son Mehmet with his dark eyes, dark lashes, and dark hair finally wailed his way into their world.

Yagiz promised her a proper Turkish wedding. He was planning on taking her to Ankara to meet his *Baba*, who had retired and moved back to Turkey. To meet his extended family, the rest of the Çelik clan. The ones in Sweden, his five sisters and three brothers, had already accepted her upon sight. It seemed the family now growing around her was taking forms she never would have dreamed of. Creating meaning out of her abyss with Yagiz, unbeknownst to him, showing her how it feels to be treasured, so she never has to tremble in fear again.

So, she keeps her memories buried, her past deeply entrenched. She's dead-scared of losing them all if they find out that Yasmiin, with her round cheeks, shoulder-length hair, and soft pear shape, sold her body numerous times for less than the cost of a *räksmörgås*. A shrimp sandwich.

Yasmiin sobs with mixed emotions. Sadness for her friend lying in front of her with no one and nothing left in this world. The other emotion, a tiny bit of relief. Of course Yagiz wasn't having an affair with her. She'd been ludicrous to think it. He simply pitied her because he'd also realized she was all alone.

She cries against Muna's bed, the younger woman unmoving, until Mehmet, who she has been cradling to her chest while he sleeps, stirs, whimpers, and lets out a piercing wail of hunger.

BRITTANY-RAE

Brittany watches him dress as she lies beneath their goose-feather duvet in a bedroom the size of a modest New York apartment. Jonny had already run ten kilometers that morning. He runs religiously every morning, rain or shine. He'd returned with cheeks flushed red from frigid temperatures.

He stands in front of the mirror, tucking a crisp white shirt into light-gray pants. He combs his wheat-colored hair with his fingers, pushing rogue strands into place. He keeps raking and raking, his way of calming his own nerves, Brittany knows.

Jonny reaches for his titanium watch sitting on a dresser. He pulls it on. He calmly strides back to the mirror, eyes roaming over his body to smooth out wrinkles and errors. He pats out an invisible crease here and another invisible pleat there.

Brittany observes him as he goes through his meticulous ritual. One he has been doing since the first time he dressed in front of her. His obsessive compulsion.

The first time they were fully intimate had been in his London watchtower—a sparsely decorated eighteenth-floor penthouse in Canary Wharf. A replica of that furniture in his hideout also graces their home here in Elfvik on Lidingö, one of Stockholm's wealthiest islands. He had studied every inch of her surface area then.

Last night, Brittany finally admitted to herself that she has become addicted to his lovemaking as they went at it wildly against their shower wall.

Jonny turns to her, fists bunched by his sides. "I have to go to work now," he says. When he inches toward her, she holds up a palm to stop him.

"Have a great day at work," she says.

He nods, gaze still on her. "Will you be here for dinner when I get back?"

When Jonny says this, something snaps within her. She has fallen so far off her track that now this man expects nothing more from her than to be there when he gets back, doing nothing, being nothing.

She bites her lower lip, willing him to disappear from her sight. He asks her again because his mind can't handle loose ends.

"Will you"—his fingers move within their fists—"be here for dinner when I get back?"

"I have to take care of Maya. Go to work, Jonny." She catches the small beam on his lips. He takes a few more steps toward her. She stops him once more with a splayed palm. "Go to work," she repeats, her eyes locked with his. He holds her gaze for a few seconds, his brows dipping.

When Jonny leaves the room, Brittany gasps in despair. She had let herself fall so deeply into a space where she lost who she was. She worked for years as a flight attendant. Had become a senior crew member at British Airways who could bid for first and business class cabins because she'd raked up years of experience. She modeled in her twenties. She still dreams of becoming a fashion designer, even though being in her forties suggests otherwise, because she has yet to inch closer to that dream.

Brittany decides she's going to stand on her own two feet once more. After a quick shower, she pulls on a cashmere sweater over dark jeans and struts over barefoot to her daughter's room. Maya's already awake, dressed like a doll by her au pair.

"Hey baby!" Brittany's face lights up as she grabs the toddler from the younger woman's arms.

"Mamma!" Maya's high-pitched squeal rings sweet in Brittany's ears. Her eyes wash over her daughter with her tight curls and large hazelnut-brown eyes. Brittany plants a kiss on her cheek.

"Mamma's here," she says and bounces her daughter on her hip, while holding back tears. For Maya's sake, she must get herself together. Pull herself out of the alternative reality she's living in where she feels the world can't touch her while bundled in privilege. In a sense, she isn't ready to release Maya into that world. A world without privilege. Not quite. Her baby would never understand.

"After breakfast, I am planning on taking her to the park to play," her au pair Vicky informs her.

She nods. Maya lacks friends. Brittany realizes she's also cocooning her child from a social life too. There are other moms on maternity leave who often push strollers in the park. They usually bring coffee, yogurt, and fruit with them. Snacks to snap them back into shape in no time. Brittany decides she'll make an effort.

She needs friends. She must practice her Swedish and not retreat into her shell like a snail anytime anyone tries to converse with her in it. Some of those fellow Lidingö latte moms could end up becoming dear friends. One skill she cherishes is making small talk. Years as a flight attendant honed this strength.

"You know what? Let me take her instead."

The British au pair gapes at Brittany, eyes squinting. "Are you sure, Mrs. von Lundin?"

"Please stop calling me that. Just call me Brittany."

"I know. Old habits are hard to shake off," Vicky says.

"Well, let's kill them here, shall we?" Brittany smiles, handing Maya back to her. "Please bundle her up in her winter gear," she directs before leaving her daughter's room.

KEMI

Kemi finally sees what had caught Jonny's fancy, as Ragnar casually put it, once they land in London. A lithe creature, barely twenty-five years old, sitting across from Kemi, a flute of champagne in hand about to toast her twenty million pound acquisition by von Lundin. A full head of wispy chestnut curls, lush skin with a hint of ethnic ambiguity, the cushiest pillows for lips, and feline eyes which shamelessly keep washing over Jonny.

Kemi's thoughts rush to Brittany. Isn't a goddess in flesh form enough for him? What on earth is going on?

"*Skål!*" Maria, media relations, leads the toast. "We will start the new year with this press release." She beams, tapping flutes with *Ms. Veronica.* Surprise, surprise. Veronica is a former model who got into design, then joined a startup with two white male co-founders, who both now chat in Swedish to Espen and Jonny. Veronica is simply their investor-luring face.

Ambient lounge music spun from a live DJ fills the upscale air of the glass-enclosed hotel rooftop on which they're currently downing overpriced cocktails. They have an incredible direct view of the Shard close by. Their party is still in suits, ties, and formal dresses, just coming in from getting the sale officially notarized and taking press photos together for the embargoed announcement.

More *skål*s are strewn out, choking Kemi. She has never felt this useless and unwanted in her life. She tries making small talk. Veronica's pop culture references fly over her head. Are her instincts getting weaker? Is her star rapidly dulling?

Kemi chugs her Chardonnay, then launches onto her stilettoed feet. "If you'll excuse me," she says.

Ragnar rushes to his feet too, scanning her face. "Is everything okay?"

"I need some air, that's all." She feigns a smile. "Congratulations, Team VEEK, welcome to von Lundin." She tucks her clutch purse under an armpit and grabs her coat.

"I'll walk you out," Ragnar offers. She rushes off, not glancing his way. He darts after her. A few feet away from their table and the curious gazes, she spins around and stamps her palm on his chest to stop him from following her. She quickly pulls it away once she feels heat. Ragnar's faster. His large palm covers hers, grabbing her hand, bringing it back to his chest, tightening his grip.

"Let me go, I need to get air," she protests.

His eyes hook hers instead. "You're angry." They darken when Kemi glares back at him, enraged.

"No, Ragnar. I'm livid. Why the fuck am I here? To gawk at Jonny's girlfriend?"

She yanks out of his grip and heads for the elevators. Ragnar follows her. The whole scene smacks of déjà vu. This time, though, if he touches her in the elevator, she'll punch him square in the face.

"Who the fuck does von Lundin think I am?" Kemi fumes as she frantically pushes the call button. "You all came for me in the States. You brought me here because you guys know what I can do. What I've done dozens of times for others."

"She's not his girlfriend," Ragnar tries to reason. "Brittany is his world. Trust me."

"I don't give a fuck who she is to him," Kemi seethes. "I will not be disrespected and treated like this. Paraded to show that you have one Black employee? Oh wait, now two?" She pauses to collect her breath. "What the heck does that startup do anyway?"

She gets into the elevator and pushes the button for the fourth floor toward her room. Ragnar hits his own floor. The twelfth. She closes her eyes and leans back against the wall. Box breathing. She breathes in deeply, holds, breathes out, and holds it once more to calm herself down.

She had seen Ragnar's eyes grow darker as her anger flamed hotter. They both seem to be seesawing between emotions, him calmly drawn to her enraged version.

Now he stands next to her in uncharacteristic silence, watching her relax her nerves.

Kemi has felt completely humiliated the entire day. Starting with their company ride from the airport where everyone bantered in deep business Swedish, excluding her from their conversation, to sitting quietly through their acquisition proceedings. Not one word had she been allowed to utter beyond bobbing her head in agreement when she was introduced as Director of Diversity and Inclusion. Veronica had simply bunched up her shoulders and muttered "Cool" in typical schoolgirl fashion, leading Kemi to question just how old she was.

Reticence isn't one of Kemi's virtues in boardrooms. Especially around tables where she clearly needs to speak. Yet, she'd simply followed along because of *his* presence. When Ragnar rushed after her from their table, she already knew why she'd been summoned to tag along to London. He'd convinced his best friend to bring her because he wanted her alone, away from Sweden's shores.

Because whatever happens in London, stays in Lon— The elevator pings and opens on the twelfth floor, breaking her thoughts. Her eyes bolt open, though she dare not glance his way.

"I'll see you at breakfast…"

Ragnar grabs her left hand instead and drags her along with him out of the elevator. They make it a few feet until she yanks out of his grasp again. He pivots to face her. She pulls her coat tighter around her shoulders. She begins picking invisible lint off the fabric.

"Shouldn't you check up on Pia instead?" she says. She catches his nostrils flare. "How many more months has Pia got left to go now?" Ragnar regards her silently from the distance she now puts between them. "You must be excited," she continues, her raw nerves exposed beneath the heavy coat.

"Saying her name isn't going to make me want to fuck you any less."

Ragnar's response is low and hard, almost a grumble. Kemi's breath catches in her throat. She clears it, so she can breathe her way through whatever unbothered mode she's about to switch on.

"Have you no self-control?" Kemi hisses at him once she finds her voice. "Don't be so shameless," she dips into a whisper. Ragnar slowly closes the gap between them in the corridor. One heavy calculating foot in front of the other, his eyes reaching her before he does. Once he stands close enough for her to feel his breath race across her face, he speaks.

"Unlike you, Kemi, I have self-control." His ultramarine eyes, now dark inky pools, suck her in. "I know what's real and what isn't."

"Oh, do you now?" Her sarcasm surfaces. She hears her voice become brittle.

He grabs her, crushing her close. His scent. Fresh forest dew. It envelops her, drowns her, fogs up her mind. He leans into her neck, his lips trailing her citrus-scented skin. She feels her legs begin to buckle.

"You smell so good," he mutters against her skin. "I want to taste you." She feels the wet flick of his tongue against her neck. *Breathe in. Hold. Breathe out. Hold.* He reaches one wide palm to cup her face. "Come." Their lips barely touch as he brushes hers lightly.

Ceiling-to-floor windows with London's sparkling lights below. Beyond those glowworms lighting up the night sky alongside a brilliant half-moon, Ragnar's room is dark. He quietly leads her to the desk next to those panoramic views. Kemi hears blood rushing in her ears.

Her brain had stopped functioning the second she splayed her hand on his chest to stop him from coming after her. All she had felt then was warm solid muscle. Now she sits as silently commanded atop his desk while he stands tall in front of her, chest cocked outwards, slowly tugging his striped tie loose, his eyes on her.

This stillness unnerves her. Her heart pounds. She can hear it clearly. That's all she hears, though. Not even the steady beating of his own heart or his deep breaths of desire. He's simply drinking her in quietly as he pulls the tie loose, letting it slither to the floor. Next, the whooshing sound of his belt being pulled free, joining his tie.

"Rag—" He swiftly kisses his name off her lips, his tongue parting her mouth, diving in deep. He steps in closer, forcing her legs apart. He tugs her with a strong kiss. She can tell he loves her ample lips. She prays he doesn't destroy them.

"I've wanted you since the day I saw you." Ragnar breaks off to whisper in her ear. He nips it, grazes it with his teeth. He caresses her broad hip, moving the roaming hand up her waist, gripping her soft flesh tightly. Kemi instantly grows self-conscious. He's gripping more fat than she would like. Images of a fat-free Pia with her barely-there baby bump flash across her mind. A squeeze from Ragnar jolts her back.

"Why?" she croaks out breathlessly.

He pulls back up to peer into her eyes, his own twinkling in low light. "I don't know," he confesses.

Kemi studies him as he gazes down at her, his palms now planted on either side of her on the desk. She reaches up for his baby-blue shirt and starts to unbutton it. Unhooking each translucent button slowly under his hooded gaze.

When she reaches the fourth button, she glances up at him, pauses, then forcefully rips it apart. The button flies across the room. Ragnar makes a grunting sound. She rips the fifth one and he grunts again.

When she peeks at him once more, she sees it clearly in his eyes. They have now taken on an indigo hue in that room.

"Was that why?" she whispers back. "*Hmm?*" His hands move to grab her hips forcefully, locking her against his brawn. "Was that why?" She watches the veins in his jaw tense. "See," she murmurs. "You have no self-control."

Ragnar answers her loudly without words on his desk. He shows her why, while she lies on her side on his bed. He tells her roughly on her knees on his floor. She hears him clearly. His heart beating, his breath dying, his grunts. Both of them still fully clothed. Though his shirt is in tatters and the side slit of her plum wrap dress now reaches past her waist. She wonders how she kept her stilettoes on through it all.

Two hours later. Silence cloaks the room once more as they lie side by side on the floor at the base of those windows, peering out across London, glimmering below for the lovers. Her eyes are tightly shut. She can't bear to look at him, to look at her reflection in his, to see what she has become. She knew he'd finally gotten her how he'd always wanted her—raw, exposed, unprotected.

Breathe in. Hold. Breathe out. Hold.

When she turns toward him, she finds Ragnar propped up on an elbow, his head resting on his palm, leering at her with a smirk that reads like victory.

FIVE

YASMIIN

When she leaves Mehmet at daycare for his first full day without her, it feels like ripping flesh off her skin. But she has to drop him off. She's going for her first job interview since being on maternity leave for over a year. Then she'll go visit Muna again. She promised the younger woman, through the grating of heart monitors, that she'll come sit by her side every week.

That Muna will never be alone again.

Forty-five minutes later, Yasmiin pulls open the door to a tiny boutique salon on Kungsholmen owned by a contact of Yagiz's. He seems to know everyone who works blue-collar. Like he's the kingpin of the blue-collar networking scene in Stockholm. The salon belongs to the wife of one of his friends. An Iraqi couple. She's meeting Salima, who has agreed to assess her after Yagiz had threatened her husband over random business.

"What business?" Yasmiin had asked him that morning, curious to know his dealings with these Iraqis.

"Small business," Yagiz had said, waving her aside, a cigarette between his lips. "He owes me small money."

"So your wife is worth small money?" she had retorted. That Yagiz roar she loves filled the room. He simply reached a hand down over her backside, squeezed a cheek, and muttered the word "*Guld.*" *Gold.*

Yasmiin steps into a quiet space and immediately realizes if she gets this job, she will die of boredom. The sole customer looks like a retiree with similar coloring to Salima. Salima pulls strands of jet-black hair upwards and deftly clips off split ends with a seasoned pair of scissors.

"Yasmiin?" Salima peers over the rim of her glasses at her. Yasmiin gives her a weak smile in response. "I've been expecting you. Sit!"

Yasmiin glances around the space, a technicolor bastion of interior decor thrown together in hodge-podge fashion. A photo of Baghdad's cityscape. Pictures of striking turquoise-domed mosques. Yasmiin isn't sure how old those photos are. A large portrait of Sweden's King Carl XVI Gustaf and Queen Silvia. A photo of Zlatan with fists in the air, running, while wearing his yellow football jersey representing Sweden. There are vases of flowers, a mix of artificial and natural blooms, and varying degrees of gilded knick-knacks hinting at someone who loves flea markets.

"So," Salima starts after five minutes. "You know how to do hair?"

Technically Yasmiin is a makeup artist, but when she lived in Tensta, she worked at an Ethiopian beauty salon and learned how to cut hair, with each new customer.

"Yes."

"White hair too? Or only Black hair?"

Yasmiin thinks back to the Serbs, Bosnians, Poles, and the occasional Russian who stumbled into that Ethiopian salon out in the suburbs looking to get a wash and blow out for a fraction of the cost in town.

"Yes, and I also do makeup. I am a certified makeup artist," Yasmiin adds.

Salima raises her brows. "White makeup or Black makeup?"

"A face is a face."

This elicits a chuckle from Salima, who turns back to the thick shock of hair she's trimming.

"I like you." Salima laughs. "You have fire. No wonder Yagiz likes you. You can handle him." Yasmiin purses her lips. She isn't sure what she thinks of Salima yet. "So, are you ready?" Salima asks.

Yasmiin furrows her eyebrows in response. Salima snickers once more before handing her the pair of scissors.

A few hours later, she pushes open the door of Salima's salon, ready to leave for the day, and steps out onto the sidewalk.

"Yasmiin?" a thickly bespectacled, sturdy-looking middle-aged white man calls out.

Her shoulders bunch up, startled by the stranger's presence. He readjusts his glasses, then takes another step forward. The hairs on her neck rise and goosebumps wash over her skin. *Middle-aged white man.* Her instincts are piqued and she backs away from him.

The stranger continues. "I am so sorry to scare you," he says in Swedish.

"How do you know my name?" Yasmiin's brows arch in suspicion as she pulls her bag tighter, taking another step backward. Is he a former customer? He doesn't look familiar. Frankly she barely looked at their faces. Is he a link to her past? A friend of Bosse's?

A chill runs through her body. A police officer?

He lifts both his hands to reassure her of his intentions. "Please don't be scared," the man says. "Your husband said I would find you here."

Yasmiin frowns. Why would Yagiz send a strange man to her?

She finds her voice. "What do you want from me?"

"My name is Mattias." The man stretches out a hand to shake Yasmiin's. "I am from Solsidan Asylcenter. I used to watch over Muna there." The asylum center where Muna had lived for months.

Yasmiin stumbles backward, her back hitting the salon's door. A solid link to Muna's past has materialized in front of her. The only words which tumble out are, "*Hur hittade du mig?*" *How did you find me?*

"I heard about what happened to Muna." He pauses to collect his breath. "I am so shocked that she would ever try to do something like this." Yasmiin gawks at him, waiting for his answer. "The police reached out to me at the center as part of their investigation. They named you as next of kin."

Yasmiin continues to stare at him, no words. Mattias begins shifting uncomfortably on his feet.

"Do you have a few minutes for *fika*?" She shakes her head, hesitating. No, she isn't going to have coffee with this stranger. She doesn't want him anywhere near her.

He continues. "I knew Ahmed Tofiq Rahim. Maybe I can provide some answers? Give you some closure?"

A few minutes later they're sitting at a nearby Espresso House.

"Tell me about Ahmed." Yasmiin demands after a sip of sweet coffee so diluted with milk it looks like tea. Mattias adjusts his glasses, then leans forward, arms crossed, resting on the table.

"I think Ahmed was her boyfriend. He was a Kurdish guy who came through Denmark alongside Muna."

"Ahmed." Yasmiin repeats his name, breathing life into it. Muna never mentioned that name, let alone acted like she knew what to do with a man. And certainly no mention of having a Kurdish boyfriend.

"Yes," Mattias confirms. "They spent a lot of time together." He pauses. "Until that horrendous night at the center."

"Horrendous night?"

Mattias sighs before pressing on. "He killed himself. Set himself on fire in front of everyone. Many of them said they saw him give Muna something before doing it."

"The box," Yasmiin gasps. "The police gave me a box filled with items. I think that box is Ahmed's past," she says. "His family, his village, his life."

"I don't understand why Ahmed gave Muna all these things?" Mattias wonders out loud before taking a sip of black coffee.

"Ahmed knew he was going to die and he probably wanted Muna to help him get justice," Yasmiin says. "Something horrible must have happened to his family and his village."

"Ahmed didn't trust anyone," Mattias chimes in. "He wasn't popular at the center either and he was a bit of a loner. Muna kept him company."

"How close were they?" Yasmiin asks.

Mattias shrugs. "I think they were together but hid it very well," he says.

This makes no sense. Is Muna a radical? Did she jump because of Ahmed? Had they even been intimate? Yasmiin ponders quietly over her tea-like coffee.

"So, what do we do now?" she asks.

"Can you please bring that box to me?" Mattias asks. "I need to see what is inside. I suggest we try to find out more about Ahmed and what happened to his village."

Yasmiin eyes him suspiciously. Does he even know Muna is still living, hanging on by a thread at the hospital, machines keeping her alive?

"Why?" she asks, narrowing her eyes at him.

"Yasmiin, the police should never have given you back that box," he starts. "An oversight on their part. They should have cared enough to hold onto it. To find out more—"

"Muna didn't die," she interrupts. Silence hangs between them for a few moments. "She didn't die but all you care about is that box."

"That is not true."

"You don't care about Muna, about Ahmed, about any of them." Yasmiin becomes agitated. "You never did."

"That is unfair," Mattias retorts. "That is why I am here. I do care and I want the police to care enough too." Yasmiin's dark eyes burrow into him, questioning him.

He presses on. "I need you to trust me, Yasmiin."

Trust me.

Yasmiin glares at him. *Trust me.* She processes those words. The very same words greasy Bosse had muttered to her before growling. A muffled sound begins to build up in her chest.

Once it reaches her lips, it morphs into maniacal laughter.

BRITTANY-RAE

Brittany counts three moms huddled around a wooden park table and benches. Steam from their mugs of coffee rises sluggishly up into the frigid air. When she had wheeled Maya out in her stroller into the cold, the toddler immediately dozed off. Now Brittany drags in a deep breath before walking closer to the table.

All three women are bundled up in layers of wool and cashmere covering every exposed limb, all topped off by burly jackets she knows aren't cheap. Her fellow Lidingö moms. Peeking out from beneath bulky furry hats are straight blonde strands and one chestnut hued. They cradle their mugs with mittened hands and chat in short bursts, conserving heat and energy.

Their conversation dies to a lull when Brittany, pushing a sleeping Maya, rolls up to them. A look she can't quite read washes over their faces as they stop to peer at her.

"*Hej*," Brittany greets, her cherry red lips widening into place. Old habits as a flight attendant do die hard.

"*Hej! Kan vi hjälpa dig med nåt?*" one of the blondes asks. *Can we help you with something?*

"Umm, *nej*!" Brittany's voice pitches higher. She knows she has to go there. Her greatest fear. Try to speak Swedish with strangers. "*Jag heter Brittany.*" The blonde she now tags leader of the pack glances at the other women before settling back on Brittany.

"*Jag heter Malin*," she introduces, palm to chest. "*Ellas mamma.*" She points to a toddler about three years old climbing up a mini-playground slide. The other two mammas introduce themselves as well.

"*Kaffe?*" Malin offers. Brittany nods. Soon enough she carries a mug between her mittens, sharing space on a bench with them. Silence washes over the group. Their flow has been interrupted but Brittany doesn't care. She's on a mission to try.

"*Var kommer du ifrån?*" Malin asks.

"USA. Atlanta," Brittany responds. "*Jag är…umm.*"

"Should we speak English instead?" Malin offers.

Brittany bites her lower lip, pleading with her tears not to show how weak and desperate she has become, in front of this pack of rich wives. She lowers her head once the first drop slips through. She wipes it away with the back of a mitten.

Brittany nods. Yes, she needs English. She hates this feeling. Simply hates having no level playing field to start on. Always at a disadvantage when it comes to Swedish. Especially when normally patient Swedes have no patience for new learners of their language.

She isn't sure what they do for money or if their husbands simply support them the way Jonny does her. Right now, she doesn't care.

For once, she's not alone.

"It's alright." Malin places a hand on her arm to comfort her. "I know the feeling. It's not easy to move to a new place and try to learn everything all at once."

Brittany wipes her eyes again. "No, it's not," she adds before stretching those lips wide.

"What brings you here? To Sweden?" Malin continues. Brittany nods her head toward Maya, who's still fast asleep in her stroller.

"Ha!" Malin smiles. "It's always a man, isn't it!" The other two women chuckle. Brittany wonders if it's at her expense or in solidarity.

"So what do you ladies do?" Brittany switches topic.

"Well, Anna here works in finance. Lotta in design. And I am in fashion," Malin says. "But we're all on *mammaledig* now until the spring." *Maternity leave.* Malin's words become a blur once the word *fashion* floats through.

"Fashion?"

Warmth spreads within Brittany as she stares at a potential lead—Malin.

"Yes, have you heard of Stockholm Fashion Week?"

Thirty minutes later, Brittany and Malin are left behind while the others take their leave.

"It's been lovely chatting with you, Brittany," Malin says and stretches out a hand. Brittany grabs it. "Here is my number." Once

Brittany pulls off a mitten to type into her phone, Malin rattles off her digits.

They bid each other "*God Jul*" and promise to connect in the new year.

KEMI

To sabotage. A deliberate act of subversion.

Before Kemi leaves Ragnar's room a little past four in the morning, she sends Jonny a text.

Rescheduling my flight. Feeling under the weather.

She can no longer stay for the rest of their superfluous meetings.

Ragnar sits topless on his bed. His dark hair, reflecting as black in that room, is in disarray as he watches her punch the keys of her device.

"I'm taking the next flight back," she says, slipping her phone into her purse then grabbing her coat. He stands up. She bolts inelegantly for the door. He grabs her, pulling her into a crushing hug before she has a chance to unlock it.

"I swear to God, I will scream," she threatens him. He tightens his grip instead. She wiggles in his arms, seeking freedom. "Let me go."

"You know I'll never hurt you," he whispers into her ear before grazing it with his teeth. "Unless you want me to?" He smirks. She feels that grin against her skin.

"Fuck you." She shoves out of his crushing hug and bolts from his darkness.

Later that morning, she texts Tobias from the airport as she waits to board her flight home, to deter him from coming to get her.

Feeling under the weather. Don't want to get you sick too.

Kemi silently cries all the way to Stockholm, the flight attendants avoiding her in discomfort.

That smirk. Had she let him win so freely?

When she lands, Tobias is there anyway. "Did you think I'd let you fend for yourself while you're unwell?" He pulls her into his warm embrace. Kemi disintegrates, her tears bursting through as she clings to his neck. And in that moment, "*Whatever happens in London, stays in London*" becomes her new mantra.

Once she pulls out of his hug, she asks him to take her to a pharmacy immediately. She must protect herself once more.

Two days later, Tobias swings by to give her a ride to the airport with her car. She's finally heading home for the holidays. He promises to take good care of her car while away. He also takes his sweet time showing her he'll miss her desperately.

Why did she have to go for two weeks? Couldn't she have spent at least New Year's with him and his family?

On the spot, Kemi decides she will indeed cut her trip short to spend New Year's with him.

Her brother-in-law Lanre makes the two-hour drive from Richmond, Virginia, to Dulles Airport to pick her up.

"Madam Sweden!" Lanre bellows before pulling her into a bear hug. "Is this your façe?! We forgot how you looked!" She smiles back and grabs another hug from him.

Soon, they hurtle down I-95 S with Lanre filling her in on her nephew and twin nieces. How much they miss her. How they're looking forward to whatever guaranteed goodies they know are in her suitcase. Kemi laughs before turning to look at the greenery interspersed with buildings flashing by.

She can't believe she actually misses this place. With all its insanity, strife, and constant micro-aggressions. At least here, she knows what she's fighting in daylight. Back in Sweden, she isn't sure what battles lurk in the shadows.

"Did you hear me?" Lanre's words jolt her back.

"What?"

"I said, how are you liking Sweden? Kehinde told me you have a boyfriend there?" He casts a quick glance her way.

"Yes, his name is Tobias," she says. "I think you two will get along." She catches his smiling profile.

"What's his mix again? She said he was from Senegal or something?"

"Gambian-Swedish."

"*Na wa o!*" *Interesting!* She lets his theatrics slide.

"But you're enjoying the place, *sha*?"

"I'm making it work, yes."

Her nieces and nephew are already on the front lawn waiting in anticipation after Lanre calls Kehinde to update her on their progress. And when Kemi steps out of the car, it is into a rain of arms hugging every available part of her, including her knees. She missed them desperately. Her closest family.

When she lived in Washington, DC, she made the trek to Richmond every other weekend to bask in their love. She still has her condo and rents it out through a management company. She envisions her and Tobias living there one day. Crafting a new life together in the States. Showing him her world, while running away from Ragnar.

When Kemi hugs her twin, it is an embrace which speaks without words. The distance has chipped away at Kemi. Spending the dark troughs of winter without proximity to her own family squeezes her soul in ways requiring action: getting up and traveling to the States to recharge.

She has so much to tell Kehinde and her sister wastes no time. Over takeout Chinese for dinner, Kemi opens up her suitcase and hands out chocolate, gingerbread cookies, T-shirts with the Swedish flag blazed across the chest, more paraphernalia and goodies. Lanre busies himself in random tasks and disappears from view once he senses the sisters want to talk. Carrying mugs of tea, Kehinde and Kemi stroll over to the living room where a large flat-screen TV plays *The Real Housewives of Atlanta* in the background.

Kehinde settles into her favorite armchair and tucks her legs underneath herself. Kemi notices her normally lean sister has gained weight. Though identical, Kehinde battles stubborn pimples while Kemi battles her weight, but this time around…

"Sweden looks good on you," Kehinde says before taking a sip of soothing chamomile tea. "You dropped, *abi*?"

"I haven't weighed myself in over a year."

"I can see it in your face," Kehinde adds.

Kemi gives her a half-smile and lifts her mug to her lips. She doesn't need to ask or comment any further. They often work telepathically, which scares them both sometimes. They instinctively know when to push or back off to give the other twin space to fully land and process individual feelings.

"It's my thyroid," Kehinde finally says. "I'm taking medication so it's under control."

"Why didn't you tell me?"

"I didn't want to scare you, *nau*?!"

Kemi takes another sip, while thinking back to their last few video chats. Kehinde's weight gain isn't much, but as her twin, she should have noticed it right away during their calls. Why hadn't she noticed? Had she been so wrapped up in herself she never noticed anyone else? Was this her weakness? Tobias had called her selfish. She's having a hard time shaking off his insult.

"I need to know these things."

"It's okay, I'm fine." Kehinde waves off her worries. "How are *you*?" she asks instead. Kemi shrugs. "What does that mean?"

She's certain Kehinde notices her aloofness.

"It means I don't know how I'm feeling these days."

"Is it because of that married man?"

"Will you keep your voice down?" Kemi snaps between clenched teeth, looking around for eavesdroppers. Kehinde holds her gaze once Kemi turns back to her.

"Where did you meet him?" Kehinde asks. Kemi stays quiet, then sips her tea. She dusts invisible specks of lint off her jeans, eyes downcast, before answering.

"At work. He's my boss's best friend," Kemi says. "He brought him in to take over my project."

"Who says Swedes don't do nepotism, *ehn*?" Kehinde chuckles over the rim of her mug. "So instead of standing your ground and fighting him, you ended up kissing him, *abi*?"

If only kissing was all they'd done.

"It's not like that."

"Please clarify then."

Kemi closes her eyes and sighs. She doesn't need this on her first day back in the States. An interrogation on why she's attracted to Ragnar Pettersen. She can't explain it even if she tries.

"Is he fine?" Kehinde jumps in to prod her along. "*Ehn?* Is that it?"

"Stop it!"

"Is he *oyinbo*?" *White?*

"That has nothing to do with anything. I just can't explain it, okay?"

Kehinde observes her. Kemi hates that particular look. A side-eye with a slight head shake, which insinuates Kemi has already bought business class tickets to hell seated right next to Ragnar.

"How is your boyfriend? Our dear *Tobi*?" Kehinde mimics, in Yoruba.

"Stop it, his name is Tobias and he's fine," Kemi says, a smile creeping onto her lips. "I'm still trying to find the right time to tell him I love him."

"Love him, *ke*?" Kehinde isn't asking. Kemi furrows her brows at her sister. "You don't love him," Kehinde continues. "Your eyes are still roaming, looking for options. Unfortunately they've landed on a dead end. You're not serious at all, Kemi."

"Now you're just being rude," Kemi says, low grade irritation broiling within her. Kehinde simply laughs before *tsk*ing and shaking her head once more.

"You know, as much as I love you, I fear your arrogance will finish you," Kehinde says before lifting lukewarm chamomile tea back to her lips.

SIX

YASMIIN

"Where did Yagiz find you?"

Salima yells those words over the whizzing of the hairdryer she's waving over the head of a woman who looks to be in her early fifties. A fellow Iraqi.

Those words pull Yasmiin away from the combs she's washing in the sink. Yasmiin turns to look at her, then returns to her task. A few days before Christmas, Salima's salon is still open for business. Many immigrants run their businesses round the clock, day in, day out, not bothering about work-life balance, or even having the privilege to stop, ponder, and decipher it.

Salima isn't deterred. "Yasmiin?" She waves her over, using the hairdryer in her hand. Yasmiin tuts with annoyance before sauntering to where Salima now runs a brush through lush black hair shining like the finest silk.

"What is it?" She half-throws the words at Salima, who responds with a chuckle.

She's still working out her boss's brashness. Boundaries remain a foreign concept to Salima, who speaks her mind freely without consequence. A woman who demands access into one's life, invited or not. Yasmiin is still undecided about her. Whether she can't stand her or if she must tolerate her because, despite her impudence, she is actually a good and fair boss.

"Come meet my baby sister, Amani," Salima half-yells as she runs her fingers through her customer's hair. The woman Salima calls Amani turns toward Yasmiin with piercing hazel eyes that sear right through her. "I was just telling Amani that you're Yagiz's wife."

"You know him?" Yasmiin asks.

Apparently everyone within various communities in Stockholm knows him. He seems to flow effortlessly through Iraqi, Somali, and Eritrean cliques with ease, not to forget his Turkish clan. She has yet to meet an immigrant who doesn't react when the name of her vibrant husband is dropped.

Both Salima and Amani laugh at her question. Anger brews up within her. Not at the two women, but rather at Yagiz, who is now making her a laughing stock for some reason she has yet to uncover.

"Everybody knows Yagiz," Salima says as she continues brushing her sister's hair. "Only a strong woman can tame him." She meets Yasmiin's eyes through the mirror. "So, I wonder how you two met." Yasmiin holds her gaze for a few more seconds.

"Is that why you called me over? To explain to you how I met my husband?"

"What? Did I upset you?"

"How did *you* meet your husband?" Yasmiin counters with her own question. Salima's husband, who seems indebted to Yagiz in some fashion. The same husband who forced his wife to give Yasmiin this mundane job.

Salima mutters something beneath her breath, a cross between a curse and a prayer for Allah to intervene.

"Where there is smoke," Salima insinuates, "there's always fire."

"You would know, wouldn't you?" Yasmiin says. "I'm wondering why I got this job in the first place."

Salima shakes her head before launching some words of Arabic at Amani, her tone tinged with frustration.

"Don't mind Salima," Amani finally speaks up. "Always poking her nose in other people's business." She finishes off with a laugh.

"Me?" Salima exclaims in an exaggerated fashion, a hand splayed flat on her chest. "Me? What about you? Stockholm's number one divorce lawyer! Talk about poking your nose deep in other people's business."

Amani laughs, a deep bellow, her shoulders dancing with the sound. Yasmiin turns back to Amani, poring over her with new eyes.

"So, Salima says you also do makeup?" Amani changes the subject, after calming herself.

"That's right," Yasmiin replies. "I'm a Master Makeup Artist certified by the Makeup Institute here in Stockholm." She beams proudly.

"Really?" This time, it's Salima scrunching her nose in mock disbelief. "I thought you only did makeup for fun." Yasmiin rolls her eyes at her.

"That is excellent," Amani chimes in. "I may need your services soon. I have a gala to attend."

"You don't have anyone else to do it?" Yasmiin half-asks.

Amani eyes her, a slow walk from Yasmiin's forehead to her stomach and back up, before ending it with a smile.

"I like you," Amani says.

After picking up Mehmet from daycare, Yasmiin arrives home to find Yagiz lifting weights, grunting as usual in the living room, veins popping along his arms. When she first met him in that reggae dancehall years ago, he was a lean character with a weasel look about him. The man in front of her is twice his size, all solid muscle.

She sets the toddler down, who scurries off toward his room the second his feet touch the floor.

"*Aşkım*," Yagiz calls out, his eyes lighting up the minute she walks into the living room. He drops his weights, wipes sweat off his forehead, before beckoning her toward him. She stands rooted in place. Yagiz lets out a sigh of exasperation. "What have I done this time?"

"Everyone wants to know how I met *Yagiz*," she says bitterly, making air quotes around his name. "They laugh every time they find out that I am your wife. What is this?"

"What is what?" Yagiz pumps his shoulders.

"I'm tired of your business." She folds her arms across her bust.

"Which business are you tired of?" he smirks.

"You know which one."

"Which one? I have many businesses." He splays his palms open.

"Yagiz?!"

"What?!" He bunches his shoulders up at her. She rolls her eyes at him. He is an exhausting man. Yet her love for him keeps her squarely chained to him.

"Salima. Amani. They were laughing at me, asking how we met."

"Ha, Amani." He rubs his hands together in what Yasmiin can only interpret as fond remembrance. "*Tigris Tigress.*"

"She's old enough to be your mother, you nasty man!"

Yagiz chuckles. "So, what is the problem? Why are you angry with me now?" He walks up to her, pulling her toward him by her wrists. He hugs her to his sweaty torso and plants a kiss on her neck.

She pushes him away. "Are you trying to be a big man?"

"Big man?"

"Yes, big man," she repeats, holding his gaze.

"I'm already a big man, *aşkım*," he brags. "I own three businesses." He spreads three fingers. His brows begin to crumble into each other as if questioning her audacity for insinuating he was anything less. "Why are you talking like this?"

As much as she loves him, Yagiz has only given her a glimpse of his depth, which he often masks with charisma. She knows his avoidance tactics. She senses she's the only one who has gotten this close to his core. He looks through her, his dark eyes scanning her face in search of clues.

"Do you know how hard I work? To give you this life? To give us something in this land?" His eyes cloud with emotion. "I wake early and take the *tunnelbana* with every single brown face before seven in the morning. Before the fucking *Svenssons*." The generic tongue-in-cheek equivalent of *John Doe* in Swedish. "I come back with them after nine at night." He catches his breath. "When my son is asleep."

She holds his gaze deeply, and for the first time she identifies what drew her so forcefully to this man.

"I am tired of working hard, Yagiz." She whispers the words softly. "I know you are too."

Yasmiin watches as his features soften, her words cutting him deep. She knows he's also tired. Of being treated as a second-class citizen. Beyond being the hardest-working man she knows, Yagiz is currently building his way to power. Some power. Any scraps of power he can firmly hold onto in this society.

He responds with a hard kiss, prying her mouth open, pulling her tighter into himself as if wanting to meld her physical being with his heart, to have his body open up and swallow her.

She receives his sudden kiss, keeping up with him, savoring him. Her Yagiz is a hard man and an even harder lover. His hand roams to her backside, giving one cheek an equally hard squeeze.

"I am not a big man," he whispers quietly against her lips. "I am a king."

BRITTANY-RAE

When it comes to feasts, the von Lundins know no moderation. Tables are lavishly set with glittering silverware and elegant tableware. They often pool their housekeepers and chefs together when they celebrate as one family, whether for their annual Midsummer ritual in Sandhamn, or Christmas with Antonia, Jonny's oldest sister stepping in as the acting family matriarch as they're doing now on *Julafton. Christmas Eve.*

Brittany's relationship with his parents Wilhelm and Astrid remains nonexistent, specifically with his mother, since the first time Jonny introduced them and Astrid made it clear she did not approve of their love. That tense lunch meeting at Berns had started with Astrid saying terse words in Swedish which left Jonny agitated and in tears. Brittany hadn't understood a word of what she uttered.

They crossed paths two or three times over the years when important family functions forced them together: Antonia's sons graduating with no plans for the future at the moment, a party Antonia threw in honor of the other sister, Svea, announcing her engagement to some financier twenty years her senior.

Now they all sit around Antonia's long table, forks and knives clacking against porcelain as they dine in silence. They have finally been graced with a white Christmas. With the dark bay as backdrop, fluffy white flurries float from the sky.

Brittany glances over at Astrid, who eats bird-like, her mouth widening only to take in tiny morsels. The true matriarch of the family, she looks leaner, older, under her signature short-cropped blonde hair. Yet well preserved for her seventies.

Antonia simply does her bidding, while Astrid metaphorically sits back and observes. She often stares with the same intensity her son has inherited, her eyes seemingly judging everything and everyone in sight.

She senses Brittany staring at her and looks up. Brittany doesn't turn away. It's Astrid who shifts her gaze away this time.

"I would like to propose a toast," Svea says, while tapping her glass with her fork. Svea always cakes herself beneath layers of makeup, her lips plumped up, her cheekbones sharp, natural wrinkles for her age smoothed out every couple of weeks. Everyone else drowsily reaches for their glasses and half-raises them. "Here's to new beginnings."

"To new beginnings," people mutter out of sync before touching glasses with each other.

Then she turns to Brittany.

"*Kära* Brittany," Svea starts. Brittany takes a sip of wine. "I know these years have not been easy for you. But we love you and we support you. Look how happy you make our brother." Brittany glances at Jonny. He is gnawing on his fingernails while leering at her. Brittany purses her lips in response.

Svea lifts her glass once more. "We are so happy to have you in our family. Thank you for choosing us." Brittany cocks her lips slightly at the dramatic speech, wondering what has triggered its delivery.

Dinner continues in low-key conversation. Afterwards, everyone mills around Antonia's villa while waiting for *Jultomte—Santa*—to show up and distribute gifts. The true gifts, money, had already been transferred into everyone's accounts. Astrid strolls toward Brittany, who sits in the heated sunroom with a mug of black coffee, looking out into the darkness.

"May I?" Astrid asks. Brittany glances at her and gives a nonchalant shrug. Astrid clears her throat and settles in a nearby chair. Both women sit in silence for a few moments.

"Brittany, I know things have not been good with us."

"You didn't see your grandchild for over a year," Brittany says, swiveling toward her. "You disrespected my parents when they visited during Midsummer. You sent Antonia to dredge up that Maya Daniels tragedy to spite me." Astrid receives her words quietly. "You have been nothing short of cruel to me."

"I thought you were one of them," Astrid counters.

"One of who? *Uhn?*"

"Those girls who always chase Johan for his money."

"So he didn't chase them too?"

Astrid falls silent. Brittany studies her. *Trust* is the furthest word from her mind. She doesn't trust Astrid and will never place any stock in her words, because the look Astrid is currently giving her says she's only tolerating Brittany's presence within her dynasty because of her son.

"He has always been different," Astrid says. "He was always wanting something exciting, something exotic."

Exotic?

"No, Astrid. You never let Jonny feel normal."

"You don't know everything." Astrid's voice grows stern. "In fact, you may not know much about this family you've married into." Astrid fixes her with a searing glare she recognizes from her husband. "My son means the world to me and I'll do everything to protect him."

Brittany shakes her head at the woman who now sits with color rapidly rising up her cheeks, the only outward display of emotion. She can't do this anymore. Kemi promised to help her find a divorce lawyer within her network but she hasn't heard from her since their brunch. This family is closing in on her faster than she can breathe.

"I know enough to know that you failed him and I'm now paying the price for it," Brittany says.

Astrid wrinkles her brows as she looks up at Brittany. "What price are you paying?" she asks. "If anything, I think you live a very comfortable life now, wouldn't you agree? Johan said you were an air hostess."

"Flight attendant," Brittany corrects her.

"Well"—Astrid waves a delicate hand—"at least life is better for you now, isn't that right? *Eller hur?*" Astrid suddenly stares past her, a smile widening on her face. "*Johan! Kom hit.*" *Come here.*

Brittany turns to find Jonny standing by the entrance to the sunroom, hands clenched into fists by his side. The stance he always takes whenever he stands in front of his mother, Brittany has observed.

"*Kom hit*," Astrid repeats. Jonny strides toward her, then dips low to give their matriarch a peck on the cheek. Brittany glares at Astrid. Then she bolts to her feet, catching the smirk on the older woman's lips, before storming off.

Astrid isn't the only one determined to pull her aside that Christmas Eve. When she tramps back into the main house, Antonia corners her.

"Have you got a minute?"

No, she doesn't have a minute. At this point, nothing Antonia can say is going to pull her out of the depths of hatred she feels for her mother-in-law.

"What is it?"

"Please?" Antonia points in the direction of her husband's study.

Brittany drops her arms to her sides and heads toward the room. It's spacious, furnished in maple and metallic gray, a color she is fast associating with the von Lundins. Antonia kept her last name when she married. Her husband Stig decided to take hers instead—Stig von Lundin. A name Brittany suspects is more powerful than his own.

Antonia shuts the door quietly behind them and offers Brittany a seat. She declines.

"What is it?" Brittany asks.

Antonia lets out an audible sigh. "It's Jonny."

Brittany rolls her eyes. His sisters protect him fiercely. Whatever Antonia plans to say will pit her as his oppressor.

"What about him?" Brittany asks.

"He's depressed." Antonia fixes her glare on Brittany.

"Okay?"

"He told me why."

"Can you enlighten me, maybe?"

"Jonny says something is wrong between you." Antonia pauses for effect. "He says he feels it."

Brittany lets the words settle to the floor between them. She holds Antonia's gaze.

"So now he's an expert at reading emotions?" she spits out, her arms moving back up to cross themselves over her chest. "I never should have married him."

"Don't say things like that," Antonia says in response. "You're devastating him."

"I'm devastating him?" Fury brews within Brittany. "You told me just weeks ago about Maya Daniels and his obsession with her ghost."

"Can't you move past it?" Antonia says. "The girl is dead. She has been dead for over twenty years."

"Move past?" Brittany fumes. "Then why would you even bring her up in the first place?"

"Because Astrid forced me to. You know this."

"So, what changed, *uhn*?"

Antonia ponders her next words quietly. Brittany can see her mind working, processing behind those gray-blue eyes all three siblings share.

"Astrid wants to give you a chance."

"Give *me* a chance?" Brittany cackles. "It's me who has to give *her* a chance. She's racist. It oozes out of every pore."

"Don't be unfair," Antonia scolds. Brittany notices her cheeks flushing red. She instantly knows they have moved into that space. The one where Antonia grows uncomfortable and society wants the likes of Brittany to back off before the tears come.

"I don't care!"

"I want to talk about Jonny instead," Antonia says. "Please leave my mother out of this." Antonia shifts on her feet. It seems the name *Astrid* rattles everyone when they hear it.

Silence settles over them. Brittany bites her lower lip, frustrated, before conceding.

"Fine, what do you want to talk about?"

"Are you planning on leaving Jonny?"

Fuck. Brittany thinks. She needs to be more strategic and reel her emotions in. She can't let them suspect her plans for divorce just yet.

"I'm not here for his entertainment. I have my own needs, my own passions, my own purpose." Brittany's voice pitches higher. "I didn't come to Sweden to be dead to myself."

"He loves you. You can't leave him. He won't be able to handle that."

"He has a fetish. He's obsessed with my image. He doesn't love me. He loves that ghost. That Maya."

Antonia sucks in a deep breath. "I know we haven't told you much about Jonny's childhood."

"I know enough to know that no one took his condition seriously."

"He was a sensitive child. He still is. He can't handle sudden changes. He can't—"

"The world doesn't revolve around your brother, okay?"

"Just don't leave him. Not right now."

"I'm done with this conversation."

"Okay, but at least you two can discuss things while you're in London for *Nyårsafton.* You don't have to worry about *söta* Maya. We'll take good care of her."

Brittany sighs. She's tired of the interventionist circle formed around her and Jonny. She only found out about London when his assistant there, Eva, texted over flight details.

Jonny, through Eva, had booked a last-minute getaway for them to ring in the New Year. A lavish experience with five-star dining at his favorite Michelin-starred restaurant, Yamamoto. Eva organized a couple's massage in their, well his, watchtower high above Canary Wharf. His wraparound floor-to-ceiling windows are going to provide a spectacular view of the fireworks.

So, when Brittany received that text days earlier with the flight information and detailed itinerary from Eva, she'd started typing instructions for her to cancel it all immediately.

Then a voice in her head said, "*Keep him close.*"

She changed the content of her text.

Tack, Eva! I need a small favor.

Eva's response had been instant:

Of course. Anything.

KEMI

Christmas arrives two days later. After all the requisite phone calls to their parents in Lagos, Nigeria, are made, she, Kehinde, and Lanre retire to the living room with steaming mugs of peppermint tea.

As they settle into their respective corners, Kemi's phone beeps. She grabs it, reading the message, squinting while taking a sip.

God jul.

R

She swallows, glances at Kehinde. Her sister regards her with suspicion.

"Is everything okay?"

"Yes, it's a—it's a work thing, I need to quickly sort this out." Kemi rushes off to the mad world of peonies, her sister's guest room and her own hideout. She shuts the door and leans against it, heaving a deep breath. Her heart is pounding at the sight of two words and a letter.

How this is enough to elicit this reaction she can't fathom.

Earlier she had gushed on the phone with Tobias, spewing words about how she missed him desperately and couldn't wait to hold him in her arms. How she was passionately going to tire him out once she got back to Stockholm. She had watched Lanre occasionally pull her sister into spontaneous loving hugs whenever they crossed paths around the house. She'd yearned for her own happy ending for years.

Then, two words and a letter, accompanied by gasoline and matches for her paper dream.

He picks up on the first ring. Kemi holds her breath.

"*Det är Ragnar*," he answers, waiting for the caller. The first time she has heard his voice since London.

"*Hej*," Kemi says. The other end goes silent for a few seconds.

"*Hej*."

"I, umm, I saw your text message." She fumbles for words. His text doesn't warrant a return call. Why is she calling him back? A reciprocal message would have sufficed, but Kemi knows why. His deep baritone already ran goosebumps across her skin when he picked up.

"It's good to hear from you." His voice drags low, heady over the line. Another agonizing pause, then, "How are you?"

"I'm fine. Just wanted to wish you Merry Christmas over the phone."

She needs to be in control. To show him he doesn't rattle her as much as he thinks he does. That London was a meaningless fluke and nothing more.

When Ragnar chuckles at her Christmas greeting, she immediately regrets her desperation for power. The phone goes quiet for a few more seconds.

"I'm glad you did," he says before pitching lower, "*God*, you felt so good."

His confession snuffs out her voice, reminding her of their lack of protection and her idiocy in the heat of the moment.

"*Hallå? Hallå?*" Ragnar tries prodding her back onto the line.

"You can't say things like that." She composes herself, her voice neutral, while every cell quakes within her. "We're colleagues."

"I'm sorry," he apologizes. "It must be the wine going to my head that makes me say these things."

"London meant nothing." She pauses for more air. "We were both bored."

"I can't stop thinking about you, being inside you. I'm trying." Silence passes between them. "I know, I know, I'm sorry." His voice grows serious again. "I've been drinking."

"Have a wonderful Christmas," she cuts in tersely. "I'll see you in the new year."

She disconnects before he spills more alcohol-tinged words. Ragnar is why she needs to flee back to the States. The ego-driven, power-hungry version of herself she becomes around him frightens her. Seeing Tobias's face will suppress the virus, which now crawls through her bloodstream, heating up her blood whenever she and Ragnar orbit each other physically or even from a distance.

SEVEN

YASMIIN

"Faaaan."

Yagiz mutters the curse word softly under his breath as he stares at Muna lying in her hospital bed. He rakes his fingers through his thick strip of hair.

"I told you," Yasmiin says before settling in a chair next to Muna, readjusting Mehmet on her lap.

"A miracle from Allah!" Yagiz continues. "Nothing but a miracle. And she survived?" He runs a palm over his mouth in disbelief.

"You're looking at her, aren't you?" Yasmiin adds.

"And her face wasn't mashed up?" Yagiz's bewilderment sails through.

"Yagiz!" Yasmiin scolds him for being crass. He shrugs. "Here, take him." She hands their son to his father before digging into the canvas tote bag on her shoulder. She pulls out a small roll of Sellotape and a brown envelope. Inside are three photos which belong to Muna. A family portrait with both Muna's parents seated while she and her younger brother stand behind them. The second is of Muna turning shyly away from the camera, but her smile is certain. Yasmiin can see why she kept this particular shot.

The last photo is of Muna's Ahmed with the sheep across his shoulders. Yasmiin lingers on his face a moment longer until she feels Yagiz's looming presence over her own shoulder.

"*Hmm*, should I be jealous?" he asks, bouncing Mehmet in the crook of his arm.

"Muna's boyfriend," Yasmiin says softly, before holding Ahmed's photo in place on the pale pastel-green wall above Muna's head. With her free hand, she lifts the tape to her mouth and bites off a piece to secure it in place. She repeats the action with the other two photographs.

"Boyfriend?" Yagiz seems perplexed. "Little Muna had a man? Wasn't she a virgin?"

Yasmiin lets out a gasp of frustration. Every inch of her wants to sweep the back of her palm across his face.

"Ahmed is dead."

"Dead?" Yagiz continues bouncing Mehmet. The toddler starts wriggling, his little chubby fists rubbing at his eyes in tiredness. Yasmiin nods. "What happened?"

"A man came to see me at Salima's salon," she starts. "He said you told him where I was."

Yagiz furrows his brows, trying to remember. "What man?"

"A man named Mattias. He said he worked at the asylum center where Muna was. Why would you give a strange man information about me? Your wife?"

Recognition floods Yagiz. He purses his lips. "Oh please, that man looked harmless," he says. "He said he had important information about Muna he wanted to share with you."

"Why didn't you get the information from him yourself?" she counters.

"*Aşkım*." Yagiz's voice turns serious. "You know I handle sensitive business. I can't just be talking to anybody." He peers into her eyes. "What did the *gubbe* want?" *Old man.*

"He told me how Ahmed died . . . He burned himself alive." She hears Yagiz curse once more as he spins around, the sleepy child in his arms. He takes a few disoriented steps, then turns toward her.

"These people are cursed." Yagiz is visibly agitated. "First he burns himself and then she jumps in front of a train? Why the fuck are we here?"

"Because I care about Muna. She's my sister. I want to help her. I also want to help Ahmed rest in peace." Her voice echoes through the room.

"But why do you have to be involved, *eh*?" Yagiz remains adamant. "I don't like this. *Aina* is getting too close. I don't like this at all," he says, using the slang word for the police.

"Mattias wants to help."

"Mattias wants to help?" Yagiz parrots her. "Why are you involving yourself again with this girl? I told you, Yasmiin, trouble follows her everywhere."

"It's the box," Yasmiin explains. "Remember the box I showed you with all those Kurdish things?" Yagiz shifts uncomfortably. Yasmiin recognizes his smoking shakes. He deposits a sleeping Mehmet into her arms, pulls out a pack of cigarettes, and slips one between his lips in anticipation of a drag. He pads toward the door.

"Yagiz," she cries out, halting his exit. He spins round to face her. Yasmiin moves toward him, her eyes behind thin films of tears. "Thank you for coming," she says, "for spending *Julafton* here with her."

He gives her a quick nod, placing a hand over his heart, before leaving the room.

BRITTANY-RAE

It has been a while since she's had a proper massage.

One making her groan with each pressure applied. She closes her eyes in bliss but her mind churns, thinking about the list Eva texted over. The dutiful assistant had found three obituaries for a *Maya Daniels*, including one for a teenager survived by parents and a younger brother. She texted back a hearty "Tack så mycket!" before instructing her to find the contact details for the parents named in the obituary.

She needs answers quickly. About how long Maya and Jonny were together. How well Maya's parents had known this stranger who swept their daughter into his universe, where people circle around him like angels carrying out his unspoken bidding. She must get close to the memories of this girl who took Jonny's heart to the grave with her. Even if they break her.

Because she can barely breathe when he's around her, unsure of how much he knows about her mission.

A third hand on her back gives her a shock. She turns to find Jonny peering across from his own massage table, his hand tracing her spine, trying to gain her attention. He grins, his eyes narrowing as he studies her. He follows the masseuse's hand movements over her back. How they dip into the hollow and rise up between her shoulder blades. He observes the slow strokes like a human motion detector.

"What is it?" she asks in a low voice as the masseuse continues with her task. Jonny drops his grin. Brittany knows that look well. He shuffles off the table and onto his feet, the white cloth around his waist falling to the floor. His own masseuse averts her eyes. Brittany gathers her own cloth around her, tucking it beneath her armpits for security.

"Thank you very much. My husband is done." The words rush out of her. Both masseuses nod and start gathering their supplies, while avoiding Jonny, who stands naked, staring at his wife. The charged air forces the women to pack up as noiselessly as they can.

"Our chauffeur will deliver your tables," Brittany assures them, pushing strands of hair behind her ears shyly. She gets to her feet and escorts both women to the door. They dare not turn around to take in the naked man who now trails them toward the front door. Brittany wonders what these English women must be thinking. That the long-held stereotype of Swedes frolicking around in the nude is indeed true.

When she locks the door, Jonny wraps his arms around her from behind, pulling her back into his chest.

"Jonny," she whispers. He runs his lips along her shoulder,

tightening his grip, pressing her closer. She leans into his touch. If this is what she must do to survive a little longer before breaking free, then, *God help her*, she must.

Eva is on her quest. For now, Brittany will ride him out in every way until she gets more information. Information which will prize her out of his . . . She moans when his hand roams lower.

"Tell me what you want," Jonny asks her breathlessly.

"Stop talking."

He kisses down her neck. She spins around to face him. He backs her into the front door. His eyes scan her face, studying her. Brittany grows nervous. Is he on to her and Eva? Had he intercepted their messaging somehow? It wouldn't surprise her. What had she been thinking to place her trust in Eva? She needs to be smarter about her exit.

Jonny's lips seek hers softly, tenderly. She strokes his cheek, letting him taste her. His tongue sweeps in possessively, his grip tightening around her, pressing her into the door with his weight.

The sharp shrill of his phone slashes through the quiet of the penthouse. Jonny pulls back robotically.

Brittany draws his face in to continue their kiss. His attention is fleeting. The moment, lost. He peels himself off and moves calmly, his hands in fists, toward the shelf where he faithfully keeps his phone in the exact same position every time.

It shrills until he taps it after exactly four rings. He always waits for that count. He holds the phone silently to his ear. No greetings or words of invitation to the caller to talk.

Brittany sneaks toward him, the cloth now a makeshift sarong around her body, waiting for his reactions as he takes the call. No doubt from one of his pixies. He listens. Almost sedately while whoever is on the line gives him news.

Then . . . *tap.*

"Jonny?" Brittany wraps the cloth tighter around her. He turns to face her, his eyebrows creased, tears filling up his eyes. Brittany freezes. Her mind runs wild. Her daughter. Their child.

"Oh my God." She starts to panic. "Is it Maya? Please don't tell me it's my baby?"

He shakes his head, his eyes drowning, standing almost motionless, his arms hanging by his sides.

"It's Ragnar," Jonny shares, calmly.

Brittany frowns. She loathes his best friend but she would never wish for his death. If Ragnar had died, it's enough to derail her husband and push him over the cliff into the—

"They lost their baby."

"What?"

"I need to go."

"Now?"

"I need to go now. Eva will take care of you." He spins to go. Brittany watches her husband disappear into their bedroom to start packing. It's late afternoon. He'll catch the last flight back to Stockholm.

Brittany turns toward the sparkling city below, processing the fact that she will never be what Ragnar is to her husband. She is fourth in line for her husband's love after Maya Daniels, their daughter, and his best friend.

KEMI

The last few days before flying back to Stockholm move lethargically.

Besides running all over Richmond stocking up on braids, makeup for brown skin, clothes that fit, and favorite toiletries, she spends the rest of her final week at Kehinde's sleeping, eating, binge-watching some shows, and contemplating that open-ended decision to move back to the States.

With or without Tobias.

She sees no prospects for advancement, she keeps telling herself. Her hastily created vanity post at von Lundin Marketing is a void of boredom. She needs a new project to work on besides the

Bachmann account which pulled the firm back from the brink of diversity disaster.

Even after over two years away, she's still revered in the industry back in the States. They followed her international von Lundin campaign which marketed the German brand Bachmann's B:GEM shoes in a creative and innovative way. But those laurels are getting tired. She can't rest on them anymore.

Besides, she no longer holds creative control over the project. Ragnar does. His simple text message and subsequent chat had mentally derailed her for the rest of the trip. She has never faced anything like this. Feelings growing deeper for a man who isn't hers and who seems to get high on her strength.

A therapist session is long overdue. Maybe she can trust her good friend Malcolm with these feelings once she gets back to Stockholm. She fires off a quick Christmas greeting to him, who responds with:

And keep being the bad bitch that you are! xoxo!

Normally she would chuckle at his jokes, but this time, she indeed feels like a bad bitch wading in dangerous territory. These thoughts, swirling with the image of Ragnar's lingering dark-blue glare, keep her awake all through her connecting flight to London.

Whatever happens in London…

Back in Stockholm, she grabs onto Tobias for dear life when he picks her up with her car at Arlanda Airport. He lets her hug him tightly, waiting till her racing heart calms.

"That bad, *uhn*?" He laughs, brushing curls off her face before dipping to kiss her.

"I've missed you, that's all," she says, finally breaking for air. "You have to come with me next time."

"Of course, I would love to meet your family." Tobias gives her a quick peck before taking over her luggage cart. Her single suitcase found three new friends in the US. He chuckles. She links her arm in his as he pushes the stack of luggage.

"So, how was Christmas?" Tobias asks. She leans in closer. "Your family?"

"I just wished you were there, that's all," she says. "How was *Jul hos Nancy*?"

"You know Nancy," is all Tobias offers.

Kemi talks incessantly all the way to Nacka across town. She shares every detail—from when her brother-in-law picked her up at the airport, the long drive to Richmond, her nieces and nephew digging into their gifts, her twin sister's penchant for calling him *Tobi* in their native Yoruba. She ate her weight in Chinese food because finding good places in Stockholm is a chore. She filled suitcase upon suitcase with everything she can't get in Sweden.

She talks about kids, her thoughts tumbling out one after another without a chance for Tobias to answer. How she would love to have kids someday. Is this something Tobias wonders about too? And if so, how many? Because two would be her maximum. She still isn't sure how people handle more than two kids. How and where would she raise them? In Sweden? Move back to the States? Sweden is built for raising kids up until twelve years old. It's clearly the better choice. If Tobias wants kids, where would he want to raise them? Obviously Sweden, right? He hasn't lived anywhere else. He has traveled to a handful of countries around Europe as well as Thailand like all other Swedes. But Tobias always stays close to home. Is it because of Nancy? she asks. Doesn't Nancy like him traveling? Speaking of Nancy, is she hounding him for grandkids yet? His celebrity singer-songwriter younger sister Tina is dating some famous football player on the Swedish national team. Nancy has been hounding them for kids for years.

By the time they get to Nacka, Kemi has fallen fast asleep mid-conversation.

Tobias has already made New Year's Eve plans for them. First, dinner on the island of Djurgården, then braving the cold with a couple thousand more souls at Skansen, the city's open-air museum, which has hosted a public gathering on the last night of the year since 1895. After songs, performances, and the reading of poems, the clock will count down until midnight and fireworks will light up Stockholm's islands, all coated in powdered sugar-like snow.

Kemi pulls on a new faux fur hat she picked up stateside and wraps herself in layers. She learned after her first winter in Sweden that bad weather didn't exist. Only bad clothes. Still, the freezing chill often stabs her nostrils like mini-knives. No amount of layers can change the fact that winter remains brutal. But she's excited to spend the last few hours of the year with a man she's sure she loves. She'll finally muster up the courage to tell Tobias those three words once the first sparks of fireworks hit the indigo night sky.

While pulling on her leather gloves, her phone rings. She peers at it, furrowing her brows at the name which pops up.

Ingrid.

She glances at the time. Seven thirty-two p.m. What could be so urgent her direct boss Ingrid is calling her on New Year's Eve?

Jonny.

Something bad must have happened to him.

Shit. She remembers her unkept promise to help Brittany find a lawyer. Had she jumped the gun and left him in dramatic fashion? Has he fallen apart at the news?

Or is it Ragnar? Has Ingrid found out about what happened in London? The others had seen Ragnar leave with her when she claimed she needed air. They never returned to their drinks.

Kemi picks up after the third ring. "Ingrid. Such a surprise," she says. Swedes are direct. She knows Ingrid will get straight to business.

"Sorry to call you on *Nyårsafton*, but I thought you would like to get this message personally," Ingrid says, her voice heavy. Worry fills Kemi. Ingrid's calling to deliver a personal message. She casts a quick glance at Tobias. He stares back at her with concern wrinkling his brows too.

"Has something happened? At the office?" Kemi asks.

Ingrid steals three seconds of silence. "It's Ragnar." Her voice sounds too heavy to simply be confirming gossip of their affair.

Kemi swallows, her legs shaky. She isn't sure she can handle news that something's happened to him. Her heart still isn't sure what it feels around him. Whether simply lust or a complicated type of budding love.

"Is...he alright?"

"They lost their baby."

"What?"

"Pia was due in March. She went into labor this morning..." Ingrid's voice tapers off. "The baby was delivered dead." Kemi's palm flies up to cover her mouth. They lost their baby barely a week after her awkward call with Ragnar. Barely two weeks after their tryst in London.

"Oh my God." Kemi finds her voice. "My heart breaks for him, for them."

"I know. It is truly terrible," Ingrid continues. "That's also why I called you."

Kemi senses the warning before it morphs into words over the line. "I appreciate you letting me know."

"So, you must understand this is a sensitive time for him and his family," Ingrid says. "It will be wise to distance yourself from whatever you have going on with Ragnar."

"This is not the time, Ingrid."

"But it is the right time to know that there's another person involved who is currently hurting," Ingrid says. "Please use your discretion when reaching out to them. We will organize a sympathy card and flowers on behalf of the team."

"Yes." Kemi's response is barely a whisper. Ragnar lost his baby. She can't think. She doesn't know what to do or say.

"I must go now, but I wanted to tell you myself." Ingrid wraps up. "He's on leave now for the next two weeks." Kemi nods reflexively at the phone.

"Thank you, Ingrid."

"*Gott Nytt År*, Kemi." *Happy New Year.*

Tap.

Kemi sits on the bed, hands resting on the sheets on both sides of her hips, her chest heaving. Tobias observes her, fear crawling all over his face.

"What's wrong? What happened?"

She shakes her head vigorously before lurching for her phone once more. She pulls up Ragnar's number, fingers shaking. She types words.

I'm so sorry

K

EIGHT

YASMIIN

Östermalm. One of Stockholm's wealthiest districts. Classic buildings close to a century old whose dark musty interiors scream old money and nepotism. Muna had spent months working as a janitor in buildings like these. Scrubbing toilets, refilling coffee, and probably slinking around like a ghost in her jilbab, Yasmiin imagines. The younger woman is never far from her mind.

"*Nassar-Berg*," the gilded nameplate reads. Yasmiin stands in front of a thick wooden door that belongs to Amani Nassar, Salima's younger sister. Yasmiin wants to know more about this Iraqi woman who flows freely among white wealth, living among them, floating in a class way above her station while her sister owns a modest salon on Kungsholmen.

Years living in Sweden and this is the first time Yasmiin has entered an apartment in Östermalm.

Amani lets her in to strong smells of lavender perfume. Yasmiin enters on unsure feet, kicking off her well-worn sneakers by the door.

"Yasmiin, come." Amani is in jovial spirits as she wafts around the apartment wearing a satin dressing gown, her thick black mane in rollers atop her head. Yasmiin's eyes dart around the fabulous living room with white leather furniture and gold trim on everything—from lamps to coffee tables.

Money on display. Rather, money wasted on display, Yasmiin thinks.

Amani leads her through two more heavy doors until they reach what looks like a dressing room. A room used only for getting dressed. Yasmiin's thoughts mill. Rows of six-inch stilettoes. A sprawling walk-in closet. A table with an oversized beauty mirror and theatrical spotlights above it. A silver sequined ball gown hangs from one of the wardrobe doors. Yasmiin pauses by the door, nervous. When she turns back to look at Amani, all she sees is possibility. Of access and the blueprint of a well-assimilated immigrant.

She wonders what Amani gave up for such deep access into Swedish society, because Yasmiin knows assimilation and integration are different beasts. The higher you climb with ease where you're not wanted, the less you are who you truly are.

Amani settles herself behind the mirror and waves for Yasmiin to come over. "I have only an hour," she says frantically. "Can you do it in one hour?"

"Why me?" Those words tumble out before Yasmiin can take them back. "I mean, don't you have special makeup people?"

Amani glares at Yasmiin, before softening her look as she regards the younger woman.

"I like your fire, Yasmiin," she says, before turning back to the mirror to rub some moisturizer on her face. "I wanted to try you out."

"Try me out?"

"I have one hour. Get to work."

Forty-five minutes later, Amani peers at her reflection, transfixed. Smoky eyes to complement her jet-black hair while making her hazel glare pop. Rosy cheeks, a nude lip with a tint of rose color. A full contour job and her hair slicked back from her face in an elegant do. She turns her cheeks to each side, assessing Yasmiin's work before making eye contact with her in the mirror.

"You're incredible!" she declares. "This is incredible. I look amazing. *Tack så mycket.*" *Thanks so much.* Yasmiin accepts her praise, trying to keep her voice steady. This exchange doesn't require tears. She needs to keep her composure. Amani, who has unprecedented access by marrying a clearly wealthy "*Berg*"—a white man with a Nordic last name—is asking Yasmiin to do her makeup. Is this Amani's way of reaching behind her to pull the next woman up? Propping her up in some way? By sprinkling this man's privilege onto others?

After taking a few phone shots of Amani's newly laid face, Yasmiin helps to zip her into her silver sequins and strap her feet into her silver stilettoes, then gathers her makeup kit in a rush.

"You will definitely be hearing from me again," Amani says as she sashays toward the door to lead Yasmiin out. "Maybe others too. I have many girlfriends who need someone quick and reasonably priced."

Once they near the door, it is Yasmiin's turn to pay a compliment. "You've got a beautiful apartment," she says, giving the place one quick glance. "Your husband?" she starts to say before Amani cuts her off.

"Thank you." A smile creeps onto Amani's face. "I won it in the divorce," she trails off with a wink.

Later that afternoon, Yasmiin studies Mattias while he, in turn, studies the stack of passport photos in his palm, his glasses resting on the tip of his nose, his mouth hanging slightly open. Her arms are wrapped around her torso, her protective wall. After she'd laughed in his face when he demanded trust from her, he'd understood his error. He needed to earn it first. Right now, this was an unknowingly insurmountable task for Mattias because the likes of him had broken her body.

They're back at Espresso House. This time, they meet at Stureplan right in the heart of Östermalm, a few blocks from Amani's apartment. He continues assessing the faces in the photos in silence. Yasmiin glances uncomfortably around her. At the patrons gliding into that space. Different shades of blond interspersed with brunettes and the occasional brown face. Sleek suits wearing no ties. Gym clothes hugging lithe frames. Casual sweaters. Skinny jeans. Deceptive exteriors masking generational wealth and new money.

She turns back to Mattias and takes a sip of her milky-sweet coffee before clearing her throat to regain his attention.

"Hmmm," he murmurs, setting down the stack of over a hundred passport photos. He mutters a curse in Swedish beneath his breath.

"So?" Yasmiin prods. "What do you think of it?"

Mattias breathes heavily before reaching for his black coffee. "Thank you for bringing this to me." Yasmiin reaches protectively for the box, but he stops her. "It's okay. You can trust me." She pulls back.

"Trust you?" It's not a question. Mattias remains silent. "If Ahmed gave it to Muna and not the police, then he definitely did not want them anywhere near these items," she says. Mattias nods in agreement. "So what do we do now?"

"I need you to leave this with me so—"

"Over my dead body!" Yasmiin exclaims before Mattias can finish his statement.

"I know it's a lot to ask you. I think I know who can help, but I need this box and its items."

"Never," she snarls at him.

Mattias pulls off his glasses, lets out a sigh of frustration, and leans back into his chair. He studies Yasmiin's face for a few moments, before leaning forward once more and settling his glasses back in place.

"Look," he starts. "I work with immigrants and refugees every single day. You don't trust me. You don't trust the police. You don't trust the system." He leans in closer. "You don't trust me as a white man. I get it." He clasps his fingers together.

Of course she doesn't. For Yasmiin middle-aged white men dredge up memories from Rome's streets that she's still struggling to scrub from her existence.

Mattias continues. "But Yasmiin, this is so much bigger than you and your suspicions. We're talking about potentially bringing justice to an entire village. Over a hundred people who can be avenged in some way."

"What's in it for you?" Yasmiin asks, holding his gaze.

Mattias's eyebrows arch, wrinkles appearing between his eyes. "In it for me?"

"Yes. Why do you care? Or do you just love playing savior? Like you do at the asylum center? The one who is always in control?"

"Yasmiin—"

She cuts him off again. "There is something in this for you. You like to play God, don't you? At the asylum center out in the middle of nowhere." Mattias grits his jaw, listening to her intently. "Now you want to come in and save Ahmed's history as the white man riding a horse," she continues. "You think you can just come and take whatever you want? Because we can't fight you?" Images surface. She bats them away. "I don't trust you!"

"Are you done?" Mattias finally says. "Are you done, Yasmiin? Because going through life with such cynicism and distrust must be eating you alive."

"You have no idea what I have been through and experienced, so shut your mouth!" Yasmiin screeches, her anger spilling over. Enough for a few of the other customers to turn their heads toward them. Mattias doesn't seem fazed by her outburst. He must be used to such sudden flares of temper and emotion. As manager and, in essence, warden of the asylum center, he must be used to people screaming in his face daily. Screams of frustration and despair. Of being locked up in a place that reads like paradise on paper, a sort of Hades in reality.

Mattias adjusts his glasses before pressing on. He reaches for her hand. Yasmiin recoils sharply as if he's burned her, and he dips his eyebrows in response.

"You're right. I have no idea," he starts. "I am not a Black woman. I cannot understand what it is you experience every day, but I can tell you this. Understanding that box and what it signifies will go farther with me than it will in your hands."

"Are you insulting me?" She narrows her eyes at him. "Are you saying that you are smarter than me?" Yasmiin glares at him, nostrils flaring in frustration, not sure if she should be offended by what he insinuates.

Mattias matches her glare with the calm of his blue eyes. "I have the right access to get this box into the right hands."

With that statement, Yasmiin suddenly feels the air shift around them. She recognizes this new aura. The density of being interrogated. Sitting in sparse rooms in Rome as officers stared her down, demanding answers.

"*Du är säpo, eller hur?*" Yasmiin finally says the words. *You're Security Police, right?*

Säpo. Säkerhetspolisen. Swedish Security Service. The special arm of the government responsible for making sure terrorists, both homegrown and international transplants, don't gain a foothold in Sweden.

Mattias remains unflinching as he stares at her, neither confirming nor denying her suspicions verbally. But his eyes tell her all she needs to know and goosebumps surface once again.

Yes.

He doesn't have to say the word for her to read it off his disposition and new fear creeps up within her. Does he know her past? In Italy? Has he followed her footprints and how she got to Sweden?

If he really works for the government, Solsidan is his perfect cover. Close proximity to newly arrived refugees. His way of sniffing out any forms of radicalization or simmering resentment. Or finding former prostitutes.

Of course it makes absolute sense. This stoic man is the system itself.

Mattias reaches for the box once more in silence, his eyes locking with Yasmiin's as he slides it closer to his end of the table.

Yasmiin lets it go, her fingers weak.

BRITTANY-RAE

Jonny returns to Stockholm on New Year's Eve, leaving Brittany behind wrapped in a sheer cloth blanket. The rest of the evening, she sits on their plush avant-garde gray sofa with a glass of Merlot, staring out into the starry night with glinting lights all over Canary Wharf and beyond.

She never envisioned spending New Year's Eve alone and without her daughter. Jonny's exit had been abrupt. He hadn't even factored her into his plans. Not even given her time to pack and return home with him.

That disconnect grates on her. While she knows he focuses intensely on one issue at a time and can't multitask, she can no longer live with his quirks.

She remembers the conversation she had with her father when her parents visited during Midsummer last year. Her father had pulled her aside and wrapped his arms around her so tightly, afraid of losing his only child to something, someone, someplace he didn't quite understand.

"His family disrespects you," her father had whispered. "I can't be at peace back in Atlanta when I know my baby is suffering in another man's country."

"Dad, he gives me everything I need. He takes care of me."

"Privilege comes in different levels, Brit," he had continued. "You have the privilege he has given you. You will never have the privilege he has just because he breathes. I know you've seen wealth beyond your dreams," he'd said, choking back tears. "But he ain't worth it. Never forget who you are, baby. Never forget."

Never forget.

She stays up all night due to the five-hour time difference, so she can call her parents before the clock strikes twelve in Atlanta. But she calls her best friend Tanesha right away once Jonny leaves the penthouse.

"Hey, Tee."

"Brit!" Tanesha screeches into the receiver, excited amid

background noise. Muffled voices. A low steady beat of music. "How's London?"

"I'm here alone."

"Alone?"

"Yeah. He left me here."

"What? Why?"

"It's Ragnar."

"Raggedy-ass Ragnar?"

"Yup." Brittany feels insensitive. Though she holds no love for Ragnar and his judgmental eyes, she'd never wish this on him. "It's really sad news."

"Did the devil finally get him?"

"Stop. It's sad. They lost their baby. Pia delivered over two months early. Stillborn."

Silence on the other end. She knows Tanesha is attempting to process the news. To pull some love out of her heart for Ragnar.

"I'm sorry, Brittany. That's horrible news. That poor mamma," Tanesha says.

"I know. I can't even imagine what she must be going through. So sad."

"So Jonny left to be with him, right?"

"Yeah, he's his best friend. They've known each other since kindergarten. I am an outsider who came in just three years ago."

"Where's your own baby?"

"Back in Stockholm. Jonny left so quickly. I'm going back home tomorrow."

Silence once again on the phone. Tanesha comes back stronger.

"So, you're in a whole 'nother country while your baby is back home with him. The same man who suspects you're trying to leave his ass, right?"

After she'd set up her brunch date with Kemi, she'd called her best friend to spill her intentions of seeking a divorce. Since then, she regularly updates Tanesha on her plans.

Brittany now falls quiet. She hasn't considered the possibility of a lockout now she's temporarily out of the picture. He has their daughter with him. Is her time up? Is this the opportunity his family was looking for? To cut her off?

Brittany's breath catches, her heart racing faster as she processes Tanesha's words. She feels her skin warming up, breaking into a sweat.

Eva has already texted her a changed itinerary for tomorrow afternoon, including sending a chef over in the morning to make her breakfast. Those aren't the actions of a concerted blackout, right?

"Tee, don't be like that. He can't think strategically."

"Says who? He's smart as fuck."

Visions of a drunk Jonny carrying Maya, singing and soothing her, rush into her mind. At that moment, he seems diabolical.

"Okay, you're scaring me and it's not helping, so stop."

"A'right. How's the digging going?"

"His assistant found Maya Daniels's obituary for me. Now she's digging up contact information for her parents."

"Get that little Swedish mole on your side immediately!" Tanesha chuckles. "I like her. What's her name?"

"Eva. She's the only one I can turn to right now."

"So, what are you going to do when you get their number? You know you can't bring their daughter back. What if they've moved on?"

"I don't know what I'll do yet. I just want closure."

"For yourself or for that poor family?"

"Both."

When Brittany arrives back in Stockholm the next day—New Year's Day—it's to a tall lean chauffeur clad in black waiting for her at the airport. Normally Jonny would be there, rigid and smiling awkwardly. This time, though, she can't reach him. His phone is switched off. She tries the au pair's phone. No answer. Tanesha's sentiments bubble to the surface. *He's smart as fuck*. Her heart races once more. Is Maya safe? How could she have been so stupid?

She reaches his other assistant Louise as the driver shuttles her from the airport to town.

"Brittany!" Louise answers.

"What's going on?" Brittany's voice is too loud. She quickly calms herself. She can't be hysterical around their staff. "Why isn't anyone picking up? Where is Maya? I can't reach her au pair either."

"Maya is fine, don't worry," Louise says.

"Where is she?"

"She's safe with Jonny in Sandhamn. What happened to Ragnar's baby must have scared him. He said he wanted to be with her alone."

Brittany swallows. Sandhamn. The family's hideaway out in Stockholm's archipelago. *Alone.*

Several scenarios, all grim, play across her frantic mind in that instant, even human sacrifice and every other crazy scene in between. The rational part of her brain knows he'll never hurt his baby. The new love of his life. The irrational part already has reason and logic in a double headlock. She has been sloppy. Too relaxed. For a woman trying to leave a powerful man, she now sees how unprepared she is.

"I need to get there now."

"No need." Louise attempts reassurance. "They're coming back tomorrow."

So, when Jonny arrives by noon the next day, cradling Maya, her chubby little arms wrapped around her father's neck, Brittany bursts out of their villa barefoot, barely dressed. She races across the lush lawn and yanks Maya out of his grip, bursting into tears the moment her daughter's sweet smell hits her.

There is no official funeral service for Ragnar and Pia Pettersen's baby son. They hold a quiet intimate gathering for family. Only Jonny demands to be there by his side. Not even his sisters Antonia and Svea, who have also known Ragnar since childhood, are invited. Not even Brittany and Maya.

Brittany sends a bouquet of white lilies on behalf of her husband

and daughter with her deepest condolences, letting them know she's available if Pia needs support.

During her first two weeks back in Stockholm, Brittany starts settling into lush comfort once more, but with a mission. Her checklist is simple:

1. Get in touch with Malin

The mom who had been into fashion. Ask her out for *fika*.

2. Find a good lawyer

Or, in Tanesha's words, "*divorce his ass and take half.*"

Lastly, find herself again.

Because the Brittany-Rae Johnson she knew left herself on that British Airways flight the day she met Johan von Lundin.

She first sends Kemi a text asking about her offer to help her. Kemi's response is immediate.

So sorry, Brittany. I haven't had a chance. It's been chaotic on my end too.

It's okay. We all have priorities.

I'm sorry. I promised to help you and I always keep my word.

I appreciate it, Kemi.

She pulls up her contact list and scrolls through to find "Malin." She dials the number, her fingers unsure. Malin picks up on the second ring.

"*Hallå, det är Malin.*"

"*Hej, det är Brittany.*"

The line goes quiet for a few seconds. Brittany prays she's trying to reassociate her name.

"Brittany? Oh, yes of course. The American lady, right?"

"Yes!" Brittany's voice pitches higher than she wants it to, surprising even herself. Is she so desperate to make friends? Malin works in fashion. She mentioned Stockholm Fashion Week. What if Malin is the door to a new independent life, yanked free from the von Lundin chokehold?

"How are you? Did you have a great holiday?"

"Yes, very low-key," Brittany says.

"We just came back from skiing in St. Moritz. It was pure magic."

Brittany has already learned that, despite a culture which generally frowns on bragging, within the circles she moves in they do so unabashedly. She has been around Antonia, Svea, and some of their friends long enough to know they boast with ease. As long as everyone brags equally, then it's acceptable. Antonia and her family are still in the Maldives. They took off the day after they handed Maya back to Jonny. Svea, on the other hand, has disappeared off somewhere in the South Pacific with her older beau, no doubt to reappear around the end of January.

"I can imagine. Are you available sometime this week to meet for *fika*?"

A few seconds of silence, then Malin comes back, "Yes, of course."

A smile etches across Brittany's face.

KEMI

When Kemi returns to the office in the first week of January, Ragnar's presence startles her.

Ingrid had informed them all he was taking a few weeks off to process the tragedy. But here he is. His eyes, often tumultuous and which she often likens to a raging sea, have taken on an unnerving calm after a squall. A man clearly in shock.

The first two weeks in January, Ragnar paces the company corridors a hollowed man, grieving in depths his colleagues can't fathom. No emotions are worn on his sleeve, of course. He simply wears a blank stare that doesn't let anyone else in. Jonny begged Ragnar not to work, but burying himself in menial tasks is what will keep him sane, he relayed to their team.

Case in point, the mundane meeting they are both currently sitting in, discussing a potential campaign for a new line of Danish luxury men's watches.

Kemi listens intently, arms folded, concentrating harder than she normally would, her chair swiveled toward the large screen. She tries calming her heart, her chest heaving faster than she would have liked in that room.

Behind her, Ragnar rests his head on a palm, his elbow on the conference table. He's always impeccably groomed. This time, he's wearing an immaculate white dress shirt tucked into black trousers with platinum cufflinks at his wrists, his dark-chocolate hair brushed off his face.

She feels his eyes searing tracks across her back.

"By getting popular Danes who have broken into Hollywood to market this brand, it will bring a whole new segment to this market," the twentysomething presenter pitches, his large azure eyes made even larger behind massive frames. Standing next to him is a lithe brunette with sand-brown skin which hints at mixed heritage. Clearly some Black in there. She looks like she's just strutted off a catwalk. Her colleague does all the talking. Kemi wonders why the mixed-race woman is even there.

"Interesting," Kemi says, breaking the unnerving silence in the room. Across the table from her, Jonny sits fiddling with a pen, flipping it with precision, first clockwise, then anti-clockwise, repeating the motion several times. He doesn't seem to have heard a word. Rather, having worked with him over the last few years, Kemi knows he's pulling out only the information he wants from the young man's speech.

Dates. Figures. Numbers. Statistics.

This is a meeting that doesn't require Jonny's presence as CEO. Yet, here he is.

"And who's your target market again?" Kemi continues.

"Teenagers who have crushes on these Danish film stars or people with actual money who'll spend over five thousand dollars on a watch?"

The presenter adjusts his frames, his brows dipping inwards at her questioning.

"They have hundreds of thousands of followers," he begins his rebuttal, "including celebrities. Of course, we would tap into the right market by pulling them into these campaigns."

"Go where the money is," Kemi counters. "Go where their friends congregate, wine, and dine. Sponsor their events, their parties. Crawl into those closed corners where only those who spend thousands of dollars an hour go to play."

"And that's why we want to work with von Lundin." The brunette finally speaks up. Her voice is husky, sultry, and catches Kemi off guard. "Maybe we can schedule a follow-on meeting to discuss this with you, Jonny?" She turns to look directly at Jonny.

Kemi pulls in her bottom lip and lowers her gaze, seething. The woman continues to ignore Kemi and directs more questions at Jonny. His gaze doesn't leave the pen he's so mesmerized by, but Louise, his assistant, feverishly scribbles notes both on her laptop and in a notepad.

When Jonny refuses to respond, Kemi chimes in, "Well, I guess you have your answer. Thank you for the presentation. We will be in touch once we decide internally if your brand is worth taking on." She notices color rise to the young woman's cheeks. She looks at her phone to check the time. Half past five in the afternoon.

The pitch team gathers their equipment in silence, while Louise mutters a few words to her boss, before escorting them out of the room. They don't stick around for the customary goodbye handshakes.

"So!" Kemi spins around to face Jonny full on, Ragnar to her side still resting his head in his palm, his elbow on the table. She flashes Ragnar a quick glance. He holds her gaze intently, his brows furrowed. She turns back to Jonny, away from his discomfort. "What are your thoughts?"

"We don't do business like that here," Jonny reprimands her, his focus still on the twirling pen. "Your tone was too harsh."

Kemi frowns. "What do you mean?"

"We don't do business like that here," Jonny repeats.

"I heard you the first time," Kemi says. "You weren't even engaging with them. They can't crawl into your head and figure out if you want to work with them or not. You have to use your words."

"I don't like that brand," he says.

"Then why did you waste their time?" Kemi spits. "Why did you waste *my* time?"

Jonny's eyes leave his pen, stopping the flipping mid-motion like a robot as he glares at Kemi.

"I wanted to see her," Jonny says, unflinching.

Kemi leans back into her chair, confused. "See her? What do you mean?"

"She's one of his exes," Ragnar's exasperated tone cuts in, followed by a deep sigh. Then he turns to his best friend and motions for him to get out.

"*Stick härifrån.*" Those are his exact words to Jonny. *Get out of here.*

Like a trained dog, his friend pushes his chair back, shoots to his feet, regards Kemi one last time with a churning stare, before gliding out of the room.

Silence shrouds them. Kemi swears she hears Ragnar's heart pounding too. The weight of the unspoken hangs so heavily Kemi has to break it, shift it, with words. Any words so it doesn't asphyxiate her.

"Does Jonny see a therapist?" she asks before turning to observe Ragnar. His head still rests on his palm, but his eyes begin to roam. Traversing her face, wandering over her features, drinking her in. He chuckles in response.

Kemi presses on. "I'm serious. He's clearly a disturbed man.

You witnessed that display." Ragnar shrugs. "He summoned that company from Copenhagen just because he wanted to gawk at his ex?"

Kemi only has to think about Ms. Veronica and the vanity von Lundin startup purchase to answer her own question. No wonder Brittany is desperate to find a lawyer. From Jonny's demeanor earlier, Kemi realizes he probably has no idea his wife is planning to leave him.

"I am not responsible for Jonny," Ragnar starts to say, leaning back into his own chair. "He's a complicated man."

"Clearly," she mutters under her breath. More silence. She never knew the absence of sound could be this suffocating. She needs words once more. "Look, as his best friend, you need to convince him to see some—"

Kemi stops once she notices Ragnar's face contorting with emotion, a gasp leaving him, his loss clearly on his mind and surfacing that instant. He coughs to prevent his tears from coming. She knows Ragnar would never recover from breaking down in front of her. His fragile ego would never permit it.

"Ragnar," she says softly. "I'm so sorry." He regards her intently before shutting his eyes and lowering his head. Maybe it's too soon? To dredge up his loss? His eyes remain closed, forehead still resting on his palm. She swallows. More silence.

Kemi glances at her phone. "It's getting late and I need to head home."

Ragnar's eyes fly open. He looks at her. She holds her breath. Then he hooks his foot beneath the base of her chair, dragging it closer toward him. Kemi freezes, her hands instantly grasping her armrests for support. She lets out a small gasp of shock, her words long evaporated, as he draws her, chair and all, to him.

Once he stops moving her chair, Ragnar speaks like nothing has happened, his pitch steady.

"We need to finish up a few items regarding the Bachmann account," he says. "I'll give you a ride once we're done."

PART TWO

NINE

KEMI

Stay away from Ragnar. For your own sake.

Kemi mulls over Ingrid's warning as Ragnar's black Porsche SUV, sleek like the man himself, pulls up in front of her waterfront building in Nacka. He delayed her for over an hour to review strategy documents for their project and insisted on giving her a quick ride home.

Despite the fact he lives several kilometers away in the opposite direction in the affluent enclave of Djursholm.

They arrive at her apartment block in the same cocoon of silence which enveloped them when he pulled away from Östermalm, veering southwards. Except the void has now sucked up oxygen, leaving her breathless when he parks.

"Thank you." Kemi turns to him. "You didn't have to."

He inches her way and nods with eyebrows furrowed into their usual frown. His eyes hold hers, dark and hooded in a sadness she has never seen him wear before. She spins away from him and fumbles for the door handle. His palm on her thigh stops her. It squeezes in desperation before loosening its grip in contemplation. Then it becomes a light pat before Ragnar pulls his hand away and places it back on the steering wheel to join his other hand.

Kemi turns to study him silently as he grips the wheel tightly, his face contorting, biting his lips to keep his composure. He seems to be holding his breath. Then he roars in despair.

"I'm so sorry," Kemi whispers.

He lurches toward her. Kemi's soothing words drag his hands from the steering wheel to cup her face, his mouth crushing hers. She tries to keep up, to match his fervor. A futile task. She tastes sorrow in Ragnar's intense kiss. A stillborn child. One he loved for months in anticipation of cradling in his arms. The son he longed for.

Now grief acts as a dam holding back his love. Kemi breaches his reservoir and he violently overflows. Like touching the tip of one's cigarette to that of a stranger's, she knows he needs her to light him back up again.

Kemi threads her fingers through his hair as he kisses her hard, pushing her against the passenger seat with his weight. When they break for air, he looks down at her through dilated eyes filmed with tears.

"*Jag behöver dig…vad vi hade i London…jag vill det igen,*" he whispers against her lips before tugging them once more. She lets him kiss her. His mouth travels her neck before returning to her lips to beg her again. "*Snälla.*"

I need you…what we had in London…I want it again. Please.

"Ragnar," she starts to say. "We can't." She feels tears welling up in her own eyes.

Ragnar pulls away to drink her in. He moves a hand back to her thigh and runs his large palm along it, eliciting a moan from her, teasing her, his eyes never leaving hers. She launches into his arms, her lips finding his until he takes over once more.

Whatever happens in London stays in London…Whatever happens in London stays…

Kemi isn't sure how long they explored each other like teenagers in his car, parked right on the street. Now she stands in front of her apartment door, fumbling nervously for her keys. She drops them, her palms sweaty, and scoops them back up again. Ragnar leans against the wall next to her, watching her confidence slip with each move.

Whatever happens…Don't bring London home. Don't bring London here.

What is she doing? Why did she let him come in after her? Married men are off-limits. Affairs never end well. Ragnar's mourning. Consoling him this way isn't going to work. It's bound to backfire. Kemi knows this.

Yet here she is, her damn mind lost. Doing it all over again.

Ragnar's breathing down her neck, his hand lightly stroking her hip, waiting for her to unlock the door to her apartment she shares with Tobias so they can finish what they started in his car.

Darkness cloaks her modest floor plan, save for low light streaming in through sheer curtains overlooking a balcony with exquisite views of the bay.

"May I?" Ragnar asks with a searing gaze. She steps aside for him. He kicks off his black brogues by the door and steps into her apartment. He sweeps his body from left to right, taking it all in. Through Louise, Kemi knows Ragnar lives in an impressive five-bedroom manor out in Djursholm. Her entire apartment is probably the size of his study.

"Coffee?"

She dashes into the kitchen before receiving his answer. She turns on a night lamp above the machine and preps espresso against a pounding heart. She can't think. Ragnar clouds her mind. Nothing she can do will wash his sorrow away. She had seen the look in his eyes as they swept across her face and down her body in his car. And she had responded in kind, fully taking him in. The same draw he must see in her. The identical thread pulling her to him. Power. They both continue to taste power and suck strength from each other with every glance.

Tobias is working his night shift. He could walk into their apartment at any minute for any reason. Ragnar doesn't need to be there. She stands with her palms rooted to the countertop as a nutty coffee-scented aroma fills the air.

She hears him moving, drawing close. His forest scent. It reaches her before she can react. He dips at her neck from behind, planting soft kisses as large wide palms wrap around to cup her, crushing her back into his pounding chest.

"Ragnar." The word leaves her lips, featherlight. "We can't. Pia—"

"*Ssshhhh*," he hushes quietly into her ear before nipping it, his hands traveling her hips. "Take me there," he whispers, pressing closer.

"I can't." She turns toward him to protest. He catches her words in a slow kiss instead, prying her lips open to receive him.

Gentle caresses now replace their initial frenzy in his Porsche. She breaks free and pushes away. She glances at him before leading the way. He follows her. She peeks over her shoulder, not meeting his eyes, to see if he still trails her. Before they reach the bedroom, Ragnar grabs and pins her against the wall, clasping her shoulders. His brawn holds her fast.

"*Jag vill ha dig.*" Those hushed words roll melodically off his tongue. They caress her cheek before he kisses her gently. *I want you.* His voice sounds taming, potent, brash in contrast with his tender touch. She gazes into eyes darkened by pupils twice their size, trying to decipher him.

Kemi's mind races as both men cloud her mind in that instant. Is her powerful social identity turning Ragnar on? The quintessential "Strong Black Woman"? Is this the same reason Tobias is drawn to her? An idealized image she can never fully live up to because she is in fact human? Are both men trying to fully possess her in their own ways? It would seem both want to tame her, with Tobias trying to prove that she needs him despite her independence, while Ragnar is simply trying to show her strength is no match for him.

She hates it. That unfair cape she has to wear on behalf of her kind. She savagely rips it off, tears it into invisible shreds, and decides she wants to be weak. She wants to be selfish.

With each advance toward her bedroom, his touch softens. The desperation which once filled him wanes. He holds her gently, gazes into her eyes intensely. After they shed their clothes and Ragnar settles his broad frame over her, not even Tobias matters to her anymore.

Ragnar threads his fingers with hers and lifts both her arms over her head. He locks her down by her hands in a gesture of control, his eyes pinning hers, before tugging her lips with a crushing kiss.

Afterwards, she cradles him quietly, tracing her fingers along his toned back. Her bedroom reeks of sweat and sex. He sobs against her already damp chest. Ragnar's tears shake her as he weeps unabashedly, his dam fully breaching, drowning her. He unravels in her embrace.

"*Jag älskade honom*," Ragnar cries. *I loved him.*

"I know," Kemi whispers.

"I-I saw his little body. No life. Just dead, blue," he sobs, the words catching on his breath in broken snatches.

Kemi rakes her fingers through his hair to calm him. Ragnar shudders against her, absorbing her caress. Parents are never meant to lose children. Witnessing him disintegrate so overwhelms her, she can barely breathe.

"I'm so sorry." Kemi traces her fingertips along his jaw, soothing him as he weeps. "I'm here," she whispers into his hair as he growls against her neck in despair.

It seems those words *I'm here* snap him open because he lifts his head to gaze into her eyes, staring straight through her. She holds her breath, unsure of what he's thinking, what he wants to say.

Ragnar says nothing. His arms tighten around her instead. His quivering mouth seeks hers with force, needing more heat to dry his tears. With her skin glistening wet from his sobbing, Kemi swallows more of his pain. Again and again, each time harder than the first, more intense than the last, because she convinces herself a grieving Ragnar needs her.

Kemi closes her eyes tightly, listening to powerful sprays of water as he showers. She lies naked under the sheets pulled up to her chin, shaking with fear.

Breathe in. Hold. Breathe out. Hold.

She fumbles for the tiny Union Jack alarm clock sitting on her nightstand. Quarter to nine. Three times in an hour. The rushing sound of water stops. She hears him in her bathroom. Ragnar strides out naked, drying his hair aggressively with a towel. He catches her eyes. She turns away.

Clothes rustle and she sneaks a look, watching him dress in that crisp white shirt and black trousers. He brushes damp hair off his face, eyebrows settling into their frown, before he swivels toward her. Kemi sinks deeper into her bed, willing it to smother her. Instead, Ragnar coasts over and sits next to her, his eyes warming her. He reaches down to plant a lingering closed-lip kiss on her. She pitches her face away from him. He gets up to go. Her voice calling out halts him by the door.

"I can't do this."

"Do what?"

"I just can't," she says. "We made a mistake bringing London here," she whispers.

"Did we?" he challenges her.

She remains quiet as he regards her from the door. She closes her eyes, sucking in air to build up her dignity.

"Yes. We did." Her eyes flutter open. She sees him bite his lips, pondering her words.

"No." He shakes his head. "No. I don't regret it."

"You will, Ragnar. When you get home and look at Pia, you—"

"Stop saying her name." His voice is curt, hard. Did guilt add that edge to his roar? Kemi wonders.

She starts to get out of bed, gathering sheets around her to hide from him. She teeters over to grab her dressing gown slung across an armchair. She maneuvers into it, then drops the sheet to tie her gown.

"I'll walk you out." She squeezes past Ragnar, who leans against the doorjamb. He grabs and pulls her back, sliding both hands over her backside to lock her tightly against him. His mouth finds hers once again, his breathing labored. Kemi isn't ready for their fourth round.

Her body is weak, her mind long lost. They already broke that dam together one ravenous night in full view of London's iconic Shard.

"Go home, Ragnar," she whispers softly.

His eyes settle on her lips before releasing her. She walks to the front door, his eyes feasting on her from behind. She waits silently while he slips his brogues back on. She unlocks the door. He pauses her with a hand to her wrist and steps closer.

"I need to see you again." Ragnar's voice dips low. Tears pool in her eyes.

"We can't," she cries.

Ragnar presses his forehead to hers, breathing heavily. He strokes a tear off her cheek, then straightens up and leaves her apartment. His slow gait is quiet confidence stretched over a simmering sun. She knows he's burning up inside while his exterior remains unbothered.

Once Kemi shuts her door, she leans against it and slides to the floor in a heap of tears.

BRITTANY-RAE

"Mamma. Bulle!" Maya points to a cinnamon bun half the size of her head. "*Bulle!*"

"Soon, darling." Brittany kisses and strokes her daughter's curls. She's sitting at a café in Lidingö Centrum. Malin had picked out the place as their meeting spot, despite the fact they live on the same street as the little playground and park where they met. Brittany's already used to this norm. Unless you grew up together, inviting strangers into your house is rare. Three years on and she still hasn't been to her in-laws' house yet.

Malin had agreed to meet her for coffee. Brittany needs a lead into Stockholm's fashion scene, and after their phone call she googled Stockholm Fashion Week, excitement coursing through every pore. She was made for more. This can't be her life. One where she does nothing while being pampered. On paper, it sounds like heaven. In reality, hell. One she unfortunately crafted with her own hands.

Now Brittany sits in a café wearing a faux fur coat, elbow-length gloves, and every other impractical piece of fashionable winter wear she has.

"Brittany!" Malin shrills on approach.

Brittany stretches to her full height to give her a hug. Maya is tucked into a high chair next to their table. Brittany had given her au pair the morning off. The young British woman had looked at her skeptically before handing the child over.

Malin, on the other hand, is dressed as if she's just come from the gym. Or woke up there, simply rolled off the elliptical machine, and jogged over, her blonde ponytail still dancing long after she stops moving. The wide smile on her face is what Brittany needs at the moment. She hadn't realized how much she misses grins. Smiles rarely come out in mid-January.

"Where's your daughter?" She remembers Malin's toddler who wobbled through the snow and climbed up the slides like a drunk.

"*Dagis.*"

"Isn't she too young?"

"Not really. She's three years old. Isn't yours in daycare yet?"

Brittany glances at Maya, who sports two braids and holds the cinnamon bun she's been screaming for. Jonny's family insists on keeping Maya home until she turns two. Brittany isn't sure if this is a family ritual or if it's their way of spoiling Maya with her own chief of staff.

Brittany shakes her head. Malin stops prodding. She excuses herself to grab some *fika*. She returns with only black coffee.

"So, how long have you been here?" Malin stirs the dark brew before raising it to her mouth, still scorching.

"Almost three years." Brittany lifts her mug of hot chocolate to her lips, waiting for signs of judgment from Malin because she's still speaking English.

Malin's smile doesn't flinch. "And do you like it here?" Malin bunches her shoulders in excitement, leaning forward.

"How much time do you have for my answer?" Brittany chuckles.

Malin laughs. "Well, it can't be easy leaving your home and moving to a whole new place, a new country with a weird language too." Malin sips her coffee.

"I'm adjusting," Brittany says. "Not as fast as I'd like, but still—"

"So what brings you to Sweden?" Malin cuts her off, her smile still not breaking stride. This question is one Brittany avoids like fried food.

"My husband," Brittany says, indulging her.

"Is he from Lidingö?"

"Well, some of his family live here, but they're originally from one of the islands. Gotland."

"Fascinating." It seems Malin's smile is doing the talking. "If I may ask"—Brittany resists the urge to say no—"what's your last name?"

"Von Lundin."

"Johan's wife?"

"You know him?"

"Well, I mean, who doesn't? But when he married a Black girl . . . I'm sorry, African American woman last year, everyone was so curious," Malin says, her eyes roaming over Brittany. "I saw some photos of you two together, but I wasn't a hundred percent sure if it was you when I met you."

"I didn't know everyone followed Jonny's business so closely."

"Well, no." Malin clears her throat. "Of course not. He's from one of the most famous families in Sweden, though, so naturally . . ." She arches her shoulders. "I can see why." Her smile returns. "You're absolutely stunning."

"Thank you." Brittany smiles weakly. "Though I'm hoping he married me for more than my body." She takes a sip of her hot drink. Malin laughs. A cackle which fades once she realizes Brittany isn't laughing along.

Malin clears her throat, looking at her closely. "I mean, every marriage does have problems," she says. "I've been married for ten years and we still wake up every day wondering why we're together. Yet, we work."

"Ten years," Brittany says, pondering the idea.

She isn't even planning to finish the new year in Jonny's arms. The harder task will be weaning herself off his lovemaking. Beyond that, all romance is gone. Extinguished instantly once the Maya Daniels news was delivered. She can't find his personality. He isn't charismatic or charming. Words don't flow easily from him. He's often nervous. Fidgets all the time. Stares too intensely. Stands suffocatingly close. Scarily meticulous. Precise. Obsessive. Compulsive. Infatuated. With access to whatever he wants to fuel his passions, his pursuits, his fixations.

And she, his wife, is the current object he's smothering with everything her heart desires so he can fully possess her.

"I think the rigors of being new parents often take their toll in more ways than we realize," Malin assures her. "Even if we can afford it and get all the help we can."

"I know," Brittany says. Keen to change the subject, she asks, "So, what do you do again? I remembered you mentioning something about fashion."

"Yes, I work with the Swedish Fashion Council and was actually a buyer for many years. I'm also on the board of Stockholm Fashion Week."

"Really?"

"I love fashion!" Malin squeals.

"Me too!" Brittany pitches higher. "I studied fashion for a while, but had to drop out. My dream is to become a designer."

"How cool! Have you worked with any designers?" Malin asks. Brittany name-drops a few. "I knew it!" Malin says excitedly. "You had to be a model. You're gorgeous and so tall."

"So you didn't read in those tabloids that Jonny was married to one?" Brittany gives her a sly smile.

"Haha, *touché*." Malin laughs. "I would love to recommend you right away to some designers in town to walk in their shows."

Brittany purses her lips. Malin can potentially open doors even

Jonny's sisters haven't been able to help her do. They have tons of contacts and the tentacles of their networks reach far. But to secure an opportunity within the fashion industry for their sister-in-law seems too challenging for them. Brittany knows they haven't even tried.

"You don't know if I'm any good."

"I saw how you walked up to us that day at the park," Malin says. "I knew then you were a model."

A wail cuts through their banter. Brittany finds Maya's half-eaten bun on the floor. She swoops to pick it up and wraps it up in a paper napkin. The little girl's cries fill the café. Brittany tries soothing her as best she can. She pulls Maya out of her high chair, cradles and rocks her, but she is inconsolable.

In that moment, Brittany realizes just how much she outsources her life to others. To Jonny's assistants, to her au pair Vicky, to her housekeeper Sylvia. Everyone orbits them, making sure her life runs seamlessly for his pleasure.

Now she can't even make her daughter stop crying.

Malin promises to set up another *fika* date. Brittany wants to get to know her; she needs someone she can confide in. Malin, whose last name she still doesn't know, could potentially fill that gap.

Brittany straps a crying Maya into the car seat in her smoky gray Range Rover. She barely drives it off the island and just uses it to zip around. She can't remember the last time she actually rode the *tunnelbana*. *Oh yes*, her brunch with Kemi, who still hasn't produced any recommendations for a divorce lawyer. There she goes again. Outsourcing her life.

Within a few moments, Maya falls asleep, exhausted from crying her lungs out. As Brittany starts the car, a message pops up on her phone. She grabs it.

> I have information about the Daniels. Parents are still around. One brother. Here are the numbers I found.
>
> Eva xoxo

Xoxo?

Why is Eva sending her hugs and kisses? Is she truly an ally? After all, Eva does know how to take care of Jonny's women efficiently. Brittany figures many of them have rolled around with him in that Canary Wharf penthouse. So, she knows the words *Eva* and *trust* are mutually exclusive.

But Brittany's desperate. And desperation always brings dignity to its knees.

A live link to his past now lands in her hands. Brittany longs to know more about Maya's relationship with Jonny, how deeply the loss still affects him, and if Maya took any semblance of his personality to the grave with her.

Before she can hop on the phone, hear the Daniels' voices, and dredge out their sorrow, she needs this information out of Jonny.

She needs to know if her husband ever loved her.

YASMIIN

Yasmiin runs her thumb over Muna's cold fingers, studying them as she sleeps, the beeping in the background keeping her alive. She tugs a finger lightly, willing a response. She craves any sign Muna listens to her, hearing her recount her day as she often does during each visit.

Speaking her life into the void.

"I hope you can forgive me, Muna," Yasmiin whispers. "I had no choice. I was afraid. He works for the government. *Säpo.* He had been spying on you and Ahmed all that time."

Shuffling of feet outside Muna's room cuts into her confession. The low hum of voices milling around. Squeaky wheels, in desperate need of oil, of hospital beds being moved from room to room.

Yasmiin sighs. "I had to give it to him. He promised to update me. He promised to bring justice, if Ahmed was innocent in all this." Her eyes dart to Ahmed's photo above Muna's headrest.

They take in the striking stranger before returning to Muna lying motionless.

"Mehmet has started *dagis*," she chuckles. "Talk about ripping your heart out. I cried and cried the first day I had to drop him off. You should see him, so handsome like his father. All that thick black hair. Well, you know Yagiz. He likes to shave everything off on the sides."

She pauses, her brows lowering as she assesses Muna. "He sends his greetings. He talks about you often. Calls you a sad little girl. But don't mind him. I think that is just his way of showing he cares about you." Her hand moves to stroke Muna's arm, praying her heat warms life back into her.

"I understand why now," Yasmiin says. "I understand why you kept going to see Yagiz at the kebab shop. Why you just won't leave him alone." She swallows her choking tears. "He was all you had. The only person who didn't go away." She bends her head to let out a few tears, her thumb brushing them away the second they hit her cheeks.

Yasmiin is tired of tears. Weeks into visiting Muna and she is still laden with such guilt. If only she had stayed in touch with her.

Muna's doctor gives her regular updates. She's healing, but they're keeping her in a medically induced coma because her pain, had she been awake, would be too excruciating even for the strongest painkillers to placate. Her doctor doesn't mention if she'll walk again, both her lower limbs shattered by the jump, and one already lost. The imagery consumes Yasmiin fully. Under those sheets lies brokenness in every sense of the word.

But Muna is healing nicely, which is all that matters to Yasmiin.

"You know, Yagiz has made it his mission to find you a man after all this." She smiles, wiping away the last few teardrops. "He has made it his mission to make sure you no longer remain a virgin." She pauses to laugh. A strained sound barely leaving her throat. "*She deserves a good fuck*. That is what he said." Her laughter dies, lips morphing into a hard line. "He thinks he is Allah's gift to women. That without a man like him, we are nothing. *Doqon!*" *Idiot!*

Silence fills the room once more. Yasmiin sinks into it. Those long quiet stretches are getting more comfortable. The need to fill every lull, evaporating. She now basks in the fact that Muna isn't alone. Even if she can't hear or feel her presence.

"Muna," she begins again. "Life feels possible now, you know." Yasmiin's ruddy cheeks spread into a grin. "I have a job. I hate it, but at least I'm meeting interesting people. Like Amani. *Tigris Tigress.*" She pauses to collect her breath. "Amani likes me."

When Yasmiin arrives home after picking Mehmet up from daycare, a dense cloud of smoke and a drunken stupor welcome her at barely five o'clock in the afternoon. Yagiz and a handful of his crew—she counts four—are in the apartment, their feet on her table, her sofa, everywhere. In varying versions of sweatshirts hugging every muscle and sweatpants wrapping bulges, leaving nothing to the imagination.

"*Yagizs Afrikalı prenses!*" one of his friends, a thick moose named Özel, yells above their cacophony. They call him Öz. The one who now runs Yagiz's former khat business. He lets out a deep matching moose-like bellow before scratching himself. The others burst out laughing while Yagiz drags in smoke and blows tendrils out without a care, barely acknowledging her. Yasmiin suspects he may be high.

She ignores Öz. He isn't deterred. He claps his right thigh, beckoning for *"Yagiz's African princess"* to come position her desirable backside on his lap.

He continues in Swedish. "Yagiz can't be selfish. He can't keep all that ass to himself."

The others snigger like weasels. Yagiz seems unfazed. Yasmiin flashes her husband a cutting glare before padding away to take Mehmet to his room. Once on the ground, the toddler finds a toy car missing a wheel and starts to play. She makes her way to the kitchen, past the leering and jeering men spread out in her living room. Someone turns on a random football match on TV. Soon, unintelligible roars punctuate burps and yelling.

She reaches into the sink and starts rinsing a few mugs left there by Yagiz's friends. Her days are filled with a certain mundaneness. *Drop Mehmet off, head over to the salon, sidestep nosy Salima, come home, do chores, rinse, and repeat*—while making sure she feeds and fucks Yagiz in between.

Now her weekly trips to Karolinska to see Muna have become a sort of craving for solitude and self-care. Those quiet moments where she sits with her thoughts and speaks whatever her heart wants to speak. Her own therapy sessions.

She feels his hand before she can react. Öz's bear-sized palm finds her backside and squeezes a cheek. He presses himself closer.

"I hear you're quite the animal." His breath is hot in her ear. She spins around and shoves him away. He sniggers and lifts his cigarette to his lips, peering at her through dark eyes. Easily clearing six feet and undeniably easy on the eyes, Öz is all muscle with a neck like an ox and a full dark beard.

"Don't you dare touch me again," Yasmiin says, glaring at him, her chest heaving. Yagiz will be livid if he finds out. Öz keeps staring at her, dragging at his cigarette. "Leave now."

"*Prenses*," he starts, naming the club where they'd all met in Akalla. "I was there when Yagiz found you. Too bad he got you first." His dark shiny eyes dance over her body.

"Yagiz!" she screams at the top of her lungs, but his name is drowned by the sports commentary and the crew arguing futilely in the living room.

"Leave Yagiz alone. I just want to talk to you." Öz inches closer to her, his large frame blocking out the light as he backs her against the sink.

"Yagiz!" she screams again. Öz cackles.

"Oh, *prenses*," he says, leaving the cigarette balancing between his lips as he rests his hands on either side of Yasmiin, trapping her between him and the sink. "Why are you acting so shy? *Hmm?*"

He languidly blows smoke into her face. "From what I've heard, you know your way around a man."

"You bastard," she spits at him, her face contorting in anger. He's picking at her old scab. He'll never know how deep his words cut close to her bone. And for this, she hates her husband. Hates that he talks too much. Hates his charisma. Hates his need to fill every lull with words and stories and noise. Including details of their life behind closed doors. All Öz knows is what Yagiz must have bragged about.

Rome remains a distant memory Yagiz is never going to unearth. He would never boast about her if he knew what she did to survive, she knows this. A piece of her wants to believe he'll understand too, because Yagiz Çelik's life is also defined by surviving. He is a man who has done surviving and is desperately trying to thrive at all costs.

"Such harsh words." Öz purses his lips in faux hurt, pressing closer to her, his voice dropping lower. "Is it true what they say?" His weight pins her against the sink, his eyes hold hers unsmiling. "The darker the berry?"

She slaps him. A solid hit so hard the TV volume and boisterous chatter among the crew instantly die down.

"*Aşkım?*" Yagiz is on his feet and in the kitchen before Öz has time to compose himself. He doesn't like what he sees upon arrival. His friend towering over his wife.

She doesn't need to push Öz back or fight him off. Within seconds, Yagiz drags him and slams him against the wall. Öz laughs in the shorter man's face while licking his lips. He pauses, placing a finger on his lower lip, staring at it to assess the light red stain.

"You come into my house and disrespect my wife?" Yagiz isn't asking. "Say it isn't so."

"*Abi*, you know I would never do such a thing," Öz says, calling Yagiz *brother* in Turkish. He isn't apologizing, though. He keeps licking his broken lip. The others gather around the kitchen door, observing, eyes darting from Yasmiin, trying to compose herself, to Yagiz pinning Öz, a much broader, much larger man, against the wall.

"Then never do such a thing again,"Yagiz says between clenched teeth. "Never." His dark eyes burrow into his friend. "That is the mother of my son. You will respect her in my house."

Öz nods. He flashes Yasmiin a glance of unfinished business. She glares back at him.

Yagiz lets his friend go, before turning to the rest of the crew. "Everyone, leave my house!"

TEN

KEMI

Back from his night shift as a security guard, Tobias tries opening the front door, but weight pushes against it. He cracks it a few inches and sees Kemi lying across the floor in her bathrobe, sleeping, acting as a door stopper. Tobias pushes it gently. She rolls over, stirring.

"*Älskling?*" he asks once he fully steps into the hallway. Kemi moves into a sitting position, wiping her face, trying to process where she is and what's happening. She remembers and draws her bathrobe tighter around her shoulders.

"What's going on?" he repeats as he drops his backpack and kneels next to her. She bursts into tears and throws her arms around his neck, sobbing. He pulls her into his broad swimmer's chest and cradles her, running a soothing palm over her back.

She feels him turn to her neck and take a sniff of her before loosening their embrace. Kemi can't think. She keeps sobbing, her body shuddering in panic with each memory as worry starts to fill Tobias.

"You're scaring me," he says. "Please tell me what's wrong."

She shakes her head. A new batch of tears bursts through. So he simply holds her until her heart slows and she breathes normally again. This is new. This territory she never dreamed she would ever cross into. And it's heavy. Too heavy for her heart to bear. She brought this anvil upon her own chest. No one else will help her lift it. Not when Ragnar holds it down so she can't move it, suffocating her. The only way to breathe through the pressure is with lies. She knows she's never going to be able to sustain them, but right now she needs air.

"How was work?" She sniffs, wiping away tears.

"You've got to tell me what's going on," Tobias insists, stroking her disheveled curls. "Are you okay?"

"I'm sorry I scared you," she apologizes. "It's nothing."

"I found you sleeping on the floor."

"I missed you, that's all." Tobias frowns at her. Kemi notices the air around them shift.

"But you don't lie on the floor for any man. You're strong. That's not you."

Kemi starts weeping again. Tobias reveres her as strong. That archetype is what attracted him to her. His mother said, in no uncertain words, that Tobias had been waiting for her all his life. It's probably the same scent attracting Ragnar to her beyond reason and common sense. She represents a different kind of ideal and an equal match.

"I'm tired of being strong, Tobias," she cries. "I'm tired. I just want to *be*. To exist without that burden of being strong, of representing every Black woman."

Tobias listens to her. She loves him deeply for this. He's so good at listening and existing.

"I love you, Tobbe," she finally says, wiping her wet nose. "I love you so much and sometimes I think I don't deserve you." He stares at her. She can see his brown eyes warming as her words fully sink in. Tobias leans in to give her a soft kiss. She loves kissing him. Besides his full lips, he never rushes. Never devours. Only savors. Making her feel beautiful. She tries quickening their kiss but Tobias slows it down once more, showing her how much he loves her.

Kemi realizes in that moment he never said those words back. She isn't sure what to feel.

He gently pulls her to her feet and walks her to their bedroom. He's exhausted after a long shift, but he settles her under the covers. Seven minutes later, he's carrying a mug of chamomile tea for her with lemon wedges swimming in the piping hot liquid. She nurses the mug between both palms, while Tobias slips out of his uniform and takes a quick shower.

Wearing only boxer briefs, he climbs under the covers with her and takes the mug from her. She starts crying again. Tobias gently kisses away each tear racing down her face.

"It's okay," he says and nuzzles her cheek. "I know you miss your family. I know it's hard to be here. It's dark and depressing." She squeezes her eyes shut. Tightly. She can't look at him. Can't bring herself to look into his eyes. "It will pass. Spring will be here before you know it."

He gathers her closer, his left palm caressing her softly. His other hand is rolled into a fist. He's holding something. Kemi looks from his closed hand to his face as he peers at her intently.

"What?" She becomes nervous, jittery. "What is it?"

Kemi waits, unsure of what he's about to say. She lets him lead. The night can't get any stranger even if she imagines it. He keeps studying her until he lifts his hand and unfurls his fist.

"Whose are these?" he softly asks her, his eyes roaming her face.

Ragnar's cufflinks. They glitter at her like a verdict, mocking her. Showing her that, once the dust settles, what they have will die because Ragnar is a virus and she, his host. She can still taste him on her skin. Smell him on her. She hadn't showered because she fell asleep by the door before she had a chance to. Tobias isn't stupid. He sniffed her when he held her by the door. Tobias can probably smell the stranger in their bedroom. That forest scent. The man who left his glimpse of wealth behind to spite him.

Seeing those cufflinks in Tobias's palm tightens the squeeze around her neck.

Kemi blinks back tears, her brain working furiously. Her airway. Lies. The first one so she can keep her head above water, while the virus ravages her body. She needs to breathe first.

"You didn't give me a chance to wrap them yet," she says.

When the words make their way out, they taste bitter, poisonous. She knows it's the beginning of the end. That didn't explain why something so costly would have been lying carelessly by the sink in their bathroom.

"I'm not even going to ask you how expensive these were," he says. Kemi's breath catches. She swallows. She looks at Tobias with wide wild eyes. Though tired from his shift, he seems elated on some odd level.

"Thank you so much. No one has ever given me something like this before." He carefully places the cufflinks on the nightstand. "Now I have my very own bling." He chuckles weakly. She gives him an even weaker smile.

Tobias turns toward her, his grin dropping. He gives her that look. He wants to dutifully thank her without words. He pulls her closer, locking her to fit his frame. His mouth covers hers. She tastes the distance on his lips. *He knows.*

And for the first time in her life, Kemi joins the long list of women who have slept with both their partners and lovers on the same night.

BRITTANY-RAE

Desperation brings dignity to its knees. Always.

She sits in front of her vanity mirror, massaging shea butter into her skin. Thirty minutes earlier, Louise texted her that he's on his way home. Her false alarm worked. She had summoned Jonny home.

Having coffee with Malin had made her wonder if she should give life in Sweden a proper chance outside of her gilded bubble. She realizes she hasn't put much effort into settling in properly, making friends, and learning the language.

If Jonny truly loves her, maybe she can rebuild their connection. After all, Maya Daniels is long dead even though the mere thought of his ex chokes her. For the sake of her own Maya and her visions of a happy family, this is her last-ditch attempt to stay and rebuild her life using his access.

She dons a bodysuit fashioned in black lace beneath her silk robe. She touches her cherry red lipstick to her mouth and presses her lips together to seal in the color. She pushes strands of hair behind both ears. She always wears her hair parted in the middle, straightened with relaxers and extensions put in to add length.

Brittany peers at her reflection, turning each cheek to properly assess her features. Maybe she can model again. She's in her early forties. Many models catch a second wind in their later years and make successful comebacks. Over fifty years old, Naomi Campbell still struts down runways. She has access, through Jonny, to whatever she needs to start her own fashion line and become a designer. Instead, she'd sunk into a plush cocoon of doing nothing.

Brittany hears him.

She knows how he often materializes silently. He stands by the door, hands in fists by his sides, peering at her, a look of confusion inside that suffocating stare. Probably wondering why she's in lingerie at midday. She turns back to the vanity mirror and picks up a compact of brown face powder.

"You're back," she says, her voice low, not looking at him as she presses powder to her cheeks.

"Louise said it was urgent." He closes the door behind him. She lets out a puff of frustration, realizing once again she's going to have to work. To explain in black and white what she wants from him.

"It kinda is," she says, her voice taking on a sultry tone.

"What is it?" Jonny asks.

She sighs. "I missed you."

He keeps quiet. She knows his brain is working furiously. His eyes roam her bodysuit and robe. They linger a few seconds before working back up to lock with her eyes once more.

"I missed you today," she continues, rising to her feet. She sees his eyebrows dip with concern. "I missed you, Jonny."

His gaze hold hers as she moves toward him. When she pushes loose strands of hair behind an ear, his eyes draw like lasers to the movement. Motion sensors. Brittany plants herself inches from his face. She searches his face before tilting upwards to give him a kiss. He receives it with closed lips and she pulls back.

"What's wrong?" he asks her, his voice low. He's been learning to read her face better.

"Nothing. I just want you, that's all."

She drops her robe at his feet, standing in only the black lace bodysuit wrapped around her long lean torso. She tries kissing him again.

Still, Jonny raises an unresponsive barrier between them. She knows he's confused.

"Kiss me back," she whispers against his lips.

His eyes settle on her mouth before landing a hard kiss which jerks her head backward. He takes over with fervor, both hands grabbing at her waist, drawing her closer. She strokes the back of his neck as his tongue seeks hers.

She needs to think. How is she going to get him to relax enough to show her he truly loves her beyond their physicality?

He breaks her thoughts when both his hands move over her backside and he pulls her closer, crushing her against his chest. Hard enough to make her gasp. She had planned a slow seduction. One where Jonny dutifully shows her how much he has memorized her body, but the Jonny in her arms only wants to ravage her.

Her plan backfires.

With her tightly locked against him, Jonny spins around and pins her to the door.

"Jonny," she says, running her fingers through his hair. He grabs both her wrists instead and presses them against the door next to her shoulders, as he steps in closer.

"I missed you too," he says, before his tongue sweeps in for another possessive kiss, one which shakes her. She murmurs against his raging mouth. He releases her wrists, his hands moving to her waist, lifting her against the door. She wraps her legs around him while his hands travel the length of her bodysuit, his eyes following as his hands caress her waist.

Then he stops, breaking off to stare into her eyes once more.

"You want something," he says, his eyes hooking hers seriously. He sets her down on her feet, her back against the door.

Brittany holds her breath. He places his right palm on her collarbone, feeling her heaving chest. Her beating heart.

"Tell me what you want from me." His fingers circle her neck, tightening. Brittany blinks back tears. He has never been this rough with her. This Jonny has never surfaced in her arms before.

"Only you," she gasps as his fingers move against her neck. He searches her face, looking for signs, trying to read her. His fingers flatten into a palm and journey down her chest as it rises and falls with each heavy breath. His lips dip to the trail his palm leaves behind. He kisses her collarbone, between her breasts, her stomach, his palm leading the way.

Brittany rests the back of her head against the door, desperately trying to calm her breathing. She simply moans as his lips explore her skin through lace, struggling not to fully surrender to him.

He straightens back up, his hand still on her stomach. His eyes pin her to the door as his palm works its way lower, between her thighs. Brittany holds her breath.

"Tell me," he asks her, barely three inches from her face. "What do you want?"

He applies pressure. She pushes against him. He explores her with vigor. This isn't how she planned it to play out. She had wanted that careful seduction, where she could tease out those words—*I love you*—as they cradled each other in bed. She feels his fingers move inside her and closes her eyes. No, this isn't what she wants. He waits for her answer. He bends low and mutters words against Brittany's stomach as he trails with his lips.

She freezes at those words. "No." Brittany shakes her head. "No."

Jonny stiffens and straightens up. Her eyes bolt open to meet his own, his eyebrows wrinkled in confusion. He peers at her quietly, his fingers frozen as well. Brittany swallows, tears pooling in her eyes as she holds his gaze. She pries his palm away.

"I don't understand." Jonny is breathless.

"I don't want this anymore." Brittany begins to cry, scared of her reaction. She hadn't been expecting this. Every inch of her skin is rejecting him, rejecting his sex, rejecting everything he symbolizes in her life. "It's over."

"Louise said it was urgent. You said you missed me." His fingers begin to dance in agitation by his sides. Brittany runs her right hand over her hair, smoothing invisible rogue strands as she cries. "Please tell me what's wrong," he demands.

Brittany shakes her head violently. She can't breathe. Marriage to him has squeezed her out of life. She'll have to confront the Danielses. Living with him from now on means reliving the fact he doesn't love her. She was dumb to think otherwise. All he probably sees is Maya Daniels whenever he makes love to her.

Now with her back pressed up against the door and him in her face, all she sees is a foreign being.

"I want a divorce," she cries out.

He furrows his brows. "Divorce?" Jonny's eyes pin hers, trying to process her words.

"I want you to go."

"Don't leave me."

"Go," she wails, her shoulders dancing with each sob.

"Why?"

"You don't love me, Jonny, you never did."

"I love you."

"No," she weeps. "You don't."

"Tell me what you want," he pleads in a soft, even-keeled voice. "I'll do anything for you."

Brittany shakes her head. "All you see is her when you touch me."

"I don't understand."

"You just called me Maya," she cries. "You just whispered her name against my body."

YASMIIN

"Should I kill him for you?" Yagiz is apologizing.

Yasmiin remains silent as she lays out a bowl of spicy *bariis iskukaris* for dinner. She spoons a large heap of cardamom-spiced pilaf rice with chunks of lamb onto his plate while he observes her, unnerved by the quiet lull.

Yagiz continues. "Did he touch you?" More silence. "Tell me, *aşkım*! I swear to Allah, I will kill Öz if he touches you again." She grabs a fork and starts digging into her own portion. "Yasmiin, please."

She drops the fork, the sound of metal hitting glass vibrating through the room. She holds his gaze. He arches his thick eyebrows upwards in anticipation of her backlash. She picks up her fork and spears a piece of roasted lamb instead. Knowing her man, the silence will grate him for the rest of the night.

A few moments of silence later, Yagiz tries again. "I know people. I can finish Öz for you."

"Shut up!" Yasmiin yells, tossing her fork at him. He catches it and puts it on the table. "Shut up! Okay? Öz is like your brother." Yagiz's shoulders bunch up at her outburst. "Why did you expose me like that?" she continues.

"Expose you? What did he say?"

"That he hears I'm an animal in bed," Yasmiin says. Yagiz chuckles, amused. "Do you brag about us? To him? To all your *doqon* friends?"

"Brag?" Yagiz seems confused. "Of course I brag about you. Have you seen your own ass?"

"Yagiz, I'm serious."

"What did Öz say? What did he do? Did he touch you?"

Yasmiin picks up her fork once more and digs into her rice. Eating is the only way to hold back the tears as she feels him studying her. She isn't ready. She realizes she may never be ready to confront and push her past away. Özel ripped her nicely healing scab off her soul. If anyone will understand, it has to be her Yagiz, right?

When Yagiz realizes Yasmiin isn't sharing more tonight, he picks up his fork too.

The next day, Yasmiin sobs silently against Muna's bed.

"They can smell it on me." Her arms are crossed on the light-blue sheets, her face buried in their nook as she cries. "Remember what I told you that night? About Rome?"

That night when Yasmiin had confessed to Muna. How she could never gather up the courage to reach out to her own family back in Mogadishu because she feared judgment once they found out. Muna had comforted her then. Trying to convince her in her own innocent way that they wouldn't judge her. They would receive her back with open arms. Their lost child. The one who had done what she needed to do to survive.

Yasmiin continues through her tears. "These men. It's like they just know. Like they come close to me and with one sniff they know what I did," she sobs. "Otherwise, they would not talk to me with such arrogance. Like they can take what they want from me when they want it."

The beeps of Muna's monitors comfort her. Even if Muna isn't sharing words of reassurance, her heart listens and soothes Yasmiin with each mechanical buzz.

"Some days I hate him so much for exposing me to his idiots," she cries. "And most days, Yagiz is my heart. He knows me. He loves Mehmet and me. He takes care of us."

He takes care of us.

That phrase breaks a nerve deep within Yasmiin. The room grows quiet once more beyond the intermittent dings of the machines. Yasmiin lets the rest of her tears run dry.

She's ready to rediscover who she is without being beholden to men. In her teenage years she had set out along a path charted by men. Now in her twenties, she's still tied financially to a man and traveling the modest lane he is carving out for them.

No. She will no longer be relegated to being his *princess*. She's ready to grow beyond those pre-defined boxes. Burst out of them with such force because she no longer wants to just survive. Yasmiin is ready to thrive.

Quruxda. Beauty.

The Somali word bubbles up right away with glimpses of her future. Salima and Amani are an opportunity she would be daft not to seize. Salima has enough space in her salon to serve more customers beyond her Middle Eastern clique. There are immigrant communities who stick to the suburbs, where it is cheaper. She'll give people a reason to venture south of Kista and north of Aspudden without being afraid it will suck up all their hard-earned funds. She will fill Salima's salon with Eritreans, Ethiopians, Somalis, Gambians. She'll bring them all out to her corner.

She plans on befriending Amani because Amani has friends in high places, clearly a powerful woman living in a palace of an apartment in Östermalm. She'll find out what had made her leave that Swedish man while keeping his life. The rented space where Salima runs her salon belongs to Amani too, "*thanks to the divorce*," she always punctuates.

If there were any reason to doubt Amani's prowess as Stockholm's top divorce lawyer, one only has to look at the wealth she surrounds herself with. Material testimonies to her work. Yasmiin plans to learn as much as she can about Amani Nassar-Berg. The older woman has stretched out a hand. Yasmiin is ready to grab onto it.

A whimpering sound escapes Muna. Yasmiin's gaze cuts to her. The first time it happened, Yasmiin went screaming in search of a doctor. It's normal, the doctor had said, calming her down. Think of Muna as being in a deep sleep with vivid dreams. Soon enough, the doctor promised, soon enough, they'll pull her out of her slumber.

Yasmiin smiles as her eyes wash over Muna's resting face. They have so much to talk about and catch up on. But first, Yasmiin will prepare. She'll learn all she can about her new sister. The one lying in front of her with no one else in the world to claim her and show her love.

The only person who has known Muna longer than anyone is a middle-aged white man working as an undercover security agent. One who promised her he'd do everything in his power to bring justice for Ahmed. One who sought, rather demanded, her trust despite her cynicism. The first white man she decides she is going to give the benefit of the doubt to, because she needs to know more about Muna.

So, it takes every ounce of will within her, pushing her pride and distrust aside, wiping images of clawing pale hands, to call him.

Mattias picks up on the third ring.

"*Hallå?*" he says gruffly, seemingly in the middle of more pressing matters.

"*Det är Yasmiin*," she says softly.

"Yasmiin?" His voice rises in surprise before tempering his response. "Hope you're doing well," he continues. "I have no new updates for you, but I assure you, we're working on it. I promise you I will—"

"Tell me about her," Yasmiin demands.

"Sorry?"

"Tell me about Muna," she repeats. "What was she like? You know, at Solsidan." She hears him sigh deeply, catching his breath. A few seconds of silence pass before Mattias speaks once more.

"*Hon var den duktigaste tjejen jag hade träffat*," he finally says.

She was the smartest girl I'd ever met.

ELEVEN

KEMI

She isn't sure how she has summoned the courage to sit in this meeting. She ponders where she found the strength. She has been awake since Tobias came home from work, staying up the rest of the night.

In the winter darkness this morning, she had put on one of her favorite pantsuits—a lean-cut plum-colored number paired with a daisy-yellow chiffon blouse. She buried it under a heavy coat and dragged herself to the bus station, leaving her small car behind. The ride from Nacka to Slussen gave her time to think. How is she going to continue this lie? She can already feel its weight bearing on her, suffocating her.

From Slussen, she rode the *tunnelbana* to Östermalmstorg in equal contemplation. This will crush Tobias once he finds out. This man who stands by her side so loyally. Who bakes fresh buns for her and makes sure she's taken care of in the little ways he knows she needs. Even if she never asks because she's too independent to do so.

Ragnar left his cufflinks behind on purpose. He came into her apartment with nothing else besides the clothes on his back. And his scent.

She pulled out her phone and scrolled through her contact list. She found his details and considered deleting them. She sighed, frustrated, and put the phone away instead because they're colleagues. She needs to be able to reach him.

Now she enters the meeting room, where some of her fellow directors are already gathered:

Björn Fältström, Head of Business Development.
Greta Ljungberg, Head of Operations.
Espen Wiklund, Head of Client Services.
Maria Larsson, Head of Media Relations.
Ingrid Johansson, Head of Human Resources.

As CEO, Jonny's also there. A rarity because he does nothing. Greta runs the company on his behalf. This time, though, Jonny leads the meeting. He sits at the far end of the long table, the room filled with low mumbling. The muttering silences when Kemi steps in.

"*God morgon!*" Espen greets her enthusiastically. Kemi nods and smiles back at him, before a low chorus of "*god morgon*" is offered. The only person who doesn't greet her is Jonny. He simply glares at her with his characteristic intensity. She knows his quirks. They often bother her. She also knows he's Ragnar's best friend, so she isn't sure how much he already knows. Once she settles into a chair, which Espen pulls out for her, all attention turns to Jonny once more.

He twirls a pen in his left hand, his fingers expertly flipping it over and over again as if in a meditative trance.

"Jonny?" Greta's stern motherly voice brings him back to their table. "*Ska vi börja?*" *Shall we begin?*

Her words break his concentration. He dives right into it in Swedish, explaining that Ragnar finally decided to take much-needed time off to be with his wife and family.

"He has turned over the Bachmann account to me," Jonny says. "He isn't coming back as a consultant with von Lundin for now." He pauses. "He was working too much." His eyes float over to Kemi.

"That was the best decision for him," Ingrid agrees. "Ragnar needs time to heal." Her words are followed by nodding around the room and that quintessential Swedish swooshing—sharp intakes of air—in agreement.

"*Stackars Ragnar.*" It's Greta again. *Poor Ragnar.*

The bastard. Those are the first words that come into Kemi's mind. Ragnar is equally complicit in their affair. Yet, he also lost his baby. She feels heartless. Another word bubbles up. *Selfish*. Can two things be true? Can one feel both disdain and empathy for the same person?

Eyes burn her skin. She turns to see Ingrid staring at her. Possibly looking for a reaction. Kemi folds her arms across her chest, eyes fixed on no particular person or object. In a world of her own thoughts. The universe is ripping him out of her path, so she won't continue to derail herself. She dare not say anything. Every single person at that table knows what happened at the Christmas party. Well, everyone except Jonny, she thinks. She suspects people keep a lot of things from him. Espen and Maria had been in London and witnessed Ragnar chase after her.

"So." Jonny faces her. "The account is yours once more."

What she worked so hard to build to show her prowess. She doesn't want it anymore.

"Maybe this is a good time to transition the account to someone else?" she says.

All eyes turn on her as if she's just confessed to killing Ragnar's baby.

Jonny's eyebrows lift in surprise. "What do you mean?"

"I mean..." She isn't sure what she means, but her ego rises up. She certainly doesn't want Ragnar's scraps, where every decision, design, and procedure currently in place reeks of him. A constant reminder. She can't work on the project anymore.

"Maybe it's time someone else took over," she continues. "You took the account from me because you said you wanted a more Nordic touch." Mumbling fills the air.

"Maybe Jonny wasn't clear," Greta says. "This isn't a suggestion." The room falls silent.

Kemi opens her mouth to reply, but Greta isn't finished.

"I know you've read a lot about our *consensus* culture"—Greta makes air quotes with her fingers—"but in the end, your boss makes the decision. Not you."

Anger brews deep within Kemi as she fights the sudden urge to burst onto her feet and quit her job on the spot. She can't act rashly now, when she's raking in twice the money doing a quarter of the work she did back in the States.

"So, is Jonny back to making all the calls now?" Kemi says. "I thought it was you who actually ran this company." She sees Greta bite her lower lip, her brows knitting, as red rushes up her cheeks. Kemi knows she's playing with fire. They aren't going to dissect her now. They're eagerly awaiting her exit, when they will free-flow in Swedish. She waits for Greta to reload.

Ingrid grabs the barrel instead. "What is your real reason why you don't want the account anymore?"

"I've already explained why." Kemi doesn't like back-pedaling. They're cornering her. "Jonny had explicitly said he wanted a Swede handling it."

"But you and Ragnar worked late on it yesterday," Ingrid pushes. "He gave you a ride home, didn't he? And then this morning, he calls Jonny and quits everything so suddenly."

"I'm not sure what you're asking me."

"We all want to understand why. What would make Ragnar drop a project overnight he has been leading so passionately?"

Kemi takes a deep breath. "Maybe the fact that he just lost his son and is grieving?" she says. "I'm surprised he's been able to work this long without completely losing it."

She remembers his cries as he fell apart in her arms, his sobs against her chest, his tight grip around her waist as he wailed. Those salty tears she tasted in his rough kisses over and over again.

They listen to her. She drags in another deep breath to pull up more buckets of courage from her well.

"I . . . I was able to get through to him," Kemi says. "To help him understand he was grieving and needed to fully allow himself to feel what he was feeling." She swallows to choke back tears.

She isn't sure what she was expecting from the room, but they continue to stay silent, hanging on her every word.

"How did you convince him?" Greta finally reloads.

"What do you mean?"

"The same way you did at the Christmas party?"

Kemi hears gasps around the room. She dare not look around, so she trains her eyes on Greta, matching her stare. Unbeknownst to them, kissing at the party is the least of their worries. Those kisses might as well have been chaste pecks compared to the raw territory she and Ragnar have already explored together in London.

"I'm not following you, Greta."

The older woman chuckles, provoking her. Kemi struggles to keep her cool. She's already burning from within trying to keep up a lie to secure Tobias in her life. Now, she needs more air to breathe through her work life as well.

"From what I've heard, you have a way of convincing Ragnar without words," Greta says. "That's quite a skill you have there. He's a very determined man." More audible gasps. This time, someone else speaks up.

"Greta, that is inappropriate," Espen says, coming to her defense. Kemi doesn't turn to look at him but continues glaring at Greta, who she now officially declares a maleficent soul.

"I would file harassment charges against you with HR, but . . ." Kemi starts. "HR is sitting right next to me." She pivots toward Ingrid, who stays quiet.

"Can we all just take a deep breath and relax?" Maria suggests.

"I'm not sure why we're having this conversation," Kemi says.

"Because we've all heard what happened," Greta retorts. "And I think that is highly inappropriate behavior."

"Greta." Espen raises his voice again. "We're not discussing anyone's personal lives here."

"So you think it's okay?" Greta's getting exasperated now. "You think what happened was okay?"

"What are you talking about? Drop it." Espen remains adamant.

"I see." Greta smirks. "You want to experience some of those skills yourself. Is that it?"

"That's enough." This time, Ingrid decides Greta has indeed gone too far. "Can we please focus on the discussion at hand? Our largest account is now at stake because Ragnar can't manage it anymore."

The room hushes.

"Can we make this meeting productive once again?" Ingrid continues. "Ragnar isn't coming back and we need to cover this as soon as possible." She turns to Kemi. "Please, can you handle this?"

Kemi nods, still in shock at what has just transpired. Greta cornered her, leaving her exposed. She had no one else to blame for this but herself. Everyone sitting around that table knows she and Ragnar had been caught kissing, passionately. The rumor doing the rounds is they had practically been fucking with their clothes on in that elevator. Others saw them leave together in a taxi.

Everyone suspects what, up until now, had only been speculation, that they're having a torrid affair. Two morally decrepit individuals with no integrity and compassion for the then pregnant wife and loyal boyfriend caught between them. That foul smell of deceit permeates the office. One which Ragnar has avoided because of his terrible loss. A part of her thinks it's a larger price to pay for their indiscretion. Nothing she would ever wish upon her worst enemy. Losing a child.

The mood in that room suggests her colleagues are only tolerating her now. Whatever respect they had for her eroded long ago. That bullet-proof confidence she built within her industry is melting away. She knows her days at von Lundin Marketing are numbered.

"So, now that everyone has settled down"—Ingrid takes over—"there will be no verbal attacks and harassment charges here, okay? We've all done dumb things after too many glasses of wine, so let's not throw stones." Ingrid looks from Greta to Björn, and back to Greta.

"Jonny." Ingrid turns back to the head of the table. "Jonny?" It's to an empty chair.

Jonny has already left the room.

BRITTANY-RAE

The room feels too stuffy to be Swedish. No airy spaces, clean lines, or minimalist decor. Every inch of that office in Östermalm is covered in polished mahogany. Bookcases, shelves, a sturdy desk which looks like it was carved directly from a tree and transported to the century-old building.

All in sharp contrast to the middle-aged woman of Middle Eastern descent sitting behind it: Amani Nassar-Berg.

Amani's dark-turquoise shoulder-padded pantsuit is cinched at the waist with a thick black belt, her jet-black hair brushed off her face, falling just above her shoulders. Hers is the only cherry red lipstick matching Brittany's shade she has seen. Silently, she takes Brittany in from beneath thick fake eyelashes, her hazel eyes soaking up every word.

For weeks, Brittany avoided searching for a random lawyer online because of the von Lundin family name. One whiff of divorce rumors, and they'll be plastered all over the tabloids within hours. She wanted a discreet connection. That was why she'd begged Kemi to scour her network.

Now desperation has taken deep root within her.

A simple search on "*divorce lawyer Stockholm*" had pulled up a picture of Amani, and Brittany was immediately struck by her. Arms confidently folded across her chest, back straight, her searing gaze. Nicknamed the "*Tigris Tigress*," a play on the Iraqi river and female tiger.

Using Google Translate, Brittany discovered she was behind some of Sweden's most high-profile divorces. From celebrities to sports stars and a couple of wealthy clients in between. Brittany sought her out right away. Amani had been busy all week but once

Brittany dropped her last name, Amani found an hour to squeeze her in.

"What about his assets?" Amani asks, her chin resting on cone-like manicured nails with glitter stones.

"What about them?"

"Do you know how much he's worth?"

Brittany presses her lips together, embarrassed that she knows nothing about her husband's finances. She isn't even sure if Jonny knows what he has. Eva and Louise handle everything for him as his interfaces with the world, his liaisons between his lawyers and accountants.

"Why would I? I didn't think it was important," Brittany says. "I didn't want his family thinking I was a gold digger."

Amani smirks. "Okay, what assets do you have in your name?"

"I'll need to check and get back to you."

"You know why I am asking you, right?"

Brittany hesitates before responding. Of course she knows why Amani's asking. With nothing to her name, she's leaving with nothing. If her name isn't legally signed on any documents, she's penniless. And Brittany hasn't signed any important-looking documents besides her marriage certificate since she moved to Sweden.

She grabs the mug of coffee Amani offered her earlier and takes a swig of the now lukewarm brew. This isn't going to be easy but she's ready to fight.

"And our daughter?"

"She would be entitled to all his assets, your assets, if both of you should die. Do you know if there are any trust funds or accounts set up in her name?"

That she does know. Once *söta* Maya screamed her first cry as a newborn von Lundin, accounts automatically opened up on her behalf.

"Yes, several."

Amani raises a perfectly arched eyebrow and reaches for a pen. She pulls her notebook closer and starts scribbling. She writes for almost a minute while Brittany swallows the silence. A lull comfortable for the Swede in the room. From what she googled online, she knows that Amani fled Iraq with her family as a young girl, so Sweden is probably all the older woman knows in her heart and soul.

"So, Brittany, I've got some homework for you," Amani says, ripping out the page from the notebook in dramatic fashion. She passes the sheet to Brittany, who grabs it with trepidation. She scans Amani's note and looks at her quizzically.

"You need a mole," Amani says, calmly clasping her hands together, leaning her elbows on the table. "You need someone on the inside who can get you all this information."

Brittany peers at the list once more.

Eva.

By the time her appointment with Amani is over and she's booked her next one, she has received two text messages from Eva. One to check on Brittany and see if she already called the Danielses. No, she hasn't. She's still gathering up the courage to rip the bandage off their loss. The second to remind her that her beauty specialist is flying in from London on Friday. She still hasn't found a hair salon she can patronize with ease. She's sure there are several dotted over Stockholm specializing in Black hair, but Brittany never goes wandering around the city.

Both Eva's messages end with *xoxo.* A budding familiarity she still isn't sure about. Had she also sent hugs and kisses to all Jonny's exes? But she needs a mole and Eva will have to do for now.

Brittany glances at her phone. Four fifty-three in the afternoon. Besides finding ways to bring her marriage to an end, another reason pushed her to venture into town today.

When she arrives at the hotel lobby, she immediately spots a banner with the American flag and a large "*WELCOME!*" sign. She had found a club online, an expat community of fellow Americans that holds regular mingle events. She decided to stop by one to check it out. She doubts anyone will recognize her here, so she saunters up to the registration desk and pulls off a brown leather glove to sign her name.

"Welcome!" The lady manning the desk seems too excitable for the Swedish winter, but Brittany relishes that American aura. One which rides out a dark depressing season with high-pitched enthusiasm. She introduces herself and stretches out a hand toward Brittany, who gives her first name.

"Nice to meet you, Brittany. Please sign your name and leave your email address so we can add you to our mailing list and let you know about our upcoming events!"

"Sounds lovely," Brittany says weakly. "What kind of events?"

"Lots of get-togethers, more mingles, potluck dinners, cookie exchanges, bowling, barbecues…"

"Wow," Brittany adds with a tinge of sarcasm.

Since moving to Sweden, her social life has only revolved around fancy dinners, social impact galas here and there alongside Jonny or Antonia. Lots of low-key family gatherings. Usually at Antonia's. This club is promising her bowling and barbecues.

She signs her name as *Brittany Johnson*.

Using her maiden name feels freeing. She promises herself to do it more often. To begin the process of detachment.

"Brittany?" She hears a familiar voice and closes her eyes. *Good God*. She takes a deep breath and spins around to face its source with a forced smile.

"*Hej*…Kemi."

She needs Kemi as an ally. But considering Kemi hasn't helped with finding a divorce lawyer after promising she would, she isn't so sure.

"Brittany, I'm surprised to see you here," Kemi says.

"Why not? I'm American," Brittany reminds her.

"Yes, but remember the last time I invited you? Last year?"

"It's a new year." Brittany shrugs. "New possibilities."

"I say we drink to that then," Kemi says.

After dropping off their winter coats and securing margaritas at the club discount from the bar, they find a cozy corner, while others mingle in that familiar cadence of home.

They sip silently for a few seconds.

"So"—Brittany tries breaking the awkwardness—"how are things?"

"I was going to ask you the same. With you and Jonny."

"You said you were going to check your network for contacts? Lawyers?"

"I'm so sorry, Brittany, I've been swamped with work and other issues." Kemi chugs a mouthful of her cocktail, spilling a few drops, intriguing Brittany.

"Issues? Is everything okay?"

"They've been better."

Brittany studies her jittery disposition. This woman who normally wears her judgmental armor of confidence seems to be skating on thin ice. Brittany needs to know why. For once in their forced relationship, she wants an upper hand. Any hand.

"Is it work?"

Kemi flinches. Brittany knows she has struck a nerve.

"Ha!" Brittany bluffs.

Kemi turns to her with wide eyes. "So you heard?"

Brittany cocks her head to the side and bunches her shoulders to throw Kemi off course. It's the only way to keep her talking on cue.

"There are rumors going around the office." Kemi takes a long sip. "About me and Ragnar."

Brittany rolls her eyes at the mention of his name. Of course it has to do with Ragnar. *Raggedy-ass Ragnar*, as she and Tanesha often call him. For Brittany, he's the worst kind of racist. One in a suit within close range.

"And what's your side of the story? Is there any truth to these rumors?" Brittany asks.

She watches Kemi take a pronounced breath, getting visibly weaker with each passing moment. Brittany looks upon her with pity. Not the good kind.

"At the Christmas party. We had both been drinking," Kemi starts. "Someone caught us kissing."

Brittany gasps with a smile on her face. The best possible news for her. She couldn't script it better if she'd wanted to. Now, she has dirt on Ragnar and is pretty sure Pia isn't in the loop.

"Now everyone thinks we're having an affair." Kemi drains the last few tangy sweet drops of margarita. A smirk creeps onto Brittany's lips as she observes Kemi. The weight on Kemi's shoulders is palpable. Brittany can smell it.

"Oh my God"—Brittany's voice dips into a whisper—"you're fucking him, aren't you?"

"Stop it," Kemi responds firmly.

"You're having an affair, right?" Brittany adds quietly.

"No. It happened only once. Twice," she corrects herself. "It was a mistake. Mistakes, horrendous mistakes. He was grieving. I was torn." Kemi begins to defend herself.

"The same mistake twice." Brittany chuckles. Kemi frowns at her. "You and Ragnar." Brittany draws out her speech. "Who would have thought it?"

"We're not having an affair, Brittany. We were both vulnerable. He recently lost his baby."

"Hmm, I knew it."

"Knew what?"

"Ragnar has a thing for you." Brittany sniggers some more before taking another sip of her cocktail. "His eyes had already had sex with you the first time you and I met at our house."

Kemi remains unsmiling. "Please stop. I need to kill these rumors. I can't concentrate at work. I can't get anything done."

"Because of Ragnar?"

"He quit suddenly, so I'm now back in charge of the project."

"I see." Brittany sips some more. "How convenient for him. For you two. Now you can continue your trysts outside the office." She laughs.

"This isn't funny."

"Oh, I wish I had popcorn for this."

Kemi hisses in irritation. Brittany continues. "I'm assuming neither Tobias nor Pia know about your affair, right?"

A long stretch of silence follows. Kemi shakes her head. "Ragnar and I are going to fix this," Kemi shares.

"How? In bed? Is he any good? Because all I get from him is *big ego, small dick* energy." Brittany lifts her cocktail back to her lips.

"We'll figure it out," Kemi says.

"*Dayum*, girl, I wish I had your gall."

"Really, Brittany? Coming from someone looking for a divorce lawyer?" Kemi bursts out. Brittany narrows her eyes at her. "Everyone knows how you ended up in Sweden, thanks to Louise, so get out of your cushy ivory tower once in a while and come toil with us in the real world. It's messy down here."

"At least I'm not the one sleeping with a married man."

"At least I make my choices. I'm not being forced to sleep with a man because he takes care of me," Kemi snaps. "I've heard all the rumors about Jonny's past." Kemi's nostrils flare. "He just can't seem to get enough of all that *chocolate*." Her eyes roam Brittany's skin.

Brittany bites her lower lip, rage bubbling, threatening to breach the surface. This dance with Kemi grates her. Two steps forward, several moonwalks backward. The very manifestation of a frenemy.

Brittany finally finds words. "I guess you're that desperate for friends, *uhn*?"

Kemi frowns, clearly confused, before saying, "Please clarify."

"I baited you so easily. To spill your guts to me. Someone you don't even like," Brittany continues. "I get it."

"Get what?"

"It's lonely not having close friends in Sweden," Brittany says, holding her gaze. The air between them shifts as Kemi's eyes begin to film with tears, her lips still pressed in a tight line. "Trust me, I get it," Brittany says, her voice softening as she finally gives Kemi a glimpse into her own isolation.

YASMIIN

Fifteen minutes later, she's still trying all combinations of Yasmiin and *Quruxda* to create her beauty account on Instagram. She even asked an unconscious Muna for suggestions, hoping she would telepathically send through ideas.

Yasmiin apparently isn't the only Somali makeup artist in Sweden. Her searches take her down a rabbit hole of a vibrant community she lives on the periphery of. She finally settles on a combination of *Quruxda*—Beauty in Somali—and *Prenses*—Princess in Turkish, before tapping and following dozens of beauty accounts, watching perfectly contoured melanated faces right here in Sweden.

She definitely has some catching up to do, but she isn't worried. The first face she posts on her account is that of Amani Nassar-Berg, a local celebrity. The one she took on her first visit to her apartment in Östermalm. Most immigrants know of other immigrants across communities who are making it in Sweden. Amani's no exception. After helping lots of Swedish celebrities, she's become one herself. TV interviews here, a guest judge appearance there.

So, within minutes of posting a swipeable slide of photos and copying hashtags from another popular Swedish-Somali beauty Instagrammer, she gets her first few likes and her first comment:

Shit! Är det Tigris Tigress?

"Do I pay you to surf Facebook?!" Salima's high-pitched reprimand cuts into her elation. Yasmiin is lounging on a chair in the salon, her right leg hooked over its arm.

"I don't do Facebook, old woman," Yasmiin spits back as she taps and scrolls. "I'm trying to bring more life into this salon. I'm creating an account so people can find me here."

Salima hisses back, pulling a brushstroke through the thick hair of a regular, "Well, don't forget the time! Amani is going on SVT at six tonight. You need to get to the studio."

"So, she's not sending a limo to pick me up?" Yasmiin asks. "I'm offended."

"*Yalla!*" Salima screams. *Let's go!*

Right on time, two hours before showtime, Yasmiin stands in the green room at Swedish National Television, settling a cape around Amani's shoulders, in awe of herself that she's in this room.

"What do you want today?" Yasmiin asks as she works on Amani's foundation base.

"Something worthy of my nickname," Amani says firmly, her eyes locking on Yasmiin's intensely through her mirrored reflection.

Her gaze tells Yasmiin more about this strong woman beneath her fingertips. Amani's motives continue to elude her, but if that look is any indication, she has just given Yasmiin a solid peek.

Both Salima and Amani moved to Sweden when they were girls. To the town of Borås, Salima shared when Yasmiin pried it out of her once. It couldn't have been easy for both women, now in their fifties, growing up in spaces where they already stuck out before uttering a single word.

An hour later, Amani sports a black eyeliner cat-eye look which makes her hazel glare more searing as she strolls over to join the revered talk show host on her couch. They discuss the latest high-profile Swedish celebrity divorce feeding the tabloids. The equation was cocaine, an intense orgy, and a surprised husband who walked into the mix to find his wife at the center of it all. While not on the case herself, Amani had been invited to provide commentary.

Once Yasmiin had finished, she'd taken a couple of after-photos of Amani, a few of the room and the set, then posted them on her account. Her second post. Her first post continues to garner a few dozen likes, her follower count now up to twenty-five since she opened the account earlier in the day. Must be the hashtags, Yasmiin reckons. A small community means you don't get swallowed up in the crowd.

Yasmiin leans against a wall, observing her work with pride. Salima's probably at home watching as well, beaming over her little sister, who etched their Iraqi name, *Nassar*, on the marble stone of Swedish celebrity.

"*Snyggt jobbat*," a voice whispers next to her in Swedish. *Beautiful work*. She turns to peer at the lanky hairstylist who has positioned himself next to her, his lean arms folded across his chest. Fashioned eye-to-toe in black including black eyeliner, his hair is bleached so blond it looks almost translucent and shocking against his olive-hued skin.

"*Tack*," she replies, accepting his compliment.

"*Du*," he starts. "*Vi behöver fler makeup artists som kan jobba med olika hudfärger.*"

Yasmiin can't believe her ears. Are they inviting her back as a makeup artist to work with different skin tones? A tiny giggle escapes her. She suppresses it. Big-shot makeup artists don't giggle like schoolgirls backstage. Especially since she has her sights on "big shot."

Is life this easy once someone else clears the way for you to waltz in behind them? Like pulling your car into the empty lane behind an ambulance rushing by? Amani is currently holding a door open for her. She'd be a fool not to wedge herself in.

"*Det låter helt fantastisk*," she effuses her acceptance. He beams and wiggles his shoulders at her in response.

By the time she gets back to Hässelby in the taxi the studio organized for her, her follower count has climbed to fifty. Her second set of photos from the studio nears a hundred likes with three comments. SVT reshared one of her stories from behind the scenes. Her new followers clearly think she's Amani's personal makeup artist.

Yagiz had picked up Mehmet from *dagis* on his rare day off work, fed him macaroni with meatballs as promised, and already put him to bed when she arrives home, beaming. She finds him topless, sitting in their low-lit living room, an arm propped behind his head, watching pale flesh moving against pale flesh. He promptly switches to a sports channel when he hears her movements.

"*Hej*," he greets, feigning drowsiness, though she'd already caught him. "How did it go?" She plants herself right next to him, a large grin spreading across her face. "Good?"

She inches closer and presses her lips against his. He opens his mouth to receive her kiss, his tongue darting in.

Yagiz murmurs against her caress. "*Hmm, aşkım.*" He reaches for her hip, runs a palm over an ample cheek, grabbing and pulling her closer to him. "Tell me," he whispers. Yasmiin traces her fingers down his chest, trailing to his V-line, before cupping the bulge of his sweatpants.

"*Hmm, fuuuuck.* You should do Amani's face every day," he says, catching his breath.

She chuckles into his kiss before slipping her hand into his sweatpants.

TWELVE

KEMI

Svenska som andraspråk grundläggande (grundläggande nivå), delkurs 1.

Kemi reads her course description while settling into her next-level Swedish class on a dark Tuesday evening after work. As she places her oversized bag on the floor and grabs a seat, someone large and sturdy hugs her from behind.

"Jose finally let you out of his sight, *ehn*?" Kemi turns to embrace Malcolm, beaming up at his wispy Afro and caramel-colored face produced by an African American father and a Swedish mother.

Her only true friend in Sweden. They initially met in a Swedish class, *Svenska för Invandrare* (SFI), and kept coordinating class schedules, so they could carry on their antics from semester to semester together.

But too many weekends have passed since Kemi has heard Malcolm's exquisite sax and danced at his funky jazz gigs in Gamla stan. Malcolm is always out with their former SFI-teacher-turned-boyfriend, Jose Lundqvist, a Chilean Swede.

Since Tobias started working the night shift she has spent most of her nights at home.

"Bitch, I've missed you," he says, finally releasing her and settling himself in the chair next to hers.

"Two weeks in the States stocking up or two weeks here with meatballs, hmmm, let me think," she says, her smile dimmer than normal. Malcolm smiles back, though she notices he caught her wince.

"Okay, okay. Hope you had a fab time with your family." He pulls out his notebook. "Jose's mother made sure I passed out from food. Those Chileans don't mess around."

Kemi laughs weakly enough for Malcolm to train his dull-gray eyes on her.

"Okay, what's going on with you?" he asks.

"A lot. Can we do dinner afterwards?" Kemi replies the second their new teacher, a middle-aged woman dressed all in black, materializes. She casually strolls in with the lethargy of someone who has lost the will to talk to fellow humans. Let alone teach them.

"You WHAT?"

Malcolm's voice cuts loud enough to turn the heads of fellow diners their way. They had strolled over to a nearby Vietnamese restaurant for hot bowls of *pho* to warm up. Kemi's eyes dart around, embarrassed. She rests her elbows on the table, blowing nervously into her clasped hands.

He grimaces and shakes his head once more. "On the same night?"

She nods.

She tells Malcolm everything. From the instant chemistry on their first meeting in Jonny's office. Their casual flirting whenever they were near each other. That fateful elevator ride where Ingrid caught them pawing each other as if it was their last dying breath. That unfortunate taxi ride which other colleagues had apparently seen them climb into together. And how they subsequently ravaged each other on that business trip to London.

She tells him how the air at work has changed, and she fears they're all waiting for her demise.

"Girl, that's messed up." He reaches for his glass of tepid water and gulps it down. "Like seriously fucked up."

"You have no idea," Kemi says, fighting back tears. "I am a shambles. I can't think. I can't concentrate. My soul is eating me alive."

Malcolm purses his lips as he studies her. Both he and Jose are fond of Tobias, this Kemi knows. Malcolm has been pushing her to propose to him, or, in his own words, "*Lock his ass down already!*"

Jose, on the other hand, simply likes grabbing onto Tobias's biceps and asking for his workout routine. Even though Jose can't lift anything heavier than a purse.

"Is he packing? Was the sex that good?" Malcolm interrogates. "Enough to stray from a fine Black brother who's *obviously* packing? *Dayum.*"

"Stop it," Kemi scolds. "It's not like that."

"Girl, I'm trying to understand. You know this is a sore spot for me."

She nods. Malcolm's mother had abandoned him and his father in the US and fled back to Sweden. She ended up creating a new family. One of all blonds with a mix of blue and gray eyes.

"I swear, Malcolm. I wasn't thinking," Kemi says. "The moment was overpowering. I can't stop thinking about this man."

"You gotta leave Vegas in Vegas, *baby*," he proselytizes. "Why did you let his ass into your apartment in the first place?"

Kemi wipes a tear which slides through. "I don't know. He was grieving." More tears begin to fall. "I don't know what came over me," she says.

Malcolm watches her cry, his eyebrows wrinkling with emotion. "Does Tobbe know?"

She shakes her head between sniffs. No, her boyfriend doesn't know and he can't find out. Not right now until she fully organizes her thoughts and feelings.

"But he found his cufflinks in the bathroom."

"He what?" Malcolm's brows arch upwards. "This is some soap opera level shit right here. He found evidence."

"He thought it was a gift from me. Those damn things look like they cost a fortune too."

Malcolm digs his fingers into his Afro, cursing under his breath. Kemi keeps wiping away tears, trying to compose herself. A different feeling washes over her. Her airways open up an extra inch. Telling Malcolm the truth is helping her breathe a little easier.

"So, are you going to tell him?"

"I don't know, Malcolm. Right now, I just need to forgive myself first."

"Have you seen this man again?"

Daily thoughts of Ragnar possess her like the virus he is. She could never see him again even if that's all her body wants right now. To touch him and feel his weight once more.

"No. He has quit the project, the company. He's taking time to heal from his loss."

Malcolm's skeptical eyes dance over her as he raps his fingers on their table. One person she knows can fully process these details is Malcolm. A man solidifying himself as her best friend in Sweden.

"This man," Malcolm starts. "What's his name? I need to start googling."

"Stop it."

"Seriously, I need to see what he looks like. He better look like a god to match Tobias, who is already fucking Adonis!"

Kemi sighs. When it comes to looks, Tobias triumphs over Ragnar, no question. Her attraction to Tobias grew over time, but with Ragnar, it had been instantaneous. The way they drank each other in, confusion over emotions neither of them ever believed the other could elicit.

She can't fully explain the searing attraction she feels for Ragnar. She doesn't know what it is or why, except she suspects they're different versions of the same person. She feels it. Sees herself in Ragnar and him in her. Like gravitational forces, they can't stop their pull toward each other.

"It's more than that," Kemi continues, trying to cobble together some form of logic. "We're very similar. I feel like this man"—she takes an audible breath—"like he's a white version of myself."

Malcolm processes her words, before a smirk creeps onto his lips.

"You're that narcissistic, *uhn*?" he chuckles. She rolls her eyes at him. "Get outta here with that bullshit!"

Narcissistic. The word pricks her skin. She hates it.

Kemi remains firm. "You know what I mean, Malcolm."

"So he's endowed in all the right places?" He points to her chest. "Like you?"

Kemi frowns at him. Malcolm always has jokes. Right now, though, she needs his adult version. She needs her best friend to listen to her and tell her she isn't this lascivious person who enjoys sleeping with married men, destroying what others took years to build.

"I see," Malcolm continues. "The cufflinks. He's got money, doesn't he?"

"It has nothing to do with that. I carry my own weight."

"But he's your equal in that regard, isn't he? Professionally? Toe-to-toe?" Malcolm digs. "Intellectually?" He taps his temple with a finger. "He's what you think Tobias is missing, isn't he?"

Kemi blows into her clasped hands once more as tears gather steam. Malcolm scrapes at the truth she isn't ready to face. Was Tobias ever going to be enough for her?

"Dude probably looks dapper in a suit, smelling like fresh bills and white privilege," he adds. "Son of a bitch probably lives on Lidingö or Djursholm." He shudders dramatically for effect. She winces at those words. "Look, Kemi." Malcolm turns serious. "Who's the polar opposite of a white man with power in society?"

"Who?" Kemi asks, though she already knows his answer.

"A strong Black woman standing in her power. You two are opposites yet similar like the earth's poles." He pauses for effect. "That man wants to conquer you. To show you he's more powerful than you could ever be." Malcolm dissects. "Don't let him anywhere near you. There are very few successful C-suite sisters in this country. Sisters making it on your level as directors."

"I know." Kemi sighs. "I feel that burden every day."

"You can't be *hoeing* around with plain as fuck Svens. What's his name again?"

"I'm not telling you."

"Let's call him Sven. Tell Sven to go fill his jungle fever fantasies through porn and leave you the hell alone!"

She laughs, feeling a bit better in ways only Malcolm makes her feel. If only a tiny bit.

"Look, swing by my gig on Saturday night. Jose will be there," he says. "Let's pick up where we left off with our kebab pizzas afterwards, okay?"

So, after dinner, when they hug each other goodbye with "*See you in class on Thursday!*" Kemi hops on the red line, hurtling toward Slussen. Pulling out her cell phone, she scrolls through her messages, looking for his contact.

Kemi takes a deep breath and types:

You left them behind on purpose.

K

Before hitting *send*, she backspaces and clears the message. She then scrolls through her phone list one more time and deletes Ragnar's contact card instead.

BRITTANY-RAE

Jonny is out on his daily ritual morning run. After pushing him away from her body, Brittany moved him out of their bedroom and into one of their guest rooms. Physically extracting him out of her life over the last couple of days has done her some good.

Brittany stares at the photos Eva sent her. The woman is resourceful. She dug up photos from the international school which Jonny and Maya Daniels had attended. Brittany's eyes roam over the girl's face, the similarity uncanny. Down to their narrow eyes hooded with heavy eyelashes. Brittany touches her throat as she takes in her competition. She isn't sure why she asked for these images to be dug up, whether it's from basic jealousy, or if she wants to know what happened to Maya during that botched abortion which claimed her young life.

There are pictures of Maya on one knee posing with her team, a basketball under one arm, her hair in a ponytail. There's also an official annual class photo with Maya seated in the front row. Brittany lifts the phone closer and zooms into the photo, to her face. Maya sports a wide smile, hands on her knees. Next to her sits Jonny. He isn't looking straight into the camera. His head is cocked to the side, his lips pressed together, his body angled toward her. Brittany doesn't need to follow his eyes.

She sets her phone down and reaches over to her nightstand, where her clutch purse lies. She pulls out Amani's list and studies it again. Amani wants details from his life before Brittany. The lawyer wants to establish his dangerous pattern of obsession to help strengthen Brittany's case for securing custody of their daughter. Having *söta* Maya under her full protection means a level of child support only his family can afford for her.

Because right now, Amani suspects Brittany has no assets in Sweden to her name. The judge would be more likely to grant Jonny and his family full custody, while granting Brittany visitation rights only.

So, she needs her mole. Eva is proving herself useful. Brittany isn't even sure why Eva's helping her, so she is still keeping her guard up.

"*Det är Eva.*" She picks up on the first ring. Barely eight on Sunday morning London time, Eva's voice sounds unnaturally chirpy. Especially since Brittany knows her name flashed across her phone. Eva must know she's on the other end.

"Eva, it's me, Brittany."

"Brittany!"

"You seem upbeat this morning."

"I'm just back from the gym and making myself a smoothie. What can I support you with?"

"Well, I wanted to say thank you for the photos. And for all the information you've been sending me."

"You're welcome. That's why I'm here. Do you need anything else?"

The phone goes silent for a few seconds as Brittany collects her thoughts.

"Actually, I do. How long have you been with Jonny?"

It's Eva's turn to fall silent. "About ten years," she says a beat later.

"Ten years? Wow, that's impressive."

"Louise has been with him longer."

"I see." Brittany pauses for a deep breath. "Why so long?"

"Jonny doesn't like change and he fully trusts us both."

Brittany listens, her brain processing and trying to parse beneath Eva's surface. No doubt this woman knows her husband better than she does. Was there something else behind Eva's unflinching loyalty?

"For a man who doesn't like change, he sure changed a lot of girlfriends before me." Brittany giggles, trying to bait her. Eva doesn't respond in the same jovial tone.

"Yes," she says firmly.

"So he did have a lot?"

"Fifty-six women made it past three weeks. I don't keep track of his casual flings."

Brittany swallows, stunned. Not by the number, but by how meticulous Eva seems to be. She sensed it when she first started seeing Jonny. When he kept chasing her from Europe to the US and back. Eva made things run seamlessly around their relationship once they left Sweden's shores. Her replica, Louise, took care of things once they landed at Arlanda Airport.

"Fifty-six girlfriends? In ten years?" Brittany's voice breaks. "The number is so . . . precise."

"Not counting casual flings." Eva's tone remains firm.

"And that never frustrated you?"

Brittany hears the sharp intake of breath as Eva collects herself, trying to stay as professional as she can. Her tone now in direct contrast with the *xoxo*'s she started adding to the bottom of her texts to Brittany.

"It was challenging logistics-wise," she says. "Once we were getting a routine locked down, they'd break up and we would have to start all over again with a new woman. Learning her routines, what she liked, didn't like."

Brittany places a sweaty palm on her chest, scared she's uncovering a new side to Jonny.

"I see."

"Is there anything else I can support you with?"

"Yes, there is." Brittany takes a deep breath. "Do you know what happened between Jonny and Maya?"

"No." Eva sounds unsure. "Sorry, I don't have information about that relationship. She was before my time."

"Okay, thanks."

"Would that be all?"

"One more thing." Brittany swallows. "All these women. Do you still have contact details for them?"

Eva goes dead silent. Brittany is certain she has overreached her goodwill, turning Eva skittish.

"What is going on, Brittany?"

"I need more information."

"About what?"

"I need to talk to some of these women. From his past."

"But they shouldn't matter. You are his world right now. Trust me, I know. I keep that world running." A light giggle escapes Eva.

Brittany remembers Amani's list. This is her first hurdle toward accomplishing that list.

"But you still have their contacts, right?"

"I do, yes."

"I just need the last six or so women. That's it."

"Why?"

"Eva, I can't explain it right now, but you need to trust me. I'm not planning on hurting him."

"You're not?"

Eva's question catches Brittany off guard. What's she saying? That all those *xoxo*'s were encouraging Brittany to help hurt her boss? Things aren't adding up.

"Why would you think that?"

"I thought you were planning on leaving him. That's what Louise told me."

"So, you were encouraging me to leave him?"

Eva remains quiet for a few moments longer. Fifty-six. It adds up now. The family knows how to fiercely protect its own. Its matriarch Astrid got rid of Maya Daniels. His pixies found ways to get rid of his girlfriends. Probably at Astrid's bidding because they were varying shades of brown and Black.

And for the first time since she's known Eva, the petite blonde, who always sports a bob cut with precision bangs, now reeks of unadulterated sabotage. Brittany is no longer sure of her motives.

The tension between them becomes palpable until Eva finally breaks it.

"Do you need anything else, Brittany?"

YASMIIN

"I thought I was the smartest girl in the world." Yasmiin chuckles as she peers at Muna. Muna's face looks better, clearing up a bit. Yasmiin counts the days until Muna is brought back to life. "Mattias thinks *you* are."

She rearranges a bunch of gerberas she bought for Muna, the first full rays of spring spilling in through Karolinska's blinds. Orange-colored gerberas. The color she always associates with Muna, the orange-ocher jilbab she often wore. Yasmiin isn't as religious as Muna. She stopped wearing her own hijab the day it was yanked forcefully off her head in Italy by her pimp when she was fifteen.

"He told me so much about you, Muna." She primps the flowers. "Said you were so shy but so hardworking. Your smile. Ahmed couldn't resist it," she adds. "I don't know Mattias." She pauses to collect her thoughts. What he might know scares her. "But I have to trust him. He didn't have many updates but said he is working on it. They have been able to locate Ahmed's village in northern Syria. Not much left except those photos and notes in that box."

A nurse comes in, interrupting her preening, to check on vitals. Light-blue scrubs, white socks tucked into rubber clogs, and bags of exhaustion under her eyes. She gives Yasmiin a quick nod before darting back out as speedily as she slid in like an apparition.

Yasmiin's phone beeps a notification. A quick glance reveals Anu, the hairstylist from SVT.

Tina Wikström äger rum på fredag på Kulturhuset. Är du ledig?

Anu

Yasmiin reads the text three times. One of Sweden's biggest popstars-turned-activists is going to appear on a panel and they want Yasmiin to doll her up for her appearance. Anu wants to try her out.

Yasmiin reads his message one last time before sending back a resounding "Självklart!" She immediately calls Anu, who spills the details. A panel discussing some sobering statistics will be moderated by an SVT host at Kulturhuset, to be streamed live on TV. Tina Wikström is their star panelist. In her past life as Sweden's pop darling, a full team of stylists followed her every step. Now Tina eschews any fussing over her. Anu wants Yasmiin there for touch ups in case Tina is open to it.

"Make me proud," Anu says before disconnecting their call. Yasmiin stares at the phone, then turns back to Muna. She folds her arms across the stark white sheets and sinks in for a good cry.

"Are you doing Amani's face today?" Yagiz half-asks a few hours later.

He slides out from behind his kiosk and comes in for an intimate hug when he spots Yasmiin, his palms wandering her curves. After her visit with Muna, she made her way to Kungshallen and his kebab kiosk. She stood in a corner, observing her charismatic man serve customers, his arms flailing with exaggerated laughs, a back pat here, a fist bump there. The whole scene playing out in slow motion.

"What you don't know won't kill you" is a refrain she knows all too well.

Secrets keep the mystery in marriages. Allah knows what secrets Yagiz hides from her. The mere mention of his name evokes emotion from within their circles. Amani and Salima. His Turkish crew. His staff. His large family spread all over Sweden, the bulk of them based in Malmö.

Beyond the Çelik clan accepting her and sending gifts to Mehmet occasionally, they've adopted a sort of Nordic distance which requires you to notify them weeks in advance of visits in lieu of unexpected drop-ins. Yagiz calls his *Baba* back in Ankara every day. The news is always the same. Nothing new. Trying to keep boredom at bay as a retiree. But Yagiz calls daily anyway.

"Hmm?" Yagiz pulls back to assess her face, a smile of expectation etched across his own. His right hand roams lower.

"Stop it. I came here to talk to you," she says, glancing around shyly.

"Talk? I'm busy, is it important?" Yagiz pulls out his phone to check the time. "I need to go back and help Nusret." He points behind him to his kiosk. "What is it?"

"It's Muna."

Yagiz curses and glances up to the ceiling, hands at his hips. "Still tormenting me here, even when she's in a coma. *Eazizi Allah*."

"What do we do when she wakes up?" Yasmiin's voice is heavy.

"We?" Yagiz frowns at her.

"Yes, *we*. You know, as her next of kin."

"Doesn't the government handle that? Why *we*?" He bunches his shoulders in question.

"Because I'm her sister now."

"*Men snälla nån*. Yasmiin, stop. I need to get back to work." Frustration oozes out of him.

"We need to talk." She remains adamant.

"Not now." He gives her a hard peck and slaps her bottom. A reverberating hit so loud it causes a nearby elderly white patron balancing her tray to freeze and stare at the couple. "Go pick up some Efes beer and lamb for the weekend. The boys are coming over." He slaps it once more, prodding her, in Turkish, to move like a donkey. "*Git!*"

With that command, Yagiz spins away, leaving Yasmiin staring after his wide gait.

When Friday rolls around, Yasmiin hops on the* tunnelbana *from Rådhuset toward T-Centralen. The panel is being held right in the heart of town at Stockholm's iconic Kulturhuset—a nebulously shaped blob of a structure often dubbed the ugliest building in town. She makes her way up several floors to where a makeshift studio has been set up.

"*Tjena!*" Anu greets her with two air kisses and beckons her to follow him toward a room. Once he opens the door, a strong waft of coconut and incense hits them. Tina Wikström had lit a stick to clear out negative energy, according to Anu. The sweet coconut smell is all her. And she's more mesmerizing in person than Yasmiin has seen on TV, sucking her in with honey-brown eyes which glitter like gold under sunlight.

"*Hej, Yasmiin heter jag.*" Yasmiin introduces herself, stepping with unsteady feet into the closet-size room. She's still reeling, reflecting on how her trajectory has landed her next to one of Sweden's pop idols and the most powerful lawyer-turned-celebrity in her own right, both in a matter of weeks.

"*Trevligt att träffas,*" Tina says politely. *Nice to meet you*. "*Jag brukar inte använda så mycket smink,*" she tells Yasmiin. She no longer uses tons of kitschy makeup. That life was her past. Tina swivels back to the dressing-room mirror while Anu settles himself behind her chair. He grabs long strands of her reddish-brown locs like small snakes, and begins wrapping them in layers atop her head, setting them into a cone-like updo.

Yasmiin gawks at her in awe. While her innards twist and fangirl, her exterior remains unbothered. After all, didn't big-shot makeup artists carry themselves like mini-celebrities too? Her beauty account has only two posts of Amani. The third post will guarantee a tripling of her follower count and bring it into three digits after one week.

"*Ingen fara,*" Yasmiin continues. *No worries.* "I'll do a nude look to bring out your eyes and lips. That's all," she says before unboxing her makeup case and spreading out its contents.

Fifty minutes later, after snapping a few after-photos and wishing Tina "*lycka till*" on her panel, Yasmiin eagerly posts the photo.

Barely three minutes later, her first comment arrives:

Våran drottning!

Our queen!

THIRTEEN

KEMI

If absence makes the heart grow fonder, then Ragnar took her heart with him when he disappeared. She sees his face whenever Tobias makes love to her. She hears his melodic lilt whenever a stranger speaks a little too loudly. She sees his face in unsmiling crowds.

Weeks have passed since he quit von Lundin. She's taken several business trips to Germany and back, trying to save an account gradually slipping into staleness. She breathes life back into Bachmann and its new line of hiking shoes which they wanted to promote using a Scandinavian touch. Ragnar and his freaking forest essence had been perfect for that line.

Now, she's forced to somehow make it work in his absence and diversify it too.

She feels like she is choking under her colleagues' judgment of her. Everyone seems to be funneling it toward her without an ounce reserved for Ragnar. The last she heard from Louise, *of course*, is that he took a month off to go hiking around Nepal, leaving his wife and daughter behind. To think. To ruminate. To grieve.

Things mill mundanely on her home front. Tobias is quieter than usual. Besides that, everything else is chugging along at its usual pace. Slowly simmering. Daylight sticks around much longer as winter begins to make way for spring. She swears she hears birds chirping one Friday morning as she lies in the crook of Tobias's arm in bed. Kemi has taken the day off to enjoy Tobias's free day with him.

"What are you thinking about?" His voice cuts through the calm in their bedroom. He gently strokes her hair as she stares out the window from bed.

"I don't know," she mutters quietly. "I don't know what I want or where I want to be in two years, let alone five."

"Do you need to know?" he says. "Why not live what's in front of you?"

She half-chuckles, though there is pain in her laugh. "You're such a romantic, Tobbe," she says. "Oh, I wish life were that easy."

He turns to look into her eyes. "We can make life easy in this room, in our lives," he says softly. "It's already brutal out there."

She closes her eyes, absorbing his words. "Was this what you wanted?" she asks him. "This life of comfort . . ." She contemplates before adding ". . . as adding, "As a security guard?"

"You mean having the smartest, most beautiful woman in my arms right now?" He gives her a peck, laughing. "Plus, curves in all the right places?" He kisses her lightly. "I have all I need, even as a guard."

She smiles weakly, receiving his attention.

In the US, she's average when it comes to body size. Here, quite the opposite. Suddenly, she feels curvier, larger, heavier than she has ever felt in her entire life. In Stockholm, people worship in gyms. They pray at the altars of vegan lunches and poke bowls. They have cinnamon buns and *fika* three times a day, yet like magicians, those calories evaporate into thin air before landing on equally thin lips.

Tobias kisses her again to pull her thoughts back to him.

"Your mother told me something," she says.

He sighs and looks toward the ceiling. "Way to kill the mood by mentioning Nancy." He laughs. "What did she say this time?"

"That you've been waiting for me," Kemi says. "What did she mean?"

Tobias swivels back to look at her, his eyebrows dipping. "Stop listening to her, okay? She's been hounding me for kids. She wants grand-minions."

"She told me something else at Midsummer last year."

"*Men herregud*," Tobias curses under his breath. "Sounds like she's planting seeds now."

"She said I was the only Black woman you've ever dated."

Silence falls over their bedroom. Tobias's grin drops as he searches her eyes. She wants to know more about him. Her boyfriend who has been peeling himself like an onion for her. She's now thirty-six. He's a year younger, but his eyes hold a lifetime.

Growing up mixed-race in Sweden hadn't been easy for him, this she knows. He had felt othered most of the time, he told her, despite growing up in a diverse neighborhood, Norsborg. Yet, she's the first Black woman he has ever gotten into a serious relationship with, according to his mother. Nancy had laughed in her usual way as she relayed the information. Kemi knew he had come out of a long relationship, but curiosity had never gripped her until now.

"I haven't had many girlfriends," Tobias finally speaks into the void. "I've had only two long-term *sambos*. One lasted six years, and the other, eight years."

"But you dated before, in between, and after them, didn't you?"

"Well, yes, but..."

"Describe them."

She catches his nostrils flaring. She wants to know what had attracted Tobias to her. Is it the very same feeling drawing Ragnar to her?

"Does it matter?" he questions her. "I'm with you now. They're not in my life anymore. If anything, it shows you I am in it for the long haul. I am loyal."

"So they weren't Black?"

"Will you drop it already? *Snälla?*" he says with irritation. This is the side of him she loves to hate. A gentleman in every sense of the word.

"Okay," she says, nestling closer. "Just trying to feed my ego."

She smiles against his lips before kissing him. Tobias takes over their kiss. She inhales audibly when she tastes Ragnar instead.

"What's wrong? Are you okay?" he asks.

"I'm fine." She sits up in bed, running both hands through her hair. Ragnar has become her haunting. Escaping is proving impossible without a proper exorcism. Tobias's eyes roam her face in worry. She has to tell him soon. She can't keep up the charade for long. It's robbing her of his love.

Tobias sits up beside her, running a soothing palm across her back, observing her as she calms her heaving chest.

A few seconds later, she pushes out of bed, the moment gone.

Later that day, Tina Wikström, Tobias's younger sister, sits on the TV panel, legs crossed. She shares the same coloring as Tobias, with brown freckles dotting her face matching his, her brown eyes several shades lighter than her brother's, somewhere between amber and honey. Her signature locs, thick reddish-brown stems, are always worn twisted into a circular beehive crown. She's wearing a golden ring looped through her left nostril. Her everyday attire is either batiked, tie-dyed, or patterned from West African fabrics.

Every surface of Tina Wikström, from her locs to her toe ring, signal to the world she's both Gambian and Swedish. She's publicly choosing to be both, despite society forcing her to choose one or the other.

According to Tobias, his sister became an activist after years of being a lauded token. Her new look is her physical statement. Speaking on her behalf when words don't come. When her voice grows hoarse from screaming through a megaphone at Sergels torg. Or from protesting against hate in white shirts and black trousers.

She still keeps her boyfriend from her popstar days, though. Tobias had chuckled when he told Kemi this. A superstar football player on the Swedish national team named Sebastian, with piercing baby-blue eyes and a butter-blond crewcut. This fact amuses Tobias for some reason.

She hadn't always been this way, Tobias told her. Tina stole Sweden's heart when she appeared on the revered Melodifestivalen music competition at nineteen. She went on to represent Sweden at Eurovision, the international singing contest that, for one week in May, wipes out Europe's borders with a metaphorical eraser. At the time, she straightened her reddish-brown hair. She wore glitter and sparkles, and her face regularly graced magazines and entertainment tabloids.

Then one day, Tina quit it all.

"I was done performing for society in every way," was all Tina told her after Kemi's probing.

After scarfing open-faced sandwiches Tobias had pieced together with cheese, cucumber, and butter, they hurry over to Kulturhuset, where Tina is presenting some statistics on a panel about what being *Afro-svensk I samhället idag* means. *Afro-Swedish in today's society.* She runs the nonprofit organization whose members identify as such, and will be sharing workforce statistics alongside representatives from Statistiska centralbyrån, the national statistics agency, and Arbetsförmedlingen, the Swedish Public Employment Service.

Tobias is loading his paper plate with charcuterie and cheese, when the moderator gets on the mic and urges everyone to take their seats. For the next forty-five minutes, Kemi is entranced by Tina. Even though she can't pick out every single advanced Swedish word, she listens carefully. Tina is eloquent, measured, and elegant. Like a high priestess sitting up there. Kemi feels her heart swell with pride and wants to learn more about this popstar-turned-protector of culture.

When she's done, Kemi's applause seems to be the only one reverberating through the room with any energy, while everyone else claps lethargically. People quietly wait their turn to ask Tina questions and share words of gratitude, encouragement, or criticism wrapped in smiles.

"Kemi!" Tina pulls her into a tight hug. She turns to give her older brother a peck. "Thank you for coming."

"It was fascinating," Kemi says. "Those statistics are depressing."

Tina cocks her head to one side. "I've got to keep working," she says, before reaching for her purse under the chair. "Sebastian is waiting for us."

They find the footballer hiding out at a back table in a new fusion restaurant on the island of Kungsholmen. He gets to his feet and pulls Tina in for a hard closed-lip kiss.

Both men give each other half-hugs with quick pats on the back.

"Sebastian." Tina introduces her boyfriend to Kemi. He stretches out a hand to shake hers.

"*Trevligt att träffas*," he says warmly. Yup. She has definitely seen him on TV aggressively chasing after balls on the pitch for Sweden. Now she has to play it cool because in Sweden people don't hound their celebrities in public.

"*Detsamma!*" she responds, before they all settle into their seats. Sebastian's arm lies across the back of Tina's chair for the rest of the evening, only taking occasional breaks to cut into his brick-oven-baked Neapolitan pizza.

The guys get into it right away in Swedish, dissecting Sebastian's last away game, some controversial teammates, their chances for making the Euros, and other football stuff. Tina picks at olives and studies Kemi, who is cutting into her pizza.

"Tobias seems happy," Tina says, before popping an olive between plump lips, savoring it, her brown eyes searing Kemi. Kemi stops chewing and swallows uncomfortably.

"He makes me happy," she says, grabbing a glass of water. Tina watches her, as if studying her every gesture, looking for deception.

"Well"—Tina reaches for another olive—"he loves you. Even if he doesn't say it often."

Kemi takes a few more sips of water, collecting her thoughts. *But he hasn't said it, though*, she wants to retort.

"What about you and Sebastian?" Kemi switches topic.

Tina chuckles. "We've been dating since high school." She glances at him as he chats animatedly with Tobias. "Before my music and before his career. Tobbe is like his brother."

Kemi nods. She does mental calculations. Together for at least fifteen years. Still dating. Boyfriend and girlfriend with no pressure of trying to seal it with a ring. Tobias has only been in two long-term relationships. This approach is all too new. A sort of blasé attitude which seems to make them happier, despite Nancy on their backs for *barnbarn. Grandkids.*

Is love this effortless if you allow it to simply run its course? To exist without restraints? Without rules? She turns to watch Tobias's profile as he talks and laughs, showing that gap-toothed grin she loves so much.

She decides Ragnar is a fluke. One which arose because she's fighting against love without restraints. The ease with which her relationship with Tobias flows feels unnatural to her, in direct contrast to all she experienced while living in Washington, DC.

She had already emotionally worked through the fact that she's a company director dating a security guard. Her fling with Ragnar, her peer and career equal, was her subconscious trying to discredit what her brain is processing. Her way of sabotaging. Like placing hands into a calmly running stream and breaking its flow.

Clarity arrives in a way she hasn't been expecting. Kemi heaves a deep sigh. For the first time since her affair, it feels like release, instead of resistance. Her airways are opening up. *Hope.*

"Listen, Kemi." Tina pulls up the large sleeves of her moumou so she can lean forward, out of earshot of the men. "If you're doubting where this is all heading with him, just hang in there."

Kemi looks at her, a smile creeping onto her lips. Tina is confirming what her heart already knows. Tobias is the one. She has found him. He's more than enough.

Tina leans back and flashes her a grin of her own, warm ambient light catching her eyes.

BRITTANY-RAE

"Brittany!" Malin's voice cuts through her thoughts. Malin is in a cheery mood as she approaches with a smile and her trademark swinging ponytail.

Brittany is sitting in the corner of a French-inspired bistro tucked away on a backstreet in Östermalm. The last few weeks, Brittany has morphed into this fragile creature who slinks around, not wanting to be touched, seen, or spoken to. She even wears sunglasses indoors like a spy, trying to collect intel to check off items on Amani's list.

She needs to be prepared before her next encounter with the *Tigris Tigress*.

Brittany pushes to her feet to give Malin a hug. The other woman isn't as tall but they share similar lithe frames. Malin's world revolves around Stockholm's fashion scene. She's ready to pull Brittany into it.

"Thanks for meeting me for lunch," Brittany says, settling back into her seat. "I really do appreciate your time."

"Don't mention it." Malin smiles. Brittany's eyes roam her outfit, taking in her gym clothes once again like last time. Malin practices gymism religiously.

"Really, if it's a bother, do let me know," Brittany begins to apologize.

"Of course not," Malin counters. "You would be perfect for Ida's fall collection. I already pitched you to her as her lead model." Malin finishes off with a giggle. "You know Ida Persson, right?"

Brittany swallows. A mix of feelings swirl within her. The overarching one bubbling to the surface is gratitude. Ida Persson is one of Sweden's powerhouse designers. Malin is essentially handing access on a platter to her.

"I'm in my early forties—" Brittany starts. Malin holds up a perfectly manicured hand with French tips to stop her next words.

"You don't look a day over twenty-five," Malin says. "All that melanin and what they say about Black skin is obviously true."

Brittany absorbs her compliment, a smile etching across her face, silently thanking her mom for uncrackable genes.

"Thank you so much. This means the world to me."

Brittany hates modeling. Her dream is to be a fashion designer, but if this is going to be her first step into Sweden's fashion scene, she'll gladly sashay those much-needed steps down the catwalk.

"You're welcome. Stockholm is ready for you," Malin says, while pulling the menu closer. "I can already see you billed as the Nordic Naomi."

"Nordic Naomi?"

"Hmm-hmmm." Malin's eyes settle on the menu.

For the first time in years, the fog blurring Brittany's vision since she met Jonny begins to clear. She can see semblances of a new future without him, standing on her own two feet in Malin's words. She can taste the spotlight on her tongue. If she does this for a few years, builds her brand and reach, then she can open her own fashion line, *BRIT RAE*. Its touch is within her grasp.

"God, this is all so exciting." Brittany beams back.

Once both women decide on salads with dressing on the side, Brittany prepares to dig. Malin must smell her desperation, she ponders. Her dire need for a real friend here in Sweden.

"So why fashion?" Brittany asks before spearing romaine lettuce and taking a bite.

"Hmm," Malin starts after a sip of sparkling water, "I've always loved textiles and fabrics since I was a girl growing up in Stockholm."

"Let me guess, you sewed dresses for your dolls?"

"You got it. I drew and designed my little heart out. Then I studied fashion for five years in Paris. I got to live and breathe the air around the finest fashion houses in the world."

Brittany soaks up her words, enamored. "My dream," she says, before launching into her own backstory. "I wish I'd never dropped out of fashion school."

Malin listens intently as Brittany describes her former life as senior cabin crew and her years crisscrossing the Atlantic.

"I wanted more out of my life, you know," Brittany stresses with a hand before turning back to her salad. Malin quietly absorbs her words. "I knew I could never stay a flight attendant for long." She grabs another mouthful of leaves. She feels herself relaxing as she shares snapshots of her life with a woman fast becoming her first Swedish friend.

"So"—Malin's voice takes a serious turn—"how did you meet Johan?"

Brittany normally avoids this question, but with Malin, she sees no harm in opening up further. Maybe the more she shares, the more layers she might be able to peel off Malin's concentric circle of an onion.

"He was a customer." Brittany lets her play on words settle, chuckling slightly to herself.

"A customer?" Malin's brows furrow, Brittany's joke apparently washing over her. Brittany clears her throat in response.

"I met him on board my cabin en route to DC from London," she explains.

"Really?" Malin seems surprised And Brittany wonders why.

"Yes. *Really.*" She pauses for air. "What do you mean by '*really*'?"

It's Malin's turn to clear her throat. "Well, the rumors are he married an American escort, so that was why I was asking how you met Johan. Because I didn't believe it," Malin says. "That was all. Hope I didn't offend you."

Brittany responds with a quizzical frown and narrows her eyes. This isn't happening. That judgmental look which often precedes the nonvocalized words—*gold digger*—is etched all over Malin's face.

Malin shrugs as if she already has a pass into their private life. Everyone wants a piece of her reclusive husband.

"I'm just curious. He's such an..." Malin picks out her words. "... intriguing man."

Brittany gives her a half-smile. "And so you assumed I must have been an escort all along? Even at our last *fika*?"

Malin's eyes take on a look of remorse. "I hate rumors and I'm so sorry I brought this up this way."

"Well, I'd say tact isn't your greatest strength." Brittany throws the words at her.

"I'm so sorry to offend—"

Brittany cuts her off. "Why are you so interested in Jonny's life? Why is everyone?"

"He's one of Sweden's most influential people. Of course everyone is curious about his exotic life. Especially since he doesn't give interviews to anyone."

"Exotic life?" Brittany stresses those particular words Malin had poured out so casually. Apparently, Jonny leads an *exotic* life. "What makes it exotic?"

She sees color rush to Malin's cheeks, flushing red out of discomfort.

"I'm sorry I upset you," Malin apologizes.

"I'm not mad. I'm just curious why everyone thinks Jonny leads an exotic life," Brittany says calmly, hiding her anger.

Malin clears her throat once more before piecing together an answer, or a semblance of one.

"It's just that..." She pauses. "Johan has a history of not dating Swedish girls, that's all."

"Not dating Swedish girls or not dating white women?" Brittany clarifies for Malin. "Two different things."

She had begun to fear this the day her sweet little Maya was born. That her beautiful brown child who bears blood from this country will never be fully considered part of it.

"Look, Brittany," Malin says. "I was out of line. I apologize. My curiosity got the best of me. I find you fascinating and just wanted to get to know you better."

"By asking about my husband instead of me?"

Malin falls silent once more. The air around them tenses. The words *Nordic Naomi* float back into Brittany's mind. She watches her chances of a second wave in life slip away with each uncomfortable wince from Malin.

She needs Malin more than Malin needs her. That fact chips away at her, pushing her once more into that space. The opaque void where she, Brittany Johnson, despite her beauty and presence, will never be fully enough in Sweden. She has been relegated to the exoticism which makes its golden son Johan von Lundin's cushy, albeit boring, life a tad more intriguing because she infuses it with a splash of color.

Her lips spread into a forced smile once again, swallowing everything, making her scream inside because Malin holds open a crack of a door into a society that, even with the von Lundins' wealth and access, is still blocked to her.

Malin is hand-delivering her to one of Sweden's hottest designers, Ida Persson. She would be a fool to burn off the lead just because Malin is equally as curious about her reclusive husband as the rest of the world.

"It's okay." Brittany softens her tone. Malin lets out an audible sigh of relief, as if that sigh had been holding her hostage all through their exchange.

"Thank you." Malin grabs onto those words like a lifeline. "Totally out of order of me."

"I mean, I don't even know your last name yet." Brittany laughs the statement out. "I mean, what's your last name?"

"Oh, it's Persson."

"Persson? Like Ida?"

"Yeah, she's my sister-in-law."

YASMIIN

Picking up beer for Yagiz from state-run Systembolaget proves pointless.

The man is dead drunk when she arrives home into a dense fog of smoke surrounding him and his equally wasted posse. She expects no less on payday Friday. Two of them work in construction. One, Nusret, works with Yagiz at the kebab shop in Kungshallen, and Özel sells khat around town.

Her arms sagging with shopping bags, Yasmiin freezes by the

door when she sees that ox of a man. Yagiz's words about getting rid of him had all been performative, she realizes. It's clear he'll always choose his guys over her. Mehmet waddles in behind her. She picked him up from *dagis* after grabbing drinks and chunks of lamb she plans on grilling for the men.

"*Prenses!*" one of them bellows at the top of his lungs the minute he catches sight of her. Soon, it's a cacophony of "*prenses*" joining the cigarette fog.

"Stop it, you're scaring him," she scolds as Mehmet steps in, his thick eyebrows arched, clutching his little backpack tighter to his chest.

"*Oğlum!*" *My son*. Yagiz staggers to his feet, swaying. Two of his friends steady him as he makes his way toward the door. He wears only boxer briefs, his whole torso a tattooed landscape. He bends low to scoop the boy up and plants a kiss on his cheek.

"How was *dagis*?" he asks Mehmet in Swedish.

"*Bra*," Mehmet replies. *Good*.

"*Bra!*" Yagiz exclaims before letting out a burp and putting him back on his feet. Once on solid ground, the toddler scurries off to his room.

Yasmiin pushes past him. Yagiz pulls her back, his hand grabbing her bicep tightly.

"*Aşkım*," he says, pressing closer to her. "Did you do Amani's makeup today, *hmm*?" He brushes his lips hard over hers, his handlebar moustache grazing her. She turns away from his kiss and he cackles. He turns to his friends. "This one!" he starts. "She's always horny after she does *Tigress*'s face!"

The room descends into various drunken bellows of laughter. She frowns at the men, her eyes roaming over and assessing each one. They settle on the only man who doesn't seem to be sneering along with the others. *Öz*.

"So, tell us," Yagiz persists. She brushes him aside and continues walking past. He yanks her toward him again. "Tell us, did you do her face today?"

"Leave me alone! I have to cook the lamb," she spits out at him.

Yagiz wraps his arms around her from behind, trapping her in his embrace in front of them.

"I'm hungry," he laughs into her ear before nipping it. "But not for lamb." More bellows escape the men. "Tell me. Did you do her face?" His hands cup her breasts from behind. "Look how big they are," he says to his friends as he caresses them.

Their snickering begins to simmer down as they watch Yagiz's spectacle. Yasmiin drops the plastic bags she's carrying and wiggles out of his grip. He grabs her once more. Her Yagiz before and after he started taking steroids are two separate beings. His lanky former self, she could handle with ease. This beefed-up version terrifies her now in front of his friends. A man so prone to bragging about anything and everything, he wants to show off once more.

She fights him off. He captures her, his eyes dark, brooding, pupils dilated from drink. He drags her toward the sofa, where both Nusret and another *doqon* friend are parked. Both men promptly clear the way. He pushes Yasmiin onto it, face down.

"Do you want to see it bounce, *eh*?" Yagiz cackles out in Swedish to the crew. "Do you?" He slaps her backside. She winces audibly from the hit. More laughter ensues. This time, though, they sound less confident, unsure.

"*Bırak!*" a gruff voice sails through in Turkish. *Cut it out.*

"*Hmm?* What? You don't want to see it?" Yagiz's words slur. "I thought you of all people wanted to fuck my wife the most?"

"*Bırak!*" Öz repeats. He gets to his feet and drags Yagiz off Yasmiin. "Don't disrespect your *prenses* this way." Yagiz sways and swings at him. Öz pushes him to the floor. Yagiz splays himself out, chuckling, before resting an arm across his face, dizzy.

Öz turns back to Yasmiin and stretches out a hand to help her up. She doesn't accept his gesture. Yasmiin straightens her floral-patterned dress back in place under silence from the other men as they observe her. She crosses her legs and settles her hands on her knee.

"Have you enjoyed your show now?" Yasmiin asks them, her eyes hard, biting the inside of her cheek to hold back tears.

"Yagiz is an idiot," Öz says, his eyes warming as he takes her in.

"So are you," she addresses each one of them. "Is this how you treat your women? The mothers of your children?"

Unnerving silence cloaks the room as four pairs of eyes settle on Yasmiin, her husband passed out at her feet. Four large men who can do with her what they want right under Yagiz's nose and keep the secret among them.

"*Bayan Çelik.*" Öz nods at her in greeting after the long spell of silence which feels everlasting.

Mrs. Çelik.

He beckons for the rest of Yagiz's boys to get to their feet. "*Haydi gidelim.*" *Let's leave.*

FOURTEEN

KEMI

The next week back at work, Kemi feels invigorated. Recharged. Her talk with Tina sparked something within her. She started pulling weeds of self-sabotage out of her system. She's mulling over the right time to confess and get it all off her chest. To move forward, she needs to set herself free. To forgive herself. Tobias is who she longed for all those years while in the States. She has finally found the man who loves her as she is.

He might never forgive her; she mulls over this possibility. But at least she can let him know she wants no one else. That she's ready and one hundred percent committed to being a long-term *sambo* if that's all he wants right now.

"Ingrid," Kemi calls out before Ingrid leaves their Monday morning meeting. She stops in her tracks and turns toward Kemi, her brows arching.

"I was wondering if I could request two weeks off work," Kemi says. "A leave of absence."

Ingrid frowns. "Of course not."

"What? Why not?"

"Because we just handed one of our largest accounts back to you," Ingrid says. "We don't have the bandwidth for this right now."

"I really need this break, Ingrid." Kemi grows desperate. "I need some time off to think and get some rest."

"Only with a doctor's official orders, but right now, we can't afford to let you take an extended break. Besides," Ingrid adds, "you're mentally strong and can handle anything."

Ingrid doesn't wait for her rebuttal. She simply leaves as if the conversation and Kemi's request never happened.

Kemi gasps in frustration. *Mentally strong? The fuck?*

Had it been Ingrid herself, she would have quickly taken *sjukskriven—sick leave*—at the first sign of a broken fingernail. Why was she supposed to push through mental stress without time off to heal?

At the end of the next day, Kemi gathers her belongings, getting ready to head to her Tuesday evening Swedish class. She's looking forward to her follow-up dinner with Malcolm and their impromptu therapy session. She needs that safe space with him where she can actually be weak and not be this idealized strong creature impervious to mental, emotional, and physical distress.

Where she's allowed to cry over a metaphorical broken fingernail if she wants to.

Her phone beeps as she shoves her laptop into her bag. An attachment comes in from some random number she doesn't recognize. She opens it and sinks back in her swiveling office chair.

A photo. In it, cobalt blue stares back at her. His normal stubble, replaced by a dark-brown beard, is peppered with snow. His hair is longer, the wind blowing snow-streaked strands of it across his face. Behind him, mountain peaks, more snow, and evidence of altitude. He carries a backpack and the photo is shot selfie-style: hand raised above shoulder at an angle. She traces her fingers across his rugged face in a gesture which startles her. He reawakens something she thought she'd deprived of oxygen.

Beneath his photo, a short caption reads:

Wish you could see this.

R

She sits at her desk for five, maybe ten minutes, cradling her phone, looking at his photo and everything he's saying to her through it. She thought she had moved past this and was on her way to ridding herself of him. But here he is. One look at him and lava bubbles within her. God knows she tries. Every single night remains a battle. Of prying off the feeling of his fingertips scorching her skin, his salty tears on her body, his exploring mouth on hers, his calculating rhythm, his grief-stricken cries, her ultimate surrender.

She fights the urge to move her fingers and type letters, to tell him how stunning that view is. How she wishes she could experience Nepal one day too. To ask him how on earth he's living with himself after their betrayal. If he ever thinks about London. What's running through his mind. If he has told Pia. What he's feeling about the whole affair.

She resists the urge to type "*I hate you*" or "*Stay away from me.*"

Kemi's eyes simply wash over his photo, settling on his eyes one more time, looking through them. Then she deletes it.

The very act stirs up her stomach. She retches and bolts toward the bathroom to throw up until bile is all she has left.

His second photo arrives a few days later. She's sitting at her dining table, poring through Swedish textbooks, pushing through a take home exam. She glances at the time on her phone. Why is he texting her this late? She does a quick Google search for the time difference between Sweden and Nepal.

He's texting her at two thirty a.m., his time.

She sighs and grabs her phone once more. She opens his message. Another selfie. Except this time in low light with him lying back on a bed with the caption:

Trying to sleep. You awake?

Her gut urges her to delete the grieving bastard and block his number. The audacity. What she explicitly told him she's never going to be. The other woman in his life.

Her ego types back instead.

Should I forward this to Pia?

A few seconds later, her phone pings again.

Funny. Miss your fire.

Asshole.

Ouch.

How is Pia doing? Doesn't she need you right now?

Needed to get away. To clear my head. So confused.

You lost a child. Most people don't function for months after such a loss.

Thank you.

For what?

For being there.

Stop it.

Trying but all I think about.

You need to go to bed.

Mmm…Wish you were here.

Stop it now.

You felt so good. Can still taste you. Need more when I get back.

Fuck off!

She immediately deletes the thread and blocks the number he's texting from. She closes her eyes and does some breathwork, trying to calm her racing heart. Texting with him is like hearing his deep baritone right next to her, lifting tiny strands of hair on her skin as he speaks.

She races to the toilet to unload the contents of her stomach once more. Tears start flooding her eyes. She needs a therapist. The mere thought of his juvenile texts triggers her. Now they seem to be inducing vomit on demand.

Within seconds, she has Kehinde on the line. Six hours behind in the US.

"What's going on?" Her twin immediately senses there's something wrong from her voice.

"I can't stay here anymore." Kemi sniffs. She wipes her nose before pressing on. "I can't."

"What's happening?"

"I feel like I'm losing my mind, losing control."

"*Kpele*, all will be well."

"I'm not sure it will."

"*Ahn ahn*, is it that serious?"

Kemi keeps crying, hiccupping, trying to calm her heartbeats, which seem to be spiraling beyond control. The weight sits once more on her chest, robbing it of air. Confessing always eases those airways. It helps her catch her breath. Even if only for a few seconds.

"I had an affair."

The phone goes silent on the other end. Kemi's cries pick up once more. She prepares herself for her sister's onslaught.

"What?" Kehinde's voice comes back low, concerned.

"I did," Kemi cries. "I had an affair with him."

"Why, Kemi? Why?"

"I don't know. *God!* I don't know. I wanted him so much."

"But you have someone good."

"I know, I know," Kemi sobs. "I don't deserve Tobias."

"Have you told him?"

"I can't tell him."

"Kemi." Kehinde draws out her name in reprimanding fashion. Kemi knows her sister is digging out Bible verses to quote to her. She waits patiently, sniffing back tears, gearing herself. No one rebukes quite like her righteous twin.

But they never come. The fire and fury she expects are replaced by caressing words instead.

"Kemi," Kehinde calls her name softly. "Don't be scared."

Kemi bursts into fresh tears at her sister's soothing words.

BRITTANY-RAE

"Lucinda Daniels." The woman's accent is a mix of Caribbean and British English. She waits patiently on the line while Brittany stays quiet.

"Hello?" the woman asks into the void which holds Brittany's silence and her rapidly beating heart. She can't do it. Not now. She doesn't know what to say.

"Sorry, wrong number." Brittany disconnects the call. She'll deal with this another day.

Right now, she isn't sure if she's ready to dredge up the past she knows she must unearth. She needs to hand Amani as much ammunition as she can. They must establish a pattern of obsession with Jonny. Right now, she's put Eva on the task of calculating all her own assets within his empire. Brittany strongly suspects she has nothing because she signed nothing.

"Who was that?"

The sound of Jonny's voice startles her. She hates him creeping around her silently. Especially when he materializes out of nowhere and she isn't sure how long he has been there observing and listening to her.

He finds her out on their covered patio where she had, at first, been reading a book before standing up and pacing, a bag of nerves, while calling Mr. and Mrs. Daniels.

"*Jesus.* Jonny." She collects herself. He strolls up behind her and hooks a hand on her waist. She wriggles out of his touch and spins around to face him. "I thought you were at work."

"I came home early." He stands in front of her like a statue.

Uncomfortable silence passes between them. She notices he starts unfurling his fingers and she knows he needs to talk.

"What is it?" she asks him.

"I want to talk about Kemi and Ragnar."

The last two people on earth she cares about right now. Doesn't Jonny realize she's indeed serious about pushing for a divorce?

Jonny continues. "Ragnar is traveling."

"Good for him," she offers nonchalantly.

"He is traveling because of Kemi." Jonny's look turns serious. His normal intensity is dialed up several notches. It makes Brittany straighten up.

"Because of Kemi?" Brittany repeats. Her mind dashes back to the American Club event and Kemi's disposition. The other woman confessed to her about their sordid little affair. Ragnar is an asshole, Brittany knows this. She's only giving Kemi time to come around to this realization herself.

"Why because of Kemi?" Brittany prods. "I thought he needed to think and get away. To clear his mind."

"He is confused," Jonny says, standing stoically as he peers at her.

"Confused? They had an affair. A mistake. Trust me, it's eating Kemi alive." She turns back to place her phone down. Jonny's eyes follow her movement.

"Ragnar told me he has strong feelings for Kemi."

Those words pull her brows into a frown. "Strong feelings?"

Affairs often start that way. *Strong feelings.* Embers of lust blow into full flames of exaggerated feelings, but Ragnar doesn't go for the likes of Kemi. He has yet to prove to her he isn't prejudiced.

She loathes Ragnar for his arrogance and self-importance, which he displays openly in contrast to the average Swede.

"He is trekking in Nepal."

"Nepal? Halfway across the world to get away from her?" Brittany chuckles.

Jonny doesn't share her amusement. He strolls languidly up to her, landing inches from her face, his favorite spot. This time, Brittany doesn't back away. Amani coached her on what to do. How to draw out what she needs from him so she can break free from his hold.

Jonny's eyes roam her features. She remains unflinching. She knows he's trying to read her for cues. He's getting much better at it. Reading faces.

"Does Pia know?" Brittany asks. Jonny shakes his head. Of course she doesn't. "So what now?"

"I don't know when he will come back."

"He has to come back sometime," Brittany reasons. "He has a wife and daughter. He can't selfishly take off because he's falling for his mistress," she adds but the imagery floods Brittany's mind once more. Powerful Kemi who Jonny idolizes, who can do no wrong in his eyes and for his company, has now been relegated to Ragnar's Black mistress.

Something breaks within Brittany. While she firmly considers Kemi her frenemy, she also isn't going to let these men tear her apart this way. Morality aside, men have affairs all the time, and somehow seem to bounce back awash with forgiveness. But women, powerful women, aren't allowed to stray. To say nothing of Black women who society defines in terms of unwavering loyalty. Black women are never allowed to make mistakes. Not one flaw.

Between Ragnar and Kemi, Brittany suspects Kemi's getting the shorter end of this affair breakdown. Ragnar is Jonny's best friend and who Jonny loves first, he protects fiercely. In that regard, his loyalty runs deep.

Jonny's unexpected lips on hers throw her out of her thoughts. He moves them softly over hers, silently begging her to open hers up to him. He tugs her lower lip. She lets out a small sigh. Jonny pries her lips apart with his, and fully possesses her, his tongue wrapping hers gently.

She pants when Jonny splays his fingers on her back and crushes her firmly to his chest. At first, she places both her palms on his chest to regain her breath, subconsciously blocking his advance. Then she relaxes.

Brittany had already blurted out that she wanted a divorce during her last failed attempt at seduction. Jonny had repeated the word to her, confused. Even though she'd moved him to a guest room, he didn't pry further.

He simply didn't take her seriously.

Jonny kisses her with vigor. Brittany lets him kiss her the way she once liked. The way she once taught him. While every pore now recoils at his touch, she needs to keep him closer, to give him access, to throw him off the scent of her full plans. Amani's words of wisdom.

Brittany receives his love until he pulls out and rests his forehead on hers.

"Don't leave me," he begs softly, his forehead still on hers. "*Snälla*," he adds. *Please.* "I'll die if you leave me."

I'll die if you leave me.

Brittany repeats those words to Tanesha minutes after Jonny dresses himself quietly and departs without a word. He left her out on the patio lying on a sheep fur throw they had pulled off the deck chair and tossed onto the wooden floor. Jonny had disarmed her like she knew he would and she had accepted his possession. Like she knew she would.

Brittany gathers her clothes against her chest to cover her nakedness. She has never been this intimate in such openness before. Thankfully, their wooded piece of luxury lies tucked away with its own private jetty and waterfront views.

She prays Sylvia, their Bulgarian housekeeper, didn't overhear her cries out on that patio. Sylvia has probably heard enough of those moans over the years whenever Jonny corners her in various parts of their villa looking to be sated. His study, their bedroom, the dining room, by the fireplace, in the kitchen while Sylvia hides in the pantry out of discomfort.

She prays the groundskeeper has left for the day, otherwise she'll never be able to look that man in the eye again. Fortunately, her au pair Vicky had taken Maya out for a stroll.

"Girl, you're flirting with crazy. Please leave that man," Tanesha says, her voice laden with concern.

"You don't think I'm trying?" Brittany retorts as she balances the phone between shoulder and ear, wiggling herself back into her panties. She switches hands as she pulls her top over her head, not bothering to rework her bra.

"So, what's the latest?" Tanesha prods.

"I couldn't do it."

"You couldn't do what?"

"I couldn't call her parents. Her mother, Lucinda, picked up," Brittany says. "That accent. Caribbean British. I couldn't do it."

"So what happened?"

"I hung up. I hung up on her, Tee."

Her friend huffs, frustrated. "You need to talk to that woman. You need to."

"I know, I know," Brittany says. She pulls on her jeans with one hand. "I feel like I need to see her, talk to her in person. A phone call feels weak."

"So you'll travel to England?"

"Yes, and I'll take Maya with me. I need to see them."

"But you look like their dead daughter," Tanesha says.

Those words hang in the air. Brittany's a walking replica of their long dead daughter. She isn't sure how they are going to react upon sight. Whether the mere vision of her in front of them will dredge up painful memories they buried long ago. Brittany isn't sure what she's trying to find out or prove, but she prays she won't hurt them a second time by digging into their past.

"Are you sure this is a good idea? Like I've said, Jonny boy is smart as fuck. The dude is on to you even if you don't think it."

Smart as fuck. She hates it when Tanesha uses those words to describe Jonny. They always paint a diabolical image of him. Yes, he's intense. Yes, he's all consuming.

But diabolical? That she chooses not to believe.

"I've got it under control, trust me." She scrambles onto her feet, finally zipping up her jeans. "I've got it under contr—"

Brittany freezes when she spins around to find Jonny leaning against the doorframe. Like a ghost once again, he has materialized out of thin air. She isn't sure how long he has been standing there or how much of her call with Tanesha he's heard.

"Brit? Brit?" Tanesha's voice comes back stronger, trying to prod their conversation along. Brittany stands solid as she glares back at her husband silently observing her.

"I'll call you back," she half-whispers into the phone and disconnects it before Tanesha can respond. Her eyes settle back on him as he stands rooted by the door, a barricade between her and the safety of the indoors.

"I thought you'd left," she says, her voice shaky, her hand equally shaky as she slips her phone into the back pocket of her jeans. The air between them suddenly chills. A few moments ago, it had been scorching as he moved against her, lying on sheepskin.

She feels a sudden draft as the tiny hairs on her arms rise. Has he been spying all through her mission? Is Eva simultaneously feeding information back to him too? Is he already several steps ahead?

Brittany swallows, trying to collect herself, pushing strands of hair behind her ear. How much does he truly know? She feels heat broiling within her because the look he is giving her sends a rush of blood to her face.

Jonny stands at the entrance to the patio, glaring at her wordlessly before calmly asking, "Where are you taking Maya?"

YASMIIN

Yasmiin is still sitting on their couch, her legs tucked beneath her. Her tear ducts have dried up long ago. After Öz and the crew left, she had collapsed back into herself, weeping, utterly exposed. Humiliation settled over her like condensation, a layer so thick she wasn't sure she'd ever recover from it. Yagiz grabbing and humiliating her in front of his friends had ripped open that long scabbed-over wound, her memories gushing out like fresh blood.

He had left her with no other choice.

Mehmet had called for her then. So, she'd kicked Yagiz for good measure as he lay passed out on their shaggy Anatolian rug, went in search of her son, fed him, bathed him, and put him down for the night. Then she resumed her perch on the couch for the rest of the night.

Yagiz wakes from his drunken slumber at two forty-three on Saturday morning. First, a low groan pours out of him as he stirs, placing a hand on his forehead, possibly fighting a headache. Still wearing boxer briefs, he pushes himself into a sitting position, eyes scanning the low-lit room. They settle on Yasmiin.

"*Aşkım?*" Her silence meets him instead. "Yasmiin?"

"Why did you shame me?" Her voice cuts hard, masking tears.

"What?" He seems confused. "What are you talking about?" He tries getting to his feet, but thinks otherwise and sits back on the rug.

"Why did you do this?"

"Do what? I don't understand." He glances around. "The boys?"

"Gone."

"Gone? What time is it?" He crawls on all fours toward the couch and props himself onto it. When she doesn't answer, Yagiz turns to her. "Yasmiin?"

The sharp sound of her slap reverberates through their modest apartment. Behind it is hurt, shame, and unexpected release. Yagiz, stunned by her assault, glares at her. His look softens when he reads her face.

She holds his gaze tightly, her lips firmly pressed together, not breaking eye contact for several seconds.

"Yasmiin, what happened? What did I do?"

She tells him everything.

From the start. How she fled the only home she'd ever known. How she crossed paths with her pimp. The girls she roamed the streets of Rome with. Foreign hands grabbing at her flesh and hair. How she'd finally been smuggled to Sweden through Bosse, a diplomat-cum-customer. Touting his country's human rights record as he fucked her for weeks as recompense. How her mind had pushed every agonizing memory into deep recesses, which Yagiz violently dug out with one idiotic act of bravado.

"You made me that girl again," she weeps. "In front of them. You made me her."

Her sobs fill the room, her shoulders shuddering, all composure melting away. "I killed her but you dug her skeleton back up." Her short ragged breaths catch on her sobs. "And I hate you so much right now."

Yagiz peers at her, his eyebrows dipping inwards, trying to decipher and understand what she's saying to him. His Yasmiin sold her body to survive. For less than the cost of a shrimp sandwich.

What thoughts swirl his mind as he processes the news? Yasmiin wonders. Her braggart.

But he has no words for her. The air around them grows dense, and her chest heaves with each breath she struggles to take beneath tears.

Yasmiin buries her face in her damp palms, letting the last few drops make their way out. She follows the action with a deep gasp, releasing the final weight trapping her for over a decade. The relief telling someone brings is one she hasn't anticipated. Now she understands why people go to therapists, an action she's often scoffed at. Pouring out your soul to any listening ear is more cathartic than shameful.

Yagiz is glaring at her as she finally calms her racing heart and stills her tears. She glances at him, his eyes dark in the dim light. Nothing. No reaction. As if he has simply frozen on the news. Part of the mystery of marriage for them is secrets. She doesn't know all of his, and he's never bothered to tease hers out.

Suddenly Yagiz sits up taller on their worn-out couch. He flexes his chest before wordlessly getting up. He pads toward the kitchen, his pounding feet the only sounds beyond Mehmet's soft snoring. A few seconds later, he comes out with a large black trash bag. Yasmiin readjusts her position, switching into high alert. He storms past her and starts clearing half-empty cans of Efes Pilsen, first tossing them gently into the bag. With each item he picks up, his pace quickens, from delicate tosses to charged throws. He grabs plates and throws them in, breaking them on impact.

He drags the bag over to the corner of the room where he keeps his supplies, a few cartons of 32-ounce bottles of pills. His steroids. Thousands of kronor's worth of inventory for customers. He casts them into the bag as well. He opens plastic bottles and pours them into the trash bag. He digs into cabinets, cupboards, and drawers, pulling out cigarettes, a few stashes of weed and khat leaves, anything and everything that matters to his current lifestyle.

Yasmiin winces and jumps with each crash of glass breaking against glass. Bottles of expensive whiskey and brandy. Cans of undrunk beer pried open and poured into the bag. Yagiz is no longer silent. Low grunts escape him as he crisscrosses their apartment, clearing out, cleaning up. Yasmiin bites her thumb, head bowed as she hears him say all he wants to say through his actions. A warm tingling feeling bubbles deep within her, rising through her stomach, burning her chest as it makes its way to her mouth. The feeling spreads across her lips as a slight grin. Semblances of a smile before making way for another row of tears.

The clanking, clashing, breaking, thumping suddenly stops.

Yagiz straightens up, lets out a loud gasp before his body begins to convulse with sobs. He drags the trash bag behind him as if it weighs a ton, inching closer to where Yasmiin sits on the couch.

Yagiz towers over her, deep bellowing sobs escaping him. He lets go of the bag and falls to his knees at her feet.

FIFTEEN

KEMI

Blues notes fill the air, wrapping around patrons swaying to the rhythm, tapping hands on thighs, stomping to drum beats.

Malcolm moves on stage, his saxophone at his lips, blowing out notes, cheeks puffing up and flattening with each sound. Kemi loves coming to his gigs. Her way of releasing the week's draining tension and replacing it with a new kind of energy. Fuel to power her through the next week. She gyrates, throwing her hands over her head, clapping along, moving her hips.

In fact, her second date with Tobias had been to one of Malcolm's gigs, over a year ago. While she was dancing Tobias had pulled her close. His kiss had been slow and gentle, and she had fully reveled in the tenderness he showed. She called it much-needed chicken soup because, up until that point, it had been a long time since she'd met a man who wanted to take his time savoring her, not devouring her.

Kemi watches Tobias as he leans with his back against the bar, mug of beer in hand. Jose perches next to him, holding some kind of green cocktail. Jose occasionally leans in and whispers something in Swedish to Tobias, who bursts into that typical grin of his before taking another swig of beer, licking residual foam off his lips.

Since regularly meeting at Malcolm's shows, they have developed a tradition where they stroll across the bridge from Gamla stan to Södermalm to their favorite hole-in-the-wall kebab joint to feast on greasy pizzas topped with thin slices of lamb and garlicky crème fraîche.

During a set break, Malcolm hops off stage and heads over to the trio. He greets his boyfriend with a quick kiss before pulling Tobias into a hug and then Kemi.

"My favorite people," he declares and grabs a mug of beer Jose secured for him right before the intermission and clinks it with Tobias's. Tobias smiles back, cocking his head to receive the compliment. Malcolm's gaze travels to Kemi. She knows she looks forlorn. If anyone is going to comment on her appearance, it's him.

Malcolm is brash yet tender. Caring yet critical. And what she appreciates the most at that moment is the fact that he has kept her confession private. Even from Jose because Jose's disposition seems unchanged from the last time they all hung out together. Malcolm, who's always joking, knows this is serious territory and is giving Kemi the opportunity to fully land in her feelings and fix it herself without the added pressure of judgment.

"So, how's our madam doing?" He gently taps her wineglass with his mug.

"Hungry." She giggles weakly. "When will you be done?"

Malcolm glances at his watch. "Forty-five minutes. Can your highness handle that or should I send Jose to go get grapes and peel them for you?"

"You may have to."

He chuckles before turning back to Tobias. "So, Tobbe, how *you* been?"

"Same ol', same ol'." Tobias takes a sip of his Carlsberg. "Work is good, life is good, I can't complain." He hooks his right arm around Kemi's waist and pulls her closer to him. She follows reluctantly. She catches Malcolm's look and watches him purse his lips before sipping again. Of all Malcolm's words that had poured out of him during her confession over dinner, the one phrase that bubbles up that instant is:

You can't be hoeing around with plain as fuck Svens!

Since moving to Sweden, she has morphed into a version

of herself she barely recognizes. Before Tobias slid into her life, Stockholm's dating scene had been as brutal as the DC scene. Except here, she worked harder and had to be more proactive.

There had been one date where the guy, Bearded Brawn, stood frozen by the restaurant door. Upon seeing her, he vanished into thin air before resurfacing via a text message, telling her she was fat and didn't match her profile picture.

There had been another she called Cheap Bastard for leaving her with half of a hefty bill at a Michelin-starred restaurant even though he'd eaten the most expensive dishes on the menu and downed the priciest wine. She had worked her way through over a dozen dull first dates with a diverse sampling of men, ending each date right away whenever she reached boring depths or was propositioned for sex before the appetizers had even arrived.

The only man she'd ever brought home on the first date had been Vicious Viking. He had instinctively smelled her long sex-free spell and challenged her at dinner, telling her to cut to the chase as he glared at her through unsmiling eyes. Their ferocious night had been her biggest sex regret in Sweden.

Until Ragnar.

"Kemi? *Hallå?*" Jose tries regaining her attention.

"I'm sorry," she says. "I've got a lot on my mind lately."

"Yeah," Tobias agrees with him. "You keep drifting away. Your mind is always somewhere else."

"She plays in the big league, Tobbe," Malcolm says. "That's her brain racking up ways to stay there." She isn't sure how to process his words. If he's actually complimenting her or taking a jab at her ambition.

He's what you think Tobias is missing, isn't he?

Malcolm's words float back up again. She takes a hard swig of wine to drown them out.

"I think she stresses too much," Tobias says, turning to look at her, pulling her even closer. "We have what we need. We have more than enough."

"Until she's running that company, I don't think she'll be satisfied," Jose chimes in.

"It's called ambition, Jose," Kemi says. "In the US, I had a clear path. Here, it's murky to nonexistent."

"So, let me get this straight," Malcolm starts. "You're making twice the money you made back in the States for a fraction of the same work and you're complaining? *Guuurl?*" Malcolm shakes his head before turning to Tobias and placing a hand on his shoulder. "Good luck, man. You need it."

"Stop." Kemi rolls her eyes. "I didn't come to Sweden to flatline. I have goals."

"Nothing wrong with that," Jose says. "In fact, I'll drink to that." He taps his glass with hers once more.

"But it can't consume your life so fully." This time, it's Tobias, a tinge of concern in his voice. "I want you to just enjoy each moment without feeling the need to prove its importance."

"That's your Swedish work-life balance privilege talking," she retorts.

"Why can't you just *be*?" Tobias's tone turns serious. She doesn't reply.

Malcolm says he'll see them later as he heads back to the stage, while Jose excuses himself for a bathroom break which Kemi senses is his guise to give them space. Tobias pulls her into a hug and presses a kiss to her forehead.

"What's wrong, Kemi? I can feel it."

She closes her eyes and wraps her arms under his armpits, pressing herself closer, her head leaning into his chest. She shakes her head against him.

"Do you still want to move back home?"

She stays quiet. She can quit von Lundin and move back home next week if she so desires. But she wants Tobias even more. What they have. What she has been looking for, for so long. She's tired of being single. She'd worn that cape with pride for years until it lost its luster. Living here is forcing her to choose between career and love.

Right now, she wants love more than anything. And Tobias isn't going to move away anytime soon. Her boyfriend doesn't make rash spontaneous decisions, no matter how much he loves her. He marinates. He ponders. He always strives for balance that way.

"Not without you," she says. "Which means I'll be sticking here for a while." She stands on tiptoes and kisses him lightly on the lips, which he receives with a grin against hers.

Over an hour later, they're sitting in their favorite joint, waiting for three pizzas and a salad for Jose to arrive. Jose nestles in the crook of Malcolm's arm with a smile across his face, which tells Kemi he's got exciting news.

"See, Jose, this is why you could never work for *Säpo*." Tobias laughs.

"What?" Jose half-asks.

"You're hiding something and your face is telling us everything we need to know," Tobias says, his voice light.

Jose shifts in his seat, pressing his lips together, his eyes widening warmly. Then he lifts his left hand suddenly to show them the thin ring and its modestly sized glittering diamond. Kemi's mouth drops open. Tobias launches into a hearty laugh.

"*Alltså?! Men grattis!!*" He gets to his feet to hug Jose and then Malcolm. *Wow! Congratulations!* Kemi stands as well and wraps her arms around them too. Once they all settle back in their seats, Kemi reaches for Jose's hand to inspect the ring.

"I can't believe you got a ring before I did," she chuckles. "You bitch!"

"Leave my man alone." Malcolm grins. "Checkmate, Tobias. Your move now."

Tobias laughs. He turns to Kemi and makes a mock show of getting on one knee, before cackling and taking his seat once more. Kemi smiles weakly. That little act pricks her. His two long-term relationships lasted six and eight years respectively.

Tobias is never going to marry her, considering he spent fourteen years with only two women without proposing to either of them. *Just hang in there.* Tina's words surface to meet her. She's been trying but is frankly getting tired of waiting.

Their food arrives, along with cans of soda and a jug of water.

"So, when is the big day?" Tobias reaches for a fork and knife.

"We're thinking sometime in August. A small summer gathering after the civil ceremony at Stadshuset," Jose says before spearing pieces of his salad.

"We want you two there by our side," Malcolm tells them. "As our witnesses, but also as our closest friends."

Tobias grows teary-eyed and he lifts his can of Coke in a toast. "My brother!" He taps it with Malcolm's.

"We would be honored," Kemi says to Jose. He beams back at her before delicately lifting lettuce to his lips.

That night, Tobias makes love to her slowly and deeply. Spending the evening with Malcolm and Jose seems to have triggered something within him. He wants to show her how much he loves and appreciates her, despite no prospects of a proposal on the horizon. She receives his love, cradling and wrapping her arms and legs around him as he shows her.

They lie on their backs afterwards, staring at the ceiling, catching their breath. She throws a glance his way, smiling. He catches her gazing at him and flashes her a smile, before turning back to the ceiling.

Her phone beeps. She starts to reach for it.

"Do you really need to?" Tobias banks his head sideways, locking eyes with hers.

"What if it's Kehinde?" Kemi says. "Getting messages past midnight makes me nervous."

He accepts her excuse with a nod and turns back to the ceiling, closing his eyes and resting his head back on a bent arm, bringing his heart down from its sprint.

Kemi grabs her phone and pulls up her messages. A photo from him taken by someone else. He stands with sunglasses over his eyes, a wide grin on his face and hiking poles in both hands. A sign for "*Everest Base Camp*" is in the frame behind him. She glimpses its snow-covered peak far off in the distance behind Ragnar.

The beauty of this place is overwhelming. Being here feels unbelievable. Seeing how small I am. Seeing how great she is. Sitting there in the distance. I'm sorry about last time.

R

She studies his photo again. He now sports a beard, his hair longer, his square jaw looking leaner. She swallows as she studies every detail in that picture. The look of elation on his face. His chest cocked outwards with pride that he accomplished that trek. Sunglasses probably hiding tears in his eyes.

She jumps when Tobias's voice cuts through her assessment.

"Who's that?" he asks drowsily. He's looking over her shoulder at the photo of a man in sunglasses up in the clouds. Tobias presses his nose to her shoulder and takes a small whiff of her scent. Reminiscent of when he'd arrived home to find her on the floor and had pulled out of their embrace after smelling her. His lips replace his sniffing nose on her shoulder as chills rush through her.

Goosebumps surface across her skin. *He knows.*

"No one important," Kemi says before deleting his message.

She feels a deep churning in her stomach. The mere thought of Ragnar seems to be provoking nausea. She can already taste the bile on the tip of her tongue. She tosses the phone aside, lurches out of bed, and rushes to the bathroom.

BRITTANY-RAE

"Hmmm," Amani murmurs, processing the information Brittany is sharing with her. She doesn't seem satisfied. She reaches for her glass of rosé and takes a slow sip, her eyes locking with Brittany's as she drinks. They're lunching at a snazzy overpriced Italian bistro in the heart of Östermalm.

Brittany shifts uncomfortably as Amani assesses her. She hates being judged and scrutinized this way.

"Brittany"—Amani crosses her bedazzled fingers and rests them on the table—"do you understand what you're dealing with?"

"Don't be condescending," Brittany snaps.

Amani remains firm. "Redirect that energy into getting what I asked you to."

"Don't you think I'm trying? He's standing too close to me. He's always circling me. He's on to me." Brittany sounds exasperated.

"What have you gotten out of his assistant so far?"

Eva the mole. Eva has been excellent so far, digging up news and sensitive details, but Eva now reeks of sabotage herself. It seems Eva, without saying the words, wants Brittany to hurt Jonny in some way. She wants to know why.

So far, she has contact information for the Danielses, including their address. Eva also gave her as much financial information as she could find. Brittany was able to dig up Jonny's estimated net worth online via a business website. She had audibly exclaimed at the number, her breath catching on the multiple zeros.

Brittany only has a personal account in Sweden which Louise set up and dutifully transfers funds into every month. Everything else is in his name. Their villa on the island of Lidingö. Their summer home. His little hobbit cottage in town. His penthouse in London. His cars and hers too.

While he lives modestly by Swedish wealth-flashing standards, there are stocks and investments in real estate around the world. Angel investments in several startups in Stockholm, London, and Singapore, looking for the next unicorn. He sits on various boards in name only—he never does anything or attends their meetings. Wealth comes to him, because his team of financial advisors, lawyers, and accountants keep bringing it to him.

Brittany only has a simple bank account. Nothing more.

"You do realize his assistant can cut off the funds at his command, right?"

"I know. And I'm thinking of what I can do."

"First things first, get another bank account and start transferring those funds out of the other one," Amani suggests. "They are signatories to the current account, right?"

Brittany nods.

"I need words, Brittany. Not nods. If we're going to do this, I'm going to be tough on you. We're in for a long fight. I don't like von Lundin's legal team. I know those guys and have avoided them for decades. They are wolves."

"Yes, they are signatories on my account."

"So get a new private account and transfer all your funds into that, once funds come into the other one."

Brittany feverishly scribbles notes down.

"What about Mr. and Mrs. Daniels? What is the latest update there?" Amani grabs her cutlery once more and slices into a large blob of buffalo mozzarella in her caprese salad.

"I couldn't do it," Brittany says. "I will, but hearing *her* mother's voice broke me. I couldn't at that moment."

Amani's eyes soften as she takes Brittany in. "I understand, but you have to make that call."

"I'm planning on actually going to London to visit them in person." Brittany sips from her glass. "I'll take Maya with me."

"Good," Amani affirms. "You need to get away for a bit too. Time to think and relax and come back ready to fight."

"Oh, I'm ready to fight," Brittany says, forking leaves in her salad. "I am tired of feeling powerless."

A smile carves into Amani's face and her eyes twinkle like quartz crystals. It seems the word *fight* turns the Tigress on.

"So tell me"—Amani takes a bite—"what is he like? He is such an enigma."

Everyone wants to know who Jonny is, because he never offers himself to anyone. Not the press, not his family, not even Brittany. Brittany only sees the parts of him he wants to show her. The parts convincing him that she is Maya Daniels's replacement.

"He's an intense man," Brittany says.

Amani chews as she studies her. "How so?"

"In every way." Brittany lets her words linger. Through Amani's eyes, she can see the other woman's mind furiously working to stay appropriate.

"There are always rumors around him, I'm sure you know," Amani starts. "That his family refuses to fully acknowledge him. Is this true?"

"His family doesn't acknowledge a lot of things," Brittany reveals.

Amani chuckles. "Well, the biggest rumor revolves around his love life."

"He isn't capable of an affair, especially when he's obsess… when he commits. Even if it's just for two weeks," Brittany says. Amani continues studying her. "From what I gathered, most of his exes chose to leave him despite his wealth. He's suffocatingly intense that way."

Amani takes another sip. "They say he's obsessed with Black women. That he has a fetish."

"I think we're crossing into more private matters here." Brittany shifts uncomfortably in her seat.

"I am trying to help you divorce this man. I need every detail including when he takes a shit. That is where we are at, Brittany. That is our relationship from now on," Amani says sternly. "So, does he?"

Brittany swallows, holding her gaze for a second or two before finally uttering the word she has been running away from since the first day she met Jonny on that fateful flight from London.

"Yes," she mouths softly.

She sees concern etch across Amani's face as her reply settles on the woman.

"Did you get the contact information for some of his ex-girlfriends?" Amani prods. Brittany closes her eyes before nodding, then saying yes. She received five names and numbers from Eva. That was all the assistant had been willing to share. She's unsure why Eva picked those particular names, but the woman moves with intent. Brittany knows careful thought was put into those selections.

Five names who could tell her more about her husband's other condition. The one constantly being swept beneath the rug by his assistants. The one they keep clearing out of view of society.

Fifty-six women made it past three weeks. I don't keep track of his casual flings.

She hears Eva's words ringing in her ears. Fifty-six had made it past three weeks. Which means possibly hundreds of women have barreled through his bed over the decades. Hundreds. Varying shades of brown and Black. Models, celebrities, powerful women, ordinary women, and those Eva and Louise had paid with von Lundin money, and been silently sneaking into his bed.

When Eva gave her those five names, Brittany immediately googled them, looking at beautiful melanin across her screen. Initial pangs of jealousy stirred within her as she glared at his ex-girlfriends, all statuesque creatures.

She noted the similarities despite their differences. A narrowness to their faces. She could clearly see why Jonny had been drawn to them. And it all started with Maya Daniels. The first woman who had looked Jonny in the eye and had loved him fully, including every dark murky corner within him.

He's eternally searching for her replacement. Brittany's the closest he has found so far.

There's a businesswoman who runs a health food brand in London. Jonny trailed her around London, randomly showing up wherever she was, until she filed a restraining order against him. Eva dished out these details.

A British lawyer now based in Dubai. A volatile relationship which regularly left Jonny with palm prints on his cheeks and fingernail scratches across his back. Eva had caught him changing shirts during that relationship run.

A retired American model he met during London Fashion Week. Eva had told her that fashion shows in Paris, London, and New York were some of Jonny's favorite hangouts. He loved staring at and being around the dark-skinned models in particular, Eva casually explained.

A kindergarten teacher whose roots are Eritrean but was raised in Sweden. She backed out of their relationship when Swedish tabloids descended upon their affair and stalked her all over Stockholm until she was forced to resign from her job.

And a notorious high-profile Afro-Swedish escort who had named Jonny as her favorite client in the past across Swedish and international media, alongside other powerful men.

"Jonny is the most intense lover I've ever had," the woman, Ebba, had said in a British tabloid video interview Brittany watched, a smile lingering across those pumped-up lips as memories surfaced within her.

"I think he has another obsession as well," Brittany whispers. Amani cranes forward, trying to catch her words.

"Another?"

"Yes." Brittany reaches for her drink.

"What do you mean?"

Brittany shakes her head.

"Is it tied to his fetish?" Amani asks, lowering her voice. "Is this something that could help us?"

Brittany catches her eyes as tears well within her own and simply nods her response.

A few days later, she meets one of his exes. Ebba stands much taller in person, much fairer than the type Jonny usually chases. Brittany watches the slender creature freeze once she steps into the hotel room at Rival. Louise had opened the door for the woman and now follows her into the room when her gaze lands on Brittany sitting cross-legged on the bed.

This is the only way Brittany knew she was going to get Ebba to come. By pretending Jonny had summoned her. Jonny was on his way home from London. Work had called him and given her more space to breathe under his absence.

Brittany had enlisted Eva to her aid. Eva planned the tryst between Ebba and Jonny, and passed information on to Louise about the meeting. Louise thought Jonny was on his way from the airport directly to this room. Eva had then rung him behind Louise's back and re-routed him home instead.

So, when Louise, with Ebba just behind her, opens the door and finds Brittany in that room instead of Jonny, the color drains from her face. A mix of shock and embarrassment. Brittany knows once Louise steps out of the room, she'll call Eva and rail down the line at her.

"Brittany?" Louise's voice cracks at her betrayal, her hands now hugging the folder she carries tightly to her chest.

"*Vad är den här?*" Ebba asks as she stops, her shoulders slack, her eyes roaming over Brittany. *What is this?*

"Thank you, Louise. That will be all," Brittany says, pushing off the bed and walking up to Ebba, who dares not inch further in. Louise nods and swiftly exits the room, leaving the two women in a standoff.

"*Jonny's fru, eller hur?*" Ebba finds her voice. *Jonny's wife, right?*

"I'm not here to fight you, Ebba," Brittany starts, softening her tone so the other woman doesn't remain skittish. "I'm here because I need you."

Ebba's skeptical eyes roam over Brittany once more. "*Skit! Vad snygg du är!*" Ebba says, a smile creeping onto her lips. *Damn! You're hot!* "This should be fun," she adds in English.

Brittany receives her compliment with a half-smile, turning up a corner of her mouth. Ebba pulls off her faux fur jacket, too heavy for the spring weather, and walks to a corner of the room to start undressing.

"So when is Jonny arriving?" she continues in English once she slings her jacket over a chair.

"He's not coming."

"He's not?" Ebba's disappointment sails through.

"This is not that kind of meeting." Brittany's voice is stern now. Ebba's excitement dies. She eyes Brittany once more.

"What do you want?" she asks, her tone frigid.

"I need your help with something."

"What?"

"Jonny."

"Why?"

"You were his girlfriend once." Brittany struggles to push those words out. Ebba's gaze scans her face. "What was he like?"

A few seconds of silence and Ebba lets out a sigh of exasperation. "Is this why you called me here? To talk about my love life?"

Brittany swallows, trying to parse her words. "I suspect he has an addiction and I need to know just how deep it is."

"What do you mean?"

"How was Jonny with you?"

Ebba glares at Brittany one last time and retrieves her jacket, cursing under her breath. "Don't waste my time ever again." Ebba spins around to make her exit. Brittany reaches for her arm, grabbing on tightly.

"Please." Brittany is ashamed of her own desperation. "Please."

Ebba regards her, her disposition relaxing slightly, before dropping her jacket once more and folding her arms across her chest.

"Fine," she concedes. "What do you want to know?"

"How was Jonny with you?" Brittany repeats.

"Why do you want to know?"

"You've described him as intense in some interviews."

"You've been watching my interviews?" Her voice turns giddy. A woman who loves the limelight.

"How was he?"

"Well, Jonny was my favorite," she says.

"In what ways?"

"That man can fuck."

Brittany winces at her words. She clearly isn't ready for all this digging.

"Was he intense in other ways?"

"In bed?"

"In general."

"Well," Ebba starts. "He didn't like being interrupted, that's for sure. I wasn't expecting him to be wild and crazy. You know, like when Swedish guys get really drunk and loosen up." She pauses to collect her breath. "But Jonny wasn't like that."

"What was he like?"

"He was never aggressive with me, but he never wanted to stop. He had such endurance. Always wanted to know what I liked. What I wanted," she says. "Like he was trying to possess me."

"Then why did Jonny stop seeing you?"

"I don't know. One day, he couldn't get enough of me. The next day, he was off to the US for business and I was instantly cut off," she says. "Jonny met you on that trip." She holds Brittany's gaze.

Brittany bites her lip and nods, holding back tears. This isn't enough. Ebba hasn't given her enough. She needs more.

"There's no middle ground with Jonny," Ebba continues. "He is either hot or cold. Black or white. When he wants you, you are all he wants. And when he doesn't..." She trails off.

"Has he ever been controlling with you?" Brittany asks.

"Well, he made me his girlfriend for a month despite knowing what I do for business." She winks at Brittany. "His assistants organized my schedule like clockwork."

"Were you exclusive that month?"

Ebba nods. "I told you, he's intense."

"So you *did* experience his controlling side?"

"Jonny needs to own whatever catches his eye. It was suffocating for a while despite the sex. I was finally able to breathe when he met you," Ebba says. "In fact, I should thank you for that."

"Ebba"—Brittany's tone turns cool—"Jonny has a fetish."

Silence falls between both women as they take each other in. Brittany wonders what Ebba thinks of her. If she sees Brittany as the one who instantly turned him cold toward her. Ebba is stunning in her own right. Light cocoa skin, a mass of dark golden curls as her crown. Her dark-brown eyes, deep and suspicious. Their only commonality, their narrow faces.

"He's obsessed with dark women," Brittany continues.

Ebba lets out a deep breath. "I've always known this," she says. "I suspected it myself."

"How did you meet him?" Brittany asks.

"Look, how much longer is this going to take? I have stuff to do." Ebba grows impatient.

"What was he like with you? What did he like to do with you?"

"You should know, you're his wife."

"You were before my time."

"Look, I wish I could help you more. I hope you find what you're looking for under all those stones you're turning." She pauses, pinning Brittany with a hard stare. "I hope you're ready."

Once Ebba whirls out of that hotel room, Brittany suddenly feels much colder, more alone, and she wraps her arms around herself.

YASMIIN

Yagiz weeps unabashedly at her feet for at least ten minutes until she runs her fingers through his strip of hair. Once again, she finds herself soothing a man when he should be wrapping his arms around her in protection.

"I'm such a fool," he sobs against her legs in the early hours of Saturday morning. "Such a fool." She listens, raking his hair to comfort him. "I swear to you. On my grave. On Mehmet's life. No one will ever hurt you again. Ever."

He lifts his head to look up at her. Silence from Yasmiin.

"I will kill that man," Yagiz grates between his teeth. "I swear to Allah I will find him and tear him apart." More silence. "Fucking *SVENSSON* white savior!" he growls in anger. "What does he look like? *Uhn?* Tell me!" His right hand rolls into a fist.

When Yasmiin continues to meet him with restraint, he presses on. "They treated *Baba* like dirt, like nothing, for years. After giving them everything he had—" His voice catches in his throat. "Everything was not enough. *Baba* had no power." A sob bursts through. "But I have power, *aşkım*, I have power." The veins on his fist surface as he pounds each word into his chest.

When she doesn't speak, he continues. "I will give you a proper wedding. In Ankara. Let us plan it." He pushes the words out through heavy tears. "Let us plan it now."

She shushes him because this is her Yagiz. Making promises he can't keep, talking too much, bragging to everyone, showing off because he matters. Even if the world around him tries to show him otherwise. He matters too.

"What secrets do you still keep from me?" she asks in a low pitch. Yagiz's sobs grow louder. "Hmm, Yagiz? Tell me." He shakes his head. "Yagiz?"

She sighs, frustrated. "Okay, have you killed someone before?" Another head shake. "But you wish you had?" A few moments of silence before he nods. "Have you stolen money before?" He shakes his head. "But you've cheated?" A quick nod, his face still in her lap. "Isn't that the same thing?" He shakes his head. She sighs. "Tell me."

He pulls himself back onto the couch next to her, exhausted. He turns to her, the back of his head resting on the sofa's crest.

"You don't want to know my secrets, *aşkım*," he says in a placid tone which deters follow-up questions from her, his eyes growing darker in the low light. "You don't need to know. What matters is now." He places a hand on her left thigh. "You and me. Us." He leans over to press his lips against hers in a featherlight gesture. He plants soft kisses on her cheek, her forehead, back to her mouth.

"I love you with everything in me, Yasmiin." His gentle kiss grows hungrier. "Let me show you," he whispers, sliding back down to his knees between her legs.

They stay in that position, him eventually sleeping at her feet, she resting back again on the sofa in sleep until Mehmet totters out of his room in search of breakfast.

Yasmiin tries getting up, but Yagiz refuses. No, he says. This Saturday, she'll be putting her feet up. He'll make breakfast and take care of Mehmet. She, on the other hand, can do whatever her heart pleases all day.

This moment with Yagiz feels different. Even when Öz stopped her husband from humiliating her, she had seen the look of newfound respect in Öz's eyes as he took her in. Because she held her head high and said without words she was worthy.

Is this how those fancy women in fashion magazines get spoiled every day? Men at their feet begging instead of taking? Moving around them with respect instead of disregard?

And in that moment, she realizes how much power she already wields in herself and how she holds her future in the palm of her hand.

So, she lets him fully spoil her for the day.

That Saturday, she sleeps in, goes for a walk, buys more makeup to add to her kit, and picks up a new ankle-length dress for the summer. Nusret sends one of the guys over with fresh kebab meat from the kiosk. The afternoon comes and goes. Yagiz takes Mehmet out to the park to kick a football around while Yasmiin snuggles with a mug of spiced *shaah* Somali tea and binge-watches episodes of *Svenska Hollywoodfruar.* That night, Yagiz doesn't let her sleep until they lie in bed spent and soaked in sweat.

"Soon I won't be able to afford you anymore," Salima yells over the crown of brown curls she's grooming when Monday afternoon rolls around. "You now have a hundred followers. Big woman!" she cackles sarcastically at Yasmiin.

Yasmiin rolls her eyes at Salima and turns back to her phone, swiping and scrolling nonchalantly.

Days later, her fingers still tremble despite her feigned indifference. Like the shuddering aftermath of an intense orgasm, she's finally free. Releasing her past to the man she both loved and hated. She now carves her own path, the shackles of her past no longer defining her future.

The salon door chimes, signaling a new customer coming in. Salima frowns at the lean dark-hued woman who looks to be in her twenties sporting box braids to her waist.

"Can I help you?" Salima asks gruffly in Swedish.

"I'm looking for Yasmiin?" The woman steps in with trepidation, her brown gaze sweeping around to take in Salima's gaudy salon.

"Over here!" Yasmiin waves for her to come over to her side of the salon. Yasmiin pulls out her makeup case and starts spreading supplies across the counter.

"What is this?" Salima isn't asking. She eyes Yasmiin, her nostrils flaring.

"Bringing more customers to this dead place," Yasmiin sniggers back to her boss before smiling at the fresh face she's about to transform. Once done, she takes her customary after-photo for her account. She uploads the photo, excited to see more comments still coming in under both Amani's and Tina's photos. It feels oddly invigorating, this validation of her craft from strangers.

Once the woman leaves, satisfied with her new look, Yasmiin turns to find a livid Salima staring back at her.

"You think this is Tensta or Rinkeby?" Salima seems to be foaming at the mouth.

"What is that supposed to mean?" Yasmiin asks.

"I work hard to bring high-paying customers here and you want to do business under the table with your Africa friends?"

"My *Africa* friends?" Yasmiin laughs. "The only people I see here are old Arab people like you, *walai talai*!" she retorts. "Where are the white people?"

Salima presses her lips tightly at her remark. Yasmiin knows she has struck a nerve. The salon is located in a prime spot in town, on the island of Kungsholmen a stone's throw from Stadshuset—Stockholm's City Hall. Yet, Salima still can't pull in the type of clientele she desires.

Yasmiin wonders when Salima will accept reality despite having moved here as a child and adopting all the country's cultural nuances and ethos over the decades. Now well into her fifties, Salima still isn't Swedish enough to draw white clientele. Yasmiin doesn't need to tell Salima this because the older woman already deduces her jab from their exchange.

"How dare you talk to me like that?" Salima rages. The customer beneath her scissors shoots Salima a terrified look. Yasmiin hears her say something in Arabic to Salima along the lines of "*let it be*."

"Truth isn't easy to swallow, *habibti*," Yasmiin adds. "If it was, we would all be better people."

"Leave this place at once!" Salima screams. Her customer tries calming her down.

"Why?" Yasmiin retorts. "You want to fire me because I'm bringing you customers too?" She strolls up to Salima, counting kronor notes. She leaves half the stack on the dresser in front of Salima. "Your share. Partner."

Salima holds her gaze. Yasmiin sees a shift behind those brown eyes, the same she witnessed behind her sister Amani's hazel ones too. She must decode that fleeting message because she didn't grow up here. They had.

Salima takes an audible breath while reaching for the money on the counter. She fingers through the notes.

"You need to love the people who show you love too," Yasmiin presses on before turning back to cleaning her brushes.

SIXTEEN

KEMI

Uncharacteristic salvation descends upon Stockholm in late March.

The season arrives much earlier than anticipated. Spring slowly begins to bloom all over the city. The fragrance of flowers starts filling the air again. People move with a light lift to their steps as rejuvenating life seeps into them. More smiles, more talking, more help when asked.

She's finding it easier to go back to work now. It feels like winter took its misery along with rumors and judgment with it, giving her a second chance through spring to prove herself all over again. Ingrid has resumed inviting her to lunch. The office hums with purpose and she has been pulled into a new marketing project. This time, a fashion line for plus-sized women. Figures considered way below average in the US, but she plays along.

Since their dinner date with Tobias's sister Tina and her footballer Sebastian, she and Tobias spend more time with them. Though as an older player, he's often benched as a substitute rather than in the starting line up, Sebastian still lives comfortably. He owns a sprawling open-plan apartment on Kungsholmen Island where he throws parties and gathers friends at least once a fortnight.

On Stockholm's streets is where Kemi witnesses the rough collision of cultures. In Sebastian's apartment is where she marvels at its gentle melding. Spoken word artists from Somalia and Gambia performing over shrimp sandwiches specially brought in from Gothenburg. Footballers on the Swedish national team twerking to Afrobeats. Friends screaming at each other over cultural trivia games. Swedes listening in a trance-like state whenever Tina speaks about her struggles despite her early success as a singer-songwriter. The occasional footballer flirting with her before Tobias elbows him out of the way. Documentary-watching parties with popcorn. Potluck dinners with Gambian, Ethiopian, Middle Eastern, and Swedish fare.

Or simple quiet weekday nights when it's the four of them, sitting in a low-lit living room, watching a movie together.

They order sushi and are watching a political thriller with Tina nestled comfortably against Sebastian's chest. The gentle waft of raw salmon and tuna incites nausea. Kemi passes on dinner, opting for some bland potato soup instead.

Her phone beeps and Tobias stares at her, his eyes shining in the dim room.

"It's Louise, Jonny's assistant," she whispers back before reading the message.

You and a guest have been invited to a garden party at Jonny's this Saturday. Dress code is casual. Please let me know of any dietary requirements or if you can't make it.

"What is it?" Tobias whispers back.

"We're going to a party on Saturday."

By Wednesday, though, Kemi finds herself in the ER.

She doesn't want to think about it. She dare not think about it. Her breathing shallows, her breaths coming in rapid succession. Panic attack? Anxiety? She isn't sure what she's feeling, except she has thrown up her guts more times in the last two weeks than in the entire year.

Kemi gingerly places a hand on her stomach and feels the warmth beneath her palm. It was while scarfing down a salad during her lunch break with Ingrid and Espen that she'd felt lightheaded and dizzy. Espen had summoned the waiter to bring her some lukewarm water, while Ingrid had ordered a taxi to rush her to the ER to get checked for dehydration.

Her fluid levels are normal. Her hormone levels are not.

She receives the news in shock. Nine weeks along. Conceived sometime in January. Kemi sits on the examination table for about ten more minutes before shuffling quietly onto her feet and leaving in silence.

Once outside standing in the sun, she lifts her face toward its heat and closes her eyes.

Who should get the news first? Her boyfriend or her lover?

BRITTANY-RAE

"Why?" Jonny asks desperately as he watches Brittany pack for her trip to England with Maya and au pair Vicky.

"I need space. Maya needs a change of scenery."

"But the party?" Jonny pleads. "I want you both there."

"I know," Brittany says, folding a bloom-patterned spring dress. "I can't keep pretending in front of others anymore. Everyone will know something is up between us. They will feel it."

"Leave Maya behind."

"You know I can't do that," she says, placing the dress in her suitcase. "I'll bring her back. I swear to you."

"I'm going to miss her." He inches closer. "I'm going to miss you."

Brittany turns to give him a half-smile and presses her lips softly against his, keeping him close. She knows Jonny will stick Eva on her tail. To trail her and his daughter all over London. Luckily for her, Eva seems to be on her side. She's not sure why, but at this point, *screw dignity*.

Her meeting with Ebba was two weeks ago. The information the other woman offered had been enough to quench her curiosity about her husband's sex life before her. Even images of an unabashed Jonny moving wildly against Ebba had been quashed. He's a slow and calculating lover. This she already knows. Jonny is intentional with every action.

Jonny strengthens their kiss instead, his hands gripping her forearms, pulling her closer.

"Pappa! Pappa!" Maya tumbles into their room. Jonny tears away from Brittany robotically and scoops his girl into his arms, bouncing her as he does, his face lighting up in the way it only does whenever he holds Maya in his arms.

"*Hej, gumman!*" He smiles his grin of a thousand teeth and pecks one of her cherub-like cheeks. *Hi, sweetie!* Maya wraps her tiny arms around his neck, burying her face in it. Her French braids curl at the tips. Her once-dark hair is morphing into a light-brown hue. Other than taking Jonny's nose and thin lips, Maya's all Brittany.

Despite his quirks and the air around their relationship constricting her faster than she can breathe, she enjoys seeing him interact with their daughter. He adores her. He gives her the world and Brittany knows Jonny would kill to protect his child, even if it were Brittany herself who got in the way.

He presses his head to their daughter's tiny forehead and spins around in little circles, Brittany's presence in their bedroom long forgotten. She cups an elbow and bites on her finger as she watches them twirl across the room, little Maya giggling at the top of her lungs in joy.

"*Kom leka med mig!*" she demands from her father. *Come play with me!*

"*Inte nu, men jag lovar,*" he promises. *Not now, but I promise.* Maya frowns at him. "*Jag kommer att sakna dig,*" he says. *I'm gonna miss you.* "*Och mamma,*" he adds, turning to Brittany.

"It's just for a few days," she assures him. He gazes at her before turning back to his child, his eyes warming once more. He mouths to her to go find Vicky and sets her back on her feet. The second those tiny soles hit the ground, she shoots off in search of her au pair.

Jonny strides to the door once she darts out, a smile on his face. He locks it and spins back to face Brittany, his smile dropping away. Brittany studies him as he moves toward her, his gait measured. He lands in his favorite spot in front of her. Inches from her face.

They take each other in quietly and Brittany fears his mind.

He reaches out a finger and strokes her right arm, his eyes following the movement like a sensor, trailing its journey until it lands on her wrist. His hand tightens around her wrist, then he locks eyes with her again.

"Louise told me you had a meeting with Ebba."

Brittany curses under her breath. Her disdain for Jonny's other assistant deepens. Of course, she ran off to squeal to him. Has Eva already been compromised too?

"Why?" he asks, pulling her closer to him. Brittany swallows. The air around her thins fast.

"What did Louise say?" She tries buying herself some time to compose something, anything in her mind. Nothing comes to the surface.

"Why did you meet Ebba?" His eyes bore into her as he holds her close.

"She reached out to me." Brittany's words are weak, her mind racing furiously.

"Why?" Jonny stands rigidly, frozen.

"I don't know why."

"Louise said Ebba thought I wanted to see her."

"Really? Well, I mean. There must have been some confusion." She fiddles with strands of her hair, twisting some around a finger.

"Louise never gets confused," he states calmly.

"I know, I mean on Ebba's part."

"Louise said she thought I requested the meeting. Why would she think that?"

"She probably didn't understand my message." An exasperated Brittany tries wriggling out of his hold.

"Louise said the message was from me."

"Louise says a lot, doesn't she?" Brittany's sarcasm lands with a thud between them before reaching Jonny.

"Yes, she does. I pay her to know a lot of things," he says, tightening his grip around her wrist.

"Look, Jonny. I need to pack." Irritation courses through Brittany. If he hadn't been on to her before, now he clearly is. Eva remains her last hope.

She must throw him off the scent. She plants a quick kiss on his lips. He crushes her to his chest when she tries to slink out of his hold. He takes over the kiss, his tongue working hers hard. She tries pulling back out again but he holds her firmly against him.

He's doing it again. Disarming her because he knows how to taste her right, tease out goosebumps and bend her to his will. He slides a hand over her backside to cup her, gripping her.

"Why did you meet Ebba?" he asks against her lips before tugging them once more.

"Hmmm." Brittany kisses him to avoid answering, though she knows it isn't going to work. It never works because he hates loose ends.

Jonny asks her again, his hand still on her rear. Why had she summoned his ex-lover? What had she wanted from her?

"Jonny, please," Brittany pleads.

"If there's anything you need to know, ask me," he says, his lips trailing her neck. "Ask me, and I'll tell you."

"Anything?"

"Anything." His teeth grazes the skin along her collarbone.

"Why her?"

Jonny stops his task and peers at her. She knows that look. Confusion.

"Why her?" He repeats her words, searching her face.

"Yes, why her? She's an escort. She sleeps with men for money," Brittany says, her eyes hard on him.

"I liked her."

"You liked her?"

"I liked her."

"You have nothing in common with that woman. She's not your type." Brittany's frustrated at herself for getting riled up over a woman who no longer matters to Jonny. As Ebba said herself, her husband went from hot to cold in seconds.

"Where did you meet her?" Brittany demands.

"Does it matter? She's not my wife. You are."

Not for much longer, she wants to scream in his face. Amani coached her to play it cool. The only way to slip out of his firm grasp is to let him believe he still has control.

"I just want to know what would draw you to a woman like that."

"I liked her and wanted to be with her," he says, matter-of-factly. "But not anymore. I don't care about Ebba."

"Did you ever care about her?"

"No."

The coldness of his response cuts Brittany. His gaze turns serious.

"No?"

He remains silent as he glares at Brittany, her heart beating wildly, her wrist still in his grasp.

"But you just said you liked her."

A few moments of silence until Jonny finally breaks it. "I liked how she looked," he says, firmly. "I liked her face. Her body."

Brittany gasps. She isn't sure if it's shock on Ebba's behalf or sadness that she didn't record Jonny's confession.

"Jonny." The sound of his name on her lips feels toxic. "Is that why you wanted me too? Just for my face? My body?" She watches his eyebrows dip to process her words. "Did you only like my face too?"

"I love you."

"You loved Maya Daniels. You still do and I look like her," Brittany says. His eyebrows arch back upwards. Then he shakes his head. He keeps shaking his head. Brittany knows he's slipping into his space for coping with too many emotions.

"You know it's true," she continues. Agitation consumes him. He lets go of her wrists and places both of his palms on his forehead, still shaking his head. "Maya Daniels is the only woman you've ever loved. As for the rest of us"—she sniffs back a tear—"you merely like our faces. Our bodies."

"No." He pushes the word out through his fog.

"Yes, only Maya makes you feel. No one else does," Brittany rails, her voice shaky with emotion. "That was why I met with Ebba. To see if you felt anything for her too." Tears break through. "You only love Maya."

"STOP SAYING HER NAME!" he shouts at her.

The room descends into silence. Jonny peers at her through translucent rage-filled eyes. A dark fear fills Brittany's core as she stares at the man-turned-stranger in front of her. His yell snuffs out her words and takes her voice with it.

"Stop saying her name," Jonny repeats firmly as he moves toward her again. Brittany takes a few steps back and away from him. In a few strides, he has her up against the wall and she yelps. The psychological scab she worked so hard to heal begins to peel off her decades-old sore, and she trembles in his arms.

A large man she had trusted, one who had promised her the world in her early twenties, had pinned her many times. On his last try, he had overcome and overwhelmed her.

Brittany shuts her eyes tightly at the world. At the man in front of her.

"Stop." He pushes a few strands off her face as she whimpers, his breath hot on her face. "Saying." He traces his finger along her jawline as she shakes before him. "Her name."

Jonny grabs Brittany's jaw and pries her mouth open for a forceful kiss.

YASMIIN

You don't want to know my secrets, aşkım.
You don't need to know.
What matters is now.

She isn't sure why Yagiz's words float right into her mind there and then as she stands waiting for Amani to push open her door. She craves more. Needs to know why Amani and Salima had reacted when they found out she's his wife. Or why Yagiz reacted fondly when she mentioned meeting the Tigress. Her first instinct had been an affair. After all, he's a beguiling man, even if he's brash most of the time.

She got the job as a favor from Salima's husband, who clearly owes Yagiz. She needs to find the connection and why both Amani and Salima hold such fire behind their eyes.

You don't want to know my secrets, aşkım.

"Yasmiin! *Kom.*" Amani is in good spirits as she opens the door. Yasmiin steps once again into her white-leather, lavender-scented, gold-trimmed apartment.

"Turkish coffee?" Amani offers.

Yasmiin cuts her a glare. Amani chuckles. She sashays toward her kitchen without waiting for a response. Yasmiin sets down her rolling makeup case and sweeps through the space, her fingers walking along shelves and picture frames. The photos are of Amani and Salima. An older pair she reckons are their parents. Lots of outdoor shots bundled up in jackets and faux fur. She picks up a frame of a young Amani and her eyes wash over the striking woman.

"If you're looking for photos of my ex-husband, you won't find any here," Amani's voice cuts through before strong spicy wafts of Turkish coffee reach her. Yasmiin gingerly places the frame back and spins round to receive her.

"No kids either. He was too old." Amani sets the tray down. "Sit." She pours coffee from a metal dallah for them.

"Don't you use that for Iraqi coffee?" Yasmiin asks, reaching for her mug and plopping into a white leather armchair.

"I like Turkish better," Amani offers, a glint in her eye, before grabbing her own mug and settling across from Yasmiin.

"Hmm, I see." Yasmiin takes a sip, her thoughts racing, her surface acting unbothered.

Amani plans on attending yet another gala later that day. This time, to support Röda Korset Sverige—Swedish Red Cross—and raise funds. She invited Yasmiin to stop by several hours earlier to relax and talk before doing her makeup.

Both women drink in silence. Outside the salon and its gossip-fueling atmosphere, they have no words for each other. Amani observes her over the rim of her mug.

"So, Yasmiin," she says eventually, putting her mug down. "What brought you to Sweden?"

"Who says I wasn't born here?" Yasmiin replies.

Amani laughs. "Of course. Remember I grew up here. I can tell."

Yasmiin eyes her. "Okay, like everyone else. Like you."

"I don't remember much when we moved, I was young." Amani takes another sip. "Maybe I don't want to remember."

"What do you remember?" Yasmiin wedges her foot into Amani's opening door.

"Cold weather. White people. Lots of snow," Amani shares. "When we arrived, the whole place looked like icing sugar. Even the people. I was eight and Salima had just turned eleven. I remember celebrating with a green cake. *Prinsesstårta*."

"Hmm," Yasmiin hums into her coffee. She wills Amani to continue.

"My aunt brought us. My parents couldn't make the journey."

"Why?"

"Army. My father was a general in Baghdad. He sent us off with his sister to Borås."

The polar opposite of Muna. Yasmiin thinks about those worn photos tacked above Muna's sleeping head. Her family had nothing, save for the warmth emanating from that modest photo. That thought squeezes Yasmiin's heart. Muna's loss must have been unfathomable, Yasmiin decides. At least she had a choice. Even while she roamed Rome's streets, she still had a choice. Muna lost deep love that money could never buy, without a choice in the matter.

"So your family had money?" Yasmiin confirms.

Amani locks eyes with her, that fiery look returning. "Very wealthy, yes."

"But you were young. What would you have remembered about your wealthy parents, though?" Yasmiin challenges.

"I was old enough." One more sip. "Daddy's princesses. We had all we needed, wanted."

"Then why leave?"

"Life is more complicated than '*stay or leave*,' '*go back to your country*,' or '*stop complaining*.' We do things to survive, out of love for our families and children. He smelled a coup on the horizon and rushed to protect his daughters."

"And your mother?"

"She loved him more."

"How can you say that?"

"Because she chose to stay with him and not us."

"But you left with your aunt. Your mother must have known you were going to be safe. Your father was all by himself."

"It's hard to explain that to young girls." Amani pauses. Yasmiin can see her trying to settle her thoughts. "I see now why she stayed. It took me over forty years to forgive her."

"But you got to Sweden safe," Yasmiin says. "Aren't you grateful?"

She watches Amani shift in her seat. The older woman takes another sip before training her eyes back on Yasmiin.

"Grateful?" Amani repeats the word, drawing out its syllables. "When you come from the upper classes and yet people from the lower class look at you like you're second class because you're brown, it starts a fire within you. That fire grows and grows until you can't contain it anymore." Amani pauses to catch her breath. "You can use that fire to burn everyone around you. Or you can use that fire to light up the world so they cower at your brilliance."

With those words, Amani explains the fire both she and Salima share behind their eyes. The room falls into a quiet lull once more. One which Yasmiin appreciates. It means getting closer to Amani. Her craving from the very start.

"I'm sure they are proud of you now. Sweden's most popular lawyer." Yasmiin downs her last drop.

"I never heard from or saw them ever again." Amani's voice dips lower. "The coup landed on their front door too quickly—" Her voice cracks. Even after over forty years, Yasmiin hears the childlike longing in Amani's words.

Visions of her own parents cloud her mind. She left them behind in Mogadishu and fled to Italy. Parents will forever remain *aabbo* and *hooyo*—father and mother—even when they leave us or we stop talking to them, Yasmiin realizes.

Even though she doesn't know if they are alive or dead, she knows where they lived and how to reach them if they are still there. Only shame prevents her from doing so. The same shame which kept her from sharing her past with Yagiz, fearing his judgment. His rebuke never came. Will her parents understand too? If she finally gathers the courage to reach back home?

"I know you want to know." Amani's words interrupt her thoughts.

"Know what?"

"About him."

"Your husband?" Yasmiin asks. "Or mine?" she adds.

Amani gives her a half-smile. "Well, I met Leif at a charity event many years ago. I was already a divorce lawyer then."

"So you helped him divorce his wife?"

"I was only doing my job," Amani adds. "I didn't expect to fall in love with him. He was much older than I was. Twenty-five years older."

"You stole him from his wife?"

"They were already divorced by the time we became a couple." She lets out a strained laugh. "His children hate me."

"Can you blame them?" Yasmiin counters. Amani shrugs off her words.

"Sometimes you can't help who you fall in love with," Amani says. "You should know."

"And Yagiz?" Yasmiin needs to know. Frankly, she's tired of not being privy to any of his secrets, including the one sitting right in front of her.

"Don't worry, I never fucked him," Amani says. "Though he can be quite persistent and looks like he has stamina." Her eyes roam Yasmiin's generous curves. "Yagiz has been good to me."

"In what way?"

"A divorce lawyer has her ways of getting information for her cases," she says. "He has his ears to the ground and his eyes open."

"Why did you leave your husband?"

She notices Amani wince before taking another sip.

"After the first and last time he called me a *sandapa*," she says, holding Yasmiin's eyes.

Sand monkey.

Yasmiin takes a sharp intake of breath and watches Amani's nostrils flare. The only physical indication of how the slur still sears through her.

"Yagiz and his boys made sure he never spoke again."

When Amani drops those words, Yasmiin freezes as her mind tries to catch up with what Amani is insinuating.

That her husband is for hire.

PART THREE

SEVENTEEN

BRITTANY-RAE

"Cabin crew, ten minutes to landing." The pilot's voice comes across the intercom as the plane banks right over the Thames with views of London Bridge and the Eye. Unusually clear blue skies, but she'll take it. London is offering her glorious respite.

Strapped in the window seat next to her in business class, Maya's fast asleep. Vicky sits in the row behind them. Brittany reaches out a slender hand to stroke her daughter's brown curls, pushing them off her face.

Her beautiful child. The reason she's going to London. She needs answers so she can save her little Maya from a kingdom hellbent on objectifying her.

Brittany leans back into her seat, tugging lightly on her lower lip. She roamed this aisle for years as a flight attendant. She knows every sound of each plane model and the best seats for the best views. She had been excellent at her job.

Until Jonny swept into her life and consumed it so fully. Rather, she let him consume it so completely. Her fingers creep up to her lips again, softly tracing their outline, remembering the taste of his anger. Afterwards, he apologized profusely, assuring her she knew he would never hurt her, right? Right?

Brittany's mind flashes back to when she confronted him and he pinned her angrily against their bedroom wall. He had wanted her to stop saying Maya Daniels's name. The rage which bubbled up from deep within Jonny frightened her. He grabbed onto her jaw, forced a kiss on her, pinned her wrists to the wall. Brittany had been terrified. He continued his fervent kiss, sucking up her breath, swallowing any sound of protest. She hadn't thought him capable of such strength and she had cried against his kiss.

Then he stopped. Almost mechanically. Robotically. As if his mind reset itself and he peered at her in horror.

His sister Antonia had confirmed it when she'd initially told Brittany about his lost Maya last year. As a boy, Jonny often used to crush snails he'd painstakingly spent days gathering, so no one else could have them. Crushed them like they had meant nothing to him. She had felt that emotion in his grip on her.

Now she can't wait to meet the Danielses. What would they say about Jonny and his obsessive relationship with their daughter? Had he been so intense he asphyxiated Maya too? Suffocated her in their own relationship?

She convinced him to go ahead with the garden party without them. To take his mind off things, she allayed his fears. Plus, Eva and his chauffeur Frank were going to take care of them, he need not worry. He invited the usual gang from his office as well as Ragnar, Pia, and their daughter Hedvig. Jonny told her that he had invited Kemi too.

Normally, Brittany would pay for front row tickets to this type of drama. Now she's about to unleash drama even Kemi and Ragnar's trysts can't compare to. Visiting Maya Daniels's parents to forcefully pry apart a wound which had taken them decades to sew up and heal.

She also plans to meet another one of Jonny's exes—the businesswoman who runs a successful health food brand. The one who filed a restraining order against him. Eva had tracked her down and scheduled a meeting under the guise of being a potential investor in her brand.

"Brittany!" Eva squeals the second Brittany and her crew step into the arrivals hall. The petite blonde launches into her arms for a hug before peeling away and squatting to exchange words in

Swedish with Maya. The little girl giggles and tucks her face shyly into Vicky's jeans. When Eva straightens back up, Brittany pulls her in for another hug.

"Thank you," she whispers into her ear. Eva peels out of their embrace and gives her a nod of solidarity. They'll talk later. Right now, Frank needs to shuttle them over to the penthouse and Eva must feed them.

Five days in London. Enough time to dredge up as much as she can. To start building her coalition of witnesses and allies to back up her fight against Jonny once she officially files for divorce. His money runs deep and hushes voices, but if those voices are pained enough, nothing the von Lundin empire can offer would ever be enough.

Every time she steps into that Canary Wharf penthouse, memories flood her. Of innocent times when she was getting to know Jonny and he was learning to explore her like the topography of a map. This had been their hideaway from the world. The two of them. Hours spent talking without words.

The caterers had already laid out lunch for them. Vicky trots off with Maya to shower off their travels. Brittany strolls up to the dining table, reaches for a piece of carrot, and takes a small nibble.

"I've prepared your daily schedule," she hears Eva say behind her. She spins around to find Eva with an open folder. "Vicky and Maya's schedule is fully booked so you can have time to get your answers."

Brittany holds her gaze and nods, the piece of carrot still in hand. It's her quiet *thank you* to the only person within Jonny's circle who has given her an opening.

Eva pulls out a printed sheet. "I have synced it with your digital calendar, but I wanted to go through each item with—"

"Why?"

Eva peers at her with what looks like confusion filling her bright eyes. "What do you mean?" she asks, her voice unsure.

"Why are you helping me?" Brittany holds her gaze, burrowing deep into the other woman. Eva closes her folder and hugs it to her chest. She stares at the floor for a second or two, taking in a deep breath. She glances back up at Brittany. This time, her eyes are behind a film of tears.

"Because you're helping him," Eva says, before twisting her mouth. "I know too much, so *she* won't let me leave." She tries to say a few more words. Her fist flies to her mouth to stop the tears instead.

The open-plan dining area descends into silence as Eva muffles her sobbing. Water pools behind Brittany's own eyes as she watches the woman in front of her unravel in uncharacteristic fashion. Eva who was always so together. Always on point and on schedule. This shedding of face instantly endears her to Brittany.

"Astrid," Brittany finally says on a sharp exhale. *The queen.*

It's obvious Eva cares about Jonny deeply. Maybe a crush even? Brittany wonders. Guilt probably eats through Eva's core, she reckons. The other woman has been complicit in all of it. Planning his trysts, taking care of his women, feeding the dark desire within him.

But Astrid won't let her leave because she knows too much.

"I'm sorry," Eva apologizes through tears, still trying to compose herself. Brittany takes a few steps forward to try to pull her into a hug. Eva holds up a splayed hand to stop her advance.

"It's okay. I'm okay," she says. "I'm just glad you're helping Jonny."

Brittany nods her solidarity through her own tears. "Can you tell me more, Eva?"

"I need to get back to work," Eva says. "Here is your schedule." She pulls out a sheet of paper from her folder.

"Eva, I need you. I've got nothing." Brittany hugs her chest in protection. Eva gazes at her, processing her words. Brittany continues. "Please tell me more about him," she pleads.

Eva glances around her to make sure Vicky hasn't come back in, then she cocks her head to the side, wordlessly asking Brittany to follow her into another room. Jonny's bedroom. With the door shut behind them, Eva sets her folder down and links her fingers nervously.

"What do you want to know?" she asks Brittany, her voice softening, losing its edge.

"All those women," Brittany starts. "What bothered you the most about his relationship with them?" Brittany sees Eva's brain furiously working behind her eyes, trying to pick the least offensive response.

"He only wanted Black and Brown girls," Eva says. "I know it's tied to his past. That Maya Daniels girl you had me investigate."

Brittany purses her lips and motions for Eva to continue.

"I hope you don't take this the wrong way, because I like you." Eva pauses to collect her breath. "But I wondered. Why only dark girls?"

"It's an obsession."

"I know," Eva says. "And I feel so guilty for being a part of it." Her voice grows shaky again. "I helped him find girls too."

"What do you mean?" Brittany needs to hear the words from Eva's mouth. She wants his assistant to fully admit she had fed his proclivity. Instead, Eva hesitates, sensing she's saying more than she should without slinking fully into shame.

"I mean, when he didn't have a girlfriend," Eva says. "We needed to fill in those spaces to keep him entertained."

"So you found escorts like Ebba, right?" Eva's silence is all the confirmation she needs.

Eventually she says, "I know I was wrong, but now I'm trying to make it right. Jonny never cared about any of them. He only used them and they were never enough. He was searching for his past in all these women. I'm tired of it and I want him to stop. I want him to get help—" Her voice breaks again. "It always feels like everything is not enough for him."

"Tell me," Brittany says. "Was he ever aggressive with any of these women? Did he hurt any of them?"

Eva shakes her head, almost too violently. "Jonny never hurt them."

"What about that British lawyer you told me about? The one that moved to Dubai?" Brittany tries jogging her memory. "You said their relationship had been aggressive."

"Ha, yes, Pasha," Eva says. "She was the only one. He never touched her that way, but she was always frustrated with him and his quirks and things got physical. That relationship was different."

"I see."

"Jonny is not a violent man," Eva tries to assure her. It does nothing to allay Brittany's nerves.

"Jonny has been aggressive with me and I'm afraid of what he'll do when I finally file for divorce." Brittany's hand moves to her chest. She glides over to his bed. She knows every surface area of that bed. Its dips, curves, and resistance. He has dutifully claimed her across each inch of it. She turns her back to the sturdy frame.

"I have nothing to my name, Eva. Nothing," Brittany says. "When we go to court, I'll leave with nothing." She begins to sob, unable to control herself. "I gave him everything. Gave up everything for him." Eva observes Brittany and lets her cry those tears.

"I can help you," she finally offers.

Brittany stares at her through hooded eyes. "How?"

"I can get some legal documents drafted. Some documents that Jonny *will* sign. You're his wife. Some assets need to be in your name as well."

"Eva?" Brittany is stunned. "You could get into trouble for this. It sounds serious."

"I have my ways," Eva says, a sly smile spreading across her face. "I will help you."

"But…"

The sound of little feet pattering across the shiny floors toward Jonny's room breaks up their conversation. Brittany glances at Eva once more, expressing the depth of her gratitude through that gaze.

* * *

The next day, Brittany sets off on her first mission in London.

How do people drink this? Brittany ponders as she stirs the dark sludge of a smoothie Ruth, the health food entrepreneur, gave her. While Brittany loves picking at salad leaves, this is a stretch even for her—the vegan smoothie of weeds, bananas, and some sort of green powder.

Ruth takes a swig of her own raw smoothie, wipes her lips delicately, and looks at Brittany. They are sitting at a small sidestreet café in Shoreditch, buzzing street noise providing the backdrop to the eclectic district.

Brittany studies the woman in front of her. Caribbean roots, Grenada is what Eva had shared. Spotlessly smooth dark skin infused with natural antioxidants which, no doubt, will guarantee her youthfulness well into her later age. Toned, well-defined arms. A woman who clearly loves Pilates and yoga. Ruth takes a bite of a raw vegan chocolate ball and smiles at Brittany as she chews. A snack Brittany had declined politely. Ruth's natural hair looks blown out, falling past her shoulders. Beyond her narrow face and heavy eyelashes, she looks nothing like Brittany.

"I've heard a lot about your brand," Brittany starts. "You're doing great work."

"Thank you." Ruth beams. "We've just opened up our third café, including this one."

Brittany looks around once more before settling back on Ruth. "And investors?"

"Still two angels. Even after years of solid revenue, we're still having a hard time securing a venture capitalist to help us scale up. You know the stats already," Ruth says. Brittany shrugs. No, she doesn't know the stats. "Less than one percent of VC money goes to women of color. Less than one percent. What kind of laughable statistics are those?!" Ruth laughs. Brittany notes the strain in that laugh.

She shifts uncomfortably. How is she going to organically segue into asking Ruth about her past? About Jonny and what had caused her to file a restraining order against him?

"Well, hopefully Johnson Ventures might be a potential home for you." Brittany's voice snags at her lie. She's now swimming beyond her depth. "We have raised a hundred million euro fund to invest in pre-seed and seed stage startups." Brittany had rehearsed her line under Eva's coaching. She sees Ruth's eyes light up at the news. Clearly a woman done trying to prove the worth of her business, even though it's successful and seems to be thriving.

"We've been trying to raise a seed stage fund for the last two years. Still no luck," Ruth says. "Did you have time to review our pitch deck? Do you have any questions? I googled Johnson Ventures, by the way, and found a few with the same name."

"We're a newly founded VC so you won't find much, but I do have some questions for you." Brittany stops stirring her smoothie. She notices Ruth adjust herself, and square her shoulders, ready to impress the potential investor.

Brittany presses on. "One of our largest investors in the fund has a few questions regarding your business and its potential market size." Brittany finds her opening.

"Okay, sure."

"Von Lundin Enterprises is interested in investing if we lead your round, but they have some questions about—"

"No," Ruth says firmly. She sits taller and peers at Brittany, wordlessly questioning her.

"No?" Brittany asks. "Have you ever heard of von Lundin Enterprises?"

"Sorry to waste your time, but I'm not interested." She begins to pack up her bag, ready to flee. The mere mention of von Lundin, and this petrified woman is running. Brittany isn't sure she's ready to face what she'll find under the stones she's turning over.

"Do you have a history with our investor? With von Lundin?" Brittany's voice is unsure. Ruth regards her intensely. She gets to her feet. Brittany is on hers as well. They stare at each other in silence for what feels like an eternity until Ruth breaks it.

"Did Jonny send you?" Ruth asks.

"Jonny? Do you mean Mr. von Lundin? Johan?" Brittany feigns ignorance.

"Did Jonny send you?" Ruth repeats firmly this time. When Brittany has no words for her, Ruth continues. "Stay the fuck away from me, whoever you are."

Then she pulls her bag tighter and storms off, leaving Brittany staring after her.

KEMI

Her instinct urged her to rescind her RSVP to Jonny's garden party.

Her ego told her to go instead. To fall back into normalcy as if nothing was amiss and her life wasn't about to be upended.

When Saturday rolls around, a feeling of unease settles within Kemi. She wishes she had declined the invitation. Watching Tobias's excitement all week about attending a fancy garden party fills her with guilt.

"Babe, the dress code said casual."

Kemi sits on their bed watching Tobias primp and prep for Jonny's party. He puts on a baby-blue dress shirt over trousers. Kemi, on the other hand, wears a floral tunic which accentuates her cleavage and a bohemian skirt. Dangling earrings match her chosen hippie look for the party.

"I know. But I also want to make a good impression." He reaches for a small chest and opens it. Kemi swallows when he pulls out Ragnar's platinum cufflinks.

"Really? Do you need those?"

"I never get an opportunity to dress up. Why not just for once?" he says, fastening the second one to his cuff. "There. How do I look?"

Soon they hurtle north up E4 toward the tunnel taking them to the island of Lidingö with Tobias behind the wheel. When they pull up to Jonny's villa in Elfvik, it's to a line of Porsches, Range

Rovers, Teslas, and one silver Aston Martin glistening under the spring sun. Tobias turns to Kemi with raised eyebrows.

"No *lagom* here, that's for sure," he says. "Now *you* look underdressed."

He squeezes her modest Toyota hybrid in between a Tesla and a black Porsche SUV she recognizes. She takes a deep breath. Of course, he's going to be there as Jonny's best friend. What was she thinking?

Over one of their lunch dates, Ingrid had informed her Ragnar had returned from Nepal, though he no longer planned on coming back as a consultant to work on their project. Kemi had simply asked Ingrid why she felt the need to tell her all that irrelevant information.

She clasps Tobias's hand tightly as she navigates the smooth grounds in wedge heels. Music, brass music it sounds like, emanates from the wide yard where two white canopies have been set up. A large one for the single long community-style table for all the guests and a small one spread over a live band playing brass instruments. She scans the guests milling around with glasses of champagne in various casual yet deceptively expensive outfits.

A small girl with dark-brown hair chases a balloon, catching then releasing it for the light spring breeze to lift it and play with her. The girl catches the balloon and rushes off to a blonde woman sitting at the table, then leaves her once more.

Pia.

Kemi pauses in her tracks, frozen, as she stares at the petite blonde. As if sensing eyes on her, Pia turns her way. For a moment, both women gaze at each other. Kemi fears the rumors have reached her because Pia's eyes speak volumes. Kemi loosens her grip from Tobias and steps forward to Pia, who reels her in with a blank stare.

"Pia, it's good to see you."

Pia nods.

"I'm so sorry," Kemi starts to say. "For your loss."

"Thank you," she says. "I appreciate it. It's good to see you too.

It's been awhile." Her gaze washes over Tobias. "We've met before, haven't we? At Jonny's house?" she says in Swedish.

"Yes." Tobias smiles before reaching to shake her hand to reintroduce himself. "*Trevligt att träffas igen.*"

At that moment, the little girl runs back up to her mother with the balloon in hand. Pia lifts her onto her lap, pulling her close.

"And this is Hedvig," she says. "Say hello to these nice people." Hedvig peers at both Kemi and Tobias from a slightly bent head and upcast eyes.

"Nice to meet you, little lady," Tobias says, leaning forward toward her. Hedvig backs into her mother's chest away from him. Kemi recognizes that look. She has been on that look's receiving end many times while riding the subway around town. From both children and elderly people.

"So"—Tobias straightens back up and away—"where's your husband?" He makes an exaggerated show of looking around.

Pia wordlessly looks past Tobias and nods in a direction. Kemi follows her gaze, turning around.

There's Ragnar, standing right behind them all along, unsmiling. His lush dark hair is back to its normal length, his jaw clean shaven, revealing its cleft.

And those dark-blue eyes suck her in with the force of a raging sea.

Tobias and Ragnar shake hands. Kemi can't touch him. She simply greets him with a brief wave, then excuses herself to go find a toilet.

Once inside the villa, Kemi spots a door ajar and gently pushes it. It opens into a study sparsely furnished in grays with nothing out of place. A shelf with books arranged by color. A simple desk with an elegant, expensive-looking chair parked beneath it. A chaise longue in one corner. And the wall, covered with lots of photos of Brittany.

Sure, there are a handful of their toddler Maya too, but it is Brittany's narrow face that graces that study. She reaches for a framed photo sitting on his desk. A black and white selfie of Brittany and Jonny taken in bed.

The soft clicking of the door shutting startles her. She almost drops the frame which she now cradles with care in her hands.

"Are you lost?"

That deep baritone she has avoided for weeks. Her stomach starts to churn as heat rushes through her.

"Are you stalking me now?" She attempts humor. Ragnar remains unsmiling. He simply regards her intensely. She turns back to the photograph in her hands, heart pounding. "Well, someone clearly loves his wife." She laughs nervously, lifting the frame up in mock show before setting it down again.

"Why are you here?" Ragnar asks firmly.

She frowns at his interrogation. "Why are you following me?" she counters. There is a charged silence in the room as they drink each other in.

"Because you've been avoiding me." His words come low, delivered softly.

She swallows, dragging in air. "You know why." Her eyes leave him and keep roaming over Jonny's shrine to Brittany. Ragnar digs both hands into his pockets and rocks on his heels.

"We need to talk," he says.

"There's nothing to talk about." Kemi reaches for another photo—Brittany lounging every bit like the model on their yacht. Jonny's yacht.

How is she going to broach the subject with him? That the child she carries must never be his in this lifetime?

Ragnar casually strolls toward her, hands in pockets. He sits on the edge of the desk, as she busies herself in pretense. He observes her quietly while she scans the photos, clearly aware of his gaze scorching her. Kemi shuts her eyes, absorbing his presence.

She blows out air and opens her eyes before studying the photos as her distraction once more.

"Have you told him?" Ragnar asks, finally cracking the fragile silence. Those words are enough to halt and swivel her toward him, brows knotted. "About us?"

"Are you insane?" Anger brews deep within her. "There's no us! He has your cufflinks on his wrists right now."

Ragnar, no doubt, deduces what she had to do and he smirks. One that doesn't reach his eyes, which warm as they take her in. Is he jealous of Tobias? His sneer turns into a pained laugh, revealing teeth. Kemi watches that wide grin spread across his face, making him more handsome. She realizes she has never seen him laugh out loud this way before. Her eyes are still on his lips when they morph back into an austere line, matching harsh eyes.

"So you fucked him?" he asks, his expression turning serious. "That night. After me?" Ragnar continues, his voice terse, eyes hard.

"Don't be absurd." Kemi resists the urge to call him a bastard.

"Did you?" He's adamant. Unrelenting. His ego clearly hovering on the edge of their affair, insecure because of her man. Kemi bites her lower lip to restrain her anger. She has no one else to blame for succumbing so desperately to Ragnar. Now he's here, his eyes churning, clearly provoking her out of jealousy.

"You were nothing special," she says, shoving his ego off the ledge.

She sees his eyebrows dip inwards into that signature frown as he glares at her through bruised pride. It seems that, even after their torrid business trip and making love three times in an hour at her apartment, the thought that he still hadn't been enough for her grates him more than she anticipates.

He gets off the desk, stretching to his full height, his hands leaving his pockets.

"You're lying," he whispers, his eyes searching her face as he moves closer.

"Don't flatter yourself," she says, hushed, inching backward. The wall stops her.

Kemi can't tell him the truth. That she has craved him every night since then. How guilt eats through her whenever she looks into Tobias's eyes or lets him touch her. How Ragnar is a virus ravaging her alive, destroying everything she ever wanted and now has with Tobias.

That a tiny part of him may have taken root inside her. She can't take it anymore.

"You wanted it too," he says, standing inches from her face. "I can't stop thinking about that night." His voice dips low. She knows he means London. His fingers move to the edge of her floral tunic, tugging at it playfully. Kemi feels her breath catch as Ragnar sucks up the air between them, his fingers toying with the fabric. Fighting him off with words seems pointless because her body keeps betraying her. She makes a last guilt-inducing effort by conjuring up his wife.

"Do you think so little of *her*?" she mutters quietly to him against her own heaving chest, summoning his wife to kill his advance. "Hmm, Ragnar? Do you?"

The irony of her words sends blood rushing to her head. He answers her with a heady kiss instead, his fingers crawling beneath her tunic, trailing her skin. She tastes alcohol on his breath, the fuel pulling him out of character. The thrill of being caught must be coursing through him. Because the sober Ragnar she knows would never do something as audacious as paw her in Jonny's study at his party.

What about the Kemi she knows?

She moans against his lips when his fingers reach her lace bra. She pulls back and shakes her head.

"Ragnar." His name lands light as a feather on her lips. "We can't." He kisses her with renewed vigor.

"*Jag borde inte vilja ha dig, men jag vill*," he murmurs against her mouth. *I'm not supposed to want you, but I do.*

His right hand works its way under her skirt, pulling the hem up along with it as he kisses her collarbone. She threads all her fingers through his thick mane, crushing him closer to her. He rises to cover her mouth with his once more, drowning out every sound when his roving hand moves between her thighs. She tenses at his touch, self-conscious. He kisses her hard, pressing her against the wall with his powerful form, his fingers teasing her.

"You like that, *hmm*?" he asks in a whisper. "Do you?" He increases the pressure. "Tell me."

She relaxes, letting his fingers in, moving against them. "*Jag borde inte vilja ha dig*," Kemi says breathlessly. "*Men jag vill.*"

She repeats his words to him. He laughs against her lips before claiming them once more. She feared this. That once she finds herself in his arms again, she'll continue to crave him in ways terrifying to her. This power play between them.

Who's the polar opposite of a white man with power in society?

A strong Black woman standing in her power.

Malcolm's words float into her mind as Ragnar's movements grow rougher against her.

That man wants to conquer you. To show you he's more powerful than you could ever be.

Don't let him anywhere near you.

She feels herself shuddering against his palm. His mouth covers hers once more to drown out her cries. Outside, the sound of brass instruments floats in through closed windows, enveloping them as they explore each other recklessly against the study wall.

"*Pappa?*"

Like lightning, the word delivered in a high-pitched juvenile voice jolts them apart. Kemi swiftly readjusts her skirt while Ragnar runs his fingers through his hair to settle the strands back in place. Kemi turns to its source. Hanging onto the doorknob as quietly as she had opened it is Ragnar's five-year-old daughter, Hedvig.

"*Jösses, Hedvig!*" Ragnar curses under his breath before wiping his mouth with one hard stroke of his hand as if trying to rid himself of Kemi's scent, gauging how much of her is still on his fingers.

"*Pappa? Vad gör du?*" She peers up at them through eyes matching Ragnar's. *Daddy? What are you doing?*

Kemi covers her mouth with the back of her palm, unable to look at the child.

"*Ingenting, gumman,*" Ragnar says breathlessly. *Nothing, sweetheart.*

He takes a few steps toward her but the girl spins and bolts out the door. Kemi hears him curse some more as he takes off in hot pursuit after her.

Kemi leans back against the wall with both hands on her head. *Don't panic, don't panic.* Tears well up but she fights them. She doesn't recognize herself anymore. This self-destruction she has slunk into with ease. Is this why she struggled to find a good man in DC? Did she sabotage solid prospects, pulling out their seedlings before they developed roots?

Once Monday rolls around, she'll find a therapist to shake off her primal attraction to Ragnar and regain her sanity before they selfishly destroy more lives. Right now, she needs to make sure she isn't carrying one more weight on her chest. The possibility of his love child.

Kemi hides in the study for a few more minutes to collect herself before leaving the main house to rejoin the lavish garden party. The brass band switches to playing Swedish folk songs.

The moment she steps outside, Hedvig's shrill voice breaks out again, cutting through the music and mindless banter between guests. This time, it's accompanied by the little girl's index finger. Hedvig is sitting on her mother Pia's lap. Ragnar is perched right next to his wife and kid. He appears to be in deep conversation with Pia about something serious because his wife's demeanor looks guarded.

"*Där är hon!*" Hedvig screams at the top of her lungs as she points at Kemi. "*Den svartingen som Pappa pussade!*"

There she is! The nigger Daddy was kissing!

The band falters to a stop, conversations drop, and the whole party dies into palpable silence at the little girl's slur.

"Hedvig!" Ragnar's deep voice reprimands his daughter. He turns to glare at Kemi, eyebrows arched, terror in his eyes. "Oh my God, I'm so sorry."

Kemi stands frozen. Her eyes move over the table where Jonny, his sisters Antonia and Svea, and their partners sit with varying degrees of red rushing up their cheeks. They remain quiet. When her eyes settle on Pia, it's on a woman clearly in pain, tears pooling in her eyes. Kemi averts her gaze to look at Tobias, who seems to be in a two-fold state of shock. The possibility he might have been dining with racists all along and, more devastating, that Kemi might have been cheating on him with one of said racists must be impossible for him to process in that instant, Kemi realizes.

"I don't know where Hedvig picked up such a word," Ragnar says, getting to his feet, apologizing. "We're not like that."

Pia's hard gaze tells her otherwise.

"Is it true?" Pia asks through tightly clenched teeth, a sneer wrinkling her nose. The disgust Kemi reads on Pia's face feels multilayered.

Kemi glares back at Pia with conflicting emotions coursing through her. Shame that Hedvig caught them. Fear she's about to lose everything. Guilt she has now caused Pia so much irreversible pain. Disappointment in herself for going this far. And anger that Pia, in all her skinny blonde and blue-eyed glory, assumed Ragnar could never desire someone like her. Never mind that he's her husband.

"Pia!" Ragnar turns to his wife, trying to calm her in Swedish, trying to explain away Hedvig being only five years old and prone to fantasy. Kemi feels warm. A burning sensation spreads through her. She must flee. Tobias seems paralyzed and, in that moment, she despises him for not saying anything, for staying quiet, for not reacting like she expects him to. Her betrayal far from her mind in that moment. Does he not realize he's also Black?

"Excuse me," she says weakly to the group as she grabs her purse, and turns to flee as quickly as wedge heels on perfectly manicured grass will allow. She tries to get away as fast as she can, tears now streaming down her face. Men like Ragnar never chased after the likes of her. Especially not when sitting next to their wives. Ones who society places on pedestals. He would never come after her. They had gone into this affair as equals.

Now she's leaving, relegated to the disgraced Black mistress. It's over and spectacularly so. She needs to piece her shattered self back together.

And Tobias. *Oh, her Tobias.* She doesn't know how she'll ever face him. But she hears him rushing after her. She dares not turn back.

She races across Jonny's driveway flanked by immaculately landscaped trees. She runs all the way out of view of the grand villa, toward the small guest parking area brimming with its Porsches, Range Rovers, Teslas, and that one damn Aston Martin. She sights her car. A strong arm grabs her, halting and pulling her into a crushing embrace.

"God, I'm so sorry," he murmurs against her neck, his lips lightly brushing her skin, lingering. That heady forest scent shocks her. She was expecting Tobias. Ragnar's grip tightens around her instead. She tries pulling out of his embrace. Ragnar's stronger. He grabs her once more.

"I'm pregnant."

The words instantly release her from his clutch. Ragnar stares down at her, irises now pinheads of fear. His lips move. No words come. His mouth hangs open, eyes pinning hers in fright—raw, exposed, unprotected.

"I need to know it's not yours," she whispers. "I need to know this isn't real."

"I swear to you, Kemi. I swear, I'm not—" He never finishes. Tobias reaches them and yanks Ragnar away from where he stands in front of her. He thuds Ragnar's chest with both hands angrily, pushing him backward.

"Stay away from her!" Tobias yells at him in Swedish, his eyebrows furrowed in rage. Ragnar runs his fingers through his dark hair, his own eyes burning with resentment.

"Let's go, Tobbe." Kemi grabs her boyfriend's arms, trying to push him along. Ragnar turns to look at her once more as she hides behind Tobias.

"I'm so sorry—" he starts to say. Tobias cuts him off in Swedish.

"I saw your eyes on her today," Tobias shouts. "You just can't stop, can you?"

Ragnar peers back at him, his face in its perpetual frown.

"Let's go," Kemi pleads. She needs to get them out of there before Ragnar's ego comes out to play.

Tobias isn't done. "You think you can have it all, don't you?" Tobias provokes him, his eyes burrowing into Ragnar. She sees Ragnar's nostrils flare, his eyes darkening more. "Hmm? You piece of shit!"

"Who says I haven't?"

Ragnar's words cut through their tension, suffocating her and stabbing Tobias right in the heart. Tobias yanks himself out of her grip and charges at Ragnar. She manages to pull him back with all her strength, crying. She wedges herself between both men and wraps her arms around her boyfriend's neck, burying her nose into his chest.

"Please," she cries against Tobias. "Please, let's go home." She feels him nod, then she turns to look at Ragnar. She sees his eyes soften as he takes her in. Ragnar swallows, his Adam's apple jumping with the movement, his chest heaving beneath the navy-blue polo shirt he's wearing. His look is one of loss and shock replacing jealousy.

Ragnar had come after her. He had waved aside what his clique thought and chased after her across that driveway in front of everyone. Kemi mulls this over as she stares at him. He belongs to someone else. Yet, she may be carrying his child. Her heart can't reconcile his daughter using a racial slur against her minutes after he kissed her so passionately and touched her so provocatively in Jonny's unlocked study. Hedvig had given her a true glimpse into what they said behind closed doors.

That public exchange leaves her feeling filthy, sordid, and used. It dredges up centuries of painful dynamics between his kind and hers. Ragnar had seen what he wanted, felt entitled to it, and simply taken it. He had done exactly what Malcolm knew he would.

Above all, she's most disgusted at herself for letting him take her so freely. That verdict tears her deeply. She feels her heart thudding as more tears come, flooding her face. Memories of him weeping helplessly against her chest in grief between lovemaking fill her mind. That's the Ragnar she'll keep close to her heart. The vulnerable one who had laid himself completely bare for her to see.

"Stay away from me," Kemi says bitterly to her lover.

YASMIIN

Yasmiin can't scale those weathered steps fast enough. She takes them two-by-two, her heart pounding against her ribcage, mouth hanging open. The phone call from Karolinska Hospital over a week ago plays on repeat in her head.

"*Yasmiin Çelik? Det är dags.*" *It is time.*

Time to wake Muna up from her medically induced coma. She had immediately called Mattias, who picked up on the first ring.

"*Det är dags, Mattias,*" Yasmiin cried into it. "*Det är dags! Alhamdulillah!*" *Praise be to Allah.*

Now the older man gets to his feet upon her approach. She flies into his arms, overwhelmed, tears pushing their way out. As if her emotions have reset themselves, she quickly pulls back out of their embrace, remembering what he represents. The pain of that touch.

"Great to see you too." He laughs, returning her initial hug, pulling her back in. "Thank you for inviting me to be here." He loosens his grip when he feels her tense up.

Yasmiin nods, accepting his gratitude. "They woke her a few days ago but she is still very weak. Now, they think she can take visitors for a very short time."

"Such wonderful news." Mattias beams. "I also have some news for you regarding Ahmed and what happened to his village. Do we have a few minutes for *fika* before we go in?"

Five minutes later, they cradle paper cups from the kiosk in the waiting area. She sits close to him, encouraging him to continue in a lower voice.

"His entire village was razed by rebels. Burnt to the ground." Mattias takes a sip. This information Yasmiin had already deduced, but hearing those words confirmed and spoken out loud doesn't make it easier to digest. "We have been able to locate an older brother, Afran, who was granted asylum in Canada. Toronto. The rest of the immediate family is gone."

Yasmiin places a hand on her chest, absorbing the details. "And the passport photos?"

"His final selfless act," Mattias says. "We have started tracking down their own family members." He swallows. "Ahmed cut all those passport photos out of their Syrian national identification cards. Ahmed wanted to make a point. They were all Kurds."

"I see why Muna's heart beats for him," Yasmiin says after a few seconds of silence.

Mattias nods. "Yeah, I told his brother Afran about Muna. That she was the one who led us to him by protecting Ahmed's memories." He pauses for another swig of coffee. "He wants to meet her in person. He wants to fly over to Stockholm to meet her as soon as she's strong enough."

Yasmiin lowers her head, her chest heaving with tears. She recognizes that sweet taste of release, of peace. She'd felt it when she shared her past with Yagiz. She'd recognized Amani's own release when she did her makeup and zipped her into her gown for the Red Cross gala, shoulders held high in pride.

Muna's awake and Yasmiin will finally see her. Mattias will grant her some peace once she starts asking questions.

Yasmiin fiddles with her fingers, wiping away the tears that land on them. When she glances up, she finds Mattias studying her intently, his eyebrows arched upwards.

"Thank you," he says, adjusting his glasses.

"For what?"

"For trusting me," Mattias shares. She sees his own eyes begin to submerge behind tears. "I can't imagine what he must have gone through to get here, knowing everyone he ever had was gone. His neighbors, all lost too."

Yasmiin presses her lips tightly and nods back at him. *No, Mattias*, she wants to say. *You have no idea*. What it took for her to open up herself to him. To let him close enough to engage.

"Here"—he shifts in his seat as he reaches for his phone—"here is Afran's number." He taps and scrolls to pull it up. "Afran Tofiq Rahim. I wouldn't normally do this, but Muna is special. This case is special, and if this is her only connection to Ahmed, she needs it."

Yasmiin's phone pings when the contact card Mattias has just shared comes through.

Muna drinks from a straw in a cup propped by a nurse when Yasmiin and Mattias step into her room. She looks frailer awake. Her lips are dry and cracked, her skin pale and ashy. Yasmiin grows irritated. During her weekly visits, she often lathered Muna's arms, face, and lips with lotion to keep her skin supple. Never mind that the hospital was keeping her alive, her skin needed moisturizing love too in between Yasmiin's visits.

"You have visitors," the nurse says in a tempered voice to Muna, following her words with a smile.

Muna glances toward the door. Her brows begin crumbling into each other as recognition washes over her, her eyes drawing Yasmiin closer.

"Muna *gacaliye*," Yasmiin says softly. *Dear Muna*.

The younger woman's face keeps contorting, trying to piece together what's happening. She opens her mouth to say something. A hoarse sound makes its way out instead as if her throat's been perpetually parched. She makes that dry sound again, Yasmiin's name on the tip of her tongue.

"Yes, it's me," Yasmiin says. "I'm here." She turns to look at Mattias waiting by the open door. "You remember Mattias?"

She watches Muna gently turn her head toward the door. Muna follows up with a half-smile and slow nod, her eyes filling with tears.

"You can come sit next to her," the nurse offers, getting to her feet and handing the cup to Yasmiin instead. "Here, you take this."

She smiles. Yasmiin grabs the cup and straw, and positions herself in the nurse's vacated chair. "Please don't ask any questions. Just let her know you're here for her," she coaches Yasmiin and Mattias before padding out of the room.

Muna's eyes follow Yasmiin all the way as she settles herself until her head perches sideways on her pillow, peering as if in shock. Yasmiin studies her face. Bruises along her left side, but her features are still intact. The doctor plans on briefing them after their visit with her. About her long-term journey toward healing herself and her heart.

Yasmiin reaches to gently stroke her face. She and Mattias had washed and sanitized their hands before coming in.

"Muna," Yasmiin calls out again. "It's so good to see you. *Alhamdulillah*."

"Yasmiin," the word pushes its way out. Yasmiin watches her struggle. "Yasmiin."

"I'm here," she whispers back. "I've always been here. Every week. You don't have to worry."

Muna presses her lips together as tears stream down her face. She gives Yasmiin a slight nod in response. "I know," she says weakly. "I heard you. Your voice."

Yasmiin looks at her, puzzled. "You heard me?"

Muna's smile is weak but Yasmiin sees it anyway. "Yes," she whispers.

Then she turns toward the door where Mattias stands, hands in pockets.

"Mattias?" Muna calls out softly. He moves closer to the women.

"*Hej*, Muna," he greets her, stepping closer to the bed and gently laying a hand on her wrist. "You look well."

She chuckles a low sound, and shakes her head. Her chuckle dies into a stern line as she keeps shaking her head.

"It's true, Muna," Yasmiin consoles her. "You look well. You look wonderful and we're here. Take some water." Yasmiin pushes the straw toward her. Muna banks her head away. "Take, you must drink."

"Sorry," Muna says. "So sorry."

Yasmiin shushes her. "Don't say that."

"Sorry," Muna continues. "Jump. Sorry."

Yasmiin quiets her down once more. "No, Muna. You have nothing to say sorry for. We're here. You're home now." Muna descends into quiet sobbing. Yasmiin holds her hand.

A bespectacled doctor, a man who looks to be in his late fifties with fluffy white hair, floats into the room, a clipboard in hand. His gaze travels from Mattias over to the two women and back, probably trying to work out their association, Yasmiin expects.

"I'm Bengt and I'll be Muna's doctor from now." He adjusts his glasses before stretching a hand toward Mattias, speaking in Swedish. Mattias shakes it, then points to Yasmiin.

"She's next of kin. You should be talking to her," Mattias tells him. Yasmiin simply glares at the doctor for his assumptions.

The doctor clears his throat while moving closer to Yasmiin.

"And what's your name?" he asks her in English. She eyes him before introducing herself and saying in fluent Swedish she's Muna's friend and guardian.

He continues, switching to Swedish. "She is recovering remarkably well. I think she has youth on her side."

Yasmiin listens, her eyes trained on him. He presses on. "We will keep her for one more month before we can let her go."

"No rehabilitation center? The last doctor told me they would transfer her there," Yasmiin questions.

"Yes, I understand. That was before we fully understood the extent of her injuries. I'm afraid she may not be able to fully walk again without assistance."

Yasmiin's hand flies to her chest. "Don't say that." Her voice dips into a whisper. "She's lying right here." She turns to look at Muna. The younger woman lets out small whimpers, clearly hearing their conversation.

She turns back to the doctor.

"Please," Yasmiin starts. "Can we just celebrate that she is breathing right now?"

EIGHTEEN

BRITTANY-RAE

She shouldn't have come. Brittany is sure of it.

She stands nervously, her fingers fidgeting by her side. A little past ten in the morning, she finds herself in front of a modest terraced house in Brixton, south London. Home to a sizable chunk of Jamaican Brits. She isn't sure what she'd been expecting when Frank, their chauffeur, dropped her off in front of the house with a low fence framing a pint-sized vegetable garden.

After ringing the doorbell, she instantly regrets her decision. She turns to flee back toward the car when the door creaks open. Brittany takes a deep breath before swiveling around.

Lucinda Daniels. Maya Daniels's mother. Despite sporting long gray dreadlocks and taut dark skin which belies her true age, the mother-daughter resemblance is uncanny.

Once Lucinda adjusts her thick glasses and takes a long look at the woman on her doorstep, her mouth drops open, trying to process the apparition standing in front of her. "It can't be—" Her voice starts to break.

Brittany jumps in. "No, I'm not Maya." Brittany's voice is low, soft. "I'm not her."

"Is this some kind of joke?" Lucinda's heavily accented English sails through. Jamaican roots just like Brittany.

"I'm so sorry to disturb you, Mrs. Daniels," Brittany starts to say. "I am so sorry for your loss." She shouldn't have come here.

"Who are you?" the older woman asks, her tone stretching out those words in suspicion.

"Umm, Brittany," she introduces herself. "Brittany, umm, Brittany von Lundin."

Uncomfortable silence spreads between them at the mention of von Lundin before Lucinda steps backwards.

"Excuse me," she says as she starts shutting her front door. Brittany wedges herself in between it and the doorjamb, surprising herself with her desperation.

"Please." Brittany begins to cry, her tears shaking her. "Please, Mrs. Daniels. Please."

Lucinda observes Brittany clutching her chest and sobbing unabashedly. She lets Brittany cry, watching her unravel at her front door. Brittany didn't anticipate this breakdown, one tearing her wide open in front of the dead woman's mother.

"I'm sorry," Brittany apologizes between sniffs. "I'm so sorry. I'm just, I'm just so tired of not knowing," she cries. "But I have no right to come here and dig up your pain."

Lucinda studies her quietly a few more moments before letting her into her home.

Her living room is low-lit and stuffy. Camel-colored faux leather sofas frame a mahogany coffee table. The light-yellow walls are covered in framed photographs of the Danielses with Maya. Lots of photographs of their daughter, as if she's still alive and breathing. Brittany studies the photos, arms crossed, her gaze squarely focused on Maya.

God, they look like they could have been sisters. Twins even.

"You have a beautiful family," Brittany says as Lucinda comes bearing a square tray with black English tea and a stack of digestive biscuits. Lucinda winces at the back of her throat before setting the tray on the coffee table.

"Please, help yourself," she offers as she pours herself black tea into a white porcelain teacup painted with green vines. Brittany rounds the sofa and positions herself opposite Lucinda before helping herself.

They chat for a bit, then drink in silence, with Brittany feeling more and more uneasy as the seconds tick by.

"So, you have a baby girl now, right?" Lucinda ends her misery. "How old is she?"

"She's soon turning two," Brittany replies. She digs into her purse for her phone, taps and swipes until she lands on her favorite shot of Maya. She passes the phone over.

Lucinda smiles in appreciation as she takes in Maya's photo. "Such a beautiful child. What's her name?"

Brittany freezes. She can't do it. Can't do that to Lucinda.

"Whitney," Brittany drops. "Whitney. Her name is Whitney." She repeats it multiple times as if trying to convince herself.

"Such a beautiful name," Lucinda compliments. Brittany nods before taking another sip. "So, how can I help you?"

"I'm so sorry for your loss. I swear to you, I didn't come to dredge up your past to make you sad," Brittany starts. "I'm...It's because I'm trying to leave him."

Lucinda stops mid-sip and sets her teacup back down. "Leaving him?"

Brittany nods, tears filling her eyes once more. "I've asked for a divorce."

"I see," Lucinda says.

"Please, Lucinda, I need to know more. I need to know more about Jonny and Maya. About what happened. His family is keeping me in the dark. They aren't answering my questions. I need to know just how dangerous he is," Brittany pours out in a single breath.

"I see Johan has possessed you too," Lucinda says calmly, locking eyes with Brittany.

"What-what do you mean?" Brittany cries, her voice brittle.

"Johan consumed my daughter. My Maya—" Lucinda's voice falters. "Except she no longer wanted him and he wouldn't let her go. Couldn't let her go. She had been trying to rid herself of him for months. He just wouldn't go away."

Brittany leans back into the sofa, absorbing Lucinda's words.

This glimpse into his past, she grabs onto tightly. She needs to know more about the stranger whose child she has borne.

Lucinda continues. "Maya called him Jonny. Up until then, Johan was just Johan. He told her names ending in 'y' like Jonny, Conny, Tommy were associated with blue-collar workers in Sweden." Lucinda chuckles at the absurdity. "So Maya started calling him Jonny in jest." She pauses. "His family didn't like that nickname. *Jonny.* That boy was convinced she was his soulmate." Lucinda finishes with a pained laugh as memories flood her mind. "Those dead eyes. Like he was staring straight through your soul."

Brittany swallows at her remarks. "I'm so sorry about what happened to Maya," she says.

"They stopped searching for her," Lucinda continues. "The police stopped searching for my baby." Silence envelops them.

"Searching?" Brittany asks, puzzled. "His mother told me about the abortion. That she hadn't survived."

She catches Lucinda's frown, her eyebrows dipping sharply inward in confusion.

"What abortion?" Lucinda asks, her tone one of surprise coupled with shock. "What abortion?" she repeats.

"His-his family told me Maya had died due to complications from her abortion," Brittany says, her voice unsure.

"Brittany," Lucinda starts, her voice hard and serious, "Maya wasn't pregnant. She went out one evening with Johan." She pauses to collect her breath. "She never came back."

KEMI

The drive from Lidingö to Nacka is the longest of her life. She leans her elbow against the window, biting at her fingernails, crying. Tobias doesn't say a word as he drives them home.

She can't look at him. The charged air in her car tells her all she needs to know.

They walk into the apartment silently. Tobias places her car keys on the shelf in the hallway. Kemi moves toward the living room, her arms wrapped around her chest, still crying. She turns around when she no longer hears his footsteps.

Tobias stands rooted by the front door, taking deep breaths, his mouth slightly open. She sees his eyebrows contorting and she hates herself for causing him pain. She knows he's fighting back those tears, using every ounce of his strength to remain calm.

"Tobbe," Kemi calls his name softly. "I'm so sorry." He glares at her, those warm brown eyes filming with tears. He purses his lips before gathering his words.

"I didn't want to believe it," Tobias says. "I didn't."

Kemi remains silent, locking eyes with him, praying he'll say something. Anything. Because his silence will break her. He glances at his wrists and laughs wryly. Then he unhooks both cufflinks in measured fashion, and cradles them in his right palm.

"These are his, aren't they?"

Kemi takes deep breaths before nodding. Yes, they're Ragnar's. At her nod, Tobias lets out a heavy gasp of despair before shaking his head, holding back the tears now pooling faster than he can stop them.

He gently sets them next to her car keys.

"I'm so sorry," Kemi cries. "I wasn't thinking. I wasn't thinking."

"How long?"

"I swear, it wasn't—"

"How long?"

Kemi swallows between sobs. She never imagined her perfectly tailored relationship with Tobias, carefully crafted for her, would be ripped to shreds by her own hands. The pain in his face as he looks at her. His sorrow is one she'll never forget.

"We…We kissed at the Christmas party. Someone saw us. A colleague. We only kissed." Tobias inhales sharply. Even her colleagues knew they had something going on before he did, he must be thinking.

"The same night you came home asking me to move back to the States with you, right?"

She nods. Tobias deserves the whole truth. The ideal image he built around her as this strong, powerful woman he wanted so much is fragile and false.

"In January." She sniffs. "He gave me a ride home…and left them behind."

"When I found you on the floor by the door? Was that when it happened?"

Whatever happens in London…

She lowers her head, crying. When she shakes her head, Tobias runs his palms up his face and over his short-cropped hair.

"I knew it," he says. "I could smell him. In our room. On you." He pauses. "I didn't want to believe it." He audibly gulps in air. "It started on that business trip, didn't it? When you came home sick?"

Kemi bursts into sobs, clutching her chest tighter, falling to her knees. She can't look at him. Can't bear to stare into his eyes narrowing as he peers at her. If he had known even back then, why had he played along with finding those cufflinks? Why?

Unless he didn't want to believe she was capable of it.

"I'm so sorry." The words leave her as a whisper.

"It was him all this time, wasn't it? The man I could never live up to?"

"Please don't say that. I love you." He shakes his head as he stares at her.

"It was him you've always wanted. What he represented that I could never give you," Tobias continues, his voice getting stronger. "Every time you asked me if I was happy as a security guard, it was Ragnar you wanted."

"No! I don't want him. I want you, Tobbe," she cries. "I chose you!"

"You can't even lie convincingly to yourself, Kemi," Tobias says. "He couldn't keep his eyes off you today."

"It just happened. We didn't plan any of this. It just happened," she cries.

"At your boss's party today…"

She buries her face in her palms, wailing into them, muffling her cries. She takes more deep breaths as anchors, before looking up at him again.

"She found us in Jonny's study," Kemi confesses. "I'm so sorry."

Tobias nods with pursed lips. He wipes a rogue tear running down a freckled cheek. It must sound insane to him. That she audaciously made out with Ragnar at a party, where everyone was. Or that she had such disregard for Tobias she would let Ragnar run his hands all over her, while Ragnar's cufflinks rested on his own wrists. The symbolism was too much for both of them to bear.

This time, Tobias lets his tears fall without restraint.

"Do you know what his daughter called you?"

She nods. Of course she knows what that vile word means. It's one of the first words she learned as a Black woman in Sweden.

"She called you the n-word in Swedish."

"Tobbe."

"Think about that. The daughter of the man you've been"—his voice breaks with emotion—"fucking behind my back." He chokes. His words settle between them. Heavy.

"I wish I could take it all back," she wails. "I wish I could make everything right again."

"I don't even know what I'm feeling right now, Kemi," he cries. "Except a deep sense of loss and disappointment." She knows what he means and she covers her face once more.

His mother Nancy's words float into her mind: *Tobias has been waiting for you all his life. A strong African woman.*

"I can't stay here anymore. You reek of him. He's all over you."

Tobias leaves her on her knees, unaware there is more devastating news for him on the horizon. She simply grips her stomach and sobs the rest of the night.

Kemi's tears run dry by Monday morning. After Tobias left, she holed herself up for the rest of the weekend. Getting up only to quench her thirst. She hadn't eaten a single morsel. There were no cravings for her usual non-judgmental cinnamon buns.

She starts the new week a shattered woman. She left the States because it had decimated her love life. She was tired of being alone. Of pretending she didn't need a man's touch because she was independent. Strong. Feminist. Self-sufficient. Proud. Every single word which invalidated the need for a man in her life, she carried proudly.

Now looking at her reflection in the mirror, what she sees she can no longer dress up. She pulls out a black turtleneck, which hangs loosely around her torso, and black pants. She shuts the closet door on her bright colors. She doesn't bother with earrings or accessories either. She adds a little bit of black eyeliner and gloss on her lips. She distills her normal twenty-minute makeup routine into two minutes.

She rides the *tunnelbana* to work with horse blinkers on. Not noticing anyone. Not observing the world milling quietly around her. She isn't even sure how to pour herself into work that week.

Once in the office, she drags her feet over to her desk, not making eye contact or greeting anyone. Her work space feels suffocating. She should have worked from home.

"Kemi." A voice startles her. She spins around to face Louise, Jonny's assistant.

"*God morgon*," Kemi manages. Louise returns her greeting. She seems jittery.

"Ingrid and Jonny would like to speak with you in the conference room."

With that, she darts off. Kemi closes her eyes and sighs. Of course they want to see her. She had been at Jonny's party that weekend. Ingrid hadn't been there, though. She dumps her oversized purse on her desk, sheds her spring coat, and walks over to the room.

She opens it to find Jonny pacing back and forth, his fingers dancing. Rolling them into fists and out again, then threading his fingers through his hair over and over again. When Kemi steps in, Jonny freezes. His arms drop to his sides like dead weights, his fingers curling into fists.

Ingrid, on the other hand, sits calmly. "*God morgon*, Kemi. Please take a seat."

Kemi regards her suspiciously. She turns her gaze to Jonny, who stares at her as if he can see through her. She recognizes that weird glare. She regularly sees it at business meetings with difficult clients. Now it's trained on her with unnerving concentration.

"What's going on?" Kemi asks Ingrid.

"I warned you," is all Ingrid offers.

Kemi swallows. The drama at Jonny's garden party. She isn't sure how much Ragnar had told him, what he had heard, or if the pain in Pia's eyes had convinced him. Right now, Johan von Lundin wants her gone. But he can't do it himself. He simply glares at her with spite.

"Effective immediately, you are no longer an employee of von Lundin Marketing." Ingrid delivers the verdict. "I'm so sorry, Kemi."

Kemi sinks into her seat, absorbing Ingrid's words. She can't think. Her mind stopped functioning when Tobias left her crying on her knees.

"We're giving you a one-month severance package," Ingrid continues.

"I don't understand," Kemi begins to say. "I'm excellent at my job. Why exactly are you firing me?"

"Jonny told me what happened this weekend."

"You mean what happened at a private party? Something that has no bearing on my professional life?"

"It was inappropriate."

"What was inappropriate was Ragnar's daughter using a racist word against me!" Kemi's voice powers up once more.

"That was unfortunate, but that is not the discussion at hand."

"Unfortunate? You weren't even there, Ingrid."

"I don't trust you." This time, it is Jonny finally speaking up. He still stands like an effigy, but his eyes tell her all she needs to know.

Ragnar shattered that luster which enveloped her like a halo in Jonny's eyes.

Jonny repeats those words, unblinking. "I don't trust you. I have to trust you."

"I'm so sorry, Kemi," Ingrid chimes in once more. "I enjoyed working with you. I liked you."

Kemi nods and gets to her feet. She has nothing else to say. She has never been fired before in her life. What does one say? Thank you for the opportunity? Give me another chance? I'm sorry it didn't work out? What protocol is she supposed to follow when fired in such deeply embarrassing circumstances? What comes next in Sweden? Maybe this is the universe's way of convincing her to finally move back home. She has no reasons to stay anymore.

"I understand."

Those are the only words that make their way out before Kemi Adeyemi turns her back on von Lundin Marketing for good.

They had casually glossed over that little girl's slur.

YASMIIN

"So they can't keep her?" Yagiz whispers into the dark.

"Hmmmm." Yasmiin stirs. She reaches for her phone. Three forty a.m.

"I mean, why do we have to take her?" he whisper-asks. "No leg. What will we do with her?"

"Yagiz, stop it," Yasmiin scolds, pulling the covers over her shoulders and wriggling, begging for sleep to reclaim her. "It's almost four in the morning," she says in exasperation. "Shut up."

Yagiz grants her five seconds of silence before saying, "Can't her boyfriend's brother take her? What's his name? Afrim? Akeem?"

Yasmiin turns over toward him, frustrated. "You like to talk, don't you? How about we talk about Amani instead? *Uhn?*" She hears him sigh before falling quiet. She presses on. "Tell me about you and Amani."

"What *me and Amani*? What are you talking about? *Fan!*" he curses.

"Since you like to talk at night, tell me, what business do you have together?"

Yagiz laughs her off. "Go to sleep, you're not making sense."

"What did you do to Amani's husband?" Yasmiin demands. She hears him hold his breath. "She told me you and your boys made sure he never spoke again."

"What do you want me to tell you? He was a racist pig. Stop digging. I told you about looking for secrets." His voice dips sternly.

"I need to know who I married," she says. He cackles. "Tell me, what did you do?"

She feels him shrug in the low-lit room.

"Yasmiin, sleep," he replies.

"I thought you wanted to talk?"

"Stop it." His voice deepens.

"Tell me!"

"We broke his jaw, okay? Is that what you want to know? We broke his jaw," Yagiz tells her. "And I will do the same when I find that maggot Bosse. Now go to sleep."

His mention of Bosse sends a chill of fear down her spine. The man has probably retired by now. No doubt living quietly next to some tranquil lake back here in Sweden. She didn't envision Yagiz now having a personal vendetta. He probably saw in Amani's ex and her descriptions of Bosse the same men who had rendered *Baba* powerless. Relegated him to meniality until he retired.

It all goes quiet in their bedroom for a while. Yasmiin marinates in his confession. She figured that was what happened, but she needed to hear the words from his own mouth. His boys, Nusret, Öz, and the others. They dabble in shady business, no doubt, but she'd never pegged them as thugs too.

"What else have you done for Amani? Do you still work for her?"

"Stop digging, *aşkım*."

"Was she a customer? Hmm, drugs?"

"No."

"So how do you know them?"

"Look." Yagiz shifts. "Amani is old enough to be my mother. Still fuckable, but old. Same with Salima. They're friends of my family."

"Family friends?"

"Yes, family friends!"

"So, no money involved?"

Yagiz turns his back to her, cutting off her interrogation.

Later that day, she finds herself back in the dressing room at SVT once more. A rap duo of Afro-Swedes with Eritrean roots are performing live after the special vegan pancake cooking segment. Anu roped her into getting them ready for the show. Soon enough, they're gyrating and krump-dancing across the stage, while Yasmiin records a short video for her account, swaying and bobbing to their beats.

Anu loves her work. He takes every opportunity to gas her up, letting her know with his theatrical flair she'd outdone herself with each face she painted. So, he booked her for more upcoming segments.

Her account is growing fast too. Her last photos of Amani before the gala caught on like wildfire. People praised Amani for being a queen, for lighting the path, for killing it on levels within Swedish society other immigrants have only dreamed of. Her inbox begins flooding with requests.

Do you do weddings? Funerals? Graduations? Proposals? Conferences? Heck, divorce celebrations?

Soon, all Yasmiin's weekends are booked until Midsummer for beauty appointments.

With each chime of the salon door, Salima's clientele grows darker in skin tone while boosting her income. The older woman finally backs off, fully embracing the lucrative business Yasmiin brings her way so easily. Soon enough, one of Yasmiin's posts is of an elated Salima grinning from ear to ear, holding up a pair of scissors in a *Charlie's Angels* pose.

The caption reads:

Partner-in-crime.

Yasmiin revels in this new grounding beneath her feet. One getting more solid with each booking, opportunity, and moment she spends orbiting Amani's celebrity.

Yet, Yagiz's secrets remain heavy on her mind. In a few weeks, Muna will come home to them. She isn't ready. Thankfully their apartment block has an elevator, albeit a narrow beast weathered by use to be ridden at one's own risk. She still needs to get Yagiz fully on board with supporting Muna.

For now, she counts down the days until Muna comes home.

Exhausted after a full day's work, Yasmiin shuffles on her feet, Mehmet dragging behind her down the hallway. She finds Öz leaning against their door and freezes. He pushes off the jamb and digs his hands into the back pockets of his jeans.

"What do you want?"

"To apologize for being an idiot."

She squints at him.

He lifts both hands in surrender. "I swear on my children. I didn't come to harass you."

"Then why are you here?"

Öz reaches for the grocery bag she carries. Yasmiin swats his hand away. Mehmet watches them.

"Yagiz isn't home. You have his numbers," she says as she fiddles with the door keys.

"I'm here for you," he says. She frowns over her shoulder at him. He corrects himself. "To speak with you."

"Then say what you want to say here. I'm not letting you in," she hisses.

"You may want to hear this in private," he whispers. She holds his gaze before sighing and letting him in.

"Tell me," Yasmiin orders moments later after Öz helps himself to a bottle of beer from their fridge. She had turned on some cartoons for Mehmet in the living room.

"What do you want to know?" He assesses her as he takes a swig of beer.

"You're the one saying you want to tell me something!" She grows agitated, looking up from the tomatoes she's washing as he drinks unhurriedly.

"First, I'm sorry about last time."

"Which last time? The last time Yagiz embarrassed me or the last time you harassed me?" She watches his Adam's apple jump at her statement.

"I'm sorry."

"Why are you here, Öz?"

"I'm worried about Yagiz." He sets his bottle on the counter and inches closer to her. She takes a step back. He halts his advance. "He's been different since that day he got drunk and acted stupid."

Since her confession, Yasmiin ponders. "Different how?"

"His business. His products are missing. His customers have already paid him and are still waiting for their delivery. Yagiz isn't returning their calls. They are now calling me and Nusret. Yagiz isn't talking." He clears his throat. "Maybe he will talk to you?"

"I stay out of Yagiz's business and he stays out of mine."

"Yes, but his customers stay in everyone's business. Including my own. They want what they paid for."

"Öz, I have work to do, please leave if you don't have anything else to say." She settles her hands on her hips. He smirks, then chugs the rest of his beer, his eyes never leaving hers.

"Talk to your husband. He's starting to make trouble for everyone else, including us." He sets the empty bottle down before spinning around to leave.

NINETEEN

BRITTANY-RAE

"He killed her!" Brittany wails into her phone. "He fucking killed her, Tee!"

"Hold up, hold up,"Tanesha tries calming her."Say what now?!" she half-asks in disbelief.

Brittany keeps wailing on the other end instead."God, this isn't real. This isn't happening!" She rakes her fingers through her hair as despair washes over her.

"Babe, what are you talking about?"Tanesha's voice comes on stronger. Brittany knows she needs to calm herself so she can relay what Lucinda Daniels told her.

That her daughter Maya went out one evening with him and never came back. Jonny, on the other hand, had left for Sweden the next day. The abortion narrative had been complete news to Lucinda. She was close to her daughter, Lucinda explained. She would have known if Maya had been pregnant. What she did know was that Johan had been stalking her daughter. Maya had even considered a restraining order against him, she'd said.

Then one night, a teenage Johan showed up at their door in tears, shaking, rocking back and forth, his fingers raking his hair. Maya had followed him to try to calm him. That was the last time Lucinda saw her daughter.

As a boy, Jonny loved to crush snails he'd collected with love.

The police investigation was over within a month. No foul play involved. The von Lundins were cleared. Maya had simply vanished into thin air. After years of searching themselves, they finally put out an obituary because they knew their daughter was never coming home. Coordinated searches for blue-eyed, blonde-haired girls carried on for decades, Lucinda had noted. The search for her brown-eyed, brown-skinned Maya had been wrapped up within a month.

"*Jesus!*" Tanesha exclaims while Brittany relays a condensed version through her sobs. "Jonny is messed up, but this?"

"He had alibis," Brittany cries. "He had several alibis that night. They couldn't charge him. There were witnesses who saw him leave her behind alive."

"This is some scary shit, Brit. What are you going to do? What are *we* going to do?"

"I don't know." Brittany sniffs, pulling tissues out of the box and blowing her nose roughly. She's hiding in one of their Canary Wharf penthouse bathrooms.

She held her composure, poker face on, when their chauffeur drove her back to the apartment from Brixton. She dismissed Eva calmly, telling her the visit to the Daniels had gone well and thanking her for her service. Then she raced into the bathroom, turned on the tap to full blast, and cried her lungs out.

"I know he killed her. I just know it," Brittany says, her voice back to a whisper. "The way he looks at me... *God*, he scares me."

"Let's not jump to conclusions," Tanesha says, trying to calm her down.

"Why would he leave for Sweden the very next day? Why was he so distraught when he visited Maya that night?" Brittany wonders out loud, thoughts swirling.

"You think his family might be behind this?" Tanesha suggests. "Maybe they're covering something up?"

"I know he blames his mother for everything that happened," Brittany says. "He blames her."

"Do you think his mother did something to that girl?"

"God, I don't know, but I need to call my lawyer right away!"

"Okay, I'm here for you if you need me, boo."

Amani picks up on the fourth ring with noise in the background. "*Hallå?*"

"I need to see you." Brittany sounds desperate, her voice vibrating with fear.

"Brittany?"

"I need to see you, Amani. I have updates," Brittany shrieks into the phone.

"Updates? Are you crying?" Amani's voice is drowned out by shrilling in the background.

"Yes, updates."

"Okay, okay, when are you back in town?"

"Late tonight," Brittany says.

"Meet me tomorrow afternoon. I'll text you an address."

Later that night, back in Sweden, their drive from Arlanda Airport down E4 toward Stockholm proper is made in excruciating silence. Au pair Vicky and Maya are both fast asleep in the back seat. Jonny drives them, his focus fully fixed on pinheads of light, cars whizzing by.

After grabbing his daughter and twirling her around in delight, he had pressed a heady kiss onto an unprepared Brittany. Goosebumps of fear had surfaced in that instant. She'd pushed out of their embrace, reminding him of the divorce. His eyes had burrowed into her. Like Lucinda mentioned, staring straight through her soul.

"London was good." Brittany breaks the silence now. Small talk to calm her rapidly beating heart. She's still in a car with a man who might have murdered his teenage girlfriend in cold blood. She needs to speed up her exit. No more crawling. She needs to sprint out of this marriage, taking Maya with her.

"I needed that getaway," she adds, breathing a little too heavily for her liking. Jonny bobs his head, listening, his eyes glued to the road. "How was the garden party?"

"Something happened there," he says stoically.

"What did I miss?" She feigns interest. Anything to slow her breathing.

"Something happened between Kemi and Ragnar," he says.

Brittany turns sharply toward his profile. "What happened?"

"Hedvig found them kissing. Hedvig called Kemi a *svarting*. I fired Kemi," he answers calmly.

"Wait, what?"

"Hedvig found them kissing. Hedvig called Kemi—" he repeats.

"I heard you the first time." She cuts him off tersely. "Did that child call Kemi the n-word?" Brittany can't believe her ears.

"Ragnar is married. She was kissing him. I don't trust her," Jonny explains.

"What?!" Brittany grows exasperated. Her hatred for Ragnar reaches new depths. She suspected this all along. Not just prejudiced, but flat out racist. She had waited for Kemi, who seemed to be blind to his assholery, to discover this on her own terms, but the n-word? From his child no less?

Jonny continues matter-of-factly. "I need to trust people. I can't trust Kemi anymore."

"But you still trust Ragnar, right?" she counters.

"He's my best friend."

"He's an asshole!" Brittany's voice pitches higher. She hears Vicky stir in the back seat and she calms herself. "His daughter used a foul word against Kemi! Don't you see?!"

"See what?" Jonny asks. Brittany swallows, confused.

"You have got to be kidding me," she says, finding her voice once more. "You can't be serious."

"I am serious."

"Do you use that word behind my back? Behind our backs?"

"What are you talking about? I would never say such a thing," he says, adamant.

"What about Ragnar, *uhmm*? Does he use that word? Does Pia use it too?"

"Ragnar would never use that word. If he did, he wouldn't have touched Kemi, right?" Jonny says.

Brittany lets out a growl of frustration which wakes Maya up. This is going nowhere. How had she gotten herself into this mess? Jonny clearly doesn't see or doesn't want to see that his closest clique doesn't want her or his brown baby in their mix. She instantly calms herself down when the terrifying news Lucinda Daniels had shared with her resurfaces again. *Did Jonny kill Maya?*

Her voice softens into survival mode. "So you fired Kemi and blamed her for everything, even though Ragnar is screwing her behind his wife's back and his daughter called her the n-word?"

Silence fills the car once more until Jonny speaks into the void. "I trust Ragnar."

The rest of their drive home to Lidingö is completed wordlessly, while she absorbs the air charged with double standards. Brittany is certain their au pair had been pretending to sleep through their heated exchange. Once home, Vicky rushes off with Maya to give her a quick bath and dress her in her pajamas while Brittany heads to their bedroom, Jonny trailing her.

She stops him by the door with a firm hand to his chest when he tries to come in after her.

"I've missed you," he says, his voice low, looking to be sated.

"I haven't changed my mind," she whispers back, avoiding his eyes. Every part of her trembles inside. She dares not meet his gaze.

"Please don't leave me," he pleads. "I'll do anything you want me to. I will."

"We can't be together anymore," she says, leaning against the door. He reaches for her waist, his grip tightening, pulling her close, his lips finding her ear.

She resists his pull. "No, Jonny."

He scans her face, studying her. She turns away, easing out of his grasp, moving toward their bed.

His voice stops her instead.

"Did you find all your answers in London?" he asks, calmly. Brittany freezes in her tracks. She shuts her eyelids for a split second to collect herself before pivoting back to him.

"What do you mean?" she asks, her pitch unsteady.

"Was Eva good to you?" he asks, glaring at her, peering through her.

"Why wouldn't she be?" Brittany's voice cracks. "Eva took good care of Maya and me, as she always does."

"Good," Jonny replies. "I fired her after you left." He pauses, trying to read Brittany's face for a reaction. "I don't trust her anymore."

Brittany's right hand flies to cover her mouth. She feels her heart beating faster, her skin crawling.

"What? Why?" Her words are barely audible.

"I need to trust people," Jonny says, his eyes roaming her face before settling on hers, hands balled into fists by his sides. "Good night."

He lingers on her a few seconds longer before retreating to one of their guest rooms for the night.

KEMI

Her world becomes an echo chamber. The only sounds floating in are whispers from colleagues and the occasional whirling of the cappuccino machine from the kitchen area. When Ingrid and Jonny fired her, Kemi quietly left the conference room. She walked into hallways which mimicked this current silence. People peered over laptops as she made her way toward her space.

Humiliation is heavy, that she knows. But this weight is unbearable. With each passing pair of eyes, a couple more kilograms are added to her chest. With each added kilo, Jonny's words are the shovel scattering the weight within her.

I don't trust you.

I have to trust you.

Beyond being told time and time again by people she loved that she's a selfishly driven woman, this new episode in her life means she's no longer trustworthy. A far heavier burden to bear.

Where's Ragnar? And why is she getting the rough end of their affair once again?

But she knows why.

His daughter had used a racial slur against her. No one had reacted besides Ragnar. Even Tobias had been stunned into silence. Yet, Ingrid dismissed that insult minutes ago.

Shoulders downtrodden, she shuffles into her corner office to pick up her bag. She begins clearing her desk. The little photo of Tobias she'd pinned up on a cork board. Awards she'd amassed over the years. That one Swedish award for marketing which von Lundin received after its successful Bachmann campaign. She reaches for her reusable water bottle when Espen materializes by her cubicle.

"*Hej*," he says weakly. Kemi meets his eyes and gives him a half-smile. He continues. "I think Jonny is making a mistake."

"I'm a big girl," Kemi says. "I'll be fine."

"I have no doubt about that," Espen says. "But *we* won't be fine without you."

Kemi bites her lip at his compliment, fighting back tears. "You're too kind."

"I'm serious," he says. "I think they are making a big mistake. They are never going to be able to replace you."

"I really appreciate that, Espen, but it is what it is." Kemi is adamant. "I thought private lives and work were separate beasts here. Clearly I was wrong." *Especially when it comes to me*, Kemi wants to add, but she doesn't.

"I'm sorry this happened." His green eyes regard her with pity. She has always been fond of Espen. He's her ally, defending her in rooms when she isn't around, he often tells her. Being married to a Cape Verdean woman has probably infused him with levels of empathy and cracked open his shell of privilege. His wife had struggled to find a job for years despite his deep connections.

Now Kemi is swan-diving into the opaque world that immigrants with no strong ties to the culture and limited

Swedish have to wade through. Especially if their last names aren't Nordic-sounding.

"I'm sorry too," Kemi adds. "I don't know how much you've heard, but something happened this weekend."

"I heard from Louise. I couldn't make it to the party because I had previous plans."

Of course he did. That strategic leaker of information. She's never far from Jonny's side and had been at the garden party as well.

Espen continues. "I heard Ragnar's daughter used a bad word against you."

Kemi stops packing, straightens up, and stares at Espen. His look is serious, his freckles making him look boyish despite his intense glare. Espen is the only one who has acknowledged that slur.

Kemi lets out a small sigh before biting her lips to contain tears threatening to spill over in front of Espen. No one else wants to talk about it. Yes, she was complicit in the affair and had no one else besides Ragnar to blame for how it all exploded in their faces. But that paled in comparison to being called the n-word by his daughter.

She can't reconcile the fact that the man who seduced her, awakened raw feelings within her, and made her lose control whenever he was near her, used racial slurs with ease within his household.

"Did you know?" She pushes the words out. She needs to know.

"Know what?"

"That he felt this way," she says. "That he spoke this way when *we* are not around."

Espen holds her gaze quietly for a few seconds. He clears his throat as red rushes to his cheeks. Through his eyes, Kemi can see his mind furiously working, trying to find the right words to say.

"I don't know Ragnar that well outside of work," Espen offers. "In my opinion, I've always thought he was an asshole."

"But what about at work?" she challenges him. "Does he speak like this when I'm not around? Do you all talk like this behind our backs?"

She watches Espen clench his jaw, the veins in his neck popping with the action. Of course they do. All those times when they waited patiently for her to leave their meetings so they could free-flow in Swedish.

"What do you guys say behind my back?" Agitation begins to grow within her. "What words do you use when I'm not around?"

"Kemi—"

She cuts him off. "I can't believe you're protecting him."

"With all due respect, you're in no position to be self-righteous," Espen counters.

Those words break her and she wipes the tears gathering in her eyes with the back of her palm.

"Fine," she says curtly, composing herself, turning back to her task of emptying her office.

"Look, you know I'm on your side," he offers. "Both Rosa and I are, so if there's anything we can do, please let me know." Kemi nods her response, not trusting herself to speak. "It's our loss," Espen says, walking up close to her. She senses he's coming in for a hug. She obliges him and finishes it off with a pat on his back.

"Thank you," she says.

He makes his exit, leaving her exposed once more and paranoid. Even her ally had participated in discussions behind her back with loaded language.

Now Jonny's words float back up to her:

I don't trust you.

I have to trust you.

And they reek of hypocrisy.

Beyond vacations, this is Kemi's first Monday in years where she has nothing to do. After leaving the office under wordless stares, she stands quietly waiting for her train to take her to Slussen, then a bus back home to Nacka. Besides Espen, none of the other directors had bade her farewell. They were probably around but avoiding her, the situation too uncomfortable even for them to attempt to navigate with civil talk.

They may never reach out to say goodbye. She had at least expected a few words after the last couple of years working side by side with them. Are they also giving Ragnar the cold shoulder? Is he also getting roasted by silence, not because of what he did, but who he did it with?

She isn't sure if it was the action itself or the fact she had been the one Ragnar had strayed with. Her ego has already shattered into pieces. She knows she's never going to be able to pick up its shards. She has made a fool of herself and if there ever was a rapid fall from grace, she is experiencing it.

She needs to get indoors, out of her work clothes, and bundle herself into a blanket for the rest of the day. She can't think, her mind turning into ash. Specks of memories she can't quite piece together. She's now jobless in a foreign country whose language she's still struggling to learn after close to three years. As for Tobias, he has radio-silenced himself forever at this point.

Once the elevator opens up to her floor, she digs into her bag for her keys. The word "*Hej*" startles her instead. She freezes, her arm halfway inside her oversized bag. He pushes off the wall he's leaning against and stands taller, tucking his hands in his pockets, his shoulders slumped.

Kemi glares at Ragnar, her blood hot with anger at his audacity.

"Kemi," he calls out to her. She returns to digging into her bag for her keys, ignoring him. She pulls them out and walks past him. He trails her to her door. "Kemi," he calls out again.

"Stay away from me," she says through clenched teeth, turning suddenly to face him. He takes her in.

"I know I'm the last person you want to see right now," he starts.

She spins away from him and back to the door. Her fingers shake as she tries pushing her keys in, failing at the simple task. He's rattling her again and she hates him for it. Yes, he's the last person she wants to see ever again as long as she lives. He inches closer. She feels his proximity and turns once more to him.

"I'll call the cops if you don't leave me alone."

"I'm sorry."

"You're a fucking racist."

Her words physically catch him off guard. His shoulders arch backward, his brows furrow as he peers down at her. Kemi matches his frown.

"I swear to you"—his voice is low, hoarse—"I never use words like that. I don't know where Hedvig picked it up from. Maybe from *dagis*."

"This is the last time you'll ever laugh in my face or behind my back," she says tersely. "Leave now."

"I'm so sorry," he says. "Please give me a chance to share my side."

"Leave now!"

"I'm so—"

Her piercing slap stuns them both, her fingers left tingling from the hit. Ragnar receives her slap, his face banking sideways with the blow. When he turns back to look at her, his cheek burns bright red. He lets out a deep sigh, his eyes drinking her fully in.

Tears begin to well up behind her eyes as she massages her wrist to soothe the pain. Behind that hit had been years of oppression and repression unleashed upon Ragnar. He just happens to be the one standing right in front of her, representing everything she hates about herself and the world.

"Leave," she mouths at him. Ragnar takes a couple of steps toward her instead, backing her up against her front door until she feels his breath on her face.

"Don't you dare," she whispers. "Don't you fucking dare."

He reaches a palm up to cup her cheek. She smacks it away from her face. His rejected palm tries for her forearm instead. She swats it away once more.

"Please—" Ragnar starts. She finishes his sentence with another slap across his cheek. This time, he grabs her wrist forcefully in retaliation, anger brewing within him. He pulls her hard toward him by her wrist, crushing her against his chest. *I'm more powerful than you*, his tight grip tells her without words, his eyes burning through her. *Don't you fucking dare*, his glare repeats her own words to her.

"Get your hands off me," Kemi snarls at him. He holds her gaze for a moment longer before releasing her.

"I wish I could make things right again," Ragnar says in defeat, his voice heavy. He swallows, pondering his next words as his eyes roam her face. "I can't stop thinking about you." He pauses for a deep breath. "Are you sure it's mine?"

Ragnar drops the words in the space between them. Kemi lets them sink right to the floor.

"Move back," she grits between her teeth, her eyes holding tears which refuse to fall. "I'll text you the location to meet me for the test."

He presses his lips together at her command and backs away from her. Once he's at a comfortable distance, she turns around, finishes fumbling with her keys, and flees inside into safety.

Kemi sends him an address. Ragnar meets her there the next day.

If the middle-aged clerk manning reception was thinking it, she certainly kept her poker face on. Two well-dressed individuals at a private fertility clinic. One white, the other Black. One wearing a wedding ring. The man in a custom-made navy-blue suit fitting his frame, cufflinks, and a white dress shirt underneath. The lady in a form-fitting royal blue suit hugging her curves with a white silk blouse underneath. For two people who didn't say a word to each other when they arrived, they'd certainly coordinated outfits.

Their silent standoff continues in a backroom. They barely acknowledge each other as a nurse draws blood samples from them both.

"You'll get your results within a week," the nurse shares with Kemi, before clearing her throat in discomfort as Ragnar stares her down.

Kemi gives the nurse a half-smile and gets to her feet, not bothering to cast a glance his way. She leaves him sitting there. Before she reaches the front door, her phone pings with an incoming message. Kemi swipes and pulls it up.

If it's mine, get rid of it.

R

YASMIIN

"One hundred million kronor?" Salima gasps, peering at Amani through her mirror. Amani is getting a quick dye and trim job to keep her raven look.

"Every year," she says, chuckling as she adjusts herself under Salima's touch. "That's what the wife wants. After digging up four girlfriends, I think we might get it."

Salima hisses and shakes her head. "These Swedish boys. So sneaky. It's those young ones running startups."

"I tell you," Amani adds. "That man was juggling girlfriends like oranges while pushing his baby stroller."

"*Sheu*, that's why I stay with my men," Salima declares. "I already know what I'm getting with them. No nasty surprises . . ." She trails off with a laugh.

"What do you think, Yasmiin?" Amani calls out to her. "Yasmiin?"

"What?" Yasmiin answers curtly. Engaging in their conversation is the last thing on her mind.

Yagiz had finally come back home reeking of cigarettes and booze, staggering with a black eye and bloodied bottom lip. He hadn't wanted her to touch him or help clean up his wounds.

Yasmiin didn't ask him any more questions. She left his secrets buried.

"Didn't you hear?" Amani reminds her. "One of the divorce settlements I'm working on. The woman wants a hundred million kronor a year."

"Can he afford it?" Yasmiin asks.

"Probably. And more," Amani says. "His family is in the shipping business. That's how they fund his startup."

"Then get the woman what she wants," is all Yasmiin says before turning back to her brushes.

Amani chuckles. "All these cases I'm working on, I'm telling you, these women hopping into bed with man-boys. I'm meeting one soon in about an hour. American woman. Brittany."

"Ooooh, *amrikiin*," Salima teased.

"Beautiful too. Supermodel," Amani adds just as the door chime announces a customer.

A timid-looking white couple—a lean man easily clearing six feet and a petite redhead—step in. They look to be in their late thirties, early forties. Their presence brings the salon to an immediate halt as the three women stare at them as if they've made a mistake.

Behind them peeks a young Black girl who can't be more than six or seven years old.

"Hello," the man speaks up, clearing his throat. "We're looking for Yasmiin."

"Can I help you?" Yasmiin asks, her eyes on them.

"Yes, we were recommended to come see you," the woman, wife maybe, says. "We have been desperately looking for someone to help us with Mercy's hair."

Yasmiin's eyes wash over the girl called Mercy. Her hair is dreadlocked and matted beyond repair. Heat begins to broil within Yasmiin.

"When was the last time you took her to a salon?" Yasmiin asks.

"We couldn't find one until now that does her kind of hair," the woman replies.

"In all of Stockholm?" Yasmiin isn't asking. "You didn't even search?"

"I mean, we've found one now. A friend sent us your account."

"I specialize in makeup," Yasmiin stresses.

"Okay, umm, can you help us with any recommendations?"

Yasmiin assesses the child once more. She shyly clings to the woman's side and Yasmiin looks at her with pity. If these are her adoptive parents, they haven't even tried.

She reaches to touch Mercy's hair, which has calcified into hard-as-rock tentacles. Yasmiin is livid.

"I'll have to cut it all off." She turns to assess the adults. "It's too damaged. We will start from scratch."

"Thank you, thank you," the man effuses. "When we adopted her from Cameroon, we knew it was going to be difficult to take care of her hair."

"It's only difficult if you don't even try," Yasmiin says, holding his gaze. "There are videos on YouTube which can teach you how to do Black hair," she adds. "So, when did you adopt her?"

"As a baby," the woman says. "We fell in love the minute we saw her."

"And how old is she now?"

"Six." The mother beams.

"And when was the last time you did her hair?" Their silence is all Yasmiin needs to know.

She smiles at Mercy and leads her to her chair, propping the child on a large padded cushion. Mercy begins to cry when Yasmiin gently touches each matted branch. She can only imagine the pain the little girl must have endured over the years.

"Mercy, what a lovely name. I am Yasmiin," she introduces herself. "Don't be scared. We're going to make your hair healthy again, okay? But first"—Yasmiin reaches for a pair of scissors—"we have to start at the beginning."

Thirty minutes later, Mercy smiles at her reflection of a buzz cut, deep dimples surfacing.

"Look how beautiful you are," her father says, running his palm over Mercy's head. Yasmiin swats his hand away angrily and applies hair butter.

"Bring her every two months until it's about two inches thick," Yasmiin orders. "Then I will start her on a growth program, okay?"

The parents simply nod, beaming their gratitude. They take their child and wave as they leave, stepping aside for a tall lithe Black woman, wearing large sunglasses, stepping in.

Yasmiin gapes at the woman as she takes her sunglasses off and scans the small salon.

"Ha, Brittany!" Amani calls out. "Over here."

TWENTY

BRITTANY-RAE

"There are other people here," Brittany mutters between clenched teeth as she leans closer to Amani, eyes darting around her. She's sitting in a stuffy salon on Kungsholmen, packed to overflowing with knick-knacks, photos, and a mix of faux and real flowers at the address Amani texted her.

Amani is in one of the hairdressing chairs beneath the touch of an older woman sharing the same raven-black hair color and similar facial features. Another woman, who looks East African, is cleaning hairbrushes in a corner.

"It's okay, it's my older sister Salima." Amani waves a nonchalant hand upwards to introduce Salima, who peers at Brittany over the rim of her glasses. Brittany gives her a half-smile. "Salima knows all my business." Amani cocks her head toward the other woman. "That is Yasmiin." Brittany gives Yasmiin a short wave.

"What about client confidentiality?" Brittany whispers back.

Amani shrugs. "Say what you can here. No names. We'll handle the rest back at my office."

Brittany looks at the duo of hairdressers once more before leaning back into her seat.

"What did you find there?" Amani asks, banking her head to the left, giving Salima access to her right side.

"A lot," Brittany says, twisting her fingers, still in disbelief. "Her parents." Amani murmurs, prodding her to continue. "There was never an abortion." Amani swivels her head sharply toward Brittany; Salima pushes Amani's head sharply back in place.

"What do you mean no abortion?" Amani asks.

"The mother said she simply went out with him one night and never came back." Brittany's voice dips lower, trying hard not to say too much around listening ears. "He ran back to Sweden the next day."

Amani gasps, falling out of character for a moment. "Can she prove this?"

Brittany shakes her head. "Several alibis."

"Can you get this information out voluntarily from him?" Amani adds.

"I don't know what to do," Brittany says. "I'm not sure how to get this information out. He already fired the assistant who was there."

"You mean the mole?"

"Yes. Fired her yesterday once we left."

Amani sighs loudly. "Sounds like he's one step ahead of you."

"He says he needs to trust people and that he doesn't trust her anymore and asked if answers were found on that trip," Brittany pours out in a single breath.

"And what is the name of this drama again?" Salima chimes in, giggling.

Amani speaks rapidly to Salima in what Brittany assumes is Arabic. Salima lifts her shoulders and turns back to Amani's hair. Yasmiin, who has now moved on to wiping surfaces, inches closer to the trio.

"Sorry about that, please continue," Amani apologizes.

"The assistant blames the *queen* for what happened. Now there's no one to help. She's gone now."

"But she can still talk, right?" Amani digs. "You can still get in touch with her."

"I tried texting this morning to check in," Brittany says, "but the number's already been disconnected."

"*Fan!*" Amani curses under her breath. "Did she help with anything else while there?"

Brittany remembers her emotionally charged first day in London with Eva. The blonde had cried, trying hard to compose herself. Wracked with feelings of guilt for feeding Jonny's inner monster what it had desired over the years. Eva promised to have Brittany sign "a few things." Brittany wasn't sure what, but she had indeed signed a few documents before Frank drove her, her daughter, and the au pair to Heathrow for the flight back to Stockholm.

"She made sure some papers were signed the day we came back," Brittany tells her.

"She may get back in touch once settled," Amani says. "Sounds like she did good."

Brittany nods. "I need to know what was done to *her* that night."

"I'll do some digging as well, call some contacts over there," Amani says. "Sounds like it's time for you to visit the *queen* during Midsummer."

Brittany rolls her eyes. As is customary for generations of his family, every late June, the von Lundin clan gather at their sprawling archipelago estate in Sandhamn on the island of Sandön. They probably all know by now that Brittany plans on leaving Jonny. In fact, since Christmas, they have quietly observed from a distance, knowing she isn't going to get far. The authorities will never let her leave with her daughter.

Why does she have to face the *queen*, Astrid, again? She doesn't want to celebrate Midsummer with them, but Maya is part of the family too.

"Visit the *queen*," Amani interrupts her thoughts. "Have your phone ready. Record everything. Tell her you know what she did. We obviously can't use it in court, but we can be anonymous tipsters," she finishes with a slight cackle.

Brittany nods at Amani's firm instructions. Midsummer is her next cover.

Salima comments, "Good luck divorcing your husband. He

sounds like a wealthy man. Is he white? He must be with all that money here in Sweden. Is he an old man?"

Brittany frowns at her, then cuts Amani a reprimanding glare. She hears Yasmiin hiss at Salima as well.

"I swear I didn't tell her anything." Amani lifts both palms up. "Like I said, Salima just knows my business."

Salima laughs. "Wasting your time with all that fake talk. Here is the place to speak. Why do you think Amani is sharp like she is? I was the one who raised her."

"*Tawaqaf ean dhalika!*" Amani snaps at Salima. *Stop it!*

"Amani, we can continue in your office another day," Brittany says, eyeing Salima, who doesn't seem fazed. "I don't plan on sharing my private life here. Plus, time is running out."

"Of course," Amani says before slapping at her sister's hand fiddling with strands of hair. Salima's wordless response is to hold both her palms up again as if to say "*What?*"

Brittany pushes strands of her weave behind both ears. That gesture piques Yasmiin's interest.

"*Vem är din frisör?*" Yasmiin asks her. *Who's your hairdresser?*

"My hairdresser?" Brittany answers in English. Yasmiin nods. "Oh, I fly her in from London every six weeks or so." She notices Yasmiin's eyebrows arch up.

"*Vad?! Och det ser fortfarande ut som det där?*" Brittany frowns at her remark. *What?! And it still looks like that?* She hears Salima chuckle.

"Don't mind Yasmiin." Amani jumps in with a giggle. "She's just looking for more customers."

"Not with that attitude," Brittany says, eyeing Yasmiin, who is giggling too.

"She's really good," Amani says. "Let her do it. And while she's at it, let her do your face too."

Yasmiin walks up to another faux leather chair and pats it, gesturing to Brittany to come and sit.

"So you're a model?" Yasmiin asks as she starts clipping Brittany's hair, strands of extensions hitting the floor.

"I used to be. I also used to be a flight attendant."

"Wow, for SAS?"

"No, British Airways."

"Hmm, and now?"

"Full-time mom."

"So, like me, but I still work."

Brittany shifts uncomfortably. "I'm grateful not to have to work," she says. "Besides, being a mother is a full-time job."

"Oh, I know. My son Mehmet is a handful. You have a son or daughter?"

"Daughter. Maya. She's so sweet," Brittany shares. Yasmiin trades a smile with her.

Three hours later, after Yasmiin takes her usual after-photos for her social media account, Brittany stares at her reflection in the mirror sporting a short pixie cut reminiscent of Halle Berry. She turns her face left, then right, assessing her new look, words long gone. Beneath her new do lies a perfectly contoured face complete with dark smoky eyeshadow which makes her already hooded eyes look even sultrier. Plum blush, darker plum lip gloss, rose gold highlights, and perfectly groomed brows.

Brittany stares at a face she hasn't seen in decades. Her fingers inch to her natural hair, which Yasmiin straightened lightly with a relaxer. Her weave lies in heaps on the floor. She fingers strands of her real hair, her touch beginning to tremble. The salon descends into uncharacteristic silence, waiting for Brittany's verdict.

"So, you like?" Yasmiin asks her in broken English.

Brittany bursts into tears, clutching her chest. They could never understand. That something so normal as changing her hairstyle is the first step toward breaking away from Jonny's gaze, ensuring he'll never touch her again.

They silently give her a few minutes to collect herself.

"Thank you so much," Brittany says, getting to her feet, wiping her tears, stretching to her full height in front of Yasmiin.

"No problem," Yasmiin says. "Now you have my number. Call

me anytime. I can come to you. Two bus tickets. No need to waste money flying anybody here," she finishes with a smile.

Brittany laughs weakly, then she remembers something. "Actually I might need you already. I have a meeting with a fashion designer next week."

"Fashion designer?" Amani chimes in. "Oh, do tell us."

Brittany beams shyly. "Nothing in stone yet. It's just an introduction by a Swedish friend."

"Tell me," Amani pushes. "I know the Stockholm fashion scene well. You think I attend galas for nothing?!"

"Ida Persson," Brittany reveals.

Amani whistles before adding, "The season's hottest designer. Work those connections, *guurl*!"

"*Guurl?*" Brittany frowns.

"Isn't that how you Americans say it? *Guurl?*" Amani says, raising her shoulders in question.

"Stay in your lane, *guurl*," Brittany fires back before finishing off with a smile and saying she'll catch Amani later.

Then she turns back to Yasmiin and mouths to her the words *thank you*.

That evening, Jonny's gaze burns tracks over her skin as they dine on fileted bream across from each other. Their Bulgarian housekeeper Sylvia keeps milling around mouse-like, moving items to and from the kitchen, clearly aware of the intense atmosphere between them.

"So beautiful," Sylvia says, placing a hand on Brittany's shoulder, refilling her Sauvignon Blanc with the other. Brittany grins at her before grabbing her wineglass and peering at Jonny over its rim. Another feeling bubbles up to the surface within her. *Power.* For the first time in their relationship, she feels powerful. Sylvia catches Jonny's look and excuses herself.

The dining room falls into a charged quiet until he breaks it.

"I don't like it." His voice comes low and firm fifteen minutes into dinner.

"I don't give a shit what you like," she retorts, spearing her fish before looking at him. Brittany sees his nostrils flare but he stays calm. She takes the mouthful.

"You don't look like you," he says.

"I don't look like *her*," Brittany bites back. "That's what you meant, right?"

There.

There it is, she thinks, as his eyes take on that flame he reserves only for his mother, and the tiny hairs on the back of her neck stand up.

KEMI

By midweek, boredom has set in with a vengeance. She gives herself until Friday to make the decision she has been dreading. Admit defeat, pack up her life in Sweden, and head back to the chaotic familiarity of the US. She eagerly awaits the test results, praying her life is at least salvageable.

She hasn't heard from Tobias since that fateful day. He has simply disappeared from her life. Radio-silenced into memories she isn't even sure she had experienced. Her Tobias. Her beautiful Tobias whose presence in her life had been exquisitely tailored for her. She had hurt him so deeply. She isn't sure he'll recover in the way she prayed he would. Each passing minute reveals the depth of her love for him. Something she has been unsure of for too long.

She knows that now. With him gone, her world feels dimmer, heavier. The man who supported her like guardrails along the sides of a bowling lane. Guiding her, directing her, helping her see reason and prioritize, silently and unassumingly.

God, she misses Tobias.

"Kemi?" She finally makes that dreaded phone call to her twin. "Kemi?" Kehinde calls out.

"I'm here." Kemi's voice is low. She's wrapped up in a blanket on her sofa, her legs crossed and tucked beneath her. She has been sitting there for the last hour, thoughts roaming her mind. Four more days to be fully convinced her life in Sweden is over with no reason for her to stay.

"How are things?" Kehinde asks. Kemi remains silent. "How are you feeling after *that thing* we discussed?"

Kemi takes a sharp breath. *That thing.* That virus. Ragnar. "Not so good." She hears Kehinde take a sharp breath inwards.

"What is the latest?" Kehinde prods. "I hope for your sake you have stopped this affair?"

"Yes, of course. It was a mistake. I am not that type of person, you know me, *nau*."

"So what is the latest?"

"I got fired."

The phone goes silent. Kemi wants Kehinde to say something, anything, to let her know that she'll be okay. To let her know her career which she meticulously built over a decade hasn't combusted into flames because she had an affair with a married man. Even admitting that fact to herself tore her apart. Ragnar chased her because she made herself available to be chased by him. She had been complicit. Dare she admit it, she had instigated it with him. Her ego had lured him to her to try to prove to herself she wasn't a second choice.

"*Kpele.*" Kehinde drops the word loaded with pity. *Sorry.*

"I have never gotten fired in my life."

"There's a first time for everything."

"Not the time for jokes."

"Sorry."

"It's okay," Kemi says. "So, this is where I am right now."

"What did they say? Was it because of the affair? How did they know?" Kehinde seems flustered, confused. "Didn't it all happen at your apartment?"

Memories of Jonny's study cloud Kemi's mind. She shakes them off. Backed against the wall. Ragnar's hands on her, his fingers working her.

"Something else happened."

"What happened, *nau*?"

"It happened again."

Another sharp intake of air is Kehinde's response. Kemi isn't sure why she called Kehinde to tell her more details, but when faced with indecision, she often waits for her twin for direction. Right now, she needs advice on whether she should keep slogging it out in Sweden and fighting to win Tobias back, or if she should lick her open wounds, pack her bags, and head back home.

She's amassed some decent savings over the last three years. She can live comfortably for a year without work. And then what? As a single mom trying to return as a blunt blade into an industry which swiftly moves on to its next shooting star? The industry has already left her behind.

"What?!" Kehinde's disbelief is hot oil splashing from a frying pan. Full of fiery judgment and deservedly so.

"I know, I know."

"You did it again with this man? Kemi, why?"

"I swear I don't know why. I don't know why *him*."

"But you *do* know why," Kehinde stresses. "You did it a second time with this married man." Kemi falls silent. *A third time.* Kehinde presses on. "Why him?"

Why him?

Why had she allowed the virus to ravage her so fully? Why did she sabotage something whole with Tobias for scraps with Ragnar?

Malcolm had hinted at a power struggle between the both of them. Had that been it? She remembers how Ragnar had grabbed her wrist so forcefully in dominance, his eyes speaking volumes when she'd slapped him twice.

"I don't know."

"You do know."

"Maybe I felt Tobias was too good, too easy for me. Love wasn't supposed to be that easy. I didn't trust it."

"So you decided to sabotage it with your own *korokoro* hands, *abi*?"

"I guess so."

"Tell me about this man. What is his name?"

"It's not important."

"So, his name is not important, but you can sleep with him left and right?"

"I don't want you to go google him."

"You think I have nothing better to do with my time?! What's his name?"

She doesn't want to say his name out loud. Breathing life into his name will make him more real. She needs him to disappear from her life, her world, her being.

"Ragnar."

"Ragnar," Kehinde repeats. "Such a white name. So, tell me about this Ragnar." A few seconds of silence pass between them with Kehinde exercising patience out of character.

"What do you want to know?"

"Why do you find him so special? Special enough to let him into your bed, hurt a good man, destroy a good relationship, and destroy his own family as well?"

It isn't a question, Kemi knows. Kehinde is fast slipping into judgment mode, donning her executioner hat.

"It was just physical."

"Just physical?"

"Yes, I can't explain it. We were just drawn to each other."

"So, just like that, you saw each other and decided you needed to sleep with each other?" Kemi senses frustration in her sister's voice as her half-truth floats between them.

"It's not like that."

"Do you know what I think?" Kehinde comes on stronger and Kemi gears up. "I think your ego drew you to this Ragnar man. You keep trying to prove to the world that, as a Black African woman, you can conquer anything, anyone. That you are not to be underestimated."

"Please, now you're reaching." Kemi waves her off while wincing at her sister's words. Malcolm's tirade about power dynamics surfaces again. Is she that transparent? Has Kehinde come to the same conclusion as Malcolm?

"You wanted to conquer this man. It seems like Swedish white people are white people on another level. Uber white people. You wanted to conquer that."

Kemi lets out a strained laugh. "So because I'm some *conqueress*, I had an affair with him, *abi*? Trying to conquer him with my Blackness? That's your reasoning?"

"What does his wife look like?"

Kehinde's question catches her off guard. She rarely thinks about Pia. Each time she flashes across her mind, all Kemi remembers is pain playing across her face alongside a look of spite. One which had questioned Kemi's audacity and her husband's choice.

"Does it matter?"

"Let me guess. She's probably a tiny blonde thing, *abi*?"

"What does that have to do with anything? I already feel wretched about what we did and how I hurt her."

"What were you trying to prove?"

"What?"

"What were you trying to prove to yourself, Kemi? That you could have this man even if society said you can't?"

"I wasn't trying to prove anything to anyone. It just happened."

"You can lie to yourself all you want, but you can't lie to me. I know you."

And with that statement, Kemi knows Kehinde has handed her deliverance. A drug for the virus within her. But she isn't sure she's ready to swallow it yet.

"I had nothing to prove by fucking Ragnar!"

"My ears. Please," Kehinde reprimands her for cursing.

"I've given myself until Friday to decide if I should leave Sweden and come back home."

"With your tail between your legs?"

"No, with some dignity left."

"So, Tobias is not worth fighting for?"

Those words shake Kemi. She never assessed her relationship with Tobias in that light before. Their low-key relationship worked because he gave her space to fully be herself. A love without fences keeping her power in, forcing her to shrink. For God's sake, the guy bakes her cinnamon buns and restocks her tampons, never pressures her to take care of him, and listens to her rants about work, her business jargon probably flying over his head.

In craving Ragnar, she was craving competition. The challenge, the fight, that survival mode she instinctively recognizes in herself and the world. That mode she had to perpetually switch on the moment she moved to the United States and became generically Black without her input.

She had prepared for a life of unease. Now she realizes Tobias's love was forcing her to thrive instead, and in that moment, Kemi decides that, *yes*, he is worth fighting for.

"Yes, he is," Kemi declares.

"Then stay and fight for him. You made mistakes. We all make mistakes. That doesn't define who we are," Kehinde tells her. "Leave that *oyinbo* Ragnar alone. He is a dead end."

Kemi bursts into tears. She has tried holding them back, but they gush as if finally finding freedom to flow unabashedly. She can never tell Kehinde about little Hedvig's slur. Kehinde would tell her she has no self-respect.

The pregnancy news can wait too. There's only so much reprimand she can endure in a single phone call.

This is what she needs. The subconscious permission to stay awhile longer in Sweden. She has already invested years in learning the language. She has started building a small professional network. She can try to find another job. She isn't sure if she'll find one at her current level, but she'll try. She'll look into what it's going to take to raise her child all alone in Sweden. Close to its father, whether that be Ragnar or Tobias.

When she eventually hangs up, more weight lifts off her chest. She feels lighter as air rushes in, filling her lungs once more, giving her hope. She's going to fight to reclaim who she was, change the narrative of *adulteress*, and find Tobias once more. She stretches her arms over her head, catlike, making the blood flow through her limbs.

Her phone rings. She contemplates letting it buzz on, but the caller seems adamant even after eight or so rings, so she gives it a quick glance.

Tina.

Kemi swallows. Tobias's sister wants to talk to her.

A few moments later, another notification ping. The test results.

YASMIIN

A week later, Yasmiin stands in front of the double doors leading into Brittany's villa on Lidingö.

"*Fy faaan,*" she curses quietly under her breath as she takes in the grounds and waterfront views. She glimpses a large speedboat at the private jetty and shakes her head.

How did she get here? she ponders.

A middle-aged woman wearing an apron answers the door.

"*Jag är Yasmiin,*" she introduces herself to the woman, who looks to be the housekeeper.

"Yes, come this way." The housekeeper weaves her through a large open-plan hall with vaulted ceilings and windows everywhere. Amani's lush Östermalm apartment is the closest she has gotten to hidden wealth, the likes of which she didn't see every day on Stockholm's streets. She marvels, rubbernecking as the housekeeper leads her toward the covered patio where Brittany is setting up a small table.

"Yasmiin, good to see you!" She seems genuinely pleased. "I figured we could use this space since it's kind of open and we can use all this lovely natural light."

"Yes, it makes sense. Good to see you too. Thank you for inviting me."

"Oh no, the pleasure is mine. I love my new *do*. Can't wait to kill it at my audition today!" Brittany is in good spirits. "Sylvia, can you please get us some lemonade? Yasmiin, are you hungry?"

"No, thank you, lemonade is enough." Yasmiin watches Sylvia

shuffle away lethargically as if she doesn't want to be the one serving Brittany.

Yasmiin pulls off her jacket and starts laying out her kit when she hears footsteps coming their way. She sees the smile drop off Brittany's face as a tall man with light-blond hair brushed off his face strolls up to them, his hands in his pockets. Yasmiin gives his outfit of a white polo shirt over khaki pants a once-over. He stops by the entrance to the covered patio and glares at Yasmiin through piercing eyes.

If she had walked past this man on the street, she would have glanced over her shoulder twice. Maybe three times.

"I thought you'd left," Brittany says to the man. He gawks at Brittany quietly. "Well, this is Yasmiin. She's here to do my hair and makeup." His gaze floats over to take Yasmiin in, still quiet.

"*Trevligt att träffas.*" Yasmiin reaches out a hand to him. His hands remain firmly in his pockets.

He nods at her before sharing his name sternly, "Jonny."

"We need to get ready," Brittany says. Yasmiin notices Brittany is not meeting his eyes and is trying to get him moving. He keeps standing there. Yasmiin observes this dynamic. Clearly this man is Brittany's husband from the way he is looking at her. The one she is trying to divorce.

"Is she the one that did it?" he finally says in a low voice, hands still in his pockets. Yasmiin notices his hands moving, his fingers dancing inside.

"Did what?" Brittany settles herself onto the bar stool she set up for Yasmiin.

"Your hair," he stresses.

Brittany doesn't respond. She simply motions to Yasmiin to come over and get to work. The younger woman grabs a comb and brush, and moves over to Brittany, her curious eyes on Jonny.

"Your hair," he repeats. "Did she do this to you?"

"It's a haircut, Jonny." Brittany's voice is on edge. "Not a bruise."

Jonny turns to Yasmiin, assessing her as if she had scarred Brittany for life.

"You don't like it?" Yasmiin chuckles, trying to make conversation. "She looks like Halle Berry now. Even more beautiful in fact."

"I don't like it," Jonny says.

Yasmiin laughs nervously. A gesture which pulls his hands out of his pockets and presses them to his sides. His brows dip toward her, clearly unamused.

"What?" Yasmiin seems perplexed.

"I don't like it," Jonny repeats as if she hadn't heard him the first time.

"As long as Brittany likes it, that's all that matters, right?" She bends low to look at Brittany. Her smile dies when she notices the older woman's discomfort. Something is clearly wrong. Yasmiin looks back up at Jonny, who now peers at his wife as if she's a stranger.

"Jonny, we need to get to work," Brittany says, stifling a sniff, which Yasmiin catches anyway. "Please."

He presses his lips tightly, looking from her to Yasmiin, spins around, and glides away at the same pace with which he materialized. The air surrounding both women instantly becomes charged. Yasmiin pulls the brush through Brittany's hair in silence.

"Was he the cause of your tears?" Yasmiin asks after a few minutes. "At the salon?"

"You don't miss much, do you?" Brittany says, her voice flat with sarcasm. "That was my charming husband."

"He doesn't like your hair?" Yasmiin is confused. "You can stop traffic with this hair. You are beautiful."

"Thank you," Brittany says softly. "He's quite set in his ways. He doesn't like change."

"But you're a grown woman," Yasmiin adds before reaching for a flatiron she'd plugged in. "You can do whatever you want with your hair."

Brittany half-smiles beneath Yasmiin's fingers. "It's complicated."

"Is that why Amani is helping you?" Yasmiin asks.

"How much do you all discuss in that salon, *geez*?!" Brittany says irritably.

"Enough to become a legal assistant." Yasmiin laughs. "Salima and I know a lot."

"I guess I need to have a chat with Amani," Brittany says as she moves her head where Yasmiin's fingers push it.

"He can stop traffic too," Yasmiin says as she starts working on Brittany's hair. "Good-looking man. Looks like proper money." She hears Brittany sigh. "Like big, big money." Yasmiin pauses. "Where did you meet him?"

"Can we talk about something else?" Brittany snaps. "I'm not digging into *your* private life, am I?"

Yasmiin sniggers. "No problem."

The housekeeper Sylvia comes in with a tray of lemonade and homemade raspberry tarts for Yasmiin. For Brittany, she brings red grapes instead. Yasmiin grabs a tart and stuffs it into her mouth before reaching for another.

"You live a fine life here, Miss Brittany," she says before picking up a glass of pink lemonade.

Brittany answers once the housekeeper has left. "I know. I know this every day. And yet, I feel trapped. Like I can't breathe. It's hard to explain. Most people would kill for the life I have."

"So what's the problem?" Yasmiin drinks her lemonade.

"I can't explain it. It's just complicated, that's all," she says. "That's why Amani is helping me with my divorce."

"Did he cheat on you?"

"No, he would never."

"Does he beat you?"

Brittany glares at her, frowning. "No."

Yasmiin dips closer to her, lowering her voice. "Has he killed someone?"

Brittany winces. "Would you stop it? He's not a monster," she says before taking a sip of her lemonade.

"So why are you leaving him?"

Brittany clears her throat. "You won't understand and I can't explain right now. Can you please just do my hair and makeup?"

Yasmiin holds her gaze before shrugging and returning to her hair.

An hour and a half later, Yasmiin snaps photos of Brittany from all angles for her beauty account.

"Can I put your name in my caption?" she asks Brittany.

"Sure, just Brittany."

Yasmiin types away in excitement. As she packs her makeup case, Brittany strolls over to her with a gold-trimmed white envelope.

"Here's your money," Brittany says. "Thank you. I love it."

Yasmiin beams, grabbing the envelope of cash and looking at it. It reads "*Johan von Lundin*" in gold italics in the top left corner. Recognition rushes in at the name. His company is one of Yagiz's biggest customers for his cleaning business. It is also where Muna had worked before she jumped.

Yasmiin glances up at Brittany and gives her a wry smile.

TWENTY-ONE

KEMI

Kemi cradles her misshapen handmade porcelain bowl of bland lentil soup.

She never would have chosen this place herself. Tina had opted for a vegan café in SoFo—south of Folkungagatan on Södermalm. The hole-in-the-wall wears its stereotype boldly—plants hanging and covering every surface area, ambient music playing low in the background, the light whiff of incense permeating the air, white Swedes sporting waist-length locs and hemp-woven armbands. Once again wearing African prints, this time Ankara fabric, Tina moves like the queen bee in this space.

And she is fuming. Piping hot with fury. Kemi knows her own ego must shut up this time around and take it.

Tina's glare blazes amber on Kemi as they sit silently, eating their soup and occasionally munching on crispbread and hummus.

But Tina hasn't brought it up yet. Her eyes tell Kemi everything she needs to know, so she waits until Kemi is ready to explain herself.

"Tina," Kemi starts to say, warming her palms around the bowl. "I-I didn't mean to hurt him." Tina continues slurping her soup. "I didn't mean to. It just happened." Tina's spoon hits the bowl. She leans back to assess Kemi. Kemi clears her throat and continues. "I swear to you. I love Tobbe so much."

"Enough to fuck a racist behind his back?" Tina says, her voice low, the words drawled out.

"I swear to you." Kemi can feel tears well up. "I never thought I was capable of this. Of hurting someone I love so deeply."

"You don't love my brother," Tina delivers with a hard glare. Kemi wipes away rogue tears which break through.

"Don't say that," Kemi whispers. "I love him with every fiber of my being."

Tina keeps eyeing her, watching as Kemi unravels at her feet. Anything else would be less than the situation deserves. She'd broken their trust so deeply she's never going to be able to work her way back.

"You've destroyed him," Tina says. "He worshipped the ground you walked on. Saw you as this Black queen. Everything he'd ever wanted and waited so long for."

Kemi clasps her hands together and sobs into them. She hasn't heard from him since that fateful day, so she holds onto Tina's intel like a lifeline.

"I'm willing to do whatever it takes to win his trust, his love back," Kemi finally says. "I swear to you."

"I need to know, Kemi," Tina continues. "I need to know why you did this."

"I'm trying to figure that out myself too," Kemi says. When in response Tina glares back at her, she starts talking. "I-I, umm, I didn't trust it."

"Trust what?"

"Tobbe's love."

Tina settles on Kemi's confession. "Why?"

"Because it felt too easy. Too effortless," Kemi cries. "I have never been with a man who made love feel this way. And I didn't trust it." Tobias had shown her in a million little ways, but his love was too quiet to overcome the clamor of Ragnar's desire.

"So you decided to go find the most taboo of relationships and indulge yourself, right?"

Kemi nods. "Yes, I did. And it was a horrible and selfish thing to do."

"You are selfish," Tina adds. "Tobbe told me you asked him to simply uproot his life and follow you to the States."

"That was between us."

"Yes, but he has a family. A small tight-knit family here in Sweden. He can't just leave us behind on a whim. We don't make decisions on a whim here, if you haven't gathered that by now."

"I know." Kemi pauses to gulp air. "I'm sorry, Tina."

"Apologize to him, not me."

"He's not picking up my calls."

"He may never."

"Then how are we supposed to talk this through?!" Kemi becomes exasperated.

"Remember, when we first met and I told you you are a rare breed here in Sweden? A Black woman in a high position who isn't fluent in Swedish yet?" Tina says.

Kemi locks eyes with her before slipping out a weak "yes."

"It's hard for women of color to rise through the ranks here. If you're not on display as the sole token, you're always being forced to prove your worth and fight off being second-guessed at every—"

"I got fired," Kemi interrupts. Her words sink to the floor between them.

"Sorry to hear that," Tina offers a few seconds later. "Now you can go back home as you've always wanted."

"I'm staying."

"Why? You have nothing to stay here for."

"For your brother," Kemi says. "I want Tobias back and I'm willing to give it one last try if he'll have me. I love him."

"And your career here?"

"I'll find another job."

"At your current level?"

"I have a lot of experience and portfolios to back it up."

"*Adeyemi* doesn't sound very Swedish, does it?" Tina challenges. "They'll throw your CV aside before even looking at it long enough to see your *experience and portfolios*." Tina makes air quotes with her fingers.

"I can't move through life being this cynical about every single thing." Kemi's snark resurfaces. "Aren't you exhausted?"

"You think I gave up my successful music career just for fun?!" Tina flares up. "Why do you think my organization is so hard at work when it comes to equity and inclusion?"

With that, Tina begins to get her things together, stuffing her phone in her cloth purse, gathering her fabric. Before she stands up, Kemi grabs her hand in desperation.

"Please wait," she cries out. "I have something else to tell you."

Tina regards her with eagle eyes and slowly pulls out of Kemi's grasp. She waits. Kemi places her own hand on her stomach while holding Tina's gaze. She notices the other woman's features finally pull back into surprise after a few seconds.

"What?!" Tina's tone is a mixture of shock, disgust and, *dare she think it*, elation.

"It's his. I swear to you," Kemi cries.

"How can you be so sure?" She hears the vitriol in Tina's words.

"I got the test results. It's Tobias's—" Kemi's voice breaks, tears overwhelming her once more as a grin spreads across her face. "Please tell him I miss him. Can you do that for me? Please?"

Tina pushes to her feet, eyeing her up and down, before exiting the vegan hole.

BRITTANY-RAE

Spring has added a certain bounce to everyone's steps in town. Since finding Amani, she has been venturing a lot more off her island of Lidingö and wandering across town. Mostly shopping to numb her mind, stopping for black coffee and no buns at quaint boutique cafés, while people-watching behind heavy sunglasses, wondering how her lush bubble morphed into a gilded cage.

Her new Swedish friend Malin texted her yesterday to say she'd brokered a meeting with her sister-in-law Ida, who is presenting her new line at Stockholm Fashion Week in August. Malin is confident she has found the next supermodel, "Nordic Naomi."

Even with her new pixie hairstyle and flawless contour makeup, which Yasmiin swung by her house to fix earlier this morning, Brittany couldn't feel farther from that label. Plus, she's waiting for the right moment to tell Malin that, *yeah*, calling her Nordic Naomi isn't for her. But fashion has Brittany's heart and she's ready to make her way back to herself again.

Brittany stops outside the doors of Ida Persson's studio on Sibyllegatan in Östermalm when her phone rings with a call from an unknown number.

"Brittany, it's me, Eva."

"Eva! I'm so sorry to hear what happened," Brittany tells her.

"It's okay." Eva's usually chipper voice has taken on an uncharacteristic heaviness. A weight Brittany isn't sure is tied to her being fired. "It was a risk I took."

"What happened?" Brittany inquires, her voice dipping lower, while strangers brush past her.

"Frank," Eva reveals. Their chauffeur in London. "He reported back to Jonny about where he took you and what we'd been doing." Brittany's heart sinks. Burly Frank whose eyes always find hers through his rearview mirror. He'd driven her to meet Lucinda Daniels.

"And those documents I signed?"

Eva sighs down the phone. "His lawyers called him to verify his signature. They encouraged me to leave quietly." Eva pauses for air. "Now they also have dirt on me too."

"I'm so sorry. It was all my fault. I never should have involved you in this."

"It's okay," Eva assures her. "Maybe a part of me wanted out because I knew what I was doing was wrong. But I did it anyway." Another long pause. "I wanted you to be free too."

Brittany shuts her eyes at Eva's remarks, absorbing her sentiment. She feels tears pooling and takes a deep sniff to hold them back.

"How?" Brittany asks. "How can I be free of him? He's my eternal haunting."

Since Yasmiin cut off her hair, Jonny has been keeping his distance. The filter of his past slipping away, making it harder for him to see his first love in the form of his wife. To keep him at bay, Brittany knows she has to keep that short crop.

A long, surprisingly comfortable lull hangs beneath them. Brittany hears her sniffs too. Then Eva comes back on, her voice gathering strength.

"Maya is your freedom," Eva announces.

"I don't understand." Brittany's eyebrows dip.

"Promise to protect your Maya and you'll be free."

"From who?"

"From her."

Brittany lets those words settle between them. Eva doesn't need to say the name. It's the same person Jonny perpetually blames for Maya's death.

Promise him you'll protect Maya from Astrid and you'll gain your freedom.

"I need to go now," Eva says, "but I wanted to call you to let you know what happened. It's been wonderful working for you."

"I'll never forget you," Brittany says.

She swears she can feel Eva's smile through the phone before she disconnects.

"There she is!" Malin squeals in excitement the minute Brittany enters the fashion studio, as if ecstatic her shiny new toy has finally arrived.

The studio is an old industrial space with high ceilings, exposed beams, and distressed walls. Racks of clothes, mostly monochrome and neutral tones, fill the space. In the middle of the open floor plan are two wide sandalwood tables covered in swatches of fabric samples, color palettes, measuring tapes, scissors, and other tailoring equipment.

"Nordic Naomi!" Malin announces. Brittany realizes now is indeed the time.

"*Brittany*." She stresses her name, her lips stretching into a tight smile as her eyes land on a svelte woman bending over one of the tables, large frames on her lean angular face, a pencil tucked behind an ear. She's wearing a loose-fitting outfit reminiscent of a burlap sack. Her butter-yellow blonde hair is slicked back off her face and falls between her shoulder blades.

"Of course, I know." Malin laughs, turning to exchange a look with Ida. "But it's just a fun nickname. Don't you like it?"

When Brittany doesn't respond, Ida stretches to her full height, clearing Brittany's by a few inches, and saunters over like a gazelle. Albeit, one wearing a potato sack.

"Malin has been going crazy about you," she says, extending a slender hand with long fingers. "So nice to meet you, Brittany."

Brittany drops the small black portfolio she's carrying, tucks her clutch purse beneath an armpit, and slips her hand into Ida's. "Likewise."

"Coffee?" Ida offers.

An hour later, Brittany finds herself standing in one of Ida's high-end shapeless sacks, twirling left and right in front of a free-standing mirror.

"I'm thinking of having you close out the show." Ida ponders, reaching for her third cup of coffee, before studying Brittany over its rim. Malin has already left after their initial ten-minute introduction.

Brittany completes another walk under Ida's gaze, swaying, her muscle memory reactivating. She glances at her black portfolio for a moment. Sketches she had taken up doing again out of sheer boredom. Her dream. *BRIT RAE*. She detours over to the case, picks it up, and spins round to face Ida. Ida sits taller on her stool. Brittany takes a deep anchoring breath.

"Can I show you something?" she asks the designer.

Ida perks up at Brittany's sketches. "I wished I'd seen all this before," she effuses as she pores over the drawings. She glances up at Brittany with a twinkle in her eye as if her mind has instantly flooded with light.

"Brittany"—Ida can't hold her excitement—"I've got an idea!"

Unlike Persson's loose-fitting cuts, *BRIT RAE* is all about elegant body wraps. Monochromatic neutrals like Persson's, but tightly following curves, dipping in the right places, strategically placed slits screaming sophistication.

One more hour with Ida and Brittany steps into the street on light feet, her heart soaring.

Ida loves her line. Brittany can't control her emotions as she struts down the sidewalk, the dipping sun hitting her sunglasses, a smile carved wide across her face.

Her last stop for the day is a dinner date two blocks away at an overpriced grande dame of a restaurant. Truth be told, the place is long overdue for a renovation. Nostalgia drives its clientele and powers its longevity. She orders a glass of Merlot once she settles in.

Barely five minutes later, a sad-looking woman shuffles over to her table. Forlorn, dressed from head to toe in black. Her normally made-up face is bloated and naked.

"Oh my God," Brittany mutters beneath her breath as the desperate apparition approaches.

When Jonny told her about the affair, she'd texted Kemi right away to set up dinner. Mostly to fill up on gossip directly from the source. As much as she hates to admit it, seeing Kemi roots her in some way. Reminding her she isn't fully alone, even if back home they never would have found each other.

Kemi pulls out a chair and sinks into it, her eyes downcast. A few moments of silence pass between them.

"Brittany," Kemi starts, finally glancing at her. "I messed up."

YASMIIN

"We will support you every step of the way," the middle-aged doctor named Bengt assures Muna, his glasses resting on the tip of his nose. He sits on a stool he's pulled over to her bedside. Yasmiin sits across from them, her arms folded over her chest. Muna looks healthier, some weight returning to her cheeks, though her speech is still slurred and her muscles weak.

"It will feel difficult at first," the doctor explains, "and you will experience phantom limb syndrome. Feelings in the limb that is no longer there. But I assure you, Muna, we will help you as you start your new life and with a prosthetic when you're ready."

Muna nods at him, probably saving her words for Yasmiin after he's gone.

"What about her wheelchair?" Yasmiin asks.

"We're preparing it and it should arrive in time before she is discharged. We will send a nurse with you to make sure your home is suitable and accessible enough for her." The doctor looks at her chart and flips through his notes. "A physiotherapist will work with her weekly to start the rehabilitation process."

Yasmiin takes an audible breath.

"So we will start with physical therapy and rehabilitation at home. We will monitor Muna every week to manage any risks or complications that may arise. And once she's ready, we will start with regaining mobility if she wants a prosthetic," he says, matter-of-factly.

"This is all too much," Yasmiin tells him, her voice low to avoid Muna's ears. "I need help."

"You will get help. A nurse and therapist will visit often to check on Muna, change her bandages so the wound continues to heal, and do some gentle exercises to strengthen the muscles."

Yasmiin bursts into tears. The doctor holds his clipboard to his chest and wraps his arms around it, waiting for her to compose herself.

"It's a hard process for caregivers as well," he adds. "But remember, there is always help."

Yasmiin accepts his words with a nod.

"Okay, so I will leave you two now to catch up. Her nurse should be here in a few minutes to go through their routine."

"Thank you, doctor," Yasmiin offers. He nods his head at her and leaves the room. Yasmiin claims the stool he vacated, sitting closer to Muna. The younger woman smiles at her. Yasmiin reaches her palm to stroke her face.

"Is asking how you're feeling a stupid question?" Yasmiin says, smiling back.

Muna shakes her head. "No," she says softly. "I am feeling good."

"You have no idea how wonderful that is to hear, Muna."

Yasmiin presses her lips together to prevent tears. The hospital staff had counseled her against interrogating Muna, even if she felt it was coming from a place of love. Muna will share in due time, they advised.

"*Aad baad u mahadsantahay*," Muna continues their conversation in Somali, thanking Yasmiin. The words strain out softly.

"No need to say thank you," Yasmiin says, waving her gratitude aside. "I'm here now. You will never feel alone again. I promise you."

Muna smiles. "Don't make promises," she says hoarsely. "Allah is always in control." Muna tries pivoting toward the photos over her bed. Yasmiin stops her with a quick hand to her shoulder and reaches to pull them down for her. She places the three photos in Muna's hands and sits back on her stool.

She watches Muna's eyes, glassy behind tears, move over each one. Her family. She lingers over each member, her fingers tracing their faces, landing on their lips as if wishing she could talk to them one last time and kiss their cheeks.

In due time.

"*Hooyo*," Muna says as her eyes fix on her mother. She repeats the word through tears.

"Rest your voice, Muna." Yasmiin reaches for her. "Don't push yourself."

"We ran," Muna starts. Yasmiin sits closer. "We ran. *Hooyo* and Aaden. The sea." Yasmiin places a hand on her chest. "The sea took them." Muna croaks out the words. "Everything hurts." Her face contorts as she writhes in pain. "Everything."

Yasmiin strokes her head, trying to soothe her. Everything hurts. Muna's heart. Her broken body too. Her muscles must feel like jelly lying so dormant for weeks.

"We have time to talk," Yasmiin comforts her. "Don't worry." Muna shakes her head. It seems like she wants to talk now. Even if she pushes out each word through the pain.

Muna glances at the second photo of herself. "My favorite photo. Aaden took it." Her voice descends, raspy once more. "My little brother."

Yasmiin nods, acknowledging, letting her know she hangs on her every word. Muna moves to the last photo. The one of Ahmed with his sheep. Her brows dip inwards as she pores over his face. She pulls her lips into her mouth once they begin trembling and closes her eyes.

"It's okay." Yasmiin strokes her arm. "Mattias told me about him."

Muna's eyes bolt open. "Ahmed?"

"Yes, he told me what happened to him and his village," Yasmiin tells her. "Mattias has promised to share more with you. He found one brother. Afran in Canada."

"A brother?" Muna's eyes widen.

Yasmiin nods. "Isn't that something?"

"I can't believe it."

"Yes, and Afran wants to meet you in person too when you're ready."

Muna's hand instinctively reaches into her hair to run fingers through it. She feels matted clumps instead.

"It's okay, I will fix it for you once you come home. I'm mad they didn't even give you lotion for your skin," Yasmiin hisses. "I rubbed lotion on you every week when I came to see you."

Muna half-smiles.

Yasmiin continues. "So . . . you really heard me? Knew I was here? While sleeping?"

Muna nods. "Yes. Your voice. Tears. I heard everything."

Yasmiin presses her lips together to stop herself from sobbing.

Maybe her visiting gave Muna the will to hang on because she wasn't alone anymore. She had heard her, felt her, even while in deep slumber.

If she doesn't change the subject, she'll break down in front of Muna. One of them needs to stay strong for the other.

"So," Yasmiin can't resist asking, "was Ahmed your boyfriend?"

Muna grins before shaking her head. "No."

"A very handsome man," Yasmiin teases. "Did you wish him to be your boyfriend?"

"I didn't really know him," Muna says.

"But you cared about him deeply enough to protect his memory," Yasmiin adds. "I call that love."

Muna gasps, then pitches her head downwards, sobbing. Yasmiin hadn't meant to upset her. She applies a little pressure as she strokes Muna's arm, trying to calm her down.

"I don't know," Muna says a few moments later. "Maybe I did. He was sad and lonely. Like me."

Yasmiin fights the urge to ask, to prod, to question why Muna did what she did. She bites the inside of her cheek to keep from talking.

Muna continues. "That feeling. I don't wish it on my worst enemy. Loneliness."

Yasmiin nods. She knows loneliness well. It comes in different shapes and sizes. It morphs within different rooms and contexts. Oh, she knows that old friend called *isolation* well. Now she'll teach Muna how to thrive against all odds.

"I work in a beauty salon now." Yasmiin redirects her thoughts.

Muna's eyebrows perk up. "Tensta?"

"No, Kungsholmen." Yasmiin beams. "I can throw a stone and it will land at Stadshuset," she adds proudly.

"That is wonderful," Muna says. "I want to visit."

"Soon. I promise to do your hair and your face too."

Yasmiin sees Muna lift a palm to her scarred left cheek before turning to her. "Mirror?" Muna asks. "I want to see." Yasmiin shakes her head. "Phone? Camera," Muna says.

"Muna," Yasmiin starts. "You need to rest."

"I'm a big girl," Muna says, locking eyes with her. Defeated, Yasmiin reaches for her phone and hands it over. She watches as Muna assesses her face, turning her head side to side to fully take in her injuries. She quietly relinquishes the phone to Yasmiin without a word.

Pattering of feet and a gruff voice distract them. The door flings open. Yagiz lets Mehmet scuttle in. He makes a beeline for his mother and she scoops him up.

"Muna Saheed," Yagiz announces, pausing by the door, hands on his hips, a wide grin across his face. He strokes his handlebar moustache before pressing on. "You like to give people heart attacks, don't you!"

Muna chuckles. "Good to see you too, Yagiz."

He inches closer to her and places a palm over her left hand. "Praise be to Allah, you're well." His eyes roam down the sheets, which flattens after her left thigh, then back to her face.

"All will be well," Yagiz adds, his voice cracking. "I swear to you, little Muna. All will be well."

When Yasmiin bids Muna farewell and leaves the hospital, she and Yagiz are hand-in-hand.

Seeing Muna lying there must have ignited a protective instinct within Yagiz, Yasmiin deduces. He clasps her hand tightly, as if letting go would yank her into a black hole and she'd instantly vanish from sight. He seems to be coming around to the idea of Muna staying with them.

"Watch Mehmet, I'll make *manti*," Yagiz offers as he transfers the sleeping toddler over to his mother. Handmade mini Turkish ravioli. Her favorite.

"And the garlic sauce?" she inquires.

"Anything for you." He smiles at her before padding into the kitchen. Yasmiin watches his wide gait. Öz's words come into her mind. His boys want her to talk to him because Yagiz is no longer speaking to them.

She bathes Mehmet, runs thick globs of hair butter through his jet-black curls, and feeds him a bottle of warm *välling*—a milky syrupy gruel made from oats—because he can barely keep his eyes open. He's spark out once his little head hits his pillow.

Yasmiin follows wafts of garlic to their simple kitchen. She leans against the wall watching Yagiz shimmy to a tune he hums as he cooks. Her eyes trail down his toned back to his lean jeans. They make their way across his buff arms, examining the tattoos snaking along them, wondering for the first time in their years together if those tattoos hold coded meanings.

Anything related to what Öz might be insinuating.

Yagiz keeps shimmying, unaware of her presence, until he spins around and catches her. He freezes his dancing and a broad smile carves into his face.

"Sneaky, sneaky," he teases her. "Come here."

"No, you smell of garlic," she protests.

"And?" He pumps his shoulders. "Who wanted the garlic? Don't worry, we will stink together after." He winks at her. "I hope you did Amani's makeup this morning." He rubs his palms together and licks his lips.

Yasmiin gives him a strained smile, which he notices. His excitement dies down.

"Yagiz," she starts.

"Is everything okay?" he asks.

"I was going to ask you the same thing," she says, folding her arms across her chest.

He wrinkles his eyebrows at her words. "What do you mean?"

"Öz stopped by the other day."

She watches him tense his jaw. Maybe she should have employed more tact. Her timing isn't impeccable.

"What did he want? Did he touch you?"

"No, he didn't."

"He knows my schedule. Why did he come when he knew I wasn't around?"

"He wanted to talk to me."

"Talk to you? My wife? Behind my back?"

"I'm not your property."

He places his hands on his hips, looks to the ceiling, and curses. "Okay, what did he want?"

"Your boys are worried."

"Worried about what?"

"That your customers are getting angry." She pauses to collect her breath. "Are they?"

He lets out a strained laugh. "My business doesn't concern you, *aşkım*."

"We live under the same roof. We have Mehmet. Your business is my business."

"Do you eat? Do you worry about bills? Do you have what you need?" he asks. When she doesn't answer, he continues. "I'm taking care of us, don't worry."

"That night when you threw everything away," she ventures, treading lightly. "That was a lot of money. Their money." His gaze locks on hers. "I'm worried."

"Don't be," he says firmly. "I handle things." He points a finger at her. "Tell Öz never to show his face here when I'm not around. You know he wants to fuck you."

"Stop it."

"Useless idiot with his five children," Yagiz curses. "Don't open the door next time."

Yasmiin simply rolls her eyes and backs out of the kitchen.

They dine in silence. Yasmiin recognizes the weight of his anger. Whatever joviality was coursing through him as he cooked them *manti* has evaporated. The Yagiz sitting across from her scarfing down the ravioli is incensed, his ego flustered. The last thing she knows he wants to look is weak in front of his posse. *Her braggart.*

He pushes his unfinished plate away as if the sight of food disgusts him and he flies to his feet. Yasmiin watches him grab his jacket and push his shoes on.

"Where are you going? It's late," she asks. Yagiz doesn't respond. "Yagiz?"

He answers by slamming the door.

For the first time since they became husband and wife, Yagiz doesn't come home that night.

TWENTY-TWO

KEMI

That look.

One of abject pity that she let herself go so quickly. She never wants to see it again. On anyone's face for that matter. Especially not Brittany, of all people.

Her pride can't take any more hits. She wishes she'd feigned a previous commitment when Brittany had texted her to meet for dinner.

> Just want to catch up. Nothing special. Dinner's on me.
>
> Brittany

Hopefully, she's found a divorce lawyer herself, Kemi mulls as she strolls along Mäster Samuelsgatan toward their rendezvous. Yes, she promised Brittany she would search within her network. No, she no longer cared at this point. Jonny had fired her. Last she heard, Ragnar was back to running the Bachmann project.

Frankly, Brittany is the last person she wants to confide in. Yet, if anyone else can understand what it's like to live under constant scrutiny of one's motives, it's Brittany.

Kemi moves lethargically toward Brittany, who looks every bit the model she is. Her new short Halle Berry hairstyle makes her narrow face look even more angular. Sitting under a dim old-fashioned lamp with flawless makeup, she looks divine.

Kemi notices Brittany's eyes widen upon her approach. They make a small crawl from her face, down the black sweater she's wearing over black baggy pants, comfortably hiding her growing bump, to the black sneakers on her feet. Kemi pulls out a chair and sits opposite Brittany, whose right hand moves to rest on her chest beneath delicate chiffon.

Her dignity is long gone, along with her job. She has nothing to lord over Brittany anymore.

"Brittany. I messed up," Kemi dives right in. "I truly messed up." She inhales deeply, setting both hands on the white linen tablecloth before finally looking at Brittany.

"Oh my goodness," Brittany says. "Are you okay?"

Kemi winces. "I've had better days."

"You didn't have to come if you weren't up to it," Brittany tells her. A waiter strolls by. Brittany flicks up a manicured finger to get his attention.

"It's okay. I needed to get out of my apartment eventually for some fresh air," Kemi mumbles as the waiter drags his feet to their table.

"Yes?" he asks, a bite to his tone, as if they'd tapped his shoulder while he was in the middle of an urgent task.

"Would you like a glass of red as well?" Brittany asks Kemi.

"I'll have what you're having," Kemi replies.

"Merlot," he confirms while pursing his lips, before swinging around and away from them.

"What's with the attitude?" Kemi asks when he's out of earshot.

"Look around." Brittany waves her hand nonchalantly before picking up her wineglass and taking a sip. "Look at us. Even with us speaking English, he still doesn't want us here."

Kemi's eyes sweep around the stuffy dining hall with heavy antique furniture and equally wizened patrons, questioning why Brittany picked this spot in the first place.

"So, how have you been?" Brittany asks, setting her glass down.

"You heard, didn't you?" Kemi holds her gaze.

Brittany clears her throat. "Well, I heard things so I wanted to confirm if they are true directly from you."

"So you can gloat, right?" Kemi eyes her suspiciously.

"Look, I'm not your enemy, okay?" Brittany's irritation is clear. "I heard Ragnar's evil spawn called you the n-word and I want you to tell me it ain't so. Jonny had me clutching my pearls when he dropped the news."

Kemi lowers her head. She isn't going to cry in front of Brittany. They aren't there yet. They might never get there. But right now, Brittany is the one in front of her.

Brittany presses on. "Whatever happened between that asshole and you is no excuse for them to accept what that child said."

"They fired me," Kemi says.

"I know. Jonny told me."

"Ragnar still has his job," Kemi continues. "In fact, he's back on the very same project."

"What did you expect?" Brittany stresses. Kemi knows it isn't a question. "They are best friends. Nepotism runs deep here. You'll forever be the outsider they can't trust. They forgive their own. They fully understand he just needed to fuck you out of his system and return home."

The waiter arrives with Kemi's wine and pulls out a notepad for their orders.

"Can you please give us a few more minutes?" Kemi requests.

He rolls his eyes and lets out an audible gasp. "The kitchen is closing in an hour."

Kemi glares through him before turning back to Brittany. "I'm not spending my money here." She digs into her bag for her wallet and pulls out two hundred-kronor notes.

"Oh, we don't take cash here," he adds as he rests on his back heel. Kemi smirks before pulling out her credit card.

"No." Brittany presses her hand against hers. "Let Jonny pay for it." She fishes into her clutch for her Centurion card, courtesy of von Lundin money. The waiter shifts on his feet, visibly shaken by the sight of the exclusive black AmEx card. He gingerly reaches for it from between her fingers.

Fifteen minutes later, they find a hotdog kiosk close to Hötorget. Cradling brown-paper-packaged *tunnbrödsrulle* wraps and wooden forks, they park themselves on the steps of Stockholm's iconic cyan-blue Konserthus to tuck in.

Brittany lifts the hotdog an inch from the rolled-up flatbread and takes a bite.

"Hmmm, I've never tried this before." She samples another bite before scooping some mashed potatoes, shrimp salad, and sweet relish from the roll. "Quite tasty."

"Don't tell me you eat like a bird to maintain that figure." Kemi laughs, before chomping on her roll. Brittany giggles in an amusingly dainty way. Kemi pops open a can of Sprite and takes a long swig. They watch as people mill around Hötorget. The fruit and vegetable vendors begin packing up for the night. Filmgoers rush next door to Filmstaden to catch a movie. Across the square, old-school jazz music emanates from the throwback hotel.

It has been awhile since Kemi has felt this relaxed. Jobless with no idea of her next steps, all that pales in comparison to simply pigging out and soaking up the moment.

With Brittany of all people.

"Why did you do it?" Brittany's question breaks her thoughts and stops her mid-bite. She inhales sharply, gathering her nerves.

"It just happened," Kemi explains. "We were both in the moment. Couldn't think straight."

"I don't get it, though," Brittany says. "Why him of all God's other gorgeous creatures on this green earth? He's such a basic man."

"I regret every moment with him." Kemi's voice dips lower as shame washes over her anew.

"Tobias seemed like a wonderful guy when I met him," Brittany adds. "Definitely better looking."

"That's why I'm staying," Kemi says. "I want Tobbe back. I really do. I love him so much."

"But you're putting your life on hold for him," Brittany tries reasoning with her. "What happened when he found out?"

"He hasn't spoken to me since then."

"And you're still holding out for him?" Brittany's eyes narrow, Kemi's words clearly striking a nerve. "I waited years for my ex to propose to me. He never did."

Kemi turns to Brittany, studying her face. She can't tell her about Tobias's baby on the way. The real reason she wants to try once more. To make it work with the man she loves. This secret she'll keep from Brittany. The last thing she needs is the other woman digging for drama and bringing Ragnar up again.

"How are things going with the divorce?" she asks, switching topic.

Brittany shrugs. "I've found one of the best lawyers in town. The process is inching along."

"It must be tough." Kemi notices Brittany has abandoned her *tunnbrödsrulle* after two more bites. Kemi envies her discipline. "What will you do about Maya when it comes to custody?"

"I can't take her out of Sweden, so I'm trapped until I find a way." Brittany sips water, her look forlorn.

"I'm sorry it's ending like this for you." Kemi reaches to rub Brittany's knee, a gesture which shakes Brittany at first until she relaxes into it.

"I got Maya out of all this so it wasn't all that bad." She lowers her gaze. "I think the hardest thing is realizing he never loved me all along. What a pill to swallow."

"What?" Kemi sits taller. "What do you mean?"

"Jonny never loved me," Brittany continues. "I look just like his dead ex. That's why he married me."

Kemi wrinkles her forehead, processing the news. "Dead ex? When? How?"

"Girl, I can't get into all that right now, but trust me, we've got time for more *fika* dates." Brittany chuckles. Kemi joins her, a feeling of lightness rushing through her back.

"I respect that," Kemi says.

"So what have we learned from all this?" Brittany's eyes settle on Kemi once more, her eyelashes looking heavier in the fading light.

"That our mistakes as Black women are unforgivable in this world." Kemi sighs before taking another sip of Sprite. "Oh, and don't fuck basic white men." She laughs.

"Exactly!"

Kemi giggles, baring her teeth before spinning toward Brittany once more. "I didn't say when I saw you earlier at the restaurant, but I like your new haircut. It suits you."

Brittany smiles, fingering her short tresses, while giving Kemi's new look the once-over. Then she reaches for her phone, taps, scrolls, and taps some more. A few seconds later, Kemi's phone buzzes with a contact card.

"Please call Yasmiin," Brittany pleads. "Let her fix you up too."

A few days later, Kemi sits in a plastic-covered swiveling chair as a songstress belts out in high-pitched Arabic falsetto over the radio. When she strolled into that pint-sized salon tucked away on Kungsholmen, she spotted Yasmiin's curvy pear shape and apple bottom right away.

Yasmiin's thick hair is lush and blowdried out to her shoulders. She stares suspiciously over protruding cheeks as Kemi walks in with her crochet braids matted beyond dignity.

"You Brittany's friend?" Yasmiin asks, her eyes traveling Kemi's length, taking in her shapeless gown in contrast to Yasmiin's vibrant floral dress belted at the waist.

Brittany's friend.

Kemi recoils at those words, her face contorting into a frown. Then her features even out and a smile creeps onto her lips.

"Yes," she confirms. "I'm her friend."

YASMIIN

A few days earlier, Yasmiin's phone pinged with a notification. Someone called Kemi claiming she'd got her number from Brittany von Lundin, Amani's super-wealthy client. She texted the Kemi lady back. Sure, she can do braids.

When Kemi shows up at the salon, Yasmiin frowns at her. The woman looks sad, like she's carrying an evil spirit on her shoulder, wearing a shapeless gown. And her hair. Goodness, what is wrong with these women? Her crochet braids are matted and way past their best-before date. Her eyes also wash over the woman's belly. Though Kemi tries to hide it, Yasmiin can clearly see there's a baby on the way.

"Come sit." Yasmiin pats her pleather hairdressing chair. Kemi shuffles in on unsteady feet as Yasmiin sizes her up. She grabs a pair of scissors and starts clipping off chunks close to the woven base. She works in silence until she needs to know why the woman underneath her shears looks this sad during summer of all seasons.

"Where are you from?"

"Oh, I'm from Nigeria. Also the US. I lived there for years. American citizen," Kemi tells her. "And you?"

"Somalia," Yasmiin says as she snips away. "What brings you to Sweden?" She hears Kemi sigh.

"A job. A really big company."

"Which one? IKEA? Ericsson? H&M?" Yasmiin prods.

"Not that big," Kemi chuckles. "A marketing company, von Lundin Marketing."

Of course, Yasmiin ponders. That's the connection. Brittany von Lundin. Kemi works for that weird husband she met.

"So that is how you know Brittany!"

"Kind of," Kemi adds. "I work for her husband. Used to," she corrects herself.

"Oh, what happened?" Yasmiin asks, locking eyes with Kemi through the mirror. Kemi purses her lips. It seems she doesn't want to go into details.

"Things didn't work out there," Kemi offers.

"But you have another job now?"

Kemi shakes her head. "Can't seem to find one."

"It's not easy in this country, I tell you." Yasmiin continues working her hair. "What did you do there?"

Kemi hesitates before responding. "I was a director."

"Director? For this von Lundin company? Sister!" Yasmiin gasses her up. "Keep representing us!" She notices Kemi wince at her glee.

"I told you I'm no longer there," Kemi says. "And I haven't found another role at the same level. Or even two levels lower."

"Sorry," Yasmiin says. "I'm sure you will find something soon, *Inshallah*. You are a smart woman. And at your level, a big director job."

"I'm not so sure," Kemi counters. "I did something unforgivable. It cost me my job."

Yasmiin frowns at her, trying to understand. "Unforgivable? Did you steal money from them?"

"Of course not," Kemi says, slightly affronted.

"So what did you do that's unforgivable if you didn't steal from them?"

"It's a private matter, that's all I can share."

"Private as in private, private with von Lundin?" Yasmiin pumps her hips suggestively. "Your friend's husband?"

"Don't be absurd!" Kemi reprimands her. "Never."

"So what did you do that's causing you to walk around like a dead woman who can't forgive herself?" Yasmiin persists. Salima is busying herself with another customer and the blaring music drowns out all noise, giving them distance from the others.

Silence hangs between them until Kemi shares a morsel. "I did something stupid with someone I shouldn't have and it cost me my job."

"So you're wearing black now and forever in mourning?"

It is Kemi's turn to frown back at Yasmiin through the mirror.

"You talk like this to everyone?" Kemi spits.

"I'm not the one here with shameful braids," Yasmiin shoots back. "I'm trying to help you, big madam. Let me help you." She watches Kemi relax back into her chair. "So you did something stupid, everyone does stupid things all the time. If it involves a man, don't let yourself go like this because of a stupid man."

"Aren't you the double stylist-therapist combo," Kemi says sarcastically.

"This is a salon," Yasmiin says. "People like to waste money. Come here. Speak your mind and go home lighter."

"Very well, what do you want to know?"

Yasmiin silently observes her as she starts loosening the cornrows beneath the crochet braids.

"He is married, isn't he?" Yasmiin breaks their standoff. "Is that his baby?"

Kemi flinches. "Why would you think that?"

"Because if he was available, you wouldn't be looking this bad," Yasmiin observes. "You can't forgive yourself. And it seems other people don't want to forgive you too."

"Shall we try box braids?" Kemi asks, changing the subject. Yasmiin chuckles beneath her breath.

"Whatever you want," Yasmiin says before combing Kemi's hair out, readying it for a wash and deep conditioner.

This is the furthest their conversation goes. It seems this Kemi woman always comports herself to project strength. Even in the salon, she doesn't want to drop her facade of pride, Yasmiin mulls.

But it seems Yasmiin's short conversation must have switched something within her. When her box braids are done, the Kemi woman lifts her shoulders higher. She straightens her shoulders, sitting taller, as if the ghost of who she once was has finally snuck back into her body.

"This is incredible, Yasmiin, thank you!" Kemi says delightedly. She gets to her feet, but Yasmiin stops her.

"Please sit. I need to do your face too."

BRITTANY-RAE

The Sandhamn Beast.

Brittany's nickname for the sprawling von Lundin estate, which takes up so much waterfront space, you'd think it is the Royal Palace itself. She observes its manicured lawns behind wide feline sunglasses as their luxury speedboat approaches its private dock, Jonny at the helm steering. White short-sleeved linen shirt over white capris, wind-tossed wheat-colored hair, his lips in a grim line beneath his own shades.

On the surface, they might as well be on a nautical-themed photoshoot, but beneath the still waters facade of their relationship lies her rapidly beating heart anxious to execute her Amani-hatched plan.

Come back with something. Anything.

Behind her, Sylvia and Vicky, hugging Maya tightly to her chest, sit huddled closely as the speedboat bobs across the soft waves of the Baltic.

Antonia's family had arrived a day earlier with their own staff to prepare for the rest, along with Wilhelm and Astrid. Svea is finally bringing her beau over the next day. As their boat nears the estate, Brittany spots a bare-footed Antonia observing their approach, both hands hidden inside the pockets of loose-fitting harem pants. Brittany gives her a weak wave, which Antonia returns, lifting her right hand.

When Brittany touches land, Antonia immediately sweeps her into a crushing embrace.

"I am so happy you came," she whispers. "This means a lot to him."

"I'm doing this for Maya," Brittany says.

"Give him a chance."

"I can't talk about this right now."

"You may want to." Antonia holds her gaze, leaving Brittany to decipher what she means, frowning at her words.

With that confusing statement, Antonia gives her a terse smile before turning to her niece with her arms wide open, her eyebrows arching into mini-rainbows. "*Raring!*" *Darling!*

As Brittany approaches the front door, she stiffens when she feels his hand on the small of her back, and she stops dead.

"You're beautiful," Jonny whispers before sliding in closer to her. He wants her to keep up the charade once they walk in to face his parents. Her plans for divorce are a silly game to keep her occupied, they probably presume. His lips brush her cheek. She pulls back from it. "Thank you for coming."

"Johan!" a voice, husky sweet, cuts through their moment. Standing at the top of the stairs is a slender white woman wearing a see-through floral halterneck dress with high slits along both thighs. She's barefoot and glows golden under the summer sun. She glides down to meet them, pulling Jonny into a hand-roaming hug, her palms splaying and moving across his back. Brittany watches Jonny stiffen into a statue. A frozen piece of marble who hates being touched if he doesn't instigate it himself.

Then the blonde settles on Brittany and stretches out a hand in greeting.

"Katarina Bernadotte," she introduces herself, adding a slight shoulder lift to the gesture.

Having hung around the von Lundins long enough, Brittany knows Bernadotte means the royal family. Figuring out Katarina's lineage within that mix now hangs on her mind as her eyes walk up and down Katarina's form.

"Brittany," she responds, finally taking her hand. Jonny's hand finds Brittany's back once more in a much firmer stance.

"I grew up spending summers here with Johan and his family." Katarina's eyes sweep back to him. "My family owns a couple of cottages across the island."

Brittany mentally converts cottages to villas.

"Jonny," he corrects, his lips barely parting to push out his name.

Katarina chuckles in response. "You know I can't call you that." She pivots to Brittany. "It's not a fitting name. He knows this."

Jonny switches to Swedish, his tone interrogating. *Varför? Why? Vem? Who?* Phrases pour out of him in rapid succession until he tenses when Katarina drops his mother's name. He tears away from Brittany's side and scales the stairs, ignoring the butler holding a tray bearing tumblers of lemonade with sprigs of mint.

Come back with something. Anything.

Propelled by Amani's words, Brittany rushes after him into the Beast, trying to keep up, but Jonny is on a mission. His eyes scan each room they move through, ignoring greetings from his nephews, his brother-in-law, the house staff, and even Wilhelm, his father. Brittany smiles in return to each person he storms past while reaching into her purse for her phone. She isn't sure what she plans on capturing, but at least she has it in her hand. She stops to pull up her voice recorder app and slips the phone back into her pocket. When others try coming closer, she holds up a hand to stop them before slipping in behind Jonny.

He pushes open the heavy door so violently Astrid yelps, her hand flying to her chest, where a string of Tahitian black pearls sits.

"Johan," she says, comporting herself and closing the book she'd been thumbing through. Brittany moves to Jonny's side. The closer she is, the clearer her phone will pick up what is about to transpire.

"*Jag vill inte ha henne.*" Jonny is standing with his hands balled into fists by his sides. "*Varför är hon här?*"

Despite her paltry Swedish, those words Brittany understands. *I don't want her. Why is she here?* She can decipher simple phrases and words, but speaking? She still hasn't summoned the courage to do so without fear of judgment.

Brittany watches Astrid suck in a deep breath of irritation.

"*Inte nu. Inte framför henne.*" Astrid nods her head toward Brittany. *Not now. Not in front of her.* Astrid turns to Brittany and says in English, "Can you please excuse us? We have a family matter to discuss."

Brittany narrows her eyes at the older woman. Three years on and Astrid still doesn't consider her family. She isn't sure if she should stand her ground next to him so she can siphon the information she needs or turn on her heels and leave the room.

Jonny answers for her. "*Hon får stanna.*" His command is firm. *She stays.*

"*Hon får inte,*" Astrid stresses back. *She may not.*

"Hon är min fru," Jonny says, his fingers escaping their fists and beginning to dance. *She is my wife.*

Astrid switches to English again. "Brittany, please excuse us."

"No." Jonny dips his head low, cocking it toward Brittany. "Stay."

"Very well." Astrid admits defeat and pushes to her feet. "I am no longer responsible for what you may hear," she continues. Jonny's eyes burn through Astrid. She matches his glare. After all, he inherited that searing gaze from her.

"I don't need to be here," Brittany hears herself say.

"I need you here." Jonny turns to take her in.

That is when she sees *him* once more. The man morphing into a boy right in front of her. The one she'd eventually fallen for, before the secrets surrounding Maya Daniels were dredged up by his family. He has no one. He has never had anyone.

"*Vad håller du på med Katarina?*" he asks Astrid gruffly. *What are you doing with Katarina?* Brittany knows precisely why Astrid dragged royalty back to her son's feet.

"*Så du inte glömmer vem du är,*" Astrid says, her tone casual. Brittany picks out "forget" and "who you are."

"*Vem är jag egentligen?*" Jonny asks her. *Who am I really?*

"*Vad sysslar du med nu, Johan?!*" Astrid seems agitated.

"*Vem.. är...jag?*" he asks again, his voice dipping lower, making the hairs on Brittany's arms stand up.

Astrid takes him in for a couple of seconds before asking, "*Vad har jag gjort fel som din mamma, hmm, Johan?*" *What have I done wrong as your mother?*

His fingers retreat back into fists. Brittany sees the veins along his hands and arms begin to strain against his skin. He presses his thin lips tight, his body trying to control itself from slipping into overstimulation.

"*Hmm, Johan?*" Astrid prods again. "*Vad har jag gjort fel?*"

"*Du tog henne ifrån mig!*" he cries out, his voice cracking with emotion. *You took her from me.*

Brittany's heart sinks after over a year of not truly knowing his feelings. She'd long reconciled herself to the fact Jonny never loved her and still pines over Maya's ghost, but witnessing his raw emotion over his loss still proves difficult to swallow.

Astrid soaks up his words, the only sign of emotion a slight tensing of her mouth.

"*Aldrig skulle jag göra sådant.*" She sounds distressed. Brittany makes out "never" and "do."

Without warning, Jonny launches into rapid bursts of Swedish, his face tinting red, spittle flying once his tears come. He is no longer talking, but screaming words at Astrid, his veins straining, threatening to burst. Astrid breaks his flow, occasionally interjecting, but he verbally overpowers her.

Brittany is lost. She can no longer follow along but she keeps recording, praying it picks up whatever she needs to hear. Amani will translate, she keeps repeating to herself as tears well up in her own eyes.

Then Jonny lets out a blood-curdling scream, a sound she'd only heard him make once before when his brain could no longer catch up with what his heart was feeling. That roar shakes Brittany to her core.

Within seconds, the study door flings open. Antonia's husband Stig, her twin sons in their early twenties, and the butler rush in. It takes all four men to restrain Jonny while his father Wilhelm floats in behind them.

Her husband keeps screaming that deafening banshee sound. Astrid stands stoically and watches as they drag him out of the room before crumbling into herself and breaking down in front of Brittany. They can still hear Jonny's muffled wails echoing throughout the mansion.

She looks at Astrid, who is sobbing in small fits like a bird. Antonia comes in and takes one look at Brittany, before rushing to bundle her mother up into a hug. Katarina Bernadotte strolls in, her arms wrapped tightly around her chest.

"Maybe it's time I went home," Katarina says in English for Brittany's benefit.

Brittany wipes a rogue tear with the back of a finger. "Yeah, maybe you should." Katarina nods quietly, leaving Brittany with Antonia, whose arms are still encircled around her mother.

The air in the study feels devoid of oxygen.

"Did you upset my mother?" Antonia snaps, frowning at Brittany, the creases in her forehead deepening.

"What?" Brittany is exasperated. "She was the one who upset him," she says and points fruitlessly at Astrid. "*She* was the one who did something to Maya Daniels!"

Astrid is still sobbing, her shoulders hopping fragilely with each pronounced inhale. Then she turns toward Brittany and looks at her in a way that frightens her.

"You were never good enough for my boy," Astrid croaks through her tears. "Never."

"Astrid!" Antonia tries to hush her mother. Astrid pushes out of her grasp instead and moves toward Brittany. Brittany reads a mixture of anger and disgust in each step of her approach.

"Just like that Black girl," Astrid says. "He threatened me," she cries, her translucent eyes near invisible behind tears. "My Johan. He was a child. He wanted to walk away from us. From his family. To leave everything we've built, *for that girl*," she snarls at the memory. "To force her on us!" Her voice is shrill now in desperation. "Whatever magic spell she cast over him, whatever Black voodoo she had, she stole my child away from me. My baby!"

Brittany swallows, her jaw slack, words forgotten. Johan had threatened to walk away from their kingdom if they didn't accept Maya with open arms. Had he put their reputation at stake? For a family which fears scandal like vampires fear sunlight, had they stooped to murder to avoid their son causing one by running off with *that Black girl*? The love of his life?

Brittany finally fishes up a few words, delivering them in a whisper. "Did you hurt her?"

The room waits in hushed silence.

"Did you hurt Maya Daniels?"

TWENTY-THREE

KEMI

It's been weeks since she was fired and she still hasn't received any responses to her resume from her job search.

Migrationsverket—the Swedish Migration Agency—says she has three months to find another job before her work permit is revoked with deportation on the horizon. She still isn't sure she wants to rebuild her career in Sweden. She reached out to advertising agencies she knows would kill to have her on board, but she might as well have run her resume through a paper shredder instead. Not a single word from any of them and she winces when she remembers Tina Wikström's words.

Adeyemi doesn't sound very Swedish, does it?

Kemi tried her luck at Arbetsförmedlingen, the Swedish Public Employment Service. But the officer—a bespectacled middle-aged woman with translucent eyes and silver hair—sitting across from her audibly sucked in air, and suggested she try a cleaning job.

"*Du vet…så att du kan vara användbar under tiden,*" she casually said. *You know…so you can be useful in the meantime.*

Kemi simply cut through her with a searing gaze, got to her stilettoed feet, grabbed her oversized bag, and strutted out of the woman's insult.

Since Yasmiin gave her chunky box braids a few weeks earlier, Kemi has noticed the change in her step. It's a style she wished she had tried before. When she had started to get out of the salon chair, Yasmiin pushed her back down again, yelling

"*Vänta!*"—*Wait!*—before proceeding to give her a complimentary full makeup session because she said Kemi looked sad.

Looked sad.

With her new head-turning braids, Kemi decides she isn't going to resign herself to *looking sad*. Because if it isn't looks of charity from the likes of Brittany, then it's looks of veneered judgment from even her closest friend Malcolm.

Which is why she has been avoiding Swedish class with a vengeance too. No one will ever look upon her with pity again if she can help it.

Malcolm had texted her earlier when she was on her way to the salon.

> You can't run from me forever, girl. You know you have to come spend Midsummer with us, right? Plus, we gotta go over the wedding arrangements. I don't need any more drama from Jose.

And when Midsummer rolls around, Kemi stands in front of their apartment door a block from Skanstull station on Södermalm. She cradles a small pot of Jollof rice she promised to add to Malcolm and Jose's international spread. *Bring something from home.* That had been their request.

Her bump is now a sizable six months.

Malcolm had been the first person she called, sobbing maniacally over the phone when she got her test results ruling Ragnar out as her baby's father. Malcolm had screamed with joy into the receiver at decibels sufficient to take out her hearing. Then he had cursed out "Sven"—his nickname for Ragnar—hoping his "*cheating-ass peen shrivels up with gangrene and drops off.*"

Above all, he promised not to say a word about it to Tobias.

Now Kemi can no longer hide her baby on the way. Frankly, she's tired of cowering in fear. She's ready to boldly step out and confidently own her mistake.

"Who else is coming?" she texts Malcolm while still on the *tunnelbana*.

"Who else needs to work the wedding," he texts back and she knows *he* is going to be there. *Tobias*. They haven't spoken or seen each other since that day four months ago.

She rings the doorbell as lightly as she can, hoping no one hears her. Malcolm yanks the door wide open, an apron tied around his torso with what she hopes are streaks of barbecue sauce across it.

"Your highness." He gives her a mock bow after taking in her new braids and steps aside. His eyes make their way down to her belly. He places a hand on it and stares back with the widest grin. "You're safe here. It's time."

She nods at him, biting her bottom lip to prevent tears, and takes cautious steps into the modest airy space, looking around, trying to catch a glimpse of *him*.

"Where can I set this?" she asks, readjusting the pot. Malcolm points to the table already laid out with six chairs around it. She sets it down next to racks of baby back ribs.

"You know your American ribs," Malcolm says before pointing to another dish. "That's Chilean *plateada*, a.k.a. slow cooked goodness. Sebastian brought some fancy-schmancy football money *Janssons frestelse*. Still got damn anchovies in them, though. Tina brought some Gambian *benachin* so we may have a Nigerian-Gambian square-off," he cackles. "And Tobias just brought his fine self and cupcakes."

Kemi swallows. That is when she catches the trio—Sebastian, Tina, and Tobias—chatting out on Malcolm's sliver of a balcony, baking in the summer sun. Tina drags at a cigarette.

"Where's Jose?" she asks, her eyes sweeping around once more.

"Ran across the park to go get tomatoes," Malcolm says as he struts back into the kitchen with Kemi trailing. "I told him the salad can survive without them. But I guess not, because he hates that park."

Kemi giggles nervously while she leans back against the countertop. She quickly drops her candor, a bag of nerves. Malcolm returns to his task of dicing avocados. He turns to peer at her over his shoulder.

"How you holding up?" he asks softly.

"Better," she offers.

"Well, you seem to be in a good place. Hair snatched. Face beat. Outfit on fleek. Sexy baby bump." He glances at her polka-dot halterneck dress. "How did you get those puppies parked that high up?!" He turns back to his task, not waiting for an explanation.

"Does he know you know?" she asks. Malcolm shakes his head. "And Tina?" Another shake of his head. Her love and respect for Malcolm grow several shades deeper.

"You know you can't avoid each other forever," he says. "Go out there and say hi."

"Right," she mutters.

She takes a deep breath and pushes away from the counter in time to see the balcony's double doors open and their small group saunter back in. She immediately avoids Tobias and her eyes seek Tina's. Still hard like their last lunch date. Tina freezes, visibly shocked at seeing Kemi.

Kemi reads it in her eyes. Did she think she'd been lying about being pregnant? Maybe Tina assumed she'd just disappear? It's clear she hasn't mentioned the news to Tobias.

"Kemi!" Sebastian is the only one who seems interested in her presence. "Kemi?" He pauses to take in her belly. "Oh my goodness! *Grattis!*"

Kemi's *hej* in response lacks weight. Sebastian gives her an airy hug filled with every awkward unsayable thing he wants to say.

She turns to Tobias. He looks different. His reddish-brown cropped hair has grown by about two inches into a styled mini-Afro. He's sporting a matching goatee, and his black T-shirt stretches across his chest, his muscles looking larger. Has he been working out since their split? He looks good, and in that moment, Kemi is grateful Brittany had intercepted her pity party and spun her around in a new direction.

"Good to see you, Tobbe," she says weakly. His mouth hangs open as if paused by a glitching universe mid-speak. He comes to and gives her a nod instead, words unspoken.

She turns to Tina. "Tina?"

"Kemi." Tina's voice is low. "I had no idea you were keeping it."

"What?!" Tobias comes on strong, his eyes darkening as he stares at his sister. "You knew she was pregnant all these months?"

Tina turns to her brother with sharp eyes. "Considering you weren't the only one she was fucking, I wasn't sure it was yours!"

Sensing the energy, Sebastian clears his throat and grabs Tina by the elbow, dragging her away from her brother to join him over at Malcolm's vinyl collection. They leave Tobias with his hands parked in his pockets, staring at Kemi.

"Uhmm, you look good," Kemi says after Tina gives them space.

"Thanks," he says. "Those suit you." He points to her braids. "Aaand you're pregnant?"

She grins slightly. She needs to fill the void with words, with anything.

"How have you been?" she asks.

"Good," he says, stretching, drawing her eyes to his torso. "And you? My God, how have you been? How far along are you?"

"I'm feeling much better," she says. A few seconds of silence. "I sent you so many voice and text messages."

"I know, I got them."

"So you didn't want to speak with me like an adult?"

He frowns at her. "You've got to be joking," he hisses. Kemi pulls in her lower lip, reeling in her ego. "Is it mine or his?"

"It's yours," she says. "I love you, Tobbe."

The words sink straight to the floor. She watches his brows broaden into lines.

"You never did."

"I swear to you. With every inch of me."

"If that was true, you wouldn't have hurt me. You don't hurt people you love that way."

"Unfortunately we do. We all do. And once we realize what we've done, we're already broken and in shards," she says. Kemi watches him as he processes her words. "I'm not going to beg you,

Tobbe. I am done groveling for anyone, no matter how much my heart aches for them. Including you."

His nostrils flare as he listens to her. "So you've finally found your dignity?" he says bitterly.

"Yes, and so much more," she says, reaching for her stomach in comfort, stroking it. "This is yours. I can prove it." They stare at each other until Tobias gasps audibly before raking his fingers through his mini-Afro. Then tears drown him.

"For weeks I couldn't think of you without thinking of his scent on you. All over you."

"I'm so sorry," she says, her voice weak. "I swear to you, it will never happen again. Ever."

"But why did it happen, though? I wanna know why." He's talking, opening up. She grabs onto that line of hope.

"I didn't trust your love. It felt too easy, too effortless."

That is when she catches it. His eyebrows relax once more with that look she has now grown to hate.

Pity.

"Damn," he mutters softly. "What has the world done to our Black women?" His voice is breaking. It's not a question. Kemi knows what he means.

"Why did you wait?" she asks him. "Your mother keeps saying you were waiting for a strong African woman like her."

"What are you talking about?"

"Were you simply looking for a replacement mother all those years?"

"Now you're being absurd." Irritation broils within him.

"Don't lie to me, Tobbe," she says with a slight shake of her head.

"Lie? Lie? You are one to talk!" he flares up again.

She launches herself into his arms. Stunned at first, Tobias stiffens, his arms held straight down by his sides. Then instinctively they wrap around her body, his hands spread across her back to pull her closer. He turns to bury his head in her neck, nuzzling into her warmth.

"I'm so sorry," she mutters against his neck. His grip tightens a little.

"You're everything I've been dreaming of, all my life," he whispers back. "A woman who fully takes up space, who lights up a room with her very being."

A sob escapes Kemi. "So you love the *idea* of me…but not me?" she asks while still in his embrace.

"Don't say that," Tobias says strongly. "I love every inch of you. I grew up in a world conditioned to never stick out. To never take up space. And I knew when I met the right woman, that life of conformity would never be for me." He's sobbing audibly now. "But I fear, my love, will I ever be enough for you?"

He doesn't wait for her answer. He simply pulls back to look at her before planting both palms on her belly, moving them gently across the surface and gazing at her behind thick films of tears.

"Is it mine?" he asks.

Kemi nods. "They're yours."

His eyes widen, his breath snatched. The word *What?* barely leaves his lips.

"Twins," she continues. "I found out at my last ultrasound."

"Are you sure?" he cries. "Please don't do this to me all over again. Please don't break my heart again."

"I swear to you," Kemi whispers before flying into his arms once more, wrapping hers around his neck.

An unexpected sob breaks out. They turn to find Tina nuzzled in Sebastian's shoulder, crying.

"Where on earth is he?" Malcolm cuts through their moment, exasperated, as he storms out of the kitchen. "He's over an hour late. What the fuck type tomatoes did he go looking for?!" Kemi notices him shifting on his feet, a hand perched on his waist. So unlike Malcolm, who always seems to have everything under control. Or at least feigned cool nonchalance.

Fifteen minutes later, they all hear the knock. Malcolm races toward it, gearing to yell at Jose for his theatrics. He catches his fiancé in his arms instead, his butter-smooth handsome face caked with blood.

"Oh my God!" Kemi screams, rushing to Malcolm's side as he props Jose by the shoulder and leads him over to their beige sofa. Tina organizes pillows to boost him. Malcolm falls to his knees in front of him. Tobias returns from the kitchen with a towel and warm water from the tap.

"What happened, baby?" Malcolm cradles his face gently, assessing him. Jose shivers, crying. His right eye is swollen shut, his lips cracked. "What happened? Please tell me."

Jose keeps shaking his head, his tears trying to force themselves out, clearly in pain. Kemi places a hand over her mouth, tears already streaming down her face. A few weeks from their wedding and she knows Jose will joke about how the universe is conspiring to make him look busted on his special day. But right now, her heart breaks as she watches him wince and writhe in pain.

"Was it the park?" Malcolm asks him. Kemi catches Jose's slight nod. She hears Malcolm breathe in deeply. "Was it them?" Another featherlight nod.

"*B…bö…*" Jose struggles to get the word out, drops of blood splashing onto Malcolm's face as he tries. "*Bög.*"

Fag.

And in that moment, Kemi understands why Jose hates that park.

BRITTANY-RAE

Jonny falls asleep in her arms because she is the only one in the entire mansion who can calm him down.

They're sitting upright in bed, backs against the headboard. Jonny's head lies on her chest, emitting a light snore. A jittery rap on their bedroom door.

"Come in," Brittany invites.

Sylvia pokes her head in. "Dinner is ready."

Brittany nods.

After they dragged him into their designated bedroom, it had taken Brittany wrapping her arms and cradling him against her to calm him from his episode. Whenever Jonny slips into his abyss, it is heartrending to witness. But she soothed him. She always does.

Her phone pings with a text from Amani.

Check your email, then call me.

She'd already emailed the voice recording to her lawyer, who had been waiting eagerly after receiving Brittany's own "I think I have something" message earlier on.

Brittany shifts carefully until Jonny slumps down to continue sleeping. She tiptoes toward the bathroom and locks it behind her. She pulls up her mail app and finds Amani's email.

Great job, Brittany!

She didn't confess, but I think we have a strong lead about a lake. Enough for my contact at the Metropolitan Police in London.

I've translated it for you:

A: Johan.

J: I don't want her. Why is she here?

A: Not now. Not in front of her. Can you please excuse us? We have a family matter to discuss.

J: She is staying.

A: She may not.

J: She is my wife.

A: Brittany, please excuse us.

J: No. Stay.

A: Very well. I am no longer responsible for what you may hear.

B: I don't need to be here.

J: I need you here.

J: What are you doing with Katarina?

A: So you don't forget who you are.

J: Who am I really?

A: What are you doing now, Johan?!

J: Who . . . am . . . I?

A: What have I done wrong as your mother, hmm, Johan? Hmm, Johan? What have I done wrong?

J: You took her away from me.

A: I would never do such a thing. Never.

J: YOU LIAR! YOU FUCKING LIAR!

A: Johan!

J: You lie and lie and lie. All my life, you all lie to me.

A: Stop this at once!

J: That night when you killed her—

A: I did not kill her. Don't ever accuse me of that.

J: You wrote that letter. She never did. I went to her house, broken, crying. She never wrote that letter to me and...she was never pregnant, was she?

A: No, she wasn't.

Brittany clutches her chest and lets out a gasp.

J: But I don't understand. You said she had a secret abortion that night, which you paid for. She died because of you.

A: She wasn't pregnant.

J: What?

A: She wasn't.

J: Then what happened that night? After the chauffeur drove her back home?

A: I don't know what to tell you.

J: What did you do to her, Astrid?

A: They got into an accident close to a lake on her way home. That's all I know.

Tears begin to carve tracks down Brittany's cheeks.

J: What did you do? What have you done?

A: She was beneath you, my son. Beneath this family.

J: Because she was Black?

A: You were too young to understand.

She tenses at those words and every piece of her heart and soul writhes in hatred for Astrid.

J: Do you want to kill my Maya too? Do you want to kill my daughter?

A: Johan!

J: Because she is Brown?

A: Stop this at once!

J: Do you want to kill my baby too? Oh my God, oh my God, oh my God!

Brittany's hand flies up to her mouth to stifle a sob.

Then a lot of screaming from Jonny and that was it.

I will send this to the police and keep you posted.

Great job, Brittany. Glad Midsommar!

* * *

They miss dinner.

Evening rays spill in through see-through curtains, casting soft patterns across the pair. When Brittany sneaks back into bed, Jonny stirs from sleep, reaching for her, his mouth seeking hers for comfort. She lets him kiss her softly, his eyes closed. When he grows hungrier, she pulls back and his eyes bolt open.

"*Snälla*," he begs her, his eyes rimmed red with tears. He presses his lips to hers again, sobbing. "*Jag älskar dig*," he mumbles against her. She shakes her head, her eyes shut. She can't look at him.

"I love you." Jonny cries those words again, burying his face against her cheek. "Please believe me—" His voice cracks under his tears. "Please love me back. *Snälla*," he whispers once more before shifting his weight over hers. He moves against her gently, soberly, crying. She lets him, both her hands sliding up his straining back and into his hair, receiving his love.

And for the first time in weeks since her pixie cut, she lets Jonny touch her. She lets him love her.

Several minutes later, they summon Vicky to bring Maya to their room for goodnight kisses. After Vicky excuses herself, the toddler heads straight for her *pappa* first. Jonny scoops her into bed with them, showering her with smacking kisses all over her face and neck as she giggles in a fit. Then she reaches for Brittany, wrapping her small arms around her neck, switching parents.

Promise to protect Maya and you'll be free.

Brittany strokes Maya's hair worn in French braids. Jonny reaches over to rub his daughter's back as she lies against Brittany. His eyes follow the movement of his hand as he studies his child, a smile resting on his lips. Brittany watches him. She knows he'll die to protect *söta* Maya. He'll do anything for her.

"Jonny," Brittany starts. He peers at her in response. "I know how to protect Maya." He regards Brittany silently, scanning her face, trying to understand. "Astrid could hurt her too like Maya Daniels. I can protect her. But you have to trust me."

"I don't understand."

"You have to let me take her out of Sweden. You have to let me go."

"I can't."

"You must. As long as we're married and I'm here, Maya will never be safe from her."

"No." He leans closer, planting a desperate kiss against her lips. "No, I can't lose her. I can't lose you too."

"Please." Brittany begins to quiver against his lips, her voice hovering over a whisper. "Let me go. I promise to protect Maya with my life. You're never going to lose her ever again."

She sees his fingers begin to dance with agitation. She threads her fingers with his, locking them together until his limbs relax.

His eyes rim once more with tears as he takes her in, and for the third time that balmy summer day, Johan sobs deeply.

YASMIIN

It's time to bring Muna home.

Yasmiin clings tightly to Yagiz as a nurse wheels Muna out to meet them. They wait next to a combi taxi, driven by one of Yagiz's numerous taxi-driving contacts in town. Muna wears one of Yasmiin's loose-fitting floral dresses, her frame too small to fill it out fully, in contrast to Yasmiin's wide hips and ample backside. She's back in a hijab, a pale blush-colored swatch of cloth Yasmiin left for her along with the dress. The base of her left thigh sports a fresh bandage.

Muna grins upon sight and Yasmiin rushes toward her, squatting low to give her a light hug, careful since her muscles are still sore. Yasmiin then turns to give her a long peck on one cheek with an emphasized *muah*. Yagiz comes in for a peck as well. The nurse informs them she'll be stopping by their place tomorrow to check on Muna.

The first of many visits, including some with a physiotherapist to rehabilitate and prepare her for future prosthetics.

Yasmiin must seem giddier than normal to Muna as she beams. She can't wait to unleash her surprise. When they roll Muna into their simple apartment in Hässelby, a ragtag welcome committee has already assembled for a surprise party.

Nusret, Mattias, her former colleagues from Yagiz's janitorial service, and a few more faces she doesn't recognize. Those three strangers step forward to introduce themselves to Muna.

Salima, Amani, and a beguiling man whose eyes Muna recognizes before he even utters his name.

"No." Muna touches a hand to her lips. "No, it can't be." Muna stares straight into his honey-amber eyes beneath silky dark chestnut-brown hair.

From the pictures Yasmiin had seen, she knows Afran is the spitting image of his brother Ahmed. What she understood from Mattias was that Ahmed had grown a full beard before he set himself ablaze. This replica is clean-shaven. He moves closer to Muna, who begins to crumble into herself, lifting her shoulders up as if not wanting him to touch her.

Afran falls to his knees in front of her, his eyes drowning in tears, turning them into specks of gold.

"Hello, Muna," Afran greets her softly. "Allah knows how happy I am to see you." Muna shakes her head weakly as tears consume her. Afran continues. "Thank you. Thank you for everything. I thought I lost them all in Syria. My family." His voice cracks with emotion. "My father, mother, sister, brothers," he sobs. "All gone."

"You look... Ahmed." Muna's lips tremble as she pushes out the words. Without giving him a chance to respond, Muna reaches to pull him close to her and he lifts himself up to hug her, burying his head against her neck as they weep. The normally boisterous crowd hold their tongues as Muna and Afran sob against each other. Yasmiin pivots toward Yagiz and buries her face in his chest. He races a palm up and down her back to soothe her.

Afran finally pulls out of their hug and straightens up. "Please, this is a day of joy. Let's celebrate."

Soon the Çeliks' living room is a mix of high-pitched Arabic tunes on full blast mixed with Somali and Turkish beats, smells of roasted lamb permeating the air, plates of bulgur being passed round, the laughter of a small group of friends becoming family. Yagiz pulls Muna's wheelchair on its back wheels and gently spins her around, laughing, until she threatens to throw up.

Yasmiin finds Afran leaning against a wall, chatting with Mattias.

"Afran, can I borrow you?"

He fully takes her in before nodding. If that is how Ahmed used to look at Muna through downcast eyes, no wonder she fell for him. She pulls Afran toward the kitchen for privacy.

"This means a lot to Muna," she says. "Thank you for coming."

He places a palm on his chest. "This is truly what I dreamed of. Muna is the one who had the last contact with my family. That makes her special to me."

"She wants to know," Yasmiin tells him. "Ahmed told her nothing. He never shared anything about his family with her. Only that box of items from Al Zawr." She sees pain wash across his gaze. Is it still too raw? She would understand if he isn't ready.

She watches him clench his jaw, trying to compose himself.

"I failed them," Afran says, his voice low. "I couldn't save them. I couldn't save him," he croaks.

"I'm sorry," Yasmiin says. "I didn't mean to make you sad."

"It's okay," he reassures her. "Muna needs to know."

Yasmiin nods and the pair go in search of Muna. They find her with Mehmet in her lap, counting fingers together, trying to convince him she has eleven fingers instead of ten. When she looks up at them and sees their forlorn looks, she motions to Yasmiin to grab and set Mehmet on the floor.

Afran falls back on his knees next to her chair. She places a hand on his forearm.

"You must be tired of not knowing," Afran says, looking up at her. She nods. Afran takes an audible drag of air before pressing on. "I watched them die."

Muna lowers her head.

He continues. "Beheaded, burnt alive before my eyes by rebels."

Yasmiin gasps. Muna remains silent. "We were simple shepherds in Al Zawr. Simple Kurdish shepherds. Ahmed was a gardener." He pushes a fist to his mouth to stop a sob. "Machine guns filled the air. Everyone ran. Ahmed and I ran into the village storehouse to hide." He lets out a pained chuckle. "Very stupid move. Imagine if the rebels wanted to replenish their supplies from our storage?"

It has been years since it happened, but it's freshly baked anew with sorrow each passing day, Afran shares with them.

Whatever the rebels' reason for not raiding the storehouse, the brothers' decision to flee there had saved both their lives but not spared Afran the sight of the rebels ridding the village of all its men and boys. He watched from his hiding place as male after male was tied up and forced into a circle.

It had taken every fiber of his being not to cry out as he watched each matching pair of honey-colored eyes belonging to his other brothers widen in shock. They wriggled and fought with bound hands until each was overpowered by their attackers and immediately beheaded. His father, despite his old age, hadn't been spared either. The hacking continued for at least an hour until they were all piled up, doused with diesel, and set ablaze in one horrifying bonfire.

Yasmiin is in tears while Muna's head is still bowed in silence.

The last Afran saw of his mother and sister was of them being dragged by their hair, now exposed once their headscarves had been ripped off, into the back of pickup trucks where more men with groping hands waited, as they rounded up all the women and girls like goats into battered vehicles.

The trucks sped off, leaving dust in their wake, and an eerie silence enveloped Afran and Ahmed. It took them a full day to emerge from their crevices in the storehouse as sole survivors in what had now turned into a ghost village. On legs weakened by trauma, they hobbled over to the pile of charred remains, making out bits and pieces of bone and metal. Everything that could be burned had already turned into ash. So both men started digging through for remains of anything they could find as keepsakes. To remember these men they'd lived side by side with since their family had emigrated from Iraqi Kurdistan to northern Syria.

The next day, against a backdrop of the lingering smell of singed flesh, the brothers combed through their empty village, hut by hut, collecting photos, chains, rings, memorabilia, and anything that seemed important or valuable.

Afran pulled out his family's donkey from their yard. Normally, the lazy beast would bray at them out of annoyance. This time, though, the donkey didn't make a sound and made its way quietly toward Afran. He latched a wooden cart to the donkey. All the memories he and Ahmed had gathered filled a small sack. His village hadn't been a wealthy one. But he filled the rest of the wooden cart with whatever food supplies he could find. Jugs of water, bread, a goat, some rice, and a change of clothes. Wrapping himself in a thick wool blanket and pulling his younger brother close, he slapped the donkey's hind, kickstarting it. He pointed their transport in the direction of where he presumed Turkey's border lay.

He wasn't sure they would ever make it there, but at least both brothers promised to die trying. And on the brink of death was how Turkish border forces found them as they shuffled on foot toward the border, their donkey having died days prior. They'd run out of supplies long ago and the only item Ahmed clung to his chest as designated protector as they crossed that border was a sack filled with memories of people they once knew.

When they saw what state Ahmed was in, the officers had expected him to have crawled toward them, as they told Afran later.

"But my brother was a proud man with eagle eyes," Afran explains. "He had a fresh cut running down the left side of his face. He stood in front of them. He swayed in silence as long as he could before a dark mist washed over him and he collapsed into unconsciousness."

He, on the other hand, had crawled on all fours toward the officers, his own dignity long gone.

They separated in Turkey. Not by choice, but by circumstance. One was physically weaker than the other.

"The guilt eats me every day," he cries. "I couldn't save them. I heard their screams, but like a coward, I hid away from them when they needed me the most."

"You saved your little brother," Yasmiin says, stroking his shoulder. "You saved Ahmed."

"Those wails followed me to Canada as nightmares," he shares. "And that smell. I will never forget it. The smell of bodies turning into ash."

Muna lifts her head sharply so she is eye-to-eye with Afran. No tears. A woman clearly tired of crying.

"Yes, that smell," Muna says. "I know it well. The last smell of my Ahmed."

Afran rests his head on her lap and weeps.

For the first few days when she came home to them, Yasmiin heard Muna sobbing every night. She wasn't sure if it was physical or emotional pain. Yasmiin figures both. Sometimes, Muna forgets her left leg is gone and tries to lift or lean on it, before realizing there's nothing there.

Besides the few occasions Muna complains about her phantom limb, she moves around well with a wheelchair, her strength returning to her arms. Yasmiin finds it hard to adjust her schedule and take care of Muna, but she doesn't complain. The last thing the younger woman needs to feel is like a burden to her. That was the feeling that caused her to jump in the first place.

Afran decides to stick around for a couple of weeks. Yasmiin relishes the company he provides for Muna. He's there when the physiotherapist and nurses visit, while she is at the salon. He pushes her around the neighborhood for walks. Midsummer approaches fast and they receive an invitation to Amani's little palace.

Afran was granted asylum in Canada and works in a factory there. But he took a long leave of absence to come to Sweden to be with Muna. The only sliver of a connection he has to his obliterated family. So their tiny apartment becomes a makeshift motel, with Muna moving into Mehmet's room, and Afran taking their couch for weeks.

Yagiz wasn't too happy with the idea. Considering he loves grunting loudly for effect when making love to Yasmiin, the presence of guests as well as Mehmet sleeping in a corner of their room makes their trysts a patience-testing exercise for him in whisperfucks.

Despite Yagiz's jovial nature and constant busyness, Yasmiin knows her husband. He detaches himself more and more with each passing day. His secrets still grate with her, but she knows him enough not to keep prodding. Yagiz always finds his way home. He'll tell her once he's ready.

TWENTY-FOUR

BRITTANY-RAE

Midsommarafton. Midsummer Eve.

Brittany and Jonny sit silently with Antonia and Stig, digging into a late breakfast. Brittany pushes granola around her vanilla yogurt. Stig scrapes at a slice of toast, tongue sticking out the side of his mouth, slathering butter so loudly Antonia cuts him a reprimanding look. He stops mid-motion and lifts his shoulders in question. Jonny watches a drop of condensation crawling its way down his glass of orange juice. Once it hits the base, his eyes scan for another drop to follow.

Svea and her fiancé still haven't arrived to join them. Antonia had advised them not to. As for Wilhelm and Astrid, they were shuttled back to the mainland before Brittany and Jonny woke up.

"Astrid needs some time away from Johan," Antonia had explained when Brittany found her with a steaming mug of coffee sitting on the steps outside, watching the rippling waters of the bay. Brittany had pulled her bathrobe tighter before planting herself next to Antonia on the staircase. They had perched in silence while Antonia took occasional sips.

That restraint now continues around their breakfast table in the open-plan great hall, panoramic windows wrapping around them like a veil with exquisite views of yachts bobbing out in the bay.

"*Hur känns det?*" Antonia asks Jonny, trying to catch his attention. *How does it feel?* He keeps watching the water droplets instead. "Jonny?"

"*Vad?*" he snaps back. Antonia falls quiet. "*Visste du?*" Jonny roars at her. *Did you know?*

Antonia holds her brother's gaze for a few moments before breaking it with a firm "no." She turns to Brittany. "I told Astrid to leave this morning," she says. "Maybe it's best if you leave too."

They don't stay for the traditional Midsummer dinner. Brittany rounds up her crew—housekeeper and au pair. Jonny moves bags, baskets, and crates back to their speedboat, while Brittany carries Maya, who clings to her neck. Antonia stands, her hands tucked into her pockets, the matriarch-in-waiting peering after as they head toward the jetty.

Brittany spins around and lifts her hand in a short wave. Antonia's own hands remain buried.

The next few days move like a blur since leaving the Sandhamn Beast in the distance as Jonny sped them away from his childhood summer tradition.

Days after Amani tipped off the Metropolitan Police, Wilhelm von Lundin's twenty-year-old sage-colored Land Rover was pulled out of a lake in England containing the skeletal remains of two people. One was still strapped into the driver's seat, its flesh and clothing long eaten away by fish and time. They had clearly sacrificed their chauffeur as well to cover their trail.

The news breaks three days later.

Well into their late seventies, Astrid and Wilhelm von Lundin are called into questioning by the police over two suspected murders two decades ago. No charges are filed due to "insufficient evidence." The news rocks Sweden. It reads like the final scene of a quintessential Swedish crime noir. Modern-day aristocrats protecting their kingdom by strategically disposing of peasants. With wealth and connections so deeply calcified, Brittany knows any superficial displays of justice are never going to stick. Not to the likes of the von Lundins. Not in this lifetime.

The other body was found in the trunk of the Land Rover.

That particular find devastates Jonny. He locks himself away in one of their guest rooms for days, only opening the door to pull in trays of food left on the floor for him. He doesn't let anyone else in. Not even Brittany. Not even his daughter. His wails of anguish punctuate each night. Like a banshee screaming eerily in the dark, signaling the death of his past so he can finally move on. All Brittany can do is listen while resting against her plush pillow, tears crawling sideways across her nose, hitting the sheets, as he mourns the love of his life.

On the fourth day, her husband emerges zombie-like, his eyes dead.

A week later, Jonny stands in a fine white shirt tucked beneath a steel-gray handmade suit in the low-lit elevator, his face paler than usual. Brittany's sporting her first *BRIT RAE*, a sample short-sleeved mauve-pastel wrap dress. Ida Persson had fashioned it for her from her rough sketch after their initial meeting. The dress falls across her lean curves in sharp angles, ending in a thigh-high slit. She smooths her hand over the fabric, removing invisible wrinkles as a smile creeps onto her lips.

He's going to do it. Sign the papers that will allow Brittany to take Maya out of Sweden. Signing even more papers to start Brittany's process of divorce while guaranteeing his daughter's upkeep. Brittany hadn't anticipated him giving in so easily. But that row with his mother had broken him out of his shell. Brittany knew reality had begun to seep through those cracks in his privilege. The Metropolitan Police had stopped searching for Maya Daniels too soon after her disappearance. His family had pretended for far too long that she'd never existed.

Despite finally settling into the fact that she'd been a replacement all along, she never once doubted his love for their daughter Maya. Though heartbreaking, she found it oddly satisfying, witnessing him coming to the realization on his own. That the world will always see his precious daughter as Black first, despite his pedigree and her lineage.

He still sleeps in one of their guest rooms, though she finds him standing out on the porch every evening, staring off into the distance. Probably wondering if he's making the right decision, she reckons. She often leans against the doorframe observing him. Her beautiful stranger.

"How are you feeling?" Brittany whispers out of earshot of Louise as the elevator takes them up a few floors. Jonny shrugs. His fingers dance. She takes them into hers. They reach the thick wooden door of Amani Nassar-Berg's office. The Tigress answers the door herself after their second buzz.

"*Välkomna.*" Amani sweeps her arm wide, inviting them into her dark mahogany-decorated, heavily lavender-perfumed space.

Once they enter, she reaches a hand to Jonny. "Amani," she introduces herself. His arms remain pinned to his sides. His response is a quick nod and a "Jonny."

"*Jaha,*" Amani exclaims. Of course he isn't going to touch her. Brittany had told her all about him. "Please sit." Amani settles herself behind her behemoth of a carved desk, her hazel gaze settling on the couple.

"So"—a smile creeps across her scarlet red lips as she links her manicured nails, decked out in acrylics and glittering studs, gearing up to do what she does best—"shall we begin?"

KEMI

Two days after Malcolm and Jose's Midsummer party, Tobias accompanies her to one of her regular prenatal checkups. Right before they walk in, Tobias kisses her hand, promising to give her another chance because he never wants to feel what Malcolm felt the day Jose came home bleeding and broken. He never wants to entertain the possibility of ever losing her again.

Kemi crosses her heart at his words. Her own promise to him.

During all her previous prenatal appointments, she never

wanted to know if it was a boy or girl. She kept her eyes tightly shut during all those ultrasounds. As long as the doctors and technicians could hear heartbeats, she was fine.

Ultimately the doctors were ethically bound to let her know she was having twins. Kemi hadn't been surprised by the news. After all, she is a twin herself, she's Yoruba, the tribe with the highest frequency of twin births in the world, and she's technically an older woman in childbearing years, when the chance of multiple births increases.

Kemi still hasn't forgiven herself for all she did. She isn't sure she deserves these twin nuggets of joy. The possibility they could have been Ragnar's makes her cringe on occasion. The mere thought of the same person who once made her shiver with desire makes her shudder with disgust.

Now they're here because Tobias the father wants to see his babies on the screen.

"Hmm, hmm." The doctor adjusts in her chair and leans forward, her eyes firmly on the screen. She glides the transducer across the gel on Kemi's lower abdomen, before sharply sucking in air. "There they are."

Kemi turns to Tobias, the terrified elation clear in his eyes. She watches him lift both his hands to the back of his head in shock.

"*Är du säker?*" he asks, begging the doctor to confirm one more time.

"*Grattis!*" is all she offers before continuing her examination.

Twins. Two identical peas sharing the same pod.

Tobias lunges toward Kemi and presses a hard kiss of joy against her lips. "I love you," he murmurs against them before giving her another chaste kiss.

Two months later, Kemi finally hears Tina Wikström perform.

Kemi has never heard Tina sing in person. She's magnificent. Wearing a floor-length vintage blush-colored lace dress, Tina is barefoot with fresh violet gerberas in her hair. Her presence is enough to gather a small crowd of photo-snapping tourists around their wedding party while they stand by the waterfront at Stadshuset.

Tears stream down Jose's face as he rests his shoulder against Malcolm's chest, absorbing her voice. His bruises have healed well, leaving only two small scars beneath one eye. That *Midsommarafton* day when he'd come home battered, he had cried for thirty minutes straight before he'd been ready to tell them what had happened.

That park. He recognized the same set of hecklers he always saw when he crossed it. Three boys, teenagers maybe, clean-shaven heads. Faded jeans rolled up at the ankles. White.

That day, they finally got into Jose's face, spat "*pretty boy!*" and "*bög!*" at him, and pushed him to the ground, promising to destroy that face, beating him until he passed out. His humiliation had been two-fold, Jose recounted. First, he was a man in his late forties who couldn't physically defend himself. Second, he lay there for over three-quarters of an hour, waking up to people strolling past him.

Beaten and bloodied, he'd lain there. No one had helped him. Not one offer. That hurt him beyond the thugs' insults. The lack of acknowledgment, like he didn't exist. Even in his weakest moments.

It was the first time she'd ever witnessed Malcolm cry. His deep guttural wails shook them all once the realization he could have lost Jose that day fully hit him.

His wailing drove Tina into Sebastian's arms and pushed Kemi's face into Tobias's chest. That was also when she knew she wanted love that deep. She deserved that type of love too and wouldn't entertain anything less than it.

Kemi is thrilled to see the smile return to Jose's lips as Malcolm hooks his arm around his shoulder, both listening intently to Tina sing.

Gamla stan glistens in the distance across Lake Mälaren. Stockholm blesses them with low hanging puffy white clouds in an azure-blue sky and temperate weather. Both Sebastian and Tobias are dressed alike in light tan-colored suits, white shirts opened at the nape, each with a violet gerbera pinned to their chests.

Kemi's box braids are piled high and styled with violet gerberas too. Yasmiin had given her a light summer touch to her makeup with lilac eyeshadow. She is wearing a dark burgundy dress with a plunging neckline. Her favorite wrap dress which Tobias was always eager to pull off her. Its fabric now stretches precariously across her eight-month bulge.

The wedding party is just the six of them. Malcolm and Jose originally planned to invite extended family, more friends, and co-workers, but the park incident shook them so deeply they wanted to spend their most special day with only their closest friends. They'll plan a small dinner for extended family another day, but today, they simply want Tina's silky, honey voice wrapping them with Tobias and Kemi by their side.

When Tina finishes serenading the couple and the curious crowd, the entire waterfront erupts in applause. She places a hand daintily on her chest, accepting their love. Sebastian moves to her side, hooking her waist to pull her closer for a kiss of pride. Malcolm plants a soft kiss on Jose's forehead before the sound of a horn interrupts them.

"The van is here," Malcolm announces, leading the way. The van will shuttle them over to Fåfängan for their wedding lunch, a hilltop restaurant with sweeping views of Stockholm's islands and ferries crisscrossing the bay.

As Kemi strolls softly toward the waiting van behind both couples, she feels a light touch on her left hand, which stops her in her tracks.

Tobias laces his fingers through hers. Kemi glances up at him, her eyebrows furrowing before arching up once she glimpses the look in his eyes. He lifts the back of her palm to his lips for a lingering kiss before placing their interlocked hands on her belly.

YASMIIN

Yasmiin brushes brown powder across Muna's cheeks in preparation for Amani's summer party. She had blown out Muna's natural hair beneath her hijab, shaped her eyebrows, and is now doing a full contour makeup job.

"I really feel so beautiful," Muna mumbles as Yasmiin dabs raspberry-colored lip gloss across her pillowy lips.

"Yes," Yasmiin agrees. "He won't be able to take his eyes off you." She winks at Muna through their mirror at home.

Muna turns away. Yasmiin gently swivels her jaw back toward Muna.

"We're just friends. We barely know each other."

"I think you know each other more than most people I know." Yasmiin pulls out a makeup setting spray. "Close your eyes." Muna follows her command as Yasmiin sprays a mist across her face.

"I am serious, Yasmiin," Muna stresses. "It is not like that. We are now family. Because of Ahmed. He's promised to call me often when he goes back, so we can talk about Ahmed and keep his memory alive."

"Hope you both talk about more than Ahmed. He's single, you're single." Yasmiin lifts her shoulders in a questioning fashion. "What is stopping you two?"

"I know nothing about his life in Canada."

"But at least he's building a life."

"Can't we just be friends?" Muna quizzes Yasmiin. "I don't see him that way."

"Well, if you ask me, you could be a perfect odd couple."

Muna smiles. "So you and Yagiz? The perfect odd couple?"

Yasmiin laughs out loud. "Yeah, perfect couple indeed. So what do you think?" She leans closer to Muna to watch her assess her new look. Muna simply purses her lips and nods her acceptance, probably not trusting herself to speak without tears.

Yagiz, Yasmiin, and Mehmet along with Afran and Muna arrive at a spread which Amani has laid out in honor of Afran's extended visit. Salima and her husband are already there, picking at dates and olives.

Amani welcomes them all with several kisses. She pauses at Afran and holds him at shoulder's length by his upper arms. "And you are very, very welcome!" She kisses him on both cheeks. "You must experience a proper Midsummer with us. This is a tradition everyone loves, even us."

Amani outdoes herself. She says so herself. Within the walls of her plush space, Amani spreads out the classics—various flavored jars of pickled herring, cured salmon, halal meatballs—alongside a mezze platter she catered for the Çeliks and their guests.

"Will you try *sill*, pickled herring?" Muna offers Afran as she grabs his plate, Yasmiin by his side.

"I eat everything," Afran says, his eyes twinkling. Yasmiin catches him smiling at Muna before the younger woman turns away shyly.

Afran returns to Canada a few days later.

Yasmiin misses his support. His absence makes her realize the magnitude of what he assisted with while visiting. With each visit from the therapist and nurses, they adapt their apartment, making it more accessible for Muna. Thankfully they already have a shower so they purchase a support stool for Muna. They install guard rails next to the toilet.

But they know it isn't enough. Muna can't stay with them forever. The pressure seems to be taking a toll on Yagiz. He's staying out later than usual. Still, she never questions his whereabouts. In due time, Yasmiin always convinces herself. In due time.

A few weeks later, Anu texts her the most amazing request.

"SVT wants you on air," he beams into the phone. "They want you to come talk about makeup for Black skin and the differences between that and white skin."

Yasmiin absorbs his words. She, Yasmiin? On TV as a beauty expert? Yasmiin who roamed Italy's streets to survive is now thriving in a way she only dreamed about.

She loses all composure and simply screams into the receiver.

Muna follows her to the TV station and squeezes Yasmiin's hand in support right before she strolls on stage in heels and body-fitting florals, her own face perfectly made up. Once the show airs, her beauty account explodes with followers. She adds five hundred more in an hour. When she posts behind-the-scenes photos, they can't wait to engage, leaving her hearts, celebratory signs, and every other emoji sharing how proud they are of her as a Black woman making it in Sweden.

When Muna and Yasmiin get home that evening, she can't wait to celebrate. The one person she wants most by her side hasn't come home yet, though. Another text buzzes from Anu before she even unlocks the door. They want her to come in once a month to provide beauty tips on the show.

Yasmiin falls to her knees in front of their door, resting her head against its cool wooden surface, while Muna reaches over from her chair to stroke her back.

Yasmiin continues crying once they move indoors.

"What a dream," she cries, turning to look at Muna. "I never would have dreamed this could be my life."

"Allah is good," Muna offers. "Look at me. I was supposed to be dead."

Yasmiin hugs her. "We must celebrate!" she announces with elation. She rushes to the fridge and pulls out two bottles of non-alcoholic cider. She cracks them open and hands one to Muna. "To new beginnings."

Muna grins. "To second lives," she toasts, holding Yasmiin's gaze before breaking into happy tears.

Past midnight and Yagiz still hasn't come home. Yasmiin sits in bed worried, while scrolling through comments on her account. She hears the soft click of their bedroom door. He pads in quietly.

"You awake?" he asks into the dark.

"Where have you been?" she whispers back.

He doesn't respond. He starts shedding his clothes until she sees his outline standing naked in front of her in the blackness.

"Yagiz?" Her voice shakes with concern. "What is going on?"

Still no response. He walks over to their bed, pulls the sheets back, and climbs in next to her.

"I haven't showered," she begins to protest. He cups her face gently between both palms and grazes his lips across hers. "Yagiz? Talk to me?" He kisses her instead, his tongue prying her lips apart to receive him. She feels him quiver against their kiss and she reaches into his strip of hair, raking her fingers through it. "What is going on?"

"He betrayed me."

"Betrayed you? Who? Özel?"

Yagiz nods against her face. "*Aina.*" *Police.*

Yasmiin gasps. Öz? A police officer?

"Kiss me, my Yasmiin."

She obliges him despite her own rapidly pounding heart, receiving the most tender kiss he ever shared with her. A few minutes later, Yagiz pulls out of their kiss and cradles her to his chest. Their room falls silent. Her Yagiz, who always has something to say, has no words for her.

But she feels the weight of the unspoken in the room. She's going to lose him. How strange life is, she wonders. A few hours earlier, she had been celebrating with Muna. Now she rests her head on his chest, hearing his heart beating, the love of her life. Two broken beings who had found their own way to love each other.

The perfect odd couple.

She splays her fingers across his muscles as she cries into his chest. She feels something sticky, viscous on his skin. She reaches for the night lamp and turns it on to investigate.

Blood.

More blood. Across his chest, a few streaks on his face, down his arms.

"Yagiz?"

"Hold me," Yagiz begs softly against her skin. "Hold me, *aşkım.*"

"What did you do?" The words barely escape her quivering lips. "What did you do?" Tears cloud her eyes.

He doesn't answer, but she already knows. A Swedish diplomat named Bosse, once stationed in Rome for decades, probably retired by now, matching the information she shared that night with Yagiz.

He wasn't difficult to find.

Yagiz kisses her forehead. "I already told you." He releases a pained smile before whispering to her, "I am a king."

They fall asleep, arms tightly wrapped around each other. Yagiz never did tell her his secrets. Yasmiin doesn't care because she knows she'll find out within days.

The next day, Yasmiin's world indeed crashes to a screeching halt as the news anchor comes on in Swedish.

Good evening. We start with some breaking news.

Stockholm Police have finally arrested a notorious kingpin who has been running one of the most elaborate networks of gangs and drug dealers in the city for the last six years. He has also been charged with the murder of former diplomat Bosse Bergström.

Yagiz Çelik turned himself in to City Police on Bergsgatan earlier today at 1:15 p.m.

And now moving on to the weather report. It's looking like sunshine all week.

EPILOGUE

BRITTANY-RAE

Stockholm Fashion Week feels like a lifetime ago. By the time it rolled around that late August, Brittany floated in a state of disbelief that her days as a von Lundin were numbered.

"*Äga det!*" Yasmiin beamed at Brittany, after dabbing her lips with plum-colored gloss and pushing her toward the catwalk. *Own it!* Brittany squeezed her arm in gratitude. She saw sadness flash across Yasmiin's eyes. Amani had told her what had happened to Yasmiin's husband. A man named Yagiz.

Swapping outfits in seconds. Last-minute hairsprays and brushes swabbed across her cheeks. Stepping from the dimly lit backstage into the light. Rows of fashion's *crème de la crème* flanking the runway. This was Brittany's muscle-memory *bike ride* after years of not cycling.

House of Ida Persson presents: The BRIT RAE Collection.

A soft accented voice came on over the speakers and filled the open ballroom at Berns, the restaurant where she'd met Jonny's parents for the first time. The symbolism didn't escape her. Once the spotlight hit her face, Brittany Johnson strutted out of her reality and into her dream.

A year later, *BRIT RAE* was picked up by Nordstrom in the US and Åhléns back in Sweden.

Brittany watches him roll in damp grass under a sweltering Atlanta summer sun. Maya keeps squealing as she aims the garden hose at him, drenching him. Brittany leans against one of the white porch pillars of her new villa, a tumbler of pink lemonade in hand. Quite modest by wealth-flashing standards. Jonny had insisted on the purchase for his little *gumman*, though Brittany had refused his attempt to send both their housekeeper and au pair along with them to the US for support. They were too close to her history with him. She needed to find her own way back home.

Now Jonny is in Georgia spending a week with his daughter. His monthly ritual performed like clockwork. He has also added one more ritual to his repertoire: seeing a therapist every two weeks.

Brittany takes a sip of lemonade and raises her glass in a toast when he glances her way. Jonny smiles that grin of a thousand teeth, his eyes which once asphyxiated her settled with ease.

"I don't think I've ever seen that boy laugh before." Her father Tyrone's bass cuts through their moment as he steps onto the porch and stands next to her. "He seems truly happy."

Brittany shares a wry smile with him and leans her head against his shoulder. Jonny staggers to his feet and chases Maya around the yard, growling like a wolf as he waddles behind her, her squeals filling the air.

Brittany inhales audibly, pressing closer into her father. He wraps his right arm around her, pulling her into him. They stand in that position for a few more minutes, watching father and daughter play. The scene playing out in front of her, a mirror of her childhood as daddy's little girl.

"Maybe I was meant to meet him on that flight," Brittany finally says, her voice barely audible. "Now we're both free."

KEMI

"Still hasn't sunk in," Tobias whispers one morning as they push their eleven-month-old twin boys, Ola and Oskar, in a double stroller along Nacka's waterfront promenade. "We're responsible for keeping them alive?!"

"Relax, they'll survive." Kemi chuckles.

It's been a year since Malcolm and Jose's summer wedding. Her life at von Lundin Marketing feels like a dream. She hasn't spoken to Jonny or Ingrid since she was fired. Ragnar slowly faded to dust, his image dulling in the deepest recesses of her mind.

Last she heard, Pia is still with him. Why she chose to stay still piques Kemi's interest. Pia must know what her husband is. Maybe she'd rather deal with the devil she knows than one she doesn't? Clearly their affair was instantly deprived of oxygen within their close circles, leaving Ragnar unscathed and Kemi without skin.

Kemi glances at Tobias. Of course she knows why Pia stayed. Tobias had stayed too. After all, he must know what she is. Ragnar's replica. Yet, he chose to show her grace. Maybe Ragnar had sobbed against Pia in shame too, begging for forgiveness, his pride finally shattering, coming to terms with the love he almost let slip away.

Maybe Pia had extended grace too.

Tobias moved back into her apartment to support her through her last trimester, which ended in a treacherous C-section and the arrival of their boys. Tobias had sobbed uncontrollably as he cradled both boys, pressing them gently to his bare chest for skin-to-skin contact.

"They're so perfect," he'd rasped out.

For Kemi, the universe had stopped her in her tracks for a while. Now on a permanent residency permit thanks to her relationship with Tobias, Sweden had forced her to embrace *lagom—balance—* in all its contrariness to her being. Jobless, rudderless, and sleepless, her new home finally slowed Kemi down. To embrace gentle walks pushing strollers, lazy afternoon *fikas*, stolen moments when the boys napped and she could finally just *be*, as Tobias had desired all along for her.

Once the twins turned nine months, though, Kemi was mentally done with maternity leave. She was ready to work.

Stockholm shimmers brightly this warm late August day, rays

reflecting off ripples in the bay, as they amble along, wearing sunglasses, pushing the boys. Rather, Tobias pushes while Kemi licks her vanilla ice-cream cone.

"Any word yet?" Tobias asks. Kemi knows what he's checking on. She's been sending out her resume at least three times a day.

"Nothing."

"Nothing?"

"Nope, not one word." She nonchalantly keeps licking, now working her way through the crispy cone. By her second jobless month of silence from all applications, she has begun entertaining the idea of a downgrade. She tells him this.

"A downgrade? Are you insane?" Tobias discourages her before giving her a quick kiss. "They know you deserve better." She beams, basking in his compliment. *Her Tobias.*

"Look, I know my job isn't enough," he says, "but at least we get benefits."

"Have faith," she replies. "I know something will—" Her phone beeps a text notification. She pulls it out.

Hej, Kemi. Are you available for a quick interview tomorrow?

Best wishes, Olle Ericsson / KLARNORDIC

She stops walking, staring at the company name in the text. *KLARNORDIC.* An advertising agency making waves across international media. She had watched a CNN breakdown of their corporate faux pas that very same morning.

Their latest campaign had photoshopped a white hand Black, including its palm, instead of hiring a Black model.

Kemi lets out a booming laugh. A roaring cackle which turns the heads of passers-by to observe the seemingly madwoman chuckling on the boardwalk.

"Here we go again," she says, before typing back her response.

YASMIIN

"Afran asked me to move to Toronto to be with him."

Yasmiin remembers Muna's words as if she whispered them yesterday.

"Let me go," Muna had cried softly to her then. "I can't burden you any longer. Let me go be with him."

Yasmiin had protested. "Don't say that! You're not a burden to me. Don't you ever think that again."

"I have all I need," Muna said. "I have you. I have Afran. I have a family now."

One glance at the younger woman and Yasmiin knew her mind had been made up. There was nothing for her in Sweden besides forcing Yasmiin to be her caregiver in addition to Mehmet's.

Yasmiin couldn't do it all, while on the cusp of a major career takeoff.

A year later, Yasmiin finds herself visiting Muna and Afran in Toronto.

Yagiz is still in jail. When the judge finally announced he was going to be deported back to Turkey in a few months and stripped of his Swedish citizenship, Yasmiin had wailed unabashedly in that courtroom while everyone else sat stoic-faced. No one else had seeped so deeply through the cracks in her soul like Yagiz. She couldn't lose him now. Not when life was beginning to make sense once more.

As they dragged him past her bench, Yagiz winked at her, threw a kiss her way, and mouthed the word "*aşkım*."

Her weekly visits to Muna long ago have now been replaced by weekly visits to Yagiz in prison, with Mehmet in tow. She'd promised him she'd move back to Turkey with him once it's time, but he had refused.

"This is Mehmet's home," Yagiz had said, waving a hand around the visiting room. "Let him know his land. He is their future, whether they like it or not," he finished with that bellow she continues to be madly in love with.

Her *aşkım*.

Yasmiin now clasps Mehmet's hand tightly as they walk behind Afran wheeling Muna toward the accessibility ramp.

"No," Muna calls out to him as they approach the ramp. "I'm ready."

Afran rounds her chair and squats to eye-level. "Are you sure?"

"Yes, I am ready." Muna smiles back at him. "Take me to the steps."

He nods, then places a quick hard kiss against her forehead. Once Afran positions her wheelchair, Muna scoots to its edge. She places her new left foot on the ground and steadies herself. Then she fully lifts onto her prosthetic, finding her balance, before taking the first staircase. What she had practiced for months during her rehabilitation sessions.

She has been granted asylum in Canada under Afran's custody. Their relationship status remains murky to Yasmiin. She suspects they want to keep it that way. The world has ripped so much from them both. They owe the world nothing else. Especially not access to their private lives.

Muna grabs the railing and takes another step up. And then another, until she reaches the door to the halls of the community college where she'll start her two-year degree in finance in her new home country of Canada.

When Muna gets home from her first full day of classes, Afran has cooked her *dolma*, a Kurdish dish of stuffed vegetables, and bought a chocolate cake to celebrate. Around his modest dining table they sit, Muna's new family, tucking into a humble meal cooked with love.

When Afran gets up to make them mint tea, Muna turns to Yasmiin, who cradles Mehmet sleeping in her arms.

"Yasmiin," Muna starts. "It's your time too."

"Time for what?" Yasmiin dismisses her prodding.

"You know," Muna says. "It's time to call them. I know they must miss you."

Yasmiin's smile drops. "You know I can't."

"Why do you fear their judgment so much?"

"You don't understand," Yasmiin says. "If they are still alive, the things I've done will break their hearts and kill them."

"I think their love for their lost daughter is more than what you have done." Muna holds her gaze. "Call them."

The phone rings and rings when Yasmiin finally tries. She knows her mother's number. She had recited it for years as she roamed, hoping she'd never forget. Praying one day, she would recall those numbers which connect her to her past.

Yasmiin prays no one picks up. Her prayers aren't answered.

"*Haye?*" a woman's voice comes on the line. *Hello?*

Yasmiin swallows. "*Hooyo*," she says softly into the phone. *Mother.*

A few seconds of silence until the same voice, now shaking with tears, comes back on stronger.

"*Yasmiin? Alhamdulillah! Yasmiin!*" she cries. *Praise be to God.*

ACKNOWLEDGMENTS

The last few years have been an incredible testimony of stepping out in faith and trusting the transitions in my life. So, first and foremost, all glory to God, my provider and protector, who continues to be merciful and gracious to me.

To my amazing family and darling kids for blessing me with your unconditional love. You continue to keep me grounded and completely loved. What a precious gift to call you my family in this lifetime. To Urban for the great memories we shared and for being a wonderful father to our kids.

To my lovely friend and writing mentor Leigh Shulman, we did it again. Thank you for your warmth, love, and for holding space for me. I am grateful for your exacting eye as we worked through the first structural edits together.

To my dear friends Lyota Swainson and Pär Johansson. Lyota's Zuzy Beauty salon in Kungsholmen served as inspiration for Salima's salon. From regularly sending each other freshly cooked food across the bridge via Pär—Jamaican jerk chicken and oxtail (from you) and Nigerian goat meat stew (from me)—to the incredibly enriching conversations we've had in the salon, thank you for being my friends and encouraging me during those times I needed it.

To my lovely beta readers and friends, especially Gerry Bjällerstedt, Angela Harris, Germaine Thomas, Sara Mansouri, Yomi Abiola, Anja Mutic, Andrea Pippins, Pamela MacNaughtan, Judi Lembke, Astrid Sundgren, Meryem Aichi, Kimberly Golden

Malmgren, Irene Nalubega, Palmira Koukkari Mbenga—thank you for all the belly laughs, soul-deep chats, long talks, and dinner antics in person around Stockholm or remotely. Thank you for bringing light into my world, especially during my darkest moments.

To my amazing agent Jessica Craig, simply calling you an agent feels inadequate. I'm grateful to now call you a dear friend. Thank you for believing in me and championing my voice when others couldn't see the vision.

To my wonderful publishers William Morrow and Head of Zeus, especially my incredible editors Lucia Macro (WM), Asanté Simons (WM), Madeleine O'Shea (HoZ), and Sophie Whitehead (HoZ), thank you for inviting me to be a member of your publishing home with fertile soil for me to bloom as an author. Thank you for modeling what true collaboration and working as one team looks like.

To the incredible Mehmet Solmaz for reviewing my Turkish words, and exquisite Sagal Jama for checking my Somali and Arabic phrases.

To my new and returning readers, thank you for your humbling support. I am truly living one of my dreams, which is writing the types of stories I have longed to read.

And for this, I am deeply grateful.

RESOURCES

Here are some supportive resources for the serious themes discussed in this book. You're never alone and always have someone to reach out to through these resources.

Suicide Awareness Voices of Education: save.org/find-help/international-resources
National Human Trafficking Hotline: humantraffickinghotline.org
Affair Recovery: affairrecovery.com
National Limb Loss Resource Center®: amputee-coalition.org

ABOUT THE AUTHOR

Nigerian American and based in Sweden, Lọlá Ákínmádé Åkerström is an award-winning author, speaker, and photographer. Her work has appeared in *National Geographic*, *Travel + Leisure*, *Slate*, *Lonely Planet*, the *Guardian*, the *Sunday Times*, the *Telegraph*, and the *New York Times*, and on Adventure.com, BBC, CNN, and Travel Channel, among other media outlets.

In addition to contributing to several books, Lọlá is the author of *Due North*, the 2018 Lowell Thomas Award winner for best travel book; the bestselling *Lagom: The Swedish Secret of Living Well*, available in eighteen languages; and the internationally acclaimed *In Every Mirror She's Black*.

She has been recognized with multiple awards for her work, including being named a 2022 Hasselblad Heroine and the Society of American Travel Writers' 2018 Travel Photographer of the Year. She was honored with a MIPAD (Most Influential People of African Descent) 100 award in media and culture in 2018. She has contributed to the National Geographic Image Collection.

Lọlá is based in Stockholm and tweets at LolaAkinmade.